HELL'S SPELLS

ORDINARY MAGIC - BOOK 6

DEVON MONK

ODD
HOUSE
PRESS

Hell's Spells

Copyright © 2020 by Devon Monk

ISBN: 9781939853196

Publisher: Odd House Press

Cover Art: Lou Harper

Interior Design: Odd House Press

Print Design: Odd House Press

This story is a work of fiction. Names, characters, places, and incidents are the product of the author's imagination or are used fictitiously, and any resemblance to actual persons, living or dead, business establishments, events or locales, is entirely coincidental.

DEDICATION

For my family, and all those who need a little ordinary magic in their lives...

CHAPTER ONE

It was Thursday morning, and I needed to hit the road to pick up the mail for the gods.

Usually I liked getting out of town. Not today.

"Is it me?" I asked the dragon pig, who was curled up on my bedroom floor. The hoard of clean socks it had gathered over the last few weeks—none of them belonging to me or my boyfriend, Ryder Bailey—stuck out from under it. The dragon pig grunted without opening its eyes.

I pulled a shirt over my tank top—early October meant layers—stuck my badge on my pocket, and nudged the little pink critter with the toe of my boot.

"Hey, are you listening?"

It rolled, four stubby legs in the air, round belly exposed, ears flopping back. Those button eyes glittered with a warning flash of fire.

"It's not just my imagination, right?" I lifted the box of aluminum foil off my dresser and waved it in the air. The dragon pig's gaze sharpened. It scrambled up to sit, curly tail wagging.

"You see it too, right? Ryder dashing out of the house every day as fast as he can?" I ripped off a length of foil and wadded it into a little ball. The dragon pig tracked my every move, eyes on the prize.

"Out of the house early every morning, home late every night. He's avoiding me." I paused. I knew what that sounded like. It sounded like he was hiding something.

I could feel it. Something between us was about to change. I groaned. "I don't want to fight," I said. "I don't want this, any of this, to change."

To end.

I blew out a breath and stared at the ceiling for a few seconds.

"He's hiding something," I said to the ceiling.

Maybe I was overreacting. Ryder hadn't told me he wanted to break up. He hadn't picked a fight, hadn't said he needed a change. What I needed was to talk to him. Really talk to him.

Find out if we'd taken a wrong turn, and if we could backtrack and make it right again. We were new at the relationship thing. It was okay if we made mistakes.

But today I had to pick up god mail, then there was the High Tea Tide event Bertie was throwing on Saturday.

"We could take the weekend and just talk. That would work right?"

The dragon pig grunted. It was standing now, little mouth open in a happy smile, and I choked on a laugh.

"Well, I can see I'm loved for my aluminum foil treats. Flame on." I tossed the ball in the air, and the dragon pig waited until it fell off the apex. Then it blew a short, white-hot burst of flame, frying the metal to a black marshmallow crinkle.

The dragon pig caught the ball and crunched it with happy grunts.

I ripped off another strip. Wadded. "One more, then we'll get mail."

The dragon pig hopped up on its back legs, flamed the tinfoil ball, and snapped it out of the air with a happy little growl.

I grabbed my holster, keys, and a rubber band so I could pull my hair back in a pony, then headed down the stairs, the dragon pig on my heels.

Ryder was already at the kitchen island, his plate empty except for crumbs, his travel mug and thermos staged on the counter.

It still hit me in unexpected moments. How much I loved having him in my mornings, my days, my life. How his hair, dark with layers of copper and gold felt between my fingers when we were curled up together on the couch. How his mossy eyes went soft when we kissed, how that wicked smile of his popped dimples in his cheeks.

I'd watched him grow up from a boy to a man.

I'd loved him every step of the way.

There was going to be no breaking up with him if I could help it.

I inhaled, exhaled, and put on a smile.

"You're up early," I said as I padded into the room. Spud, Ryder's half chow, half border collie doofus of a dog, came over from where he'd been sniffing around for toast bits and sat in front of me.

I gave him a good scratching behind the ear and a face rub. "Morning, Spuddo. Where's my toy?" He wagged and wiggled, then bounded off toward his box of toys by the fireplace.

"Morning, Delaney." Ryder stood and pulled his coat from the back of his chair, the timing of his escape carefully planned.

"Busy day?" I nodded toward the thermos and coffee.

He had the good grace to look at his travel mug a little guiltily. "This build is a pain in my ass. No one can get their damn act together. If I'm not there, I'm going to get fined and sued for half a dozen code violations."

"Sure," I said, walking toward him.

He hadn't looked up, his gaze and hands going to the zipper on his Carhartt jacket.

The problem with knowing a person for almost your

3

entire life is that they can't hide what they're feeling. Not really. Not for long.

He was nervous.

I stopped in front of him and there was this moment where we were both waiting for the other to reach out. Time hung suspended.

Then he turned toward me, almost unconsciously, smoothly, like we'd been this way all our lives, like we'd always been.

Together.

His arms lifted, and those eyes, the shadow green of a forest in winter, came up to meet my gaze.

The question lingered between us.

Were we still good? Should we be worried? Should we talk?

Just like every morning for the last month, I moved forward into him, needing contact. Needing to tell him with my body what I couldn't say with my words yet.

We were good. We were everything.

We fit, our arms finding their familiar positions, my head turned sideways so I could smell the sweet sawdust and deep woodsy notes of his soap mixed with that scent that was his, only his.

I inhaled deeply, and he tipped his face down, burying his nose in my hair. I felt him inhale, exhale, felt his arms shift and tighten, as if he didn't want to go. Didn't want to let me go. "Miss you," I mumbled.

He hummed. "Build's not gonna last forever."

Spud arrived and bumped his head between us, trying to wedge his way in with whichever stuffy he had clamped in his mouth.

I could feel Ryder's smile. "I'll be home late," he said, letting me go and moving toward his coffee in one smooth move, eyes averted again.

He snapped his fingers for Spud, who dropped the toy donut I'd bought him for his birthday at my feet. The dog rushed over to Ryder.

"I'll be out of town today," I said.

"God mail?" Thermos in one hand, travel mug in the other, he was already halfway to the door.

"Yup. Thursday," I said. "Do you want to meet for lunch?"

He stopped. "I'm meeting with the…investor today. Sorry, Laney. Raincheck?"

He looked back at me. Hopeful and apologetic.

He was hiding something.

"Raincheck," I agreed.

"Sorry, baby," he said, emotion punching each word.

"We need to talk," I said. "When you have time."

"Yeah," he said. "Sure. As soon as this job stabilizes, we'll talk. I promise. It shouldn't be too much longer." He and Spud were out the door so fast, I couldn't have said a word if I'd tried.

I pressed cool fingers against my eyelids, let out a slow breath, then picked up Ryder's plate, took it to the kitchen, and found a note on the coffee pot. "Full pot. Omelette in the oven." He'd drawn a little heart on the note. I stared at that heart for a long time. Then I carefully folded the paper and dropped it in the drawer with all the other morning notes.

CHAPTER TWO

I HADN'T EXPECTED the werewolf blockade.

I slowed my Jeep on the narrow, two-lane highway just outside Otis and turned down the radio.

A dozen members of the Wolfe family, all wearing flannel and denim, stood on the sides of the road talking to cars stopped on the shoulder. It looked like they were handing out flyers.

"What are they doing?" The dragon pig, in the passenger seat next to me, grunted and propped its feet up on the window, its too-hot breath steaming little circles against it.

"Chief?" A knock on my window followed, so I rolled it down and came face to face with Jame Wolfe.

Jame was a good-looking guy. Built like a cement truck, he was a firefighter who also put his lycan strength into helping out with the gravel business his family owned.

He and Ben had caused quite the stir in Ordinary because werewolves and vampires usually didn't get along, much less dated.

I thought there might be wedding bells in their future, and for one unreasonable moment, I was insanely jealous.

Jame's heavy eyebrows went up. I knew he heard the spike in my heartbeat and the rush of heat through my body.

He'd be able to smell jealously, no matter how brief, and I was embarrassed about that. Which he'd probably be able to smell too.

"All good, Chief?" His strong hand gripped the top of the door, but he gave me a puzzled smile.

"How's Ben?"

"Still gay. Why? Tired of Ryder?" The smile was teasing, but his nostrils were wide. He smelled emotions on me.

I sighed. "I am not after your boyfriend, for gods' sake. And before you get nosey, we're fine. Ryder and I are fine. Every relationship has its ups and downs. We're in a..." I lifted my hand and did a flat wavy motion that was supposed to mimic a roller coaster.

He could smell uncertainty, even though I worked to keep it out of my tone, out of my body language.

"Uh-huh." He glanced at the interior of my car, spotted the dragon pig, then focused on me again. "You've been acting different lately, Chief." Blunt. That was another trait of most werewolves. "I keep thinking you're dealing with," he took a moment to inhale, his eyes narrowing, "something you want to hide."

"One, stop sniffing up in my business. Two, I'm not hiding anything. Three, now's the time to give me a good explanation for why your crew is blocking traffic."

"We're not blocking traffic, just catching a few cars coming in and out of Ordinary."

"I can see that." I nodded toward the two cars and one motorcycle stopped on the shoulder, the driver of each vehicle being addressed by someone from the Wolfe pack. "Why?"

"We've been robbed."

"What? What's missing? When did this happen? And who's 'we'?" I threw on my lights, unbuckled my seat belt.

He stepped back to give me room to get out of the car.

"Here?" I scanned the area.

Otis Junction was a tiny blip of a place. On one side of the road stood a diner that sat twelve people, max. The other side of the road offered a gas station and corn dog stand. Kitty-corner to that was a swampy field where the occasional flea market and swap meet broke out during the summer months.

Not exactly a spot where I'd expect a robbery.

"Not here." He held up a flyer, and I took it from him. "This. It was stolen. Early this morning. From the office at the pit."

The carving of a pack of wolves was familiar. Beautifully made out of one knotted and gnarled burl, it was old, the curves and dips of wood darkened by years of hands touching it. Those wolves almost fully free of the burl were carved fine and elegant: exquisite. The ones hidden within the rugged knots of wood, were howling and wild.

But it was the small black wolf in the center of the carving that really drew the eye. That wolf looked like it could move at any moment, come alive and shake off the wood surrounding it to run, to hunt. That small black wolf was Granny Wolfe, the matriarch of Ordinary's pack.

"Oh, Jame. The Heartwood?" I glanced up at him. "I did a drive by last night, went through the pit."

"Why?" The word was drawn out, even. He tipped his head just a little, waiting.

For a moment—just a split second—my mind went blank. Why *had* I been there so late? What was I doing driving around when I should have been home, in bed, asleep?

Then that moment washed away, the doubt, the tiniest tick of panic, all gone almost faster than I could process.

Jame was frowning now.

The memories came back to me, though they seemed foggy, at a distance, as if I were seeing myself from the outside.

"I saw a flicker of light through the office window where it shouldn't be. I checked it out."

"And?"

I pulled on memories that felt sticky and unclear. Why was this so hard to remember?

"No one was there. I couldn't pin down exactly where the light had come from, but I tried the door. It was unlocked."

"Unlocked?"

"No. Wait. It wasn't unlocked." I frowned. Something felt wrong about that. I had been there just hours ago, really. Drove the main area, checked the parking. Got out of the car and checked the office. First, with my flashlight through the window, then I tried the handle.

It had stayed shut, right? If it had been open, I would have gone inside. And I didn't go inside. Had no memory of that.

The only thing that had happened was I got out of the car, tried the door, got back in the car.

Everything had been fine. Everything had been normal.

"So which was it? Locked or unlocked?" he asked.

"Locked." I met his steady gaze with one of my own. "I didn't see anything missing. The Heartwood was on the mantel over the fireplace like it always is."

"You noticed it there, or thought it was there?"

"Know."

"So you saw it there."

"I saw it there."

"On the mantel."

"On the mantel." I smiled. "If you ever wanted to pitch in as a reserve officer, let me know. You've got the calm, slightly intimidating demeanor down flat."

"So, here's the thing," he said, ignoring my comment. "It wasn't on the mantel."

Everything in me went a little cold and itchy. Something about this conversation wasn't right. If reality were a sweater, it was wool that had shrunk so small it didn't fit me anymore.

It was a feeling I'd been having lately. Ever since I'd gotten back my—rather beaten and bruised—soul that had been in the hands of a demon for over a year, I'd been...out of step somehow.

I knew there would be side effects to having my soul possessed by a demon. Everyone knew there would be side effects. But no one knew exactly what would happen to the soul of the person who could Bridge god powers into Ordinary when that soul had been in a demon's hands for so long.

The possibilities kept me up at night.

But I was good at my job. Being a police officer in Ordinary meant I had to follow all the laws and rules of the mortal world, and also all the laws and rules of the supernatural world. I was not above the law. No one was above the law.

But with or without a soul, with or without a demon-touched soul, I knew how to do my job.

"It was on the mantel when I was there." Firm. No doubt.

He didn't so much as twitch, but something about him changed. If I were a werewolf, I probably would have known exactly what that meant. But I was just human.

Well, mostly.

"It's been on the book shelf for the last six months."

Time *tickticktick*ed while I went over my memory again. "Behind the desk?"

"Behind the desk."

Nope. I could see it there, clearly. On the mantel. "You sure someone didn't move it recently?"

"We're sure."

"Well, someone must have moved it. It was on the mantel when I looked through the window."

"The window on the door?"

"Yes. I didn't take your carving. Why would I take something so valuable to the pack?"

His eyes widened a fraction. "I wasn't accusing you of taking it. You're…you're looking out for us, Delaney." He said that last bit like he was checking to make sure I knew it.

Right there—that was the thing. People had been acting differently around me ever since the whole demon-soul-return. I saw the way my sisters looked at me.

I saw the way the other people on the force: Hatter and Shoe looked at me.

I saw how Death, who preferred to be called Than while vacationing, looked at me.

No, scratch that. Than looked at me the same way he'd

always looked at me. Sort of amused and slightly disinterested.

But I'd seen how quickly the other vacationing gods had spotted me on the street, in a shop, and had made it a point to stop and talk. To check in on me.

And I'd seen how Ryder looked at me too.

All of them (except Than) thought something might be wrong with me, or might go wrong with me and they needed to check in to be sure.

And...okay, I did have the weird little memory issues every now and again.

But whatever side effects I had from the soul thing, it wasn't like I was broken.

"I know I'm looking out for you," I told him. "I'm looking out for everyone. That's number one on my job. You sure you don't want to volunteer for reserve officer? You have the right attitude."

He flashed me a sly smile. "Nope. Fighting fires and dating a vampire brings more than enough excitement into my life."

"How is Ben?" I asked. "Really?" Ben was tough and strong, but he'd been tortured not so long ago, and it had taken him time—a lot of time—to heal.

Vampires could take massive damage, but even the undead had their limits.

"Good." His smile was a little softer, as were his eyes. "Really good. He's back at work now. Light duty. Has been for a couple weeks."

"How's that going?"

"Complains constantly. We don't see eye to eye on what actually constitutes light duty. But the make-up sex is great."

I laughed, and he winked, then lifted his head like he'd just caught a scent.

"Something?" I asked.

"Maybe?" He turned his head north, then south, his nostrils flared. "I thought I smelled strawberries and fire. It's gone now. Probably just someone's perfume or a vape." He waved one hand low, dismissing his reaction and, I knew, letting the other wolves know everything was okay.

"Have you filed a police report on the Heartwood?"

"Yeah. Fawn went to handle it. Mantel, huh?"

"It's where I saw it. Maybe someone moved it, took off when I got there, then circled back?"

He shook his head. "Maybe. We didn't smell anyone who shouldn't be there."

So he'd known I'd been there.

A car rolled by slowly, the driver rubbernecking. I gave a reassuring wave, and he engaged the gas pedal and went on his way.

"So how long are you going to be out here?" It was early, and traffic was light, but the road would soon get busy with the valley-to-coast and casino-to-coast traffic.

"Just an hour or so. We're only stopping people who are pulling over for gas or food."

"You're a traffic hazard."

"Noted," he said.

"I'll be back by in an hour. What am I going to find here?"

"I have no idea," he said gamely. "We won't be here by then."

I flipped a thumbs up. "We'll follow up on the theft."

"Oh, before you go," he said. "I heard Bertie was looking for some volunteers for Saturday's event."

"Really?" I feigned innocently, "Isn't that interesting? I had no idea. Too bad I'm out of town."

He didn't have to be a werewolf to catch that lie.

It was Jean's turn to volunteer, anyway. My youngest sister had once again, wriggled out of helping with the last festival, the Slammin' Salmon Serenade, leaving our newest reserve deputy, Kelby, who was a giant, to deal with it all. Kelby had taken it in stride. She'd even stood in as the queen of the parade, earning buckets of respect from me.

And from Bertie.

We were all secretly hoping Kelby would volunteer for all

of Bertie's community events since she'd handled the first one so well.

"Have you posted this at the casino?" I held up the flyer.

"Not yet."

"Consider it done."

"Thanks, Chief."

I got back in the car and flipped off the lights. True to their word, the Wolfes were only pulling over cars stopping for gas, food, or general curiosity.

The Wolfe pack were solid, down-to-earth kind of people. Easy to make conversation, easy to laugh.

I mean, they were scary as hell when they were pissed off or wolfed-out, but when they walked the moonless days with the rest of us, they were easy to mistake as human.

Which was why I wasn't worried about what would happen if they found the thief before we did. I knew they'd follow the law and bring the person—supernatural or otherwise—to the station.

Everything would be handled according to the rules.

A car pulled off to the side and rolled down the windows. A voice shouted good naturedly at Jame, and he laughed, jogging to close the distance.

I recognized that voice. It was Ben.

I left them to it and eased into traffic headed east. It was twenty-two miles to the casino and I wanted to get there before the early crowds arrived.

The dragon pig turned around and growled at the back seat.

"We don't eat werewolves." I glanced in my rearview mirror. "And we aren't stopping for corn dogs."

It growled again, and this time smoke rolled up from its nostrils.

I glanced in my rearview mirror again. "What are you so—?"

A unicorn popped up in the back seat. She shook her shiny mane, threw her hooves in the air, and shouted: "Ta-da!"

"Holy shit!"

I didn't slam on the brakes because I wasn't about to start a mile-long fender bender, but I did pull off to the side of the road, narrowly missing a mailbox and blocking a driveway.

Luckily the cars behind me were slow-rolling and rambled past, no collisions imminent.

"Really, Delaney," the unicorn scolded. "Your driving skills need work. You almost ran us into that," she stretched her neck so she could see out the front window, "wooden fish? Is that a mailbox?" She blew air through her lips, making a rude sound. "Tacky. Give it a little gas. Trust me, the homeowners will thank you for it."

I inhaled, exhaled, considered my gun, but really, a gun wasn't going to do much damage to a demon. Even a demon the size and shape of a Shetland pony. A pink Shetland pony. With a stupid sparkly diamond horn in the middle of her stupid glittery forehead.

"Xtelle, why are you in my Jeep?"

"Because you have no taste in cars? Would it kill you to invest in a nice Mercedes? There aren't even seat warmers." She wiggled her butt back and forth, then sighed. "So pedestrian. I expect better of you. For me."

"Get out of my Jeep."

"Wonderful idea! A unicorn strutting across the street. With all this slow traffic, too. Imagine the news it would make. I bet reporters would come here, so close to Ordinary, just to see if the pink unicorn is real. Wouldn't that be so much fun, Delaney? All those eyes looking right here into your tiny corner of the world where gods are trying to vacation without being disturbed. And my goodness, just think of how the supernaturals in town would enjoy the scrutiny!"

Her eyes got big. "I *love* this idea. Last time we talked you were *so* self-righteous and for-the-good-of-my-people. But look at you now. A little streak of evil." She wiped one shiny hoof under her eye. "I'm so proud."

"Xtelle," I warned.

"Busy! The world must see my brilliance! Call the press!"

She grabbed the handle—not something a hooved creature should be able to do, but she was a demon. A very annoying one. If she could take the shape of a unicorn, she could make her hoof bendy enough to open doors.

Luckily, I controlled the locks in the car.

"You aren't going out there to blow some kind of supernatural cover, and we both know it," I said. "You also aren't really a unicorn. If there's a reason you're here, spit it out. Because in exactly ten seconds, I'm going to tell my dragon to drop you into the nearest volcano."

"Mount St. Helens?"

"The nearest volcano on the ocean floor."

The dragon rumbled its approval. My sister Jean and I had found the dragon in a cave on the edge of the ocean. I figured it wouldn't mind a little deep sea homicide.

The waterproofness of the demon, however, had yet to be proved.

"You are no fun. At all. Not even a little. I don't like it." She stuck her nose in the air and crossed her little pony arms across her little pony chest.

"Nine," I said, "eight. Seven seconds until splashdown, Xtelle."

She shook her head, just the tiniest of motions, like she was trying not to give in. Then she made a frustrated sound. "Fine. I want back into Ordinary."

I heard her, really I did. But it was just so preposterous, such a ridiculous request, I responded the only way I could. I laughed.

"No," I said. "Absolutely not."

"But...why?"

I held up a finger. "You lied about being a demon. You didn't sign the contract all demons are required to sign if they want to enter into Ordinary." Another finger. "You messed with my sister." And one more finger, though this one a little less willingly. "You messed with her boyfriend."

"My son? My demon son, Bathin? That boyfriend? You won't let me spend well deserved—very well deserved—vacation time in your crappy little beach town because I was curious about my son's love life?"

"You made a weapon he thought he had to use on himself."

"*Pffft.* It was just a little pair of scissors."

"That he thought would kill him."

"But they didn't, did they? I get no credit for being considerate about my betrayals."

The dragon pig growled again, and this time it sounded hungry.

"I don't know why you stay with her," she said to the dragon pig. "You can see she's going to turn on you, too, someday. Humans are so predictable."

The dragon pig roared, a sound entirely too large for an animal that small, and a space this enclosed. My ears rang, but it made me smile.

"Eeep!" Xtelle scooted behind my seat. "Delaney? Delaney?" She fluttered her impossibly long eyelashes at me in the mirror. "You know you and I have so much in common."

I shouldn't. I really shouldn't encourage her. "Name one thing you and I have in common."

"We both want to live in Ordinary, we enjoy ruling over our family, we agree that butt warmers are a necessity."

"I don't want butt warmers."

She tipped her head so that her mouth curved up in a weird little smile. "Delaney, I am a demon. I can see mortal desires. You want butt warmers."

"I don't." But I kind of did. Especially since she kept talking about it.

"But you do. You want a warm butt. Ooooo. So warm. Mmmm. Warm butt."

"Six, five, four, threetwoone," I said. "Out. And don't go tramping around as a unicorn where mortals can see you."

"You're not the boss of me. Not here outside Ordinary."

"All right. Forget about the volcano. I'll just tell my dragon to eat you."

"I...you wouldn't. That thing..." Her eyes were wild, jotting from me to the dragon pig.

The dragon pig seemed happy with her state of panic. It growled constantly, a low rumbling purr.

"In one bite, Xtelle," I said. "Horn to hoof."

She sucked in her bottom lip and the top one wobbled for a moment. "You're mean."

I was going to agree, but she disappeared in a puff of pink smoke.

"Huh," I said. "Strawberries and fire. Jame was right." I twisted to look in the back seat. I wouldn't put it past her to turn into a floor mat or pebble or a fly.

I had no idea how Myra had put up with her for the short time we'd actually believed she was a unicorn and not a demon in disguise.

I readjusted the mirror, then glanced over at the dragon pig. "Is she in the car?"

The piglet tippy-toed a little circle, then sat with its back against the seat, facing forward. It made a squeaky sound.

"I take it that's a no?"

The dragon *oink*ed.

"Good dragon." I dug in my purse and pulled out a broken screwdriver. I dangled it in front of its little nose, and the dragon pig slurped it down like a tasty noodle. "We've had enough of demons for one day, haven't we?"

It grumbled a little and I decided we were on the same page. With one last pat on the dragon pig's head, I rolled away from the ugly fish mailbox and headed toward the casino.

CHAPTER THREE

THE CASINO WAS NESTLED in a valley surrounded by hills covered in evergreen trees. The parking lot was dotted with deciduous trees and bushes that created shady spots in the summer and flashes of colorful leaves in the fall.

I maneuvered the Jeep to the far side of the parking lot and gave the dragon pig one more pat. "You're going to stay right here while I pick up the mail."

The dragon pig *oink*ed.

"You're not going to eat any of the vehicles, signs, or poles, right?"

Another enthusiastic *oink*.

"That means no nibbling on my Jeep. No buttons, no visors, no mirrors will be missing when I return."

The *oink* was a little quieter.

"No floor mats or soft stuff either."

The dragon pig wrinkled its nose, and a puff of smoke came out of its nostrils. It flopped dejectedly down on the seat, soft ears flipping to the side. It grunted.

I grinned. "Good. I'll get you some nice scrap metal once we get back to town. Maybe even a rusty old golf cart."

It sighed, though at the mention of the golf cart it perked up a little.

I rolled down the windows, even though the dragon pig liked hot cars—the hotter the better—locked the Jeep, and strolled across the parking lot.

It was a mild day for mid-October, almost warm with only a few clouds streaking the blue sky. A light wind pushed and tugged just enough to stir the remaining leaves and send a random piece of dry grass scooting across the pavement.

The group of four lingering by the door were gray haired and laughing as one of the women went on about a breakfast incident involving beans and a grandchild.

I smiled and excused my way past them and through the sliding doors.

Music—soft and folksy—lingered just behind the murmur of voices and the sweet chimes of machines. Someone cheered, an applause followed, and I threaded my way to the cashier waiting behind the counter.

"Hey there, Delaney. Mail run?" Walt was human, a heavy guy with a really impressive set of curly sideburns and a pompadour hairstyle. Whether on purpose or not (I'd never gotten a straight answer out of him), he looked like an Elvis impersonator who just happened to be slumming in Oregon.

The mail was delivered to the casino in two ways: either a large envelope addressed and postage paid with smaller, simply addressed letters inside, or individual letters, which to the sight of humans were addressed and stamped correctly.

"Every Thursday," I said, "Thanks, Walt." I handed over the key. "How are things?"

He walked back through the open door to the safe where mail for the deities was deposited. It used to be delivered to a little gas station near here, but when the big casino came in a couple decades ago, it seemed like a better drop point.

"Still above ground," he said, "so I ain't complaining." He disappeared from sight then came back, tapping a single envelope in his hand. He set it on the counter, the key on top. It looked like a regular letter to humans, but to me there was no stamp, no return address, and the only deliverable address was a single name: BATHIN and the town: ORDINARY, OREGON.

Interesting. I'd never picked up an envelope for Bathin before.

"Emily still excited about college?" I asked.

He rolled his eyes. "She can't wait. I think she just likes the idea of having her own car and a bedroom she doesn't have to share with her sister."

"Well, that might be what she's telling you, but there are plenty of pretty boys in college. Or pretty girls."

He pressed his palms against his ears. "La-la-la. I refuse to get involved in my daughter's love life."

I laughed and picked up the envelope, pocketing the key.

He dropped his hands. "She has a phone. Our number's on speed dial. She's gonna do great."

"Yeah, she is," I said. "If you need anything, if she needs anything, I know some good people in Eugene. I can call in a drive-by or wellness check."

"I'll keep it in mind. But with our girl, it's more likely she'll have her nose so deep in a book, she'll forget part of college is meeting people—boys or girls—and having fun."

"She'll figure it out."

He smiled. "Yeah. Edith and I are thinking about a road trip. Route 66. Maybe next year, or the year after. We've thought about it for years. Might be time to finally go. Have some fun of our own."

"Eat the weird stuff, make faces in your selfies, and send a postcard, okay?"

He chuckled. "Will do."

I turned and nearly ran into a unicorn wearing dark glasses.

"Oh. Delaney," she exclaimed. "Imagine seeing you here. Isn't this a surprise?"

"What are you doing?" I hissed.

She leaned forward and put one hoof by her ear. "What's that? What are you whispering?"

"Take human form, Xtelle. Before someone sees you."

"You need a form?" Walt asked from behind me.

I pivoted. Smiled. "No, I'm good." I held up the envelope. "Thanks again."

He waved and moved over to help a woman looking for the restrooms.

"He didn't notice you," I said.

"I am certain he must have." Xtelle sounded offended and also like she was lying.

"No. He didn't."

I was walking toward the little coffee shop. Even though I hadn't gotten a message from any new god that wanted to come vacation in Ordinary, I usually checked to see if one might be in the area and looking to contact me.

Xtelle trotted behind me, huffing and muttering, and—I noticed—not turning a single person's gaze. She shoved up alongside me.

"He's just stunned into silence by my magnificence."

"Uh-huh." I waited for the young, beanie-wearing couple coming our way to comment on my horned pink pony, but they just walked past me like Xtelle didn't exist.

Or like she was invisible.

"Clever."

"I don't know what you're talking about." She lifted her nose, and her sunglasses slipped askew.

She looked ridiculous. I carefully locked down the smile that threatened to break out.

"Invisibility," I said. "No one else can see you, but you can pester me."

"I'm not pestering. Demons know your name, Delaney."

"So?" I moved closer to the wall, crowding her up.

"Even though you're a pedestrian, plain, boring, rule-abiding, mostly-mortal, you aren't quite as stupid as we've heard."

"Thanks." I changed my trajectory once again, and she had to pull up fast or risk running into a potted plant.

She did neither of those things. Instead, she just trotted right through the plant.

Okay, that was different.

"Also, you aren't quite as ugly or pasty as everyone says. Your teeth could use work, and those tiny boobs…"

"What do you want, Xtelle?"

"I'm sure I don't know what you're talking about."

We were close to the bathroom, so I sped up, opened the door long enough for her to precede me, then stepped in behind her and threw the lock.

"This." I waved my finger in a circle. "You following me because you want to talk to me. Wrap it up."

She shimmered and became just that little bit more solid looking, her eyes flashing pink for a moment before returning to the fake sweet-as-spring blue.

"You won't let me into Ordinary to talk to you, so this is my only option. Although," she glanced around the restroom and curled her lip, "it's very…you."

"The dragon pig is right outside in the parking lot."

"I don't know what that has to do with…"

"Ten," I said.

"You are so tedious!"

"Nine."

"I want to visit Ordinary. And stay."

"Why?"

I shouldn't consider her request, not after all the havoc she'd caused. But the rules of entering Ordinary were too long established inside me. If a supernatural wanted in, all they needed was Reed approval. We didn't even ask most supernaturals to sign contracts, like we did for the gods.

Demons were the exceptions. They preferred breaking rules and sowing chaos. It was in their nature. Above all else, Ordinary was a vacation town. A place of rest and relaxation.

Demons had to sign a contract binding them to the rules of Ordinary. But the only demon who'd agreed to sign that contract was Bathin, Xtelle's son, and Myra's boyfriend.

He'd only agreed to it a month ago when he'd almost lost everything, including my sister.

I found it hard to believe that after centuries of breaking

laws and ruining souls, Xtelle wanted to settle down to a nice quiet beach life.

"It's…you won't believe me," she said. "You've already made up your mind."

"This is your chance to convince me to change it." I rolled my finger again.

"Fine. I…liked it in Ordinary. Okay? Are you happy? I *enjoyed* myself in your *stupid* backwater town." She was breathing hard, challenge in her eyes. Then, a little softer, she added, "I want to enjoy it again."

"You entered into Ordinary on a lie, told us you were a pink unicorn who had lost her herd."

"I *am* a pink unicorn." She trotted a circle, swished her tail, and glanced over her shoulder so the horn sparkled in the fluorescent light.

"I've seen your real form, Xtelle."

She finished the turn so she was facing me again. "You really haven't, Delaney. I've taken thousands of forms, a million million faces. This form is as real as any other. Sometimes I think it's nice just to be a pink unicorn for a while, don't you?"

That sounded dangerously close to real emotion, the sort of weary fatigue I'd heard from gods and immortals. Beings who had been alive long enough that the living of life had become a chore instead of a joy. It was one of the reasons gods and supernaturals liked Ordinary. It was a way to have a fresh start, to be something else for awhile, to be someone else.

But that wasn't enough for me to let a demon—correction: *another* demon—into my safe little town.

"You're going to have to give me more than that. Why now, Xtelle?"

"I'm tired of the everyday of my kind. Torture, trickery, temptation. Boring. But Ordinary? What a shiny little jewel. I want to spend time there. I want to swallow it whole."

Her hoof came up to her mouth, and her button eyes went moon-wide. "Did I say that out loud?"

"Yes. Thank you for being honest about wanting to devour my home. My answer is no."

I unlocked the door behind my back, then held it open for her. "Run along now like a good little unicorn."

I wiggled my fingers in a tiny wave.

"You are a pain in my neck, Delaney Reed."

"I have that on a T-shirt *and* a cup."

She snorted, which shot pink glitter out her nostrils. The sunglasses had fallen all the way down her nose, so I could see the humor in her eyes.

She might think Ordinary was a fun new place to cause trouble, and she might want to swallow it whole, but it was obvious she had fun bothering me too.

"You are insufferable," she proclaimed.

"Thank you. Good-bye, Xtelle."

She tossed her head and pranced toward the door, doing a parade two-step I'd seen at the State Fair horse competitions.

"You. Are. The. Worst," she said, step-step-stepping. "I. Don't. Like. You." Step-step-step-swish.

I laughed, and she neatly butt-checked me as she pranced out the bathroom door and into the carpeted hallway.

For a moment, I kind of wished she weren't invisible, because she was acting like such a stuck up diva, it was a sight to see.

Then the moment passed, and I angled toward the coffee shop again.

The hiss and gurgle of the espresso machine grinding through orders, and the delicious, rich scent of coffee and caramel, made me pick up my pace.

The coffee shop was small. Even though it was in a casino, they'd tucked it far enough away from the machines and the hubbub that it felt like a nice quiet retreat.

I took my place in line behind two other people who didn't appear to be together. One was ordering the most complicated cup of tea I'd ever heard of in my life, and the other was tapping his phone with both thumbs.

I scanned the tables. Two young guys who looked like

they were between jobs but had the family inheritance to make up for it were arguing over football. One couple in their thirties, both with hair dyed goth black, scanned a screen, laughing.

But it was the single figure who sat in the booth by the window that set off all my Spidey senses.

She was a goddess.

Beautiful too, her hair pulled back in a thick knot, her eyes the color of burnt amber, and her skin a rich brown. She raised one eyebrow at me, and I nodded.

When a god wanted to talk, it was best not to make them wait. I took a step away from the line, but she shook her head and made a little shooing motion. She wanted me to get on with my order before joining her.

So I did. The guy on the phone didn't even speak to the Barista, Erika, who called him by name, smoothly scanned his screen, and grabbed his cup for his order.

He shuffled to one side, eyes on the phone as he waited.

"Hi. Can I get a dark roast with room for cream?"

"Sure thing, Delaney. How's it going?"

"Good. Thanks. How about you?"

She poured my coffee while I tugged a few bucks out of my wallet.

"High Tea Tide Saturday," she said. "I'm excited for that. Have a fancy dress picked out and everything. We have new desserts and drinks we want to try out."

"Bertie has you on the vendor list, right?"

"We filled out the forms months ago."

"Then I'll see you there."

"I'll save you one of our new chai-pumpkin cream scones."

"Sounds amazing. Thank you." She dropped a vanilla-coated coffee bean on top of the lid and moved on to the pack of women who had filed into the room.

I popped the bean in my mouth and headed to the goddess.

"May I have a seat?" I wasn't sure which goddess she was

yet, but it was best to be polite when having coffee with beings of ultimate power.

"Please do." Her voice was easy and kind, and I found myself wanting to sit across from her for hours just to hear it.

God power. I was not immune, but I was pretty resistant to it. I could only imagine what effect her voice would have on a regular mortal.

"I'm Delaney Reed, the Bridge to Ordinary, Oregon. As you might know, I come here every Thursday to pick up mail and messages. Did you have a message for a deity inside Ordinary?"

That wouldn't be unusual, but it would be very old school. There was a time when my grands and great-grands had to memorize, word for word, every message some god wanted to pass along to the deities vacationing inside Ordinary.

Every one of them complained about it in their journals. Guess who got blamed if they got one word wrong?

The almost-war between Eirene and Živa had changed the oral tradition to pen and paper.

That was how it still worked today.

"No, not a message," she said. "More curiosity about the place."

"Sure. What do you want to know?"

"How blue is the ocean from the shore?"

That was not what I expected, something so mundane.

"Ordinary's ocean changes almost moment to moment along with our winds, weather, and seasons. Sometimes the water is as green as jade, other times as blue as sapphire. To be fair, it runs gray a lot of the time, storms whipping it into white foam edges."

She picked up a glass that seemed to have water in it. But just like demons, gods could make a person see what they want them to see. For all I knew, she was drinking the cosmic honey from some planet in some universe I'd never heard of.

I took a drink out of my own cup. Just plain ol' Earth coffee, which I'd put up against any drink in the heavens.

"You like it very much," she said.

"Coffee?" I asked, wondering if she had read my mind.

"Ordinary. You love it."

"Yes."

"Enough that you have suffered for it."

I held very still. But my heart pounded, *drum-drum-drumm*ing. It was fear, it was sorrow. It was knowing gods could see more of me than I could hide: my mistakes, my regrets, my bruised up soul.

"Suffering isn't my first choice."

"I see that."

I waited. This was a part of the job. To get a feel for the gods and goddesses who wanted to vacation. To help them understand what living life as a mortal was like, especially if they'd never tried it before.

I'd have to check the records, but I was pretty sure she'd never been to Ordinary.

"May I ask which goddess you are?"

"I'd enjoy you guessing."

I took another sip of coffee and studied her. This wasn't easy. If I'd ever Bridged her power before, I'd recognize her in a dark room, blindfolded. But I'd never met her.

God power could be sensed in different ways by different beings. My Dad had seen it—bright and twisting, blinding in beauty. I could see it, not as well as my Dad, but oh, how I heard it—clear and aching, rolling through me like a primordial chorus. It could be deafening. So when I was outside of Ordinary, I kept my god senses on mute.

I opened my senses to her. Carefully, slowly, ready for that rush of sound, that cosmic shout.

But instead I heard silver, bright and pastel, a soft, distant green fire. Her power was a song made of the arc of sky blushed by dawn, a held whisper between night and day.

I exhaled and dropped my guard. This goddess was gentle, beautiful. A guiding light, a star, a path.

"Tala?" I asked. Tala was the Tagalog goddess of the morning and evening star.

"Yes," she said with a soft smile. "How did you know?"

"Despite what my sister Myra might tell you, I have studied up on deities and their powers. Spent all my life doing it, actually. You've never been to Ordinary."

"No."

"Do you want to go there now? Vacation?"

She swirled the glass again, and I caught a glimpse of stars rotating, throwing off galaxies of dust, fire, spinning in a distant dark.

She sipped. The glass was empty now, no water or whatever had actually been filling it. With one tiny sip, she'd drained it dry.

But when she set it down, the glass had immense weight. It looked as if it had fused to the wood of the table and the earth below it.

Tala had made a decision.

"Is Death there?"

"He…um…is. Do you want me to take him a message?"

Those eyes, brown and glinting with star fire, pulled up at the corners as she smiled. "I think I'd rather deliver it in person."

"So that's a yes for some fun in the sun? Vacation time," I explained when she frowned slightly. "Beach, sunshine, relaxation."

"It sounds very wholesome."

"It can be. There are some rules you'll need to follow if you're going to stay."

"Of course."

"And you will be expected to follow all mortal laws too."

"I understand."

"Only by my approval may you enter, only by my approval may you stay. I can kick you out at my discretion."

Her fingertips tapped on the table, a soft, rolling motion.

"Acceptable." She nodded for me to continue.

"I will Bridge your power and give it to the goddess who is currently storing the powers. That responsibility changes from deity to deity once a year. If you stay long enough, you will be expected to store the powers for one year."

"Who is caring for the powers currently?"

"Frigg."

"Acceptable."

"You must get a job or otherwise be involved in the community. One of the original intentions of Ordinary was for gods and goddesses to experience a mortal life. That means you'll need to follow mortal norms."

"A job."

"Or volunteering."

She nodded. "What else?"

"You'll need to choose your name."

"I think Talli would be fitting, don't you?" A small smile played across her lips.

She was teasing me. None of this seemed like news to her. "You've been thinking about this for some time, haven't you?"

"Many years."

"Excellent. You need to sign the contract. Let me call my sister and have her bring it over."

I pulled my phone out of my pocket, but before I could dial, a manila envelope landed on the table in front of me.

"Hey, Delaney," Myra said.

I glanced up. Myra was the middle sister out of the three of us. While my build was athletic and lean, hers was curvy and compact. The most I ever did with my hair was pull it back in a braid, and I didn't bother with makeup.

Myra liked the rock-a-billy look, short straight bangs, and a bob that brushed her shoulders. She did that cat-eye thing with eyeliner and got it right every time which completely baffled me because there was no magic involved.

Her lips, which were currently curved in a smug smile, were a deep, deep red.

"I was headed out to the derby meeting," she said, "and thought you might need this."

Myra's family gift was that she was always in the right

place at the right time. So her turning up wasn't really a surprise.

Still, it was always cool to see her gift in action.

"Myra, this is Tala. She'll be vacationing in Ordinary. Tala, this is my sister, Myra Reed."

Her eyebrows went up. "Keeper of the Library?"

"Yes," Myra said. "Our father passed it on to me. Why?"

"You are also the lover of the demon Bathin?"

One of the drawbacks to the Reed lineage was that our skin was pale enough to blush like crazy. Hot spots slapped Myra's cheeks, and she tipped her chin up defensively.

"Does that impact your decision to vacation in Ordinary?" Myra asked, no emotion in her voice, all business.

I drank coffee and watched the force of a goddess meet my very immovable sibling.

"He is the Prince of the Underworld," Tala mused.

"I'm aware. He is also a citizen of Ordinary and follows the same laws and rules the other mortals, supernaturals, and deities follow."

"Are you aware there is a price on his head?"

"Yes," she said. "But what happens outside Ordinary is of no concern to us." It was delivered it in her cop voice: calm and confident. It sounded true.

But I knew her. The relationship with Bathin was very new. Myra did not give her heart easily or often or, really, ever.

This was her first real relationship. One she'd almost missed because he wouldn't surrender my soul. One she'd almost missed because she was not good at being vulnerable with anyone.

Well, except her sisters.

"There is a war coming," Tala said.

Cold shivers rattled through me. I'd been hearing that same refrain from the gods for almost two years, whenever they had their guards down. I had thought the war had been settled when we, assisted by some sleight of hand on Death's part, killed an ancient vampire.

I'd thought the war they kept talking about had already come to Ordinary.

"Which war is coming?" I asked. Because I was done with mystery. Putting it all on the table was my style now. I was done going with the flow when deities wanted to be enigmatic.

"The King of the Underworld searches for his son. All of the Below will rise to devour the Above."

It almost sounded like prophecy, even though she was not the goddess of such. She was a goddess of orbs of light that guided men, and she was said to shine in the night and morning sky to signal safety from the sun god.

She had warning powers, powers of evasion. I just wasn't sure she had the power of divination.

I shot a look at Myra. She caught my gaze and gave me the slightest shake of her head. No, Tala wasn't a prophetess, as it were.

Well, that was something.

"We know about the demon king," I said. "He's not welcome nor allowed into Ordinary. No demon is, unless they sign a very strict contract."

Her eyebrows rose while she put two and two together and came to the conclusion that Bathin had signed the contract.

"He's the only one," Myra said, answering the look on Tala's face.

"Isn't that surprising?" the goddess murmured, giving Myra a new sort of attention. "What one will do for love."

If Myra was blushing before, now she flashed red hot. Even so, she didn't change her stance, didn't look otherwise uncomfortable under the statement and scrutiny.

"This contract," I tapped the envelope, "is for you to sign. Please read through it and ask me any questions before you sign it. The contract is the same for every deity. If the terms aren't acceptable, then vacationing might not be in the cards."

She drew the envelope toward her and retrieved the papers. A pen, made of gold vines twisted around a black core, appeared in her left hand. Instead of leaves, clusters of stars glittered with tiny, bright sparks along the vine.

She quickly read through the contract, then signed on the last line. "What is next?"

I accepted the papers and slid them back into the envelope. "You show up at the edge of Ordinary. Any place you choose. I'll meet you there and welcome you in, then we'll take your power to Frigg and set it down."

She nodded and glanced around the little café. Or maybe she was looking through dimensions, time, realities.

"It sounds...lovely. I will come. Not now, but soon. Thank you, Delaney Reed."

"My honor and pleasure," I said. "It is nice to meet you, Tala."

"And you."

Myra turned and strode out of the shop, scanning the hallway beyond the door. Like she needed to be somewhere immediately. Now.

I got to my feet. If Myra was moving fast, that meant there was trouble going down.

"Sorry for the rush," I said, tucking the envelope under my arm. "I hope to see you soon."

Tala gave me an understanding nod as I swigged my coffee, two, three mouthfuls, getting as much of it down as I could before I hurried after Myra.

A loud crash filled the casino, something big falling over, like a machine or a table or a display case. I tossed the coffee in the trash and sprinted down the hall, right on Myra's heels.

"What happened?" I asked, just as we cleared the corner of the hall and rushed into the main room.

Xtelle—still a pony-sized unicorn, still wearing those ridiculous sunglasses—trotted out in front of us and waved a hoof, sending glitter through the air.

"Delaney, is that you?" she asked. "Oh. And I see Myra is with you." The way she said Myra's name made it sound like a particularly contagious disease.

"You see her, right?" Myra asked.

"Yep."

"She sees us?"

"Yep."

"But no one else sees her?"

"Nope."

I took the measure of the room. A craps table lay toppled on its side, a crowd circling it from a safe distance. No one had been hurt—not that I could see—but it was clear they were shaken.

I itched to spring into crowd control mode, but the casino staff were already doing a great job ushering people back and away, and making sure everyone was okay.

Three craps dealers stood, shocked, eyes wide, glancing at the table, then at the crowd, then back at the table.

"You," I ordered Xtelle, "stay."

"I've got her." Myra stuck her hand in her pocket to access whatever she had there. I was confident it'd be just the thing to stop a demon in her tracks. "Stay right there, Xtelle."

"I don't know what all the fuss is about," Xtelle said. "Delaney, yoo-hoo, Delaney! Are you paying attention to me now?"

No. I stopped next to the huddle of dealers. "Your table?"

The two women and a man nodded, not looking at me. "I don't know what happened," said the woman whose hair was pulled back in a fashionable twist to show off strong cheekbones. "I was just starting my shift and the whole thing just…" She pushed her palms forward.

"No one was near it?"

She shook her head.

"An earthquake?" The other woman was spindly and barely looked legal. "Do you think it was an earthquake? It had to be an earthquake, right?"

"Delaney! Yoo-hoo! Yoo-hoo! Pay attention to me!"

"It might have been an earthquake," I lied. This hadn't been an accident and this hadn't been an earthquake.

"It wasn't an earthquake," Xtelle shouted. "Delaney? Delaney!"

"One more step, and I'll throw." Myra's words were quiet enough to be swallowed by the general murmur of the crowd.

"It fell over. It just fell over," the woman repeated.

"Hey, it's okay," I said.

The big bosses arrived, telling everyone it was an accident and not to worry. Two beefy guys in security uniforms corralled the crowd. Another employee, who appeared to be in management, showed up and escorted the dealers, still wide-eyed and shaky, off to the private elevator.

Maintenance arrived and righted the table.

One of the many security cameras would have caught what happened. I might be able to push my way in until someone let me see it. But this was tribal territory, and I didn't have authority here.

I walked over to Myra. She was casually pointing a carrot at Xtelle, who was just as casually ignoring her.

"Any idea?" Myra asked.

"Earthquake seems to be the contender."

"It wasn't an earthquake."

"I know."

"Delaney!" Xtelle stomped her foot and charged over to us, narrowly missing a man with a walker who was making his slow way toward the exit. "Pay attention to me!"

"You know what would be great?" I asked Myra, taking great pains not to look at Xtelle.

"What?"

"If she had a mute button."

"Oh, yeah. That'd be really great. But you know what would be better?"

"What?"

"If she had a go away button."

"Nice."

From the corner of my eye, I saw Xtelle's nostrils flare and her big glossy eyes burn with pink fire. She growled—a weird sound coming from a unicorn—and muttered something that sounded like, "Fine, we'll do it the fun way." She trotted off, shedding invisible pink fire and glitter over everything she passed.

"Since when did she do the fire thing?" I asked.

"Since when did she do the show up here thing?" Myra replied.

"She was in my car just outside Otis. I think she's following me."

"Really? Following you? I never would have guessed."

"All right."

"Do you think that's why she keeps shouting at you?"

"Har-har."

"Do you think that's why she keeps demanding you pay attention to her? Following you," she mused. "Golly, you really are an amazing detective, Delaney."

"This is so funny you should sell tickets," I said.

"What does she want?" she asked. "Bathin again?"

"Maybe. She told me she wants into Ordinary."

"Why?"

"Well, since I'm such an amazing detective, here's my guess: I'm the Bridge, and as you may not know, demons don't get into Ordinary without signing contracts and getting my okay first."

"Boo. Okay, I deserved that. Did she tell you why she wants in?"

"Vacation time. Don't give me that look, that's what she said. Also, she'd love to eat it whole, which I'm pretty sure is impossible, even for a demon."

"Eat Ordinary?"

I nodded.

"You told her no, right?"

"Do you see a dotted line with her signature on it?"

"Good."

Myra had history with Bathin's mother. None of it good.

I started toward the private elevator. "Let's see if they'll give us a look at the security footage. Make sure whatever happened here isn't something supernatural we need to take care of."

I got about three steps before Myra grabbed my elbow and hurried us off toward the slot machines.

"Problem?" I asked.

"Maybe."

"Family gift?"

She pressed her lips together and nodded. "We need to move."

"I'm with you."

She let go, and we navigated the crowd, shoulder to shoulder. Neither of us were in uniform, but people saw us coming and made space.

Myra stopped next to an empty machine, tipped her head, then took a left. I moved with her.

A woman screamed. We bolted toward the sound, boots thudding across brightly colored industrial carpeting.

Then a cheer rose up, whistles, applause, and the happy *ding-ding-ding* of bells.

The woman was laughing now, and someone who might be her daughter held a phone, taking selfies of the two of them in front of a machine that was paying out big.

"Okay," I said slowly, scanning the scene then looking at Myra for confirmation. "This is the reason we hurried?"

She scowled and tipped her head again as if she were trying to tune into a distant conversation.

"Yes!" shouted a man two machines down. A murmur of surprise and applause filled the space as his machine *ding-ding-dinged* and rolled out the win. He pushed away from the machine to do a little victory dance and that's when I spotted Xtelle.

She stood in front of the machine. One of her hooves was stuck all the way inside the casing, manipulating the guts of the thing.

"Stop it," I warned, quiet enough I hoped people assumed I was talking to Myra. "Knock it off."

"I'm sorry," Xtelle cooed. "Are you paying attention to me now?" She withdrew her hoof and barreled around three machines, found the one she wanted and wedged herself between the woman on the stool and the machine. She stared at me over those stupid sunglasses."Don't," I warned.

She stuck her hoof in the cabinet.

"Xtelle."

She opened her mouth and widened her eyes, the image of innocence. Then she jiggled her hoof.

The machine went wild.

Xtelle pulled her hoof out and rocked back on two legs so she could make jazz hooves. "Ta-da!" She sprayed pink glitter in a three-foot circle.

The woman jumped to her feet. "Thank you, Jesus!"

Xtelle dropped back to all fours. "What about 'Thank you, demons? Thank you, Xtelle!' Just because I don't have a book written about me…"

"Stop." I clapped my hands and smiled like everyone else, moving toward her. Myra turned and headed back the way we'd come. I didn't know why she was leaving, but I trusted her instincts.

Staff arrived, a mix of polite smiles and narrow eyes. They knew the machines were malfunctioning. They knew a table had just mysteriously fallen over. They knew someone had to be behind all this.

I suspected the table had been shoved by a pink demon throwing a hissy fit. But they didn't know that.

Xtelle stuck out her tongue and trotted *through* the machine. Lights flickered, sounds warped, then she popped out the other side.

The crowd was growing, drawn by all the noise. I pushed through it as quickly as I could, while running through my options. How was I supposed to stop an invisible demon on a chaos spree?

I finally made it around the bank of machines and into the next row. I heard an "Eeep!" and the weird *thunk* of a carrot breaking in half, then spotted Myra pointing two jagged chunks of carrot at one snarling unicorn.

"Hold it right there," Myra ordered.

Two people passing by slowed to get a better look at what

was going on. Since Xtelle was invisible, it looked like my sister had lost her mind.

"All right," I said, loud enough for the snoopers. "You've had your fun. Let's take this outside. We can talk."

"I'll sign the contract," Xtelle said.

"Bullshit," Myra said.

"What?" I said.

The snoopers had multiplied, and people at machines turned to give us a good look too.

"Outside," I repeated. "C'mon." I grabbed Myra's shoulder and smiled at the people bug-eyeing the scene.

Myra pointed one of the carrots toward the exit. "That way."

"Yes," I said, for the crowd and for the sulking unicorn, "that way."

Xtelle huffed, tossed her shiny mane, and clopped off, wagging her butt and swishing her tail.

"You might want to put the carrots down," I said.

Myra dropped the carrots into her pockets and gave the onlookers a little wave.

"Sorry," she said. "I just get a little over-excited about fresh produce."

"Good save," I said. "That didn't sound crazy at all."

She huffed a laugh and I patted her shoulder, following her into daylight.

CHAPTER FOUR

"TALK." I crossed my arms and leaned against the Jeep's bumper. Myra had parked the cruiser in front of my car, but she was leaning next to me.

Xtelle rested her haunches on the back bumper of a neon-green VW bug. The combination of glittery pink unicorn and German whimsy was eye watering.

"Oh, now you want me to talk? Now you want to pay attention to me? I tried to talk, I really *tried* Delaney, but you and your thick-headed sister wouldn't listen. You *ignored* me. Me! The Queen of the Underworld. Well, you can take that mute button and shove it up your..."

"You kicked over the table," I interrupted. "You hacked into the slots."

"Winning! Those people won a lot of money because of me."

"Because of you cheating."

"It's a casino. Cheating is a line item."

"You're not a line item, Xtelle. You interfered," I said.

"Yes, Delaney. Yes. I interfered. I am a demon. It's what we do. Meddle. Tempt. Thumb the scales of fate. Out here? Out in the real world?" She waggled her head like a goose, daring me to throw a punch. "You have no say over what I do. You have no rules or laws over me that you can enforce unless you want to try hauling a unicorn to jail."

"Does that bother you?" She minced up a little closer to me, then back, like a boxer in a ring. "Does it bother you that I'm out here in the big, wide world doing all manner of naughty things?" Step, step, retreat. Step, step, dodge.

"Dude," Myra said, "why are you dancing?"

Xtelle stopped, and her nostrils flared wide. "I'm not dancing. That was…a fight. I was ready for a fight."

"Looked like *Footloose* to me," Myra said.

"More like foot *lose*," I said.

Myra held out her palm, and I slapped it.

"Rude!" Xtelle said, but there was something in her eyes that looked like mirth. She was enjoying this. "If you want any sort of power over me, you are going to have to let me into Ordinary."

True. I didn't have powers over demons, gods, or any supernatural creatures outside Ordinary's boundaries. If I allowed her into Ordinary, she'd have to follow the laws and rules, and I'd be the one enforcing them.

Which would make Xtelle *my* problem.

Like I needed more problems.

"You can't stay in Ordinary," Myra said.

"I can if I sign the silly contract you keep going on and on about."

"It's more than signing," Myra said. "You'll have to follow the rules and conditions of the contract. You'll be bound by Ordinary's laws."

"Hello," Xtelle said, "demon. I know more about contracts than you ever will."

"Hello, dating your son," Myra said, pointing at herself. "I know you won't follow the rules. We're done here." Myra turned, headed to the cruiser.

"I'll do it."

I blinked.

Xtelle raised her chin, her gaze level. "I'll sign the contract. I'll follow Ordinary's rules."

I rubbed at the headache starting behind my eyes. Myra opened the cruiser door, then it clanked shut.

"Let's be serious for a minute." I dropped my hand. "This isn't a game, Xtelle. Not this part."

Xtelle considered me for a moment, then seemed to make up her mind. She shimmered, becoming pink fire and smoke, burnt strawberries, then reformed into her woman shape.

She was tall, taller than me, her long, dark hair braided over one shoulder, her skin flawless. Her eyes flashed pink before going dark again. She wore a simple, cream cashmere sweater and a pair of wide-legged cream slacks.

If I didn't know she was a demon, I'd think she was a model or heiress.

"Perhaps you'll take me more seriously in this form. I want to sign the contract, Delaney. I want to be a citizen of Ordinary. I will follow the rules."

Lie or truth?

"What form are you going to take in Ordinary?" I asked.

"Does it matter?"

"Yes."

"Is that part of the contract terms?"

"Yes."

"But I can choose?"

"Within reason and with my approval."

"You must so enjoy telling people what they can be. Controlling other living beings."

"Move it along, Xtelle. I'm just doing my job."

I'd never forced any person—supernatural or otherwise—to change who they were on a whim. It wasn't like I told Bigfoot to shave. And he hadn't.

But since he'd chosen to keep his Sasquatchy shape, he couldn't wander town without getting a lot of questions, at best, or being shipped off to some kind of experimental lab, at worst.

He stayed away from town in daylight, and our "there's a bear in the area" cover story worked well enough. Still, he had a spell necklace he could wear that would hide his true form if he needed to.

"How about you show me which form you prefer," I said.

She glanced at Myra, who had rejoined us. I don't know what she was looking for there. Myra was on my side.

"This form is pleasant." She ran her fingertips down her sides before bracing palms on hips. "But being human is...tedious."

"Any day now, Xtelle."

She rolled her eyes. "Fine." Pink smoke, a puff of glitter, and she was once again a little pink unicorn.

"Nope," I said. "That won't work. We told you that before."

"But I *like* this form. It's so...me."

"You agreed to the pony form the last time you were in town. How about we just go with that?"

"Boring."

I waited.

She looked between Myra and me again.

"Fine. But I refuse to be happy about it." She shimmered, no glitter and only a thin wisp of smoke. And there stood a pony. She was a palomino, her tawny color a little on the pink side, but not so much as to draw attention.

Was her sun-bleached mane a little shinier than normal? Maybe. Were her hooves polished with a subtle iridescence? Definitely.

Frankly, that was a lot easier than I expected.

"Are you happy now?" Xtelle moped.

"Not yet." Myra flipped out a clipboard with a very familiar looking document attached.

Of course, she'd brought the demon contract with her. Right place, right time.

Xtelle wrinkled her long nose. "Did you have to use three-point type?"

I glanced at the page, glanced at Myra, then back at Xtelle. "That's fourteen, at least."

"And double spaced," Myra added. "Oh, that's right.

You're ancient. Here, let me help." She dug in her pocket and pulled out a pair of over-large, high magnification, tiger-striped reading glasses.

"I...you...she's mean," Xtelle yelled at me.

"Ponies don't talk," I reminded her. There was no one around. I'd chosen this parking spot for a reason.

"I'm not a...you're not the boss of me here."

"As soon as you sign that contract and come to Ordinary, I will be. But if you want to run around out here in the big world being a talking pony, all the power to you. I'm sure the lab where they'll dissect your brain will be very cozy."

She stomped her front hooves. Both of them. Then she turned a little circle stomping each hoof down on the pavement as hard as she could, while she muttered, "Smash you, smash your head, smash your rules, smash, smash, smash."

When she was facing us again, her eyes were wide and watery and crazy looking. The weird fake grin she wore was troubling.

"I'm so happy," she burbled. "Just, happy, happy, happy. Let me read that contract and sign on that line. Happy, happy line. Just so happy." She yanked the clipboard out of Myra's hand.

"Let me see, happy agreement...between happy parties..." she mumbled through the high points of the document.

Myra took a couple steps forward and plunked the reading glasses on Xtelle's nose.

Xtelle froze. Then her head moved in that slow-motion swivel usually only seen in horror movies.

"Since the type is so tiny," Myra said.

Xtelle's eye twitched.

I had to bite the inside of my cheek to keep from laughing. My sister wasn't afraid of anything. Not even an ancient, vindictive demon who was the mother of the man—well, demon—she was dating.

"You are so *thoughtful*," Xtelle ground out.

Myra grinned wildly at me over the top of the pony, and I flashed her a thumbs up.

"Pen," Xtelle demanded, flipping out a hoof.

Myra offered a pen. Xtelle picked it up with her lips. The demon pony initialed, initialed again, then signed on the dotted line, a flicker of pink smoke rising up as she finished her name with a flourish.

A thread of awareness hooked into my chest. She was only the second demon in history who had signed the contract to live in Ordinary. The connection between us was a physical thing.

I didn't usually feel a connection with other supernatural beings who came to town, but demons were new. It was going to take time for me to get used to how they fit into our town.

"All right." I reached for the clipboard. "My turn." I read through the document, looking for any changes she might have made.

The contract was solid. Ryder had gone over it with a fine-toothed comb, plus we'd done all the normal blessings and magical anointments to demon-proof the thing. Bathin had even pointed out a loophole in language so tiny, a gnat wouldn't have been able to stick a wing through it. Since demons were even more persistent than gnats, we'd reworked the language.

This contract was solid. Rock and earth and mountain solid.

"Stupid contract." Xtelle lifted her nose and the glasses slipped back up toward her forelock. "Stupid Reed sisters. Stomp them. Stomp them in the hoof hole."

"What was that?" I asked as I signed my full name and added my initials.

"Shotgun," she said. "I call shotgun." She sassed off to the front of the Jeep, opened the door, and wedged her wide butt up into the front.

"Just so you know," Myra said, "she is not staying at my house."

There was a shriek, a growl, and the Jeep rocked on its wheels as Xtelle scrambled over the front seat and landed with a thump in the back. A little pink snout pressed against the side window and smoke fogged the glass.

"She can't stay at mine." I thumbed toward the car. "Dragon pig."

Myra nodded. "Reasonable. So, Jean?"

I grinned. "Oh, yeah. Totally Jean." I gave Myra the clipboard, and she tucked it under her arm.

"I'll be back in a few hours," she said.

"Why isn't Bathin going with you to the derby meeting?"

"One, he's not attached at my hip."

"Uh-huh."

"Two, we have our own hobbies, thank you."

"He's afraid to leave Ordinary, isn't he?" I asked.

She shrugged. "He's still hiding. And not from his mother."

The headache spiked for a second, and I rubbed at my forehead. "I know. His father."

"Did Tala say anything else about that?"

"No. Maybe she'll say more when she's in town."

"I like how optimistic you've become," she said with a grin.

"That's me. All hope and butterflies."

She lifted the clipboard in a salute. The Jeep rocked again, and a quiet roar cut a shriek short.

"Good luck with that," she said, nodding toward my car.

"Could I interest you in an annoying demon?"

She laughed. "Nope. I've got one of my own."

"Yeah, but you kind of love the guy."

She waved over her shoulder and swung into the cruiser.

I took a deep breath and opened the Jeep's driver side door.

"Delaney, that thing—"

"Not a word."

"But it—"

"Nope."

"You can't—"

"What I *could* do is let you walk to Ordinary. It's only about thirty miles or so. A little pony like you should make it there by nightfall."

"I—"

I held up a finger and fixed her with a look in the rearview mirror. "Thirty miles, Xtelle."

Her eyes welled up with tears, and her big horsey lips quivered.

I didn't blink.

"Oh, fine," she said, the tears instantly dry. She threw her head back in a position I didn't think a real pony could have managed and wriggled down into the seats, crossing her stubby arms over her chest.

"I'll just sit here silently and suffer the presence of that… that…thing, even though there are no seat warmers."

The dragon pig was paying zero attention to the drama queen in the back seat. I thought I should take a cue from it.

"You good?" I asked it.

It grunted once and propped front feet up on the door handle so it could see out the window. It *oink*ed again and wagged its tiny curly tail.

"All right then. Let's get this pig and pony show on the road."

The dragon pig squeaked, the demon pony scoffed.

"Fine. Let's get this dragon and demon show on the road." They both made agreeable sounds. I rolled my eyes and headed back to Ordinary.

CHAPTER FIVE

JEAN WAS NOT AT WORK.

"Is there a reason you have another pony in the back of your Jeep?" Hatter, a cop we'd poached from Tillamook, had that long and lean cowboy thing going for him. He liked to talk with a bit of an accent that moseyed between Texas and Kentucky. I was pretty sure it was completely fake.

He held the station door open for me while I walked through and bent, putting the dragon pig down on the floor.

"It's Xtelle."

The dragon pig trotted adorably to my desk where it rooted around in my trash can, looking for tasty metal.

From the little squeak it gave, I figured it had found the coffee can I'd tossed in there for just this very thing. I grinned.

"The demon again?" Hatter glanced over his shoulder. "I thought we threw her out for good last month."

"She just threw herself back in. Signed the contract and everything."

"Oh-kay," he said, the word stretching like molasses. "So our demon population just doubled. How do you want us to handle that?"

"First, we find someone to foster her. She's a pony. She

can't just wander through town ordering fancy cocktails and buying knock-off designer bags without drawing attention."

"Plus that would break the rules. Ponies don't do that in the outside world, so 'ponies' don't do that inside Ordinary," he said.

He strolled behind the counter, scanned the phone system, which was quiet, then sat in Roy's chair and put his feet up on the desk.

It was still strange for Roy not to be at the desk. His big, steady presence had left a hole in the department, though Shoe, Hatter, and our newest reserve officers, Kelby and Than, had done a lot to fill his place in their own way.

"Yep, but she gets the three-strikes we give to every other supernatural who tries living among mortals and gods for the first time." I walked back to the little table in the hall where we kept our coffee and poured myself a cup that looked like it'd been on the burner since Christmas.

"You know she's going to be trouble," he said.

I blew across the coffee then took a small sip. Tar. Tar would be thinner. And tastier. I took a second sip anyway, because I had the feeling it was going to be a long day.

"Sure," I said. "But she's not going to be *my* trouble. At least not until she has to be."

"You know I'm no good with pets, Boss. Or horses. Or demons."

"You say that, but I haven't seen any proof."

He pulled his boots, one at a time, off the desk and gave me a narrow look. "You wouldn't."

I shrugged. "I'm going to foist her off on Jean, since she wriggled out of helping Bertie with…well, with everything. I think it's time she pitches in with something more strenuous than beating her boyfriend at video games."

"Good. Yes, that's smart thinking, Chief. She's at Hogan's bakery."

"How do you know?"

"She's always there this time of day if she's not on duty."

I tipped the coffee cup in thanks, then took it into the bathroom and poured it down the sink. Hogan had better coffee anyway.

"...Bertie wants to talk to you," Hatter said as I came back down the hall.

"Why? Who does she want to rope into volunteering this time?"

"Shoe. Which is a damn shame, because that man could not keep his fingers off a sweet if it was rolled in rat poison. But that's not what I was talking about."

"All right, what's up with our one and only local Valkyrie?" I tugged the stapler out of the dragon pig's mouth, wiped the ash off it, and returned it to my desk. "Bad dragon pig. You're going to spoil your appetite for dinner. We have a nice park bench you can demolish."

The dragon pig made squeaky, chew-toy sounds and scratched its little butt against the corner of my desk.

"Robbery," Hatter said.

I straightened. "She stole something?" At his look, I amended, "Someone stole something from Bertie? Our Bertie?" Just the idea of it was staggering.

She might look like a little old lady, but I'd seen her "accidentally" stab the mailman with her apple knife when she thought he'd left her mailbox open in the rain.

"She came in and made an official report and everything."

He dug around in the paper on the desk, leaned back, and offered a sheet to me.

I scanned it. "A feather. She's reporting a missing feather."

"Yup. Says it's important to her. Capital F Feather important. Large, too, 'bout yea big." His hands marked off three feet or so.

"Pearl, opal, diamond dust, and gold," I recited. "Was it locked up?"

"It was on a shelf in her office. Out in the open. You've seen it."

I frowned. Had I?

I'd been to her office two days ago, when she'd informed me she was going to invite some new businesses from outside

Ordinary to show their wares at the High Tea Tide. She'd, of course, already *done* all that, but she still filled me in like it was news just the same.

I pulled up an image of her office in my mind. Big wooden desk in the center of the room, shelves behind her, windows to the sides. Her chair wide at the head and cushioned. Two visitor chairs, plain dark wood.

Her nest was made to be comfortable for her, which meant it was set up so she could shove visitors out the door when she got tired of them.

Her desk had all the normal things one would expect of someone who kept the town busy with outreach and events—computer, pen holder, stapler, a little hourglass on a swivel.

Behind her were a scattering of certificates and awards in gold frames.

I thought about the shelves. Had I seen a big sparkly Feather?

My headache cranked down again. I stuck my thumb against my temple and pressed.

Yes. I remembered now. She'd walked out of the room to deal with a delivery, and I'd gotten up to stretch my legs.

I'd seen the Feather. Hatter was right. It was long, sparkling, and beautiful. She'd set it on the shelf with other little items, all of them special, but none of them looking particularly valuable.

The Feather was pretty but didn't seem more valuable than the gold-and-jewel-encrusted trinket box, or the carved crystal falcon in flight, or the antique, filigreed silver sewing kit.

"Chief?"

"Yeah," I said, shaking out of my mental drift, the headache receding. "I saw it on her shelf Tuesday. When did she notice it missing?"

"Yesterday. She said the High Tea Tide has kept her busy until now. Wants you to call her when you get the chance."

"All right. One thing at a time. I'll track down Jean and

offload the demon. Let me know if you get any leads on the Feather."

He gave me that quick grin. "Got it, Chief."

I pulled out my phone and texted Jean. *Where you at?*

Her reply was quick. *Day off, rembr?*

You at home? I have something for you.

No

It's a present.

No

I waited for her curiosity to get the better of her.

Hogan's shop. What is it?

Bingo.

Be right there.

This better not be work. I have 2 days off, D. TWO

I thumbed the screen and picked up the dragon pig who was sniffing the desk lamp cord.

"Let's go, buddy. Keep me in the loop, Hatter."

"Can do, Boss." The phone rang and he picked it up just as I left the station, the door swinging shut behind me to cover the conversation, which from first blush sounded like it had something to do with a sea lion and a bathtub.

Hogan's bakery, the Puffin Muffin, was just a couple minutes away. In just a few minutes I'd be rid of the demon and have a couple interesting cases to take up my time.

Suddenly the whole day seemed brighter. I whistled a little tune as I strolled across the parking lot to my Jeep.

"Hello, Delaney."

I stopped in my tracks, my heart racing, sweat instantly pricking under my arms. The headache was stronger now, an avalanche of jagged edges pounding inside my skull.

But the bigger thing filling me was fear. Fear of that voice and the creature behind it.

CHAPTER SIX

I KNEW the day was sunny. I knew there was a salty breeze blowing strands of my hair across my face. Vaguely, I could feel the weight of the dragon pig in my arms. I could see the Jeep, right over there, as distant and maddening as a locked exit in a horror movie.

It would only take me walking, one step after the next, just a few short feet, and I'd be in that vehicle. Door locked. Safe.

But my feet would not move. It was everything I could do to breathe against the fear, to break the rust off my lungs and inhale.

"It's been awhile, hasn't it?"

His voice was soft. That's what I noticed first this time, and every time I'd heard him. Because I had heard him before. Hadn't I?

Yes.

A nightmare, a dream, a forgotten darkness right behind me, unflinching in the sunlight.

"You can speak," he said. It was what he always said, I realized.

And just like the other times—

—*how many? One? Three? Ten?*—

—I did not speak. There was power in words. I didn't want him to steal my power away.

Correction: I didn't want him to steal any *more* of it away. Because he had taken something from me. I knew he had.

The dragon pig in my arms shifted a little. Maybe looking up at me. Maybe restless to go home so it could eat a bench.

It did not hear the voice. I knew that too.

Which meant he was not a demon. Which meant he was not real.

That was so much worse.

"Still so silent," he said, this voice in my head, this aberration, this manifestation of my creeping insanity, of the injury to my soul that hadn't healed properly.

That manifestation walked around me, I could hear his footsteps, the heavy heel as if he needed weighted boots to keep him in contact with the ground. As if it took some effort for him to move in this reality, this state of my mind, my madness.

Not real, I told myself. *He is not real.*

"What's this now?" He was beside me, somehow moving while all the rest of the world stood still. "Are you ignoring me? Because, Delaney…"

…he was at the edge of my vision. *Don't look, don't look, don't look…*

"…we both know that's not going to work, don't we?"

Then he was there. Right in front of me.

My height, which made it worse because his eyes—gold with deep umber flecks—were level with mine. His lips were thin and disapproving. His shoulders were wide, made even broader by the severe uniform he wore. It was not from any military I'd seen in the mortal world.

The gray, tailored jacket and slacks with slashes of red stitching made me think of cooled coal, lava cracking, burning.

At each shoulder, a hard black stone held back the flow of a cape that was also gray and black, licks of red flame shooting up from the hem. There were medals on his chest, made of the same black stone.

"Still shy?" he asked. "How cute."

I scowled and lifted my gaze to his eyes. Met them straight on.

Not real. This is not real. He is not real.

"There, was that so hard?" His smile slid over his lips like oil. His gaze calculated every emotion on my face.

I made sure there wasn't enough for him to add zero to one.

"You have been doing so well, Delaney. We're almost there."

Not real. I pushed my foot, trying to walk through the hallucination, but I was stuck, welded flat, frozen.

"You have impressed me. Your resourcefulness. Your strength. No one knows, do they? That you see me? That you hear me?"

A flicker of panic fluttered under my skin. I wanted to call out for help. Wanted to tell him to get away from me. Wanted to scream.

"Shh," he said, raising his hand to my mouth and pressing one black-gloved finger to my lips. "This is just for us, our special time."

I could feel the warmth of the leather against my lips, the soft pressure of his finger gently silencing me. Could smell the burn of stones and some other scent that reminded me of lightning.

I wanted to squirm out of my skin.

His eyes widened slightly, and as if sensing my revulsion, he pulled his finger away. Then he dropped his gaze to the ground, his shoulders pulling back. Almost as if he were putting space between us.

I sucked in a hard breath. Had I been breathing? Had I been holding my breath all this time? Panic was doing weird things to my brain, and time skidded like a rock skipping over flat water.

The dragon pig in my arms wasn't moving. The leaves in

the trees weren't moving, even though this was the coast and there was always a breeze.

"You only need one more thing," he said, bringing my attention back to him.

He'd stepped back a pace and pulled his hands behind his back, in parade rest. His intensity had been dialed down several hundred ticks.

Even his eyes looked different, brownish swimming there in the yellow, softening that hard glare, humanizing it.

Still not nice, I thought, *and still not real.*

But even that small space between us helped. The feathery fingers of panic receded, the need to scream was gone.

I felt like myself, well, as much of myself as I could be while hallucinating. I felt like I had ground to stand on.

"When you have that one last thing, then this," he used two fingers to wave between us, "will no longer be necessary."

I could ask. Just open my mouth and make him tell me what the hell *this* was. What he wanted from me, and what he was.

There was more I could ask. That thought tickled the back of my brain. This was familiar. We'd been here before, he and I. I didn't know how many times, but I knew I'd seen him before and forgotten.

Just like that, my heart was beating too fast again, my breathing going reedy.

How long had this been going on? Had it been years? All my life?

No, someone would have known. There were too many people in this town with too many gifts and powers. Someone would have known that I was…whatever this was. It couldn't have been going on for long.

Maybe only since…something flickered there. A clue. Something had happened recently, and that's when this had started.

It hadn't been long ago either. It had been night, I remembered that, I'd been awake because Ryder was gone, because Ryder was always gone...

"Now, now," he said again. His voice buzzed through my memories, and scrambled the pieces I'd almost put together.

"There's no need to think so hard," he said. "All we need is for you to find one more thing. And you know what that is, don't you, Delaney?"

I had no idea what he was talking about.

"Ah, well, you will. Once you see it, you'll understand. And I'll be there to guide you. Then..." He clapped his hands in a soft *whump* and rubbed his palms together. "Everything is going to change. Big, big, change."

"Boss?" Shoe's voice was sudden, loud, and too close. I jerked as if I'd been shot, and twisted toward him. He was walking my way from the far side of the parking lot, and all I could do was stand there breathing too hard, blinking too fast, and shaking.

"Shoe?"

He gripped a coffee carrier with two big cups in one hand and his phone in the other. He was not a tall man, built like a pallet of bricks with a few extra bricks stacked in the middle. Shoe had a wicked sense of humor, didn't say much unless he had something to say, and was ten for ten finding the good chocolate Myra thought she could hide from us all in the station.

"Something wrong?" He scanned the area around me, sharp eyes clear. He was a good cop. If there was something weird going on, he'd see it.

Was there something weird going on? I was just...walking. Right? Walking out to my car?

"There's, well, no. Just..." A moment, a flash. A man's hard yellow eyes, his eggbeater voice, and then nothing but that damn lingering headache. "...gotta take care of something," I said.

His gaze ticked over to my Jeep. "A pony?"

"Xtelle."

"Again?"

"Signed the contract this time."

"Think that's a difference maker?"

"We'll find out."

"I'm allergic."

"To what?"

"Whatever she is. Can't take care of her. No fenced yard. Hives. Systemic shock."

"I'm unloading her on Jean."

His left eyebrow twitched up for a second. "You need a hand?"

I knew he was asking if I was okay.

"With anything?" He nodded toward the Jeep.

"Thought you were allergic."

"Only on contact." That eyebrow quirk again, and a smile.

This was good, normal, and whatever strange moment I'd had, whatever memory I'd been chasing...

...*a man with yellow eyes*...

...faded away. I dug my thumb into my temple, the pressure welcome against that low-level throb.

"Working the theft case with Hatter?" I asked.

"Just got back from canvassing Bertie's neighbors."

I waited.

"If I had found something other than coffee," he lifted the cardboard carrier, "I would have led with that."

"Keep me updated." I started to the car, and just before I opened the door, there was something else I knew should tell him. About a robbery. Something missing.

A quick flash of Jame stopping me on the way to the casino for a chat filtered through my head, then was gone, as quickly as liquid sucked up by a sponge.

"Am I forgetting something?" I asked the dragon pig in my arms. It grunted and wriggled, impatient to get into the car.

"Right. Fine." I unlocked the door, tossed the dragon pig down into the driver's seat so it could hop over to the passenger side. Then I slid into place behind the wheel.

"...can *not* believe you made me wait out here for so long.

This is neglect. You're neglecting me. I will file charges." Xtelle moved around and I heard the distinct crinkling of wrappers being shoved between the seat cushions.

I readjusted the rearview.

Still a little blonde pony. Still the big, wide, eyes.

But now her face was smeared with chocolate.

"Where did you get the candy?"

"I don't know what you're talking about." She turned her head, then ducked out of my line of vision.

"I can hear you trying to wipe it off."

"What? What's that, Delaney? I'm certainly not eavesdropping on *your* private business with that swarthy police officer who didn't even offer us the latte he was carrying."

"Xtelle."

She sat back up. "Fine! I ate chocolate. Is that against your boring Ordinary rules?"

"Depends on where you got it from. I didn't have any in the car, so you'll want to think real hard about what you're about to tell me next."

"You are a terrible dresser," she said.

"That's one. Three strikes and you're out, Xtelle."

"And your hair is stringy."

"Two. Gonna go for the whole enchilada?"

She narrowed her pony eyes, and her hooves clicked together as she crossed her stubby arms. "I...acquired it."

"Details."

"With magic."

I waited.

"What?" she asked in false outrage. "I just told you the truth. The *truth*, Delaney," she moaned. She stuck her tongue out several times like she was trying to get rid of a bad taste. "I hope you're happy."

"I'm not. Where did you magically get this chocolate from?"

She mumbled something that sounded like "your butt."

"And we're just gonna go for three and a miss," I said.

"The store! Okay? I got it from the..." she waggled her hoof north, "sweet shop place right down the road."

Gods, I was so glad she wasn't going to be my charge. "Everyone pays for what they want in Ordinary. I hope you're ready to wash dishes for a week."

Her horsey mouth fell open, and her eyes went so wide, she looked like a cartoon. I bit the inside of my cheek and counted down from thirty to keep from laughing.

Then her eyes narrowed. "You *wouldn't*."

"I absolutely *am*." I started the car.

"But I'm a...a little pony." She jumped up and did a little prance in place. "I am to be admired while I frolic the days away. I am to be petted and fed sugar cubes from the palms of muscular, naked men. I do not do menial tasks."

"If you thought taking that form would get you out of work, you are mistaken."

"Pony work," she said.

"And?"

"Ponies don't do dishes."

"Demons posing as unicorns posing as ponies do. Unless they have something else they can use as payment."

"Oh! I have this cursed—"

"A form of payment within Ordinary's rules and laws for supernaturals, mortals, gods, and others."

Her pony lower lip wobbled. "You're mean."

"This? This is me being lenient. You know the ways of mortals, Xtelle. You know the ways of the mortal world. You might be able to meddle and cheat and steal out there." I pointed north. "But inside Ordinary you must follow the law. Stealing gets you jail time."

She paused, and I wondered if she was weighing the merits of being locked up for a few months against doing dishes.

"You'd lock up a pony?"

Ah. She thought that form was going to get her out of all sorts of human things. Wrong. Clever. But wrong.

"I would."

"In a...barn?"

"In a jail. You don't think the holding cells are the only place we put criminals?"

She drew back in horror, her whole body sinking back into the seat, as that realization hit her. "You have...a magic jail?"

"Something like that."

"Why haven't I ever heard of it?"

"You've been in Ordinary for all of three minutes. Frankly, I think you just set a record for how quickly I've threatened to throw someone into it."

"Perhaps I'd be treated better there," she huffed.

"Yeah, no." I put the Jeep in reverse, drove out of the parking lot, and onto Hwy 101, the main drag through town. "Start thinking about how you're going to apologize for those chocolates, and how you're going to pay Stina back for them."

"Ponies don't have money!"

"Looks like you've got a dilemma on your hooves. Better figure it out in the next couple minutes. We're almost there."

She scowled and stared out the window, muttering under her breath quietly enough I couldn't catch anything except the expletives.

I ignored her and rolled right up to the red and white-striped Sweet Reflections, parking a short distance from the door.

"If there are customers in there, you'll remain outside the building. Quiet as a pony. A real pony. We'll go around back. Stina is local and a gorgon. You can talk to her because she knows about the supernaturals. You are not to speak unless it's just Stina and me there. Got it?"

She crinkled up one eye ridge, stared straight at me, and pawed the back of my seat once.

Dear gods, save me from sarcastic unicorn pony demons.

"That's a yes?"

She waited, then pawed the back of my chair again.

"Good pony."

And oh, the look she gave me. I ducked out of the car before she could aim a kick at my head. I strolled around to the back of the Jeep, opened the tailgate, and pushed a cardboard box covered with a moving blanket to one side, looking for the length of rope I kept there.

A cool shiver ran down my spine, pooling in the small of my back. I paused and carefully studied my surroundings. Wide old graveled parking lot, three cars parked along one side—two from around the area, one with out-of-state license plates. Traffic moving normally, business across the street—a small motel and an office building—showing no unusual activity.

The shops next to the Sweet Reflections were a realtor to the north, and a trio of shops under one long, shared roof to the south: resale clothing, a clock store, and a touristy beach collectibles place.

Nothing seemed out of the ordinary.

So what was this feeling of wrongness?

I picked up the rope and closed the tailgate. I mentally backtracked my movements. I'd been talking to Xtelle, then felt a chill, then pulled the rope out of the trunk.

For a moment, I thought, something…something about a box and a blanket, but then the headache snapped behind my eyes, pounding to the beat of my heart. The wind picked up, buffeting my shoulder like someone buddy-punching my arm, and for the life of me, I couldn't remember what thought I'd been chasing.

Just in case I'd missed a message, I pulled out my phone. Nothing. If something was really wrong, if something really bad was about to happen, Jean's family gift would kick in, and she'd call me.

The Jeep rocked, and through the window I saw the dragon pig taking an exploratory nibble out of the seat back.

"No," I said, striding up and yanking open the dragon pig's door. "No eating the car. Seriously, if I have to keep telling you that, I'm just going to leave you in a shed at home. Or at the bottom of an empty swimming pool. Or somewhere a dragon pig can't get out of."

I honestly had no idea where that might be.

The dragon pig removed its mouth—which had been stretched way too wide and had too many pointed teeth for a real piggy—gave a little grunt, then sat in the chair, its butt pointed my way.

"Pout all you want. Vehicles are off limits. You know how much it cost to find a new bumper for Ryder's truck."

"Ryder Bailey," Xtelle said. "Where is that man of yours, Delaney? Did he dump you for someone smart or someone with better boobs?"

I inhaled, exhaled, then shut the front door and opened the back. "This is a rope." I held it up.

"I know what a rope is."

I took a quick moment to indulge in a hogtying fantasy, a blindfold fantasy, then a gag fantasy.

"I am going to tie this rope loosely around your nose and head so I can lead you around back."

I waited. "Rules, Xtelle. I need to know you're okay with this."

"As if I'd say no to some casual bondage." She extended her neck and turned her eyes demurely downward. "Am I doing it right, master?"

I pinched the bridge of my nose. Definitely a gag. Industrial strength. That was my favorite fantasy now.

I twisted the rope into a temporary halter and moved aside so she could hop out. She did so and followed me with mostly believable pony-ness to the wide gravel parking area at the back of the store.

A short bleating sound made me turn.

There was a goat in the parking area. A male, with luxuriant white hair and strong, thick brown horns that stuck out over the top of sideways ears. His eyes were yellow, his hooves were polished, and he was staring at Xtelle like he'd just seen the sun come out.

"Nothing to see here, Panny. Nothing to worry about."

Panny was also Pan, the god of the wild and frequent lover to...well, almost anyone if his bragging was to be believed.

Xtelle had also taken notice of the goat who was sticking out his chest and tipping his head so the sunlight hit his horns at just the right angle.

"Who is that?" Xtelle breathed.

"That is not what we're here for."

"His horns are so…large."

Panny bleated again in a deep, hey-baby tone. Then he winked.

"Nope. No." I pointed at him. "Stay. This is business, not pleasure." I tugged Xtelle up to the shop's delivery door and knocked.

Xtelle shifted her stance, crossing one leg in front of the other so her hips were canted toward Panny. She swished her tail in lazy little flicks.

Dear gods, save me from demon ponies trying to flirt.

Panny bleated once more and ended it with a little whistle.

I knocked again. Harder.

"Delaney?" Stina's voice floated out before her shape was visible through the screen door.

"I need to talk to you about a theft," I said.

Stina opened the door. She wore jeans and a short-sleeved, off-the-shoulder blouse covered by a red apron. She wasn't a tall woman, barely brushing five foot or so. But her eyes, a swirling turquoise made tropical against her naturally tanned skin, and her waves of shiny corded black hair, gave her a presence. Those eyes were captivating, powerful.

She was a gorgon, and that had a little something to do with the captivating, powerful thing too.

Her sisters, Dusi and Euri lived in town, but Stina was the one who had run the taffy shop for years. She was immortal and could make people forget how long she'd been around.

It came in handy for the mortals who aged while she remained looking a strong thirty-five or so.

"I didn't take whatever was stolen," she said.

The goat *baa*'d again. It sounded like a laugh.

Her eyes flicked to Pan, then me, then the pouting-but-also-flirting pony next to me. "Why do you have a pet demon?"

"I— What?" Xtelle exclaimed. "Queen demon, excuse your lying mouth! I am no mortal's pet."

"Ponies don't talk," I reminded her.

The goat said, "Ha! I mean: *baa*."

Xtelle bunched up her lips and sucked her nostrils shut, one eye twitching.

"She's not a pet," I said to Stina. "She's a new resident in Ordinary. You can stop holding your breath, Xtelle. I know lack of oxygen won't kill you."

She twisted her head to make sure I was paying attention to just how hard she was holding her breath, then stomped a tiny circle, tail slashing angrily against my leg.

"Queen? *The* queen?" Stina crossed her muscled arms over her chest. She might be the candy shop owner, but that didn't mean she was soft. She was one of the strongest people in town and had taken home local and regional bodybuilding competition prizes.

"Heard of her, have you?" I asked.

"Sure." Not a lot of emotion in that word. They weren't friends but I couldn't tell what level of adversaries they might be.

"She stole chocolate from you. Just now. And ate it."

"I saw it disappear. Thought it was Panny. Again."

Pan, obviously tired of being out of the conversation or just dying of curiosity, moseyed our way, stopping now and then to take a bite of this weed or that, goating it up.

Xtelle remained facing stubbornly away from all of us, legs locked, tail swishing.

"She's new here," I explained. "This is her first strike. So she's come to apologize and make amends."

"Uh-huh."

Yep. Stina had demon experience.

I raised my voice. "Xtelle. You owe Stina an apology for stealing her product. You'd better make it a good one."

Xtelle swished three more times, then turned, but I was already stepping back so her hoof missed my foot by an inch.

Xtelle stared at Stina. Stina gazed back with an expression that made it clear a dead gnat would be more threatening than the demon queen posing as a pony-corn holding her breath.

I smiled. Stina knew how to get under Xtelle's skin.

"Fine!" Xtelle blew out a lungful of air. "Talk, Xtelle. Don't talk, Xtelle. Pony, Xtelle, don't pony, Xtelle. Your rules are exhausting and stupid, Delaney Reed."

"Apologize."

"I will not be ordered around like a…like a pet!"

"Apologize, or I'll skip this part and just take you to jail. If Stina decides to press charges, that's where you're going anyway."

Xtelle tossed her head, flipping her mane away from her eyes.

Pan choked. It sounded like he'd swallowed his tongue.

"Stheno," Xtelle said.

"It's just Stina here."

"Fine. Steeeena."

"Xtelle."

"Your chocolate was…adequate."

"Apologize," I said, "not criticize."

"I'm sorry your chocolate was only adequate."

Pan couldn't wait any longer. He slow-clopped up to us and stood on the opposite side of me, mirroring Xtelle's pose. He snuck looks at her while trying to make it seem like he was just super-interested in the siding.

"You owe me a debt, Xtelle," Stina said. "I will collect it when and if I choose."

"Snake!" Xtelle accused.

"Coward," Stina replied.

Pan did the high-school you're-in-trouble-now, "Ooooh."

Xtelle gasped and clutched at her neck, searching for pearls.

Duct tape, I fantasized. That'd be even stronger than a

gag. They call it 100-mile-per-hour tape for a reason. I bet it could keep a lockdown on one demon mouth.

"You are speaking to the queen!" Xtelle announced. "Now you will pay!" She took several steps back, then lowered her head and plowed ahead, ready for a ramming.

"Nope." I set my stance and yanked on the rope right as she came up to me.

She squawked and twisted awkwardly to the side.

"Terms are set," I said. "You will abide by them." I reeled slack, drawing us so close we were eye to eye.

She tried to shake me off, but this wasn't my first rodeo. Literally.

Bertie had made me work the rodeo once. I'd been eight. For some reason, she had thought I'd make a terrific mule handler.

She was not wrong.

Unfortunately, a lot of the gods had shown up to the rodeo extremely drunk and willing to try every event. Every. Event.

There had also been a Category One hurricane that weekend that may or may not have been courtesy of Poseidon who had not been invited. In any case, no out-of-towners had shown up, so Bertie had deemed it a one and done and canceled it for good.

"I do not give debts to gorgons."

"You do if it remunerates the crime you committed."

"No," Stina said. "She owes me a debt for insulting my chocolates. There's another price for theft."

"Outrage!" Xtelle said. "Extortion!"

"Cool your jets," I said. "What's the other price?"

"Petting zoo," Panny blurted.

"Goats aren't supposed to talk, Pan."

"We're among friends here, aren't we, Delaney?" He twisted his neck to look up at me. "The queen is new to this land. A tiny bend in the no-speaking rule seems appropriate."

"This once. Otherwise…"

"Understood. Goat actions when in goat form, human when in human form."

While Pan liked to hang out mostly as a goat, there were days when he'd shed the four-legged form for his more human form, who was short, bearded, and a hell of a dancer. He played music sometimes with a rag-tag band, usually at Jump Off Jack's, or Mom's Bar and Grill.

"Petting zoo," Panny insisted.

Stina stared at him. I could tell she was surprised, because she blinked once, slowly, before looking back at me. "Starts in the morning of the High Tea Tide. Goes all day," Stina said.

"There's a petting zoo?" I asked. I didn't know Bertie had decided on that.

"Oh," Xtelle said, looking coyly over at Panny, "you flatter me. Although I'm not sure I can go *all* day. It's been a while since I've been so rigorously engaged."

"It's for children," Stina clarified. "A petting zoo for children to pet tame, docile farm animals. Not the X-rated demon thing you were just talking about."

"Chill-dren." Xtelle tried out the word like it was foreign to her.

"Petting docile farm animals. All day." Stina hadn't changed her stance, her arms still locked over her chest like she was ready to rumble.

"Touching me?" Xtelle sounded horrified. "Over your dead, stomped body!"

"My Queen." Panny stepped sideways to face her. He bowed, and made it very pretty with one foot kicked out in front of him, the other bent. His thick, twisted horns were impressive balanced on top of his head, and the breeze brushed through his soft, white fur, making it float.

"I am not *your* queen, godling," Xtelle said. But she'd lowered her voice, that bow of his apparently pleasing her.

"More's the pity," Panny murmured. "But may I be so bold as to suggest you partake of this quaint Ordinary custom? A petting zoo is a wonderful time to catch up on local gossip. Judge the inhabitants as they move about. There may be other ways to assess the people of a town, but none quite so covert as a petting zoo."

"Go on," she purred.

"While we would *never* do anything untoward or harmful," he threw a meaningful side-eye my way, "being a barn animal allows a bit of leeway when it comes to manners."

"Pan," I warned. "She's trying to fit in."

He drew up out of his bow. "Yes. As a pony. All the world knows ponies are assholes."

"Not in a petting zoo," I said.

"No, no. Of course there will be no harm done to those darling little mortal grubs. But if she lays her ears back, the children will be warned to step away, lest she swish her sharp tail over their tender knees."

Xtelle perked up, her entire countenance lifting.

"That *is* how a pony behaves," she stated. "I have seen it with my own eyes. They're assholes. I would be well within my pony rights to nip a little finger—lip only, Delaney, you don't have to get your badge in a wad."

"They'll feed you," Panny said, laying it on thick. "Sugar cubes right out of the palms of their plump, nubile hands. Crisp fresh apples offered from young, soft fingers. Honeyed grains paid for out of their meager allowances."

Xtelle shivered. "This is…pleasant."

"I am humbled you think so."

"Yes, you were very…tolerable."

"So I've been told."

"I assume you will be at this…petting?"

"Zoo," I inserted. "Petting zoo."

"I wouldn't miss it for the world." He winked at her.

She tittered, a high, girlish giggle. "Oh, you."

Then they just stood there, staring at each other.

I cleared my throat. "You know you don't have a choice, right?"

Xtelle didn't even look up at me or Stina. "I accept my penance."

"I'm overjoyed." Stina's delivery was so dry, I couldn't help but grin.

"Well, there you go then," I said to Xtelle. "I guess you

won't have to do dishes after all. And a petting zoo is one hundred percent pony work. Lucky you."

"Be here just after dawn Saturday," Stina ordered. "If you're late, you will accumulate additional debt."

Frankly, I didn't think this could have gone better. Pan trotted off.

Xtelle was no longer paying any attention to Stina. She'd turned her back completely and was now staring out at the gravel parking area.

Pan oh-so-casually trit-trotted into her line of sight, tossing his head to make his white beard flow in the wind, horns slashing the air as if ready to bash heads with any poor goat who happened by.

His *baa* was deep and suggestive.

Xtelle hummed, obviously liking what she was seeing.

Duct tape. For my eyes.

"Thanks for your understanding, Stina," I said, giving the rope a little tug. "It's generous of you not to press charges."

Xtelle snorted, but followed the tug on the rope, even though she continued staring at Pan over her shoulder.

"Good-bye, Delaney," Stina said. I heard the jangle of the bells over the front door that signaled someone had entered her shop.

"Most people would have been happy to see you sitting in jail." I picked up the pace.

"Most people wouldn't have the audacity to sell such mediocre candy." She was still half twisted around so she could keep her eyes on Panny.

"Why did you pick Stina's shop, out of all the candy shops in Ordinary?"

"Because it's delish—" She untwisted and glanced up at me. "Disgusting. She should be ashamed of it."

"Don't do it again."

"What if I have a craving for subpar confections?"

"Earn some money and buy them."

"But I'm a pony! Ponies have no earning potential."

We were at the Jeep. I opened the back door. She hopped

inside and I slammed it shut. The very short walk around the front of the vehicle to the driver's side was blissfully silent. I savored it.

I slid into the driver's seat and started the engine. "You can earn money, and you should." I backed out of the parking lot and flicked on the right-turn indicator.

"But, *pony*," she said stubbornly.

"Yes. Ponies can give rides to children. Ponies can be a part of a petting zoo."

She perked up, and I clarified, "You're not getting paid for the one on Saturday, but if someone wants a pony for events, holidays, business openings, sales events, you can work it as a pony. If not that, there's always pulling work on farms, carriage rides, that sort of thing."

"What if I don't want to do any of that?"

"Then you can shift into a human form and work a human job somewhere."

"Boring."

"Nope," I said easing into traffic. "It's just Ordinary."

She did not laugh at my joke.

CHAPTER SEVEN

JEAN WAS NOT SURPRISED, and that worried me.

"What do you mean, you knew Xtelle would end up back here again?"

My sister was currently covered in a thin patina of flour, which was weird because there was no way she'd done any actual work, despite the Puffin Muffin apron she was wearing.

"She got a taste of Ordinary and didn't want her son to have all the fun. Of course she'd come back. I'm just surprised you let her back in."

"She signed the contract."

"Still. You were pretty furious at her."

"She lied to me. To us. She cheated her way into Ordinary so she could spy on my sister and try to force her own son to kill himself."

"Those tiny magic scissors wouldn't have killed him."

"He didn't know that."

She nodded, her green hair flashing neon in the sunlight that was breaking through the clouds. The Puffin Muffin parking lot was relatively empty for this time of day, but Jean said she'd been helping Hogan bake all morning.

Jean was lying.

Xtelle sat in the Jeep, pouting.

"You tend to hold a grudge, Delaney," she said.

"I do not."

"What about that time I switched all the heads of your dolls with meatballs?"

"That wasn't a grudge. It was property protection—and I'll never forgive you for it. What did you bake today?"

"What?"

"It's your day off. You said you were helping Hogan bake. I know he gets up at dawn. What have you baked so far?"

"Puff things and…um…coffee cake…and a strudel?"

"You haven't done any of that."

"No, but I'm in charge of quality control."

"You're just eating batter and getting in flour fights with Hogan, aren't you?"

She smiled. "It's been a good day."

"Good. Because I need you to take on a small job."

She dragged one hand over her two high pony tails, making sure they were where she wanted them. "I'm not going to like this, am I?"

"It's not volunteering for Bertie."

Her entire face lit up. She was the youngest of us three Reed sisters, and when she smiled like that it reminded me so much of my mother, I couldn't help but smile back.

"I'm leaving Xtelle with you."

She glanced over at the Jeep. "What? Here?"

"I'm on duty, Myra's at the derby meeting. I don't trust anyone else to keep her in her place."

"What form did she pick?"

"Pony."

Her mouth quirked up. "So, pony-only rules, right? No talking in front of the unaware, no demon tricks, just hanging out and eating grass?"

"Yep. Stina wants her over for the petting zoo on Saturday, but otherwise her calendar is open."

"When did Stina get involved?"

"When Xtelle stole her 'mediocre' chocolate and ate it."

"Ooooh. Old pals?"

"So close."

"I don't have a yard to keep her in."

"I was thinking maybe Hogan's place? The fenced-in side yard?"

"I'll ask. Myra won't take her?"

"After last time, I'm surprised Myra didn't shoot her on sight."

"And she's not staying with you, because you and Ryder are fighting."

Were we? She said it so casually, I almost glossed it over without a thought. Didn't someone have to be present in some way to actually be fighting?

"We're not fighting. She's not staying with me because I have a dragon pig and its pet dog/brother/worshiper—whatever Spud is to it—in the house. That dragon pig and demon unicorn do not get along, and I don't want Spud to become a casualty."

"Right. And also you and Ryder are fighting."

I tucked my fists into my jacket and gave her my cop's glare. "Who told you that?"

"It doesn't take anyone to tell me what I can see with my own eyes. Police officer." She pointed at her face. "Keen observation skills."

"And what can you observe?"

"He's never home when you are. Scheduled a job that takes him out of town on the days you're home. Only gets one day to sleep in his own bed. A day when you're on duty."

"That's not—"

"Isn't it?"

I didn't know.

Yes, he'd taken the build out of town. Said he needed the extra money. Said the dragon pig was eating us out of house and home. Not strictly true, since it was eating us out of junkyard, and there were plenty of junkyards we could scavenge.

He'd been really focused on money, and quick to change

the subject whenever I brought up how we were doing together, or when I tried to check in on our goals.

Maybe having my soul possessed by a demon for over a year was just too much. Maybe I'd changed. I knew I was having...blackouts? Some kind of foggy memory moments. I figured that would get better as my soul healed.

But there was no guarantee on that.

Maybe I was broken this way now.

Permanently.

"Wow. That is one long-ass pause." Jean leaned away from the side of the building and wrapped her arms around me.

"Don't."

"It's a hug. You can handle it."

"I'm fine."

She squeezed.

"Jean, you're making a big deal out of nothing." Her hair smelled like key lime pie.

"You're confused about you and Ryder, but it's okay. It's a fight. After a fight you get to make up. Making up is the best."

"I'm not confused."

The squeeze again.

"Making up after a fight is awesome. You'll see."

"Get off me, you perv."

She snorted a laugh into my shoulder and finally stepped back, one hand catching my fingers.

She'd done that ever since she was a little kid.

"Go away," I said.

"I'll take on the pony demon. You do some work facing your doubt demons, okay?"

I tugged my hand away. "We're fine."

"That's what I said. It's just a fight. He loves you. You know he's crazy about you."

"We're not fighting."

"Oh, you're fighting, you're just never in the same place long enough to realize it. What?" she searched my face, her eyes wide and worried. "Delaney?"

That was it, wasn't it? He didn't even want to put in the energy to fight me. Or he was hiding something. Something he didn't want me to find out about. Maybe something unforgivable.

"Hey, I'm just shooting off my mouth," she said, catching at my hand again. "You know how I am. Talk first, brain later. You and Ryder are good. You just said you're good. He's...he really loves you. Trust me, Delaney."

I had to clear my throat before words could happen. "We are good."

She squeezed my hand. "Sometimes work gets in the way. I bet he's going to surprise you. Do some big romantic gesture, like a dinner or something. If he does, you just let me know and I'll switch a shift so you can do that big romantic making up. Okay?"

"You just switched to days. I don't want to throw a wrench in the gears until we get into a steady work flow."

"We're pretty close to steady. If you just had some time together to talk, I'm sure you'd see everything is okay. If you give me time for a quick nap, I can take your afternoon into evening shift."

"I wasn't going to work—"

"Yeah, you were." She held my gaze until I looked away. Maybe Ryder wasn't the only one avoiding at-home time.

"I'd have to see if he can get home for dinner tonight. Then order in something. Or cook."

"Definitely order. You'll try to make the perfect meal and burn something, then end up ordering five-dollar pizza from the gas station."

"That was once."

"Let's not have it be twice. I'll be on shift at four. Should give you plenty of time to sweet-talk your man into coming home."

"This won't get you out of watching Xtelle."

"Cynical. If she gets out of hand, I'll ask my half Jinn baker boyfriend to grant me a wish. Maybe turn her into a little pewter charm I can keep on my bracelet."

"You only get what? Two actual wishes a year from him?

"One big wish and a few tiny ones."

"You aren't going to waste those to turn Xtelle into a charm."

"Ha-ha, of course not. Ha-ha, see how much I was joking? I've never ever thought of something like that before. Taking advantage of my half Jinn boyfriend. Why just the idea. Heavens, no."

"Jean."

She strolled toward the Jeep, flour drifting off her in little wisps, the breeze teasing her bright hair. "You really need a day off. I was joking."

"No, I mean, I know. But have you had any doom twinges?"

"I'd tell you. You know that, right?"

I nodded. It was a comfort I held onto tighter than she probably realized. As long as she didn't feel like something massively wrong was about to happen, then the memory fades I'd been experiencing couldn't be something deadly.

I'd told her about them. Told Myra, too, because I'd promised both of them I wasn't going to do dumb things that might get me hurt without consulting them first.

Everyone we'd talked to in town, who might know about the aftereffects of having my soul in a demon's possession for more than a year, was pretty sure we were in a wait-and-see kind of situation.

Wait and see if my soul could knit back together.

"No change with the memory thing?" she asked.

"I think the fog is happening less." That was true. But still...

...*a dream-like voice, telling me I had to find something, steal something*...

"You're noting when they happen still? So Myra and Bathin can make sure there's nothing weird going on?"

"Yes, Mother. Now if you're done babysitting me, how about you babysit her?"

I unlocked the door.

Xtelle stood on the floorboard her head hanging, her mane and tail drooping. She looked comically miserable.

Jean fought down a smile. "Hey, Xtelle. No one's here so you can talk if you want."

She just sniffled and sighed.

Jean made big eyes at me, and I shook my head and mouthed *drama pony*. Jean swung her fist around by her shoulder like she was working a lasso.

"Xtelle, are you okay?" Jean asked.

Xtelle raised her head, and the calculating look she gave me quickly turned into big, fat, fake tears. Oh, she was gonna give Jean the floorshow and encore.

"She's been so mean to me!" Xtelle gave a hiccupping wail. Jean turned to punch me lightly in the shoulder, mostly so she could hide her choking laughter.

"I've been fair," I said. "You're not in jail."

"I'm expected to do manual labor. Do you understand how hard that is…? Uh, which sister are you?"

"Jean."

"Right. The boring, childish one."

A blush slapped Jean's cheeks, and I stepped in front of her to grab the rope before Xtelle tangled in it and broke a leg.

"Don't listen to her," I said to Jean. "She says that kind of thing to all of us. Xtelle, you are acutely aware of the differences between the three of us and each of our powers and gifts."

Xtelle paused, then hopped out of the Jeep. "Yes, well. I find all of your differences and gifts boring."

"No." I slammed the door. "You don't." I handed Jean the rope.

The heat in Jean's cheeks had cooled, and she nodded once, giving Xtelle a steely glare.

A lot of people saw Jean as the happy sister. The funny sister. The geeky fan-girl sister. And yes, she was all of those things. She was also smart as a whip. A sunny disposition was easy to interpret as naiveté.

How much strength did it take to keep a happy attitude

and caring heart in a world full of as much darkness as ours? How much strength to know that disaster and death were always right around the corner?

The answer was: a Jean's worth of strength.

"Hogan's got a side yard with a door straight into the kitchen," Jean said. "He's still working, and I'm not on duty for a couple hours, so you can hang out here behind the bakery while I get things together, and you can meet him."

"Hang out." She glanced back at me. "There must be a better choice than this... Reed."

"Nope." Jean looped the rope over her shoulder and headed toward the front of the shop. "I'm the best Reed you're gonna get. Let's go find out if my boyfriend is down with you pooping up his side yard."

"Poop?" Xtelle said. "Delaney. Delaney. Does she expect me to poop in public?"

I waved. "Bye, Xtelle. Be a good pony. Poop in all the right places."

"Wait. Wait. Jean!" She trotted closer to Jean. "Surely, I can stay indoors when no one's around. I won't need much more than a king-size bed, full bathroom, spa, sauna, and three servants. What? Fine. *Neigh, neigh, I will also require room service, neigh.*"

Jean stuck her head in the door. "Hey, Hoges. Can I have a minute?"

She waved me off with one hand without even looking over at me.

With her choppy laugh and Hogan's ridiculous giggle filling the air, I knew they were going to do just fine with our little problem demon.

I got behind the wheel and started the Jeep.

"This is so much better now that we're alone."

The voice was behind me. Right behind me. So close I should be able to feel the puff of each syllable on the back of my neck.

My breath hitched. I was frozen, staring straight ahead,

hands clenched around the steering wheel, the world fogged at the edges, unnaturally still.

"It was difficult with her so close to you. I've been looking for her for a long time. Did you know that?" The voice sounded different, almost hungry or fond, though neither of those were quite right.

Longing was closer. Lonely.

I didn't know how to process that.

"I suppose you couldn't know. I'd had one glimpse, so brief all those months ago, and I knew. I knew how I could finally get to her, reach her. After all these years."

My pulse hammered, sweat pricked at my hairline. How could I be sweating when I was so cold, frigid, arctic?

"Did you know I was looking for her?"

Words had power. My words had power. If I asked who he was talking about, if I guessed it was Jean he'd been trying to find, he'd have something.

Ownership. Leverage.

Power over me, or over my sister.

"Such muscular silence." A strange thread of laughter stitched through his words. "Well, that will change soon. The last piece. Find it. Then the spell will be complete. Enjoy yourself until then." He leaned forward, close, closer, until I felt the shivery brush of lips against my skin. "I do mean that, Delaney Reed. Because soon, you will be begging for your freedom."

A horn blared out on the street as someone waited a second too long before gassing it through the green light.

I blinked and blinked, trying to remember what I'd been doing. Sweat trickled down my temple, prickled across the top of my lip, my breathing was hard, like I'd just been running. Like I'd just been crying.

Hadn't I just left Jean laughing with Hogan? Hadn't I just gotten into the Jeep? I turned and inspected the interior of the car. Nothing. No one to startle me. Just that horn.

The Jeep was still in park, the dragon pig sleeping on its back in the passenger seat, stubby legs stuck straight up. I peeled my fingers off the steering wheel, my knuckles aching and stiff.

I pushed back out into the open air and sucked down big lungfuls of fresh, salty air buttered and sweetened by the bakery.

Jean and Hogan were leading Xtelle around the other side of the shop where I'm sure they were going to stuff her into one of their vehicles.

I'd just lost a second or two. That was all.

"You're working too hard, Delaney," I muttered to myself. "Jean said a day off would be good. She's right. Tonight is all about sitting at home and having a nice dinner with Ryder."

I leaned against the Jeep, pulled out my phone and hit the icon. The call dumped into Ryder's voice mail.

"Hey," I said after the recording. "How about you and I take the evening off? Jean said she'll pull my shift. I'll order in or make something. I mean, cook. Cook dinner. Or we can get take out. Either's good. Um... Call. Let me know."

I thought about saying more. Telling him I missed him, asking if he was all right, or if he was hiding something.

But I'd rather ask those things when I could see his face.

"Love you." The message beeped, cutting off the words. I wasn't sure if he'd hear them, but it was too late to fix.

I opened the car again, dropped into the seat, and jiggled the dragon pig's leg.

"Listen, buddy."

The dragon pig opened one eye, peering up at me upside down.

"I need you to ride shotgun while I hit a couple more stops."

The other eye slowly opened. Then both blinked independent of the other. The dragon pig huffed steam out its nostrils, warm where it brushed my wrists.

"I'm good. Just...distracted, I guess. Make sure I don't miss a stop sign or something."

It growl-*oink*ed, then hopped up on the dashboard.

"Hey, you're not quite small enough... Oh, okay then. I see you got that covered."

There really wasn't enough room for the dragon pig to perch comfortably on the dash, but it was a dragon. Once it had settled into the space, it just sort of…fit.

"Is it a magic thing?"

I got a snarl for that.

"Okay," I chuckled, "dragon thing it is."

CHAPTER EIGHT

Turned out grocery shopping was also a dragon thing.

"What do you think about lasagna?" I asked the dragon pig in the grocery cart. "Or maybe some pot stickers? I could try sushi? Can't burn what you don't cook."

The dragon pig sat transfixed in the metal cart practically vibrating with joy.

"I think a pot pie. I can make pot pie without burning it." I turned down the aisle then backtracked the way I'd come in. "Or maybe a sexy soup? What's the sexiest soup?"

"Something with sausage, meatballs, and a good, heavy cream."

My almost-uncle, Crow, dropped a loaf of rye in the basket hanging in the crook of his elbow and grinned at me.

He'd gone full Mohawk about a week ago. It looked great with his thick black hair and made the square of his jaw and cut of his cheeks stand out.

Myra had teased him about it not being traditional Siletz, and he'd pointed at Jean's pink hair and said, "Traditional clown," then at Myra's bob cut and said, "traditional flapper." She'd laughed, he'd flipped her off companionably, then done a few more runway struts so we could all thoroughly appreciate his new do.

"Hey, Crow."

"Or a good chicken. Lots of breasts and thighs?"

"Never gonna talk sexy soup with you. I've changed my mind anyway. Definitely some kind of noodle dish."

Crow was the god Raven. A trickster who mostly behaved himself while he was vacationing in Ordinary and running his glassblowing business in the Crow's Nest.

"Special occasion?" He pointed at the bottle of wine I'd spent fifteen minutes trying to decide on, and which I'd finally chosen because the label was pretty. His fingernails had gray dust embedded at the cuticles. That was different. Glassblowing didn't usually leave his fingers dirty like that. Like…dust? No, something else.

"The wine?" he asked, bringing me back to his question.

"Just dinner at home. Something simple."

"Simple like hand-rolled sushi and homemade pot pie."

"Or lasagna. Maybe I'll just go with lasagna."

"Uh-huh." He leaned his basket on the edge of my shopping cart, effectively pinning us in place.

"What's wrong?" he asked.

"We're blocking the aisle."

He didn't move.

"You're in my way, Crow."

He leaned harder. Hard enough I heard the plastic of his basket crack.

"It's just dinner."

He stuffed his boot under the edge of the wheel.

"I think Ryder's mad at me. There. Happy?" I yanked the cart. He'd been expecting it, and let go. That thing really moved.

It careened into a display of cheese puff balls, sending gallon barrels of safety-orange snack food clattering across the linoleum clear to the apple cases.

A few people looked up, including the checker at the closest stand, Mr. Manly. He'd been my third-grade teacher and had never forgiven me for spreading mayonnaise on the blackboard in an attempt to make it shiny clean.

"Clean up in the bread section," he croaked over the store's PA system. "Clean up for Miss Delaney Reed." Underlying that tone was the unspoken *again*.

"Why is Ryder mad at you, Boo Boo?"

I shrugged. "If I knew, I wouldn't be shopping for last-minute lasagna."

I must have sounded frustrated enough his uncle tendencies took over.

"All right. You are not cooking lasagna." He moved me to one side, dropped his basket in mine next to the dragon pig and took over driving.

"I can make las—"

"You'll try to make it perfect, except somehow it will catch on fire. Or explode."

"Lasagna explodes?"

He stopped the cart and gave me a look. "Remember the potatoes?"

"That was only one time! Okay two. But lasagna is easier than baking a potato."

Crow wasn't listening. He was taking the aisles at a speed that made me stretch my legs or switch to a jog. He pulled up sharp at the deli counter.

"No," I said.

"Hold your horses." He studied the options behind the curved glass display cases, the cart blocking a young man with an armful of toilet paper who was trying to squeeze past the kiosk of pretzels and hummus.

"Sorry." I shifted the cart so the kid could get through.

"Baked lemon pepper chicken, some of that pasta salad with the peas..." Crow looked over at me. "Peas?"

I gagged.

Crow grinned. "Oh, yeah, *extra* peas, no, a little more. A little more. And...good. Those rosemary garlic rolls too. Thanks, Heath."

"There," he said. "All taken care of. The baked chicken is delicious, and you can serve it cold if you want. Now you go pick out a dessert."

I glanced toward the baking aisle.

"No. Nothing from scratch, nothing out of a box. Hie thee to the bakery section. That-a-way. Cheesecake, pudding cake, donuts, pie. Baked by someone who knows how to turn off an oven before the fire department shows up." He made shooing motions.

"I can bake," I muttered to the dragon pig. It just *oink*ed and wagged its tail.

"You'll have plenty of time to sulk in the bakery department." Crow dug around in his pocket and held up a bottle cap for the dragon pig. It pecked it out of his fingers in one quick swipe, chewed and swallowed.

"Stop bribing my pig," I said.

Crow laughed and made more shooing motions.

I worked my way back to the bakery, much more slowly than the speed-run-power-walk Crow had just performed.

Chicken wasn't a bad idea, and serving it cold left some leeway if Ryder got delayed. I pulled out my phone and checked for messages. None.

I thought about calling him again, decided that was too much, but maybe a text wouldn't be a bad idea in case the job site was too noisy for him to hear his phone ring.

Dinner tonight? Picking up enough for two. Dessert too.

I read it over again, added a little heart and sent it before I did any more second guessing.

"All right," I said to absolutely no one, "what dessert says, 'Hey, we need to talk'? Pie? Crullers?"

I took my time to case the joint. I waffled between the key lime pie and the raspberry sour cream pudding cake. Finally decided on the cake, which would go well with whipped cream.

I toted my bounty back to the deli aisle, but Crow wasn't there. A quick scan down the rows, and I finally spotted him by the wine.

"Dessert." I dropped the plastic box of cake and spray can of whipped cream next to the dragon pig. "Are you done sticking your nose in my personal business?"

"Hardly. Beer—he likes the Haystack, right?" Crow held up our local brew made by Chris Lagon—our local gillman.

"Wine—you like red, right? Not what I'd pair with chicken, but it will make the lemon pepper pop." He put a bottle of red with a boring label in the basket.

"Good-bye, Delaney," I said. "Didn't mean to take over your life like you aren't an adult who has been shopping for herself since she was seventeen. Didn't mean to treat you like you don't know how to put one simple meal on the table."

Crow grinned, and there was a flash in his eyes. Not god power exactly, because he'd put that down to vacation here, and I knew it was stashed out at Frigg's place. But all the gods had a little something that made them stand out from mortals if you knew how to look for it.

Crow's looked a lot like bossy busy-body.

"Maybe it's that attitude of yours that's pushing him away," he mused.

"Watch it."

"Or your cooking skills. The lack of them."

"Go away."

"Or that your job gives you more power than him, and his masculinity feels threatened."

"Now you're just—"

"My masculinity feels just fine, thanks."

I couldn't help it, my heart went all fluttery. My cheeks and neck seared hot as a fire-red blush rushed under my skin. Ryder had that effect on me. Ryder had had that effect on me since we were in grade school.

Crow gave me a big wink. "Ryder, I didn't see you there."

I turned. It took me several seconds before I had the brain to speak.

He wore dark blue flannel over a grey Henley that hugged the muscles of his broad chest. He'd ditched the Carhartt jacket and shoved both sleeves up his arms to show off his strong forearms.

Streaks of sun-bleached blonde threaded his brown hair,

making those green eyes of his sparkle like slow-flowing water.

He looked like summer and warm sand and everything I'd ever wanted in my life.

"Hi," I said.

"Hey." He glanced away from me to assess the basket. "Looks like someone's got plans."

"I do. Have plans."

"Aw...isn't this sweet? You two kids are just the bee's knees."

"Go away, Crow," we said at the same time.

He chuckled. "See you two around. And Ryder? Stop making my girl sad. Or I'll make time in my schedule to have words with you."

Great. An over-protective almost-uncle threat. That was just super great.

Ryder shot me a look. "You're sad?"

"If there's a chance to stir up trouble, Crow's got the spoon. You know that."

"Sure," he said, though the way he said it meant he also knew Crow liked it best when the trouble was based on truth. "You..." He took a breath and changed tactics. He stepped forward and took both of my hands in his. "Dinner sounds great. Thanks for the beer."

"Crow picked out the beer," Crow called out from halfway across the store.

"Right," I said. "Can we agree to keep the gods out of this?"

"What gods?" He returned my smile.

"All of them," I said. "I'd like to have a nice meal with you and no one else."

The dragon pig *oink*ed.

"Dragon pigs and Spuds excluded," I added.

Ryder was still smiling, but a shadow crossed his face. I waited, not ready to jump to some kind of conclusion. Not ready to think he was already figuring a way to cancel the date, a way out of it.

"Uh, one god," he said.

"Which?" Calm. I was calm. The ocean in summer, no wind, no waves calm. The sand blown clean and smooth, not a footprint to be seen calm.

"Mithra."

Now there was wind, waves, churning sand.

"Mithra is joining us for dinner?"

"No not, well, in a way, but no. Not…um…physically."

"'In a way' because you're tied to him, or because he's trying to use you to do something he wants? Like get into Ordinary without having to follow the rules. Like ruling Ordinary."

"He's a god of rules, Delaney."

"Oh, I know. He's a god of contracts who tricked you into signing a contract with him. A god who hates that a Reed is standing in his way of taking over a town he won't even enter legally."

Ryder cleared his throat and glanced around to see if we were gathering a crowd. Okay, yeah, I'd been a little loud.

I followed his gaze and noted both Odin and Frigg trying to look very interested in quiche and dog biscuits, respectively.

Frigg, a trucker hat on backward, her button-up short sleeve with FRIGG'S RIGS embroidered across the pocket, glanced over at me. She tipped her chin at Ryder and held up a bag of treats, offering to peg him in the back of the head.

I took a breath, held it for a second, searching for that calm water, that smooth sand somewhere inside me.

"Delaney." Odin pushed his cart between us, forcing us to step back. "Ryder." Odin's eye patch was forest-green leather today, the band tight enough it made his wild gray hair go mushroom shaped at the top.

He was a trickster god, but also a god of wisdom and poetry, among other things. Here in Ordinary, without his power, he was a chainsaw artist. And not a very talented one.

"Odin," I said.

"Did I overhear a dinner being planned?" He focused his

one eye on Ryder and leaned toward him. "Something *special* going on tonight?"

I frowned.

Ryder cleared his throat. "Delaney and I are having a nice dinner. *Alone*," he added. "Just a nice dinner."

"Just a nice dinner?" Odin asked. He threw a look at Frigg, and I thought I caught her dragging her finger across her throat in the "kill it" signal, but she scratched at her collarbone instead.

She flashed me a toothy smile.

"Well, that's nice," Frigg said, louder than needed. "You two have a nice, private dinner. C'mon, Odin. Let Ryder and Delaney," and she upped the volume just a bit, "have a nice *private* dinner."

There was a split second of silence in the store, then I heard shopping cart wheels spin and clack, voices mumble, and the general commotion of people moving through the store toward the exits.

Odin made a short *humph* sound then reached around Ryder and snagged a six pack of Pirate Stout. "Have a good dinner, you two. Frigg?" He held up the beer. "Cold one?"

"I'm not buying a statue," she said.

"Did I say I wanted you to?"

"Every time I see you."

He aimed his cart toward the check out, and Frigg strolled along next to him.

"I can find someone else who likes beer," he grumbled.

Frigg chuckled. "You are so easy sometimes." She tossed a bag of chips into Odin's cart, plucked up a jar of salsa, hesitated over cheap queso, then grabbed it.

"Oh, and Ryder?" Frigg spun. She was walking backward, still pacing Odin. "Don't be such a jerk to Delaney, or Crow won't be the only one having words with you." She waved, turned, then they were around the corner and out of sight.

Ryder scowled. "How am I the bad guy here?"

I bit back a small smile. "Gods, right?"

He cleared his throat. "Any chance we can go back to

being annoyed at Crow? Maybe add whatever that was with Frigg and Odin?"

"Yeah. I'm still angry about Mithra. But you know that, I remind you about it enough. And Crow's always been a little…" I wobbled my hand back and forth to show he was walking a thin line too.

"We're good then?" he asked.

"We're good."

We stood there like a couple of dorks, staring into each other's eyes.

Then a woman, who was not a god, came down the aisle. She had a cell phone pressed to her ear and was reading off every brand and name in an east coast accent.

"Dinner, right?" I asked, uncomfortable with how hopeful it sounded.

"Yes. Absolutely. I just have to deliver one thing. No, don't glare. It's a part that didn't get out to the job site and they need it ASAP. I'll be back in an hour, hour fifteen tops."

"Great," I said, and it didn't sound great at all. "I'm off at four. Plenty of time."

"Delaney."

"No, it's good. Works with my schedule too. Dinner at five."

"I could take it out there maybe in the morning…"

"No. Go. I'll keep the chicken warm and throw the beer mugs in the freezer."

He paused, eyes zagging to measure my mood. "You sure?"

"I'll see you at home, Bailey." I closed the distance and gave him a kiss on the cheek which felt a little weird, but I just couldn't shake the sadness sitting lead-heavy in my stomach.

He gave me one last puzzled look, which I couldn't decipher, then raised one eyebrow. "You know we're okay, right?"

That was a landmine I refused to set off in the middle of a grocery store. I smiled. It was fake, but I wasn't sure he would notice.

"Sooner you leave, sooner we get chicken," I said with forced levity. "Fair warning, you're eating all that salad. It's full of peas." I stuck my tongue out and that seemed to erase the worried look on his face.

His hands, which had been clenched at his sides, relaxed, the lines at the corners of his eyes smoothed out. "Hour, hour and a half," he said, relieved.

"Drive safe."

I watched him go, enjoying the swing of his toned shoulders and the way those work jeans cupped his ass and made his long legs look even longer.

"Think he's going to get home before midnight?" I asked the dragon pig. It *oink*ed.

"Yeah, me neither." I sighed and headed to the checkout.

THE GLASS of wine was still half full. I'd taken three sips from it, just to see if Crow had any idea how to pick out wine.

He did. It was delicious.

When eight o'clock rolled by, I stabbed a piece of cold chicken with a fork and ate it over the sink. Then I packed away the food and placed the beer mugs back in the freezer.

The wine glass was still on the table, a testament to the "soon" that hadn't come.

When nine o'clock rolled around, I lifted the glass, took one more small sip, then poured the rest of it down the drain.

I ran the water, staring as the deep maroon liquid went crimson, rose, blush, and was gone. Diluted into nothingness. Weaker than water.

Was this how our days would go? Moments of something wonderful watered down by the mundane until we were thinned out, invisible?

I turned off the water and dried my hands. Maybe that was the way other relationships ended, but not mine. Not with the man I'd loved for so many years. If we were going down the drain, we weren't going down without a fight.

Spud and the dragon pig were sprawled across the big leather couch taking as much room as physically possible. Both were sleeping, a soft buzzing snore coming out of the dragon pig.

"All right, you slackers, scoot to one side. We're gonna watch a movie."

Before I could wedge my way into the corner of the couch, my phone rang.

"Delaney," I answered.

"Perhaps you could assist me." The voice was stuffed up, as if the speaker couldn't get any air in through his nose.

"Than?"

"Yes, Reed Daughter."

"You sound different."

"I am aware."

I pushed the dog's butt. He rolled over, leaving about three inches of couch free. I wriggled in next to him, crossed my legs and picked up the remote. "What can I do for you?"

"I require your attendance."

"Oh...kay. Where?"

"At my abode."

I just sat there with my thumb stuck in the down position on the remote. The TV flashed soundlessly through channel choices.

"You want me to come to your house?"

"Did I not just say as much?"

"You did, no you did. All right. That's— Why?"

"If you would come, we could speak in person."

Alarm bells went off. Death might be a lot of things—and he was. But he was rarely cagey about what he required of a person.

"Are you all right?"

"Quite."

"But are you in danger?"

"Delaney." The sigh said it all.

"If there's someone in your house holding you at gunpoint just say you want pepperoni with extra cheese. If you're tied to a chair, tell me to add pineapple. And if it's more of a hostage situation, tell me you like the thin crust so crisp a fly can crack it."

"I regret this immensely."

"Is that code for something? Something embarrassing? Do you have a body part stuck in something, or something stuck in a body part? Did you accidentally handcuff yourself naked somewhere? The roof?"

"If I had—" And then the weirdest thing happened. He sneezed. "If I wanted—" He sneezed again. "Good-bye, Reed Daughter."

He hung up, the little click as loud as a coffin lid slamming in place.

"No," I said. "No way. You're not getting out of this that easily. Plus, you invited me to your house."

I sprang up and put on my coat and boots in a flash. I grabbed my purse. As an afterthought, I detoured to the cupboard for a can of chicken soup, a box of tissues with the menthol lotion in it and—after dithering for a second—decided not to pack the cold chicken.

My phone rang again.

"Yo."

"Are you okay?" Myra asked.

"Yes. Well, Ryder stood me up, but I'm good. Why?"

"I just had this overwhelming urge to call you. Are you doing something stupid?"

"Maybe. I'm going to go visit Than. At his house. He sounded sick."

The length of the silence was telling.

"I know!" I said. "Finally. I'll take as many pictures as I can."

"Wow, is he…I mean I know he can't die…"

"He sneezed. So…allergies? Cold? Wanna put some money on it?"

She laughed. "No. But take some cold medicine just in case."

"Oh, good idea. I have soup."

"You didn't make it, did you? Because I'd hate to be the sister of the woman who killed Death. Think of the headlines."

"Har-har. It's in a can."

"Only one can of water. They mean the can it comes in, Delaney."

"That was once!" I suddenly realized I'd been saying that a lot.

"And you have to take it off the stove before the noodles dissolve."

"Good-bye, Myra. Too bad you're not going to see any of the pictures of the inside of Than's house."

"Don't throw crackers in it while it's heating up," she added in a rush.

I hung up on her. She rang me back. I jabbed the red button with glee, then silenced the phone.

"You two be good," I said to the creatures snoring away in the living room. "I'll be back soon."

I paused at the door, thinking maybe I should leave a note for Ryder. Let him know I was out on a wellness check of sorts. I unsilenced my phone and decided that would have to be enough.

CHAPTER NINE

THE HOUSE WAS CHEERFULLY AQUA, framed in white, with a white picket fence around it. A twisted shore pine marked the point on the property where SW 10th collided with Ebb, split into two and flowed around the home. On one side of the street was a Dead End sign, on the other, No Turnaround.

Fitting.

I hadn't known Than was looking to buy a house until Barbara, Roy's wife, mentioned she'd heard it had closed. I could only assume it had been sold fully furnished because none of us on the force had seen any signs of Than moving in, even though we'd been diligently driving by on the regular.

We'd totally been snooping, but if anyone had asked, we'd just say we were making sure a member of the community was settling in.

The curiosity was killing me. Myra, Jean, and I had all promised we'd share pictures if any of us got through the front door.

Looked like I was the lucky one.

I parked the Jeep on one side of the house. Than hadn't bought a car yet. We had an office pool on when and what model.

Before getting out, I checked my phone—Myra's messages

of fake outrage about me hanging up on her, Jean's complaint about the unicorn flushing a quilt down the toilet, and then, more excitedly, squees and demands for pics as soon as I had them.

I pocketed the phone, picked up the bag, and strolled through the little white gate, up the steps and onto the porch.

I pressed the doorbell.

The bell sang out a little tune about blue skies.

I waited for a minute, then half a minute more. Maybe he wasn't home. The front windows were dark.

I tried the bell again. Blue skies. Nothing but.

Footsteps, heavy enough to hear through the solid wood door came near and the curtained windows went yellow. A light over the door clicked on, punching a cone of light into the darkness.

The handle turned—no lock—and the door swung inward.

"Reed Daughter."

Than looked terrible. Well, he looked like he always did—pale skin, dark hair, and eyes that carried the cold light of a thousand dying stars.

But those end-of-the-universe eyes were bloodshot, his chapped nose looked painful, and his hair stuck up at weird angles.

So this is what Death warmed over actually looked like.

His over-stretched pink T-shirt had a picture on it of two beach balls which fell over the bra zone. The words: Big Girls Love Big Balls were written across the bottom of the shirt.

But it was the fuzzy pajama bottoms with little yellow ears of corn on them, and the…

"Holy crap. Tell me those are fake."

He slowly peered groundward and shifted his foot. The slippers he was wearing—because gods help me, they'd better just be slippers—were huge furry spiders. Eight bent legs, a row of googly eyes.

He shook his foot again. The eyes swirled.

"They are not fake. They are house slippers."

"The spiders are…never mind. Let's try again. Hey, Than." I lifted the bag. "I brought you some stuff. Nice slippers."

The sallow light from the room behind him and the yellow light from the porch did his complexion no favors. He narrowed his eyes, probably trying to suss out if I were lying, then he shrugged. "They are warm."

I worked to keep my gaze on him and not peek behind him into the house. I was here because he was sick. Because he needed food. Not because I finally had a chance to case the joint.

I motioned to the bag. "Chicken soup, soft tissues, medicine if you have what I think you have."

"I see." Still the pause, the hesitation as he decided if his privacy was worth a can of soup. "Won't you come in?"

Shivers plucked my spine and the hair on the back of my neck stuck up. When Death invites you in—even Death who looked like he'd been run over by a truck—you felt it in your bones.

"Thank you. Shoes or no shoes?" I stepped into the foyer.

"Remove them."

I toed them off and nudged them against the wall. "This is for you." I held the bag up again.

He took a big step backward—spider eyes a-googling, spider legs a-jiggling—and pointed down the hallway. Then he lifted his other elbow and sneezed into it. Hard. Twice. Even the spiders trembled.

"How long have you been feeling like this?" I asked.

"I am sure I don't know what you mean." He sniffed into his elbow.

"You're sick."

"I am not—" He broke off into a coughing fit, his elbow still over his mouth.

The coughs kept coming so I set the bag down on the little statue of an armadillo holding a silver tray near the door, and took Than's free elbow.

"Couch or bed?" I powered us forward.

He sneezed and waved generally leftward. We went down the hall and through a wide archway into the living room.

I was expecting quirky. I was expecting funeral home chic, but that's not at all what I got.

What I got was understated elegance. What I got was summery ease, splashes of eye-catching colors against lovely neutrals. Here a bit of red, there a bit of orange, and over there blue, and green.

The furniture—couch, loveseat, and recliners—looked brand new, well built, and comfortable. One entire wall was covered with a huge flat-screen monitor. The west-facing wall was all windows.

Soft music with wind chimes and the flow of water played from hidden speakers.

But the thing that really caught my attention were the flowers.

Hanging in pots, tucked into corners of the windows, stacked across the mantle, hooked into frames against the walls, trailing up the side of that huge monitor, were little blooms and buds. Beautiful. Fragile. Familiar and exotic, there were more than I could name.

And all of them so green, green, green. The scents should have been overwhelming, clashing. But somehow there was only a sweetness in the air that was almost too faint to catch. The kind of fragrance that made me want to stop, close my eyes and take a sniff just to see if I could breathe a little more of it.

This felt personal. Private. All these tiny pots, carefully planted, lit, watered.

This music, wind, water, and softness.

This room, furniture and comfort, inviting ease.

I was standing in the middle of Death's garden.

The urge to take pictures for my sisters faded. This was his place to vacation, to be something he was not when he carried his power. And what else would Death want but the one thing his power never allowed: to nurture life.

"Here," he said, taking over the driving and getting us around the oversized couch.

I helped him sit, then stepped back so he could recline if he wanted to. Instead he just stretched out his long, long legs —spiders jiggling—for miles, and leaned his head back against the cushion. He sniffed loudly, eyes closed, and after a quick scan, I went back out into the hall.

I ripped the cardboard off the top of the box and popped two tissues out for him.

"Thank you." He took the tissues then held them up with a questioning look.

"They're...uh...for you to blow your nose."

"Whatever do you...? Oh, I see." He folded them neatly, blew, folded, blew. "That's... Yes. Quite."

I sat on the coffee table, trying to stay out of his sneezing distance, hands on my knees. "I'm sorry you have a cold."

He wiped under his nose, looked down at the tissue, then back up at me. "Do I?" He shivered and cleared his throat. "Ah. How unpleasant. I am feeling extremely unpleasant."

"Yeah, that's how it goes." I removed everything else and set the bag beside him. "Drop the used tissues in there. Pull new ones when you need them. Have you eaten anything?"

"Ever?"

I held back a laugh. "Recently. Today."

He made an offended face. "Why would I? I am feeling extremely unpleasant. Have you not noticed, Reed Daughter? Extremely unpleasant."

"Don't be a baby about it."

His mouth fell open with a little *pop* from his tongue against the roof of his mouth. "You are not very nurturing. Is that not the role of a..."

"Woman?" I asked with my eyebrows quirked and a dangerous tone.

"...employer." He blinked those bloodshot eyes, and I couldn't tell if he was trying to look contrite or pulling my leg.

"All you get out of an employer is a request for a note from your doctor and a dock in your pay."

"You don't pay me, as I recall."

"See how smart I am? Since you're sick and not coming into work anyway."

"Would you prefer that I—?" Face to elbow again for another round of sneezing.

I really wanted to wash my hands. I stood.

"No. I do not want you at work. You'll get germs everywhere, and you look gross."

"I— What?"

"Everyone looks gross when they have a head cold."

"I am hardly gross. Are you familiar with decomposition, Delaney? Intimately familiar? With decomposition? With things that have rotted down to a primordial ooze? The ending of organic life?"

"Like old cucumbers in my refrigerator?"

He blinked, and almost, almost smiled.

"I am not a vegetable." He sniffed and laid his head back on the cushion.

"Right, so I'm going to make you chicken soup. You need lots of liquids. Tea or water?"

"Tea. With honey and lemon. Please."

There was a hint of something in that request, almost laughter, almost fondness. He was enjoying this. A little too much.

"Well, you're getting water first." I stood, took a wild guess at which direction the kitchen lay, found it beyond a small, but well-appointed, dining area.

The kitchen was less modern than the living room. The walls were covered with white-washed wood cabinets that had hand-painted tulips, irises, and some sort of herb that might be rosemary etched across the corners. The little drawings added a feeling of spring, of living, growing things.

There were real flowers here, too, and other plants—herbs poking up along the window sill, pots of succulents, and a spray of orchids. Some kind of vine crawled up the molding near the ceiling, and a pot in the corner held blossomless sunflowers that were almost as tall as I was.

I opened doors, pulled out a glass tumbler, filled it with water from the door of the fridge, and carried it back into the living room.

Than hadn't moved.

"This is unpleasant, isn't it?" he said.

"What? Life?" I came around in front of him, opened the box of cold tablets, and dropped two in the water.

They fizzed medicinal lemon tang into the air.

"No, a head cold."

"Yeah, they're no fun. But it will be over soon."

"Quite like life, then."

I sat on the coffee table again. I couldn't tell if the conversation had just turned dark, or if the subject of mortality was his go-to comfort convo when he was sick.

"Colds end sooner than a lifetime."

"Within the hour, I should hope."

"More like four or five days."

"How disappointing."

"Here, don't be sad."

He lifted his head, blinked to pull the room into focus, then noticed the glass I was holding out for him.

"Drink. It will help."

"Offers such as that do not usually end well for the recipient."

I grinned. "It's medicine, not poison. It will help with the sneezing and aches."

He took the glass, held it up to the light, then drank it down in one long, sustained pull.

He dabbed a tissue against the corners of his eyes. "Hideous. I regret requesting your assistance."

"Too bad. That's going to take a few minutes before it works. Stay here. I'll make soup."

"And will there eventually be tea?"

"Yes. Still regret requesting my presence?"

"Less so, Reed Daughter."

I raided his kitchen for a pan, can opener, and bowl and got the soup heating. This kind didn't even need me to add water, which I totally would have nailed, anyway.

So there, *Myra*.

I filled the electric kettle with fresh water, turned it on, and mooched my way through tea tins until I found one that smelled like chamomile and lemon. Honey was at the front of the cupboard, local stuff in a half-full glass jar.

By the time I'd gathered a wooden cutting board, a mug with a bee in sunglasses tanning in the center of a sunflower with the words: LIFE'S A BEE-CH on it, and sliced a lemon, it was time to pour hot water into the little ceramic tea pot.

I remembered to turn off the soup, then carried the tea out, setting it on the coffee table.

Than still had his head back, eyes closed. He'd tossed a tissue over his face. It fluttered slightly as he exhaled, contracted on the inhale, forming to his nose, mouth, and chin before fluttering outward again.

"Tea," I said. "Be right back."

He moaned softly, the wuss.

I left him to it and got busy with the soup. Crackers too.

"And here's the soup."

"Chicken soup?" his muffled voice asked from beneath the tissue.

"With stars."

I set the soup down next to the tea and dropped into the wingback chair. I scooted it closer to the couch so I didn't feel like I was halfway across the room.

Than sat and drew the tissue away from his face with the kind of dignity no one should be able to pull off with a nose that red.

"Stars?"

And oh, how his eyes glittered.

"In the soup."

He picked up the bowl and brought it to his lap. He scooped a spoonful and stared at it.

"It's soup," I said for what felt like the millionth time.

"Chicken and vegetables and broth and little star noodles. You eat it by putting that spoon in your mouth, not by staring at it."

He flicked a look my way, and okay, yeah, there was a death glare.

I pointed my finger at my open mouth.

He twitched one eyebrow upward. Sniffed. "I know what soup is, Reed Daughter."

"Delaney, remember? Or Boss, if you'd rather."

"Yes. Well."

He lowered the spoon, gave the liquid a slow stir, scooped again. Just when I thought he was going to do nothing but stare at it, he opened his mouth and took a deliberate mouthful.

Not every god fits into Ordinary seamlessly. Some refused to give up their names and their bombastic mannerisms. Some walked around like they owned this universe and collected rent from all the others.

But even the gods who tried to play it cool, who fit into the mortal world easily, like Crow, like Cupid, still had this little something that shone through every now and then. Something that set them apart.

I was very aware that I was watching the god of death try a new thing: canned chicken and star soup. Watching him experience the world was fascinating.

He lowered the spoon back into the soup, stirred, and tried a second bite.

Then he placed the spoon and bowl back on the coffee table.

"You don't like it?"

"I can't like something I am unable to taste. Isn't that the pleasure of consuming? Isn't that the point?"

"Sure," I said, nodding at the tea, which he proceeded to pour, then dollop honey into. "But food is more than just consuming. More than just the pleasure of taste. It's necessary for a mortal body to function. Especially when a body is fighting a cold."

He hummed, pinched and nasal, and sipped tea. "Much more pleasant."

His eyelids drooped, and his normal complexion—somewhere between fish belly and snow melt—had an uncharacteristic blush over his cheeks.

Fever?

"I need to touch your forehead."

He froze, both eyebrows lifting.

"To see if you have a temperature."

He opened his mouth.

"A fever," I corrected. "Because if you have one that's too high you could need more than just soup. You might need stronger medicine. Or to go to the hospital. People your age…"

"My *age*?" He drew himself up, shoulders pulled back. "People? There are no other *people* such as I, Reed Daughter. The god of death is not some kind of…of plastic membership card handed out at street corners for all comers. My temperature—"

He bent to the side and sneezed again into his elbow, careful to hold his tea up to keep from spilling.

"—is of adequate joules. Fever. Indeed."

"I'm not even going to comment on that little tirade. Where'd you learn to cover your sneeze?"

I pressed the back of my hand against his sweaty forehead. He was hot, but not burning up. I didn't know what his normal temp might be, but if it was anywhere in human range, I'd say he was in the clear.

"I am Death," he said, his nose all stuffed. He blew again, folded, blew, then dropped the tissue in the bag. "I am familiar with sickness and disease."

He sipped tea, and those eyes over the top of the cup were sharp. Had this all been a lark for him?

"Tell me you didn't just invite me over so you could show off your cold."

"Delaney. Such cynicism. Now, tell me why you are unhappy."

Nope. Not falling for it. Not going to tell Death my problems. "Like I was saying, you might be running a slight fever, so drink liquids—more than normal. Get plenty of rest."

I plucked a tissue out of the box and wiped the dampness of his sweat off the back of my hand.

"Perhaps you would stay awhile."

"I have a life."

"And yet, you are here. So late in the evening. When you should be home with Mr. Bailey."

I stood there, crumbled the tissue in my fist, then stuffed it in my pocket.

"Ah," he said.

"You have any coffee in this house?"

"Yes."

"Good coffee?"

"I've been told."

There was a carafe by the refrigerator. Full. I poured thick, black coffee into a cup that said GET MUGGED. He'd brought it into the station once and told me he'd picked it up as swag from some alternate universe.

I should be home with Ryder, and I'd tried to be. I'd tried an entire chicken dinner with pudding cake's worth of trying. I'd tried cold beer mugs, nice wine, and a side salad I didn't even like's worth of trying.

He hadn't called, hadn't texted.

It was pretty clear he didn't want to be home. Not while I was there.

The rich scent of coffee calmed me, easing the tightness in my shoulders and the annoyance at myself, at my boyfriend, and at Mr. Sick Guy over there.

"Reed Daughter?" his voice drifted back. "Perhaps you could brood in the living room where it is more comfortable."

I rolled my eyes, then took a sip. A deep roast with something spicy at the end, maybe nutmeg or ginger. I approved.

"One," I said, coming back into the room, "I'm not brooding. I was just reading your stupid coffee cups."

"And what is two?"

"No more putting on the show. You have a cold. You know it. You know about diseases. You know how to sneeze into your elbow instead of all over the place. So why am I here? Really?"

"In a cosmic sense? You are the Bridge for Ordinary's god powers. I'd go so far as to say your conception was fated."

"Don't change the subject. Why did you call me over tonight? Really?"

"Myra."

Not what I'd expected.

I settled in the chair. "Is she all right?"

Than had partnered with Myra when he had first joined the force as a reserve officer. They'd developed a friendship that seemed to consist of a begrudging approval of the other's tea choices and arguing over books.

As far as I knew, he was the only person she had invited to the magical library. And she'd done so weekly.

"She is."

"So this is about the book club?"

"Book club?"

"Yes. The one you and Myra are in. Just the two of you, giggling over the naughty bits in the marginalia of ancient texts and magical scrolls. Getting buzzed sniffing fermented ink and snorting archaic mold."

He settled back, his tea at the ready. "Do tell me more."

"I'd love to join your clubhouse. What old, moldy book do I have to lick to be part of the fun? Is there a dress code? Please tell me it's silly hats. It's silly hats, isn't it?"

"There is no book club."

"Right." I gave him a big, exaggerated wink.

"She called me."

"About the book club?"

"About you."

Mayday. "Well, isn't that nice? I'll be going now. Call me if you need anything. No. You know what? You can call your book club buddy, *Myra*, and she can make you soup."

"Delaney Reed." That voice. Those chills. "Please be seated."

I could leave. He had no power over me here. Not that kind of power. It would be easy to go home.

To my empty house where the leftovers of a dinner that never happened sat in the fridge.

I flopped down into the chair. "What?"

"She is...concerned."

"She is nosey. You know that, don't you? She is really a big ol' busybody."

He sipped tea, watched me.

"Fine," I said. "What is she worried about this time? My work quality? My attendance? My tattered old soul?"

"Your happiness."

I ran my fingers through my hair, which I'd forgotten to pull back in my usual pony tail before heading over here. "I know she wants what's best for me, and I know she's seen me make some pretty hard and maybe even wrong decisions lately. So I mean this from my heart—with all the love— please tell her to buzz off."

I stood.

His eyebrows quirked up, and he leaned in and placed the teacup carefully on the wooden cutting board next to the teapot.

"She is concerned you haven't seen Ryder Bailey on an adequately regular basis. Is this true?"

"That's really not your concern. Or hers."

He refilled his cup and reclined with an aggressively patient look.

"I live with him. Of course I see him. I saw him just a few hours ago."

"At your home?"

"At the grocery store."

Than sipped tea and watched me.

Civilizations probably gave up and crumbled to dust under the weight of that stare.

"He's got a job. A build. Outside of town. The client is

demanding. He's...it won't go forward without him there. Making the decisions. Talking his client into doing the right thing. And I understand it. I do. I have a job that sends me out at all hours of the day and night. Unexpectedly." I pointed toward him, and he lifted his cup in toast and acknowledgment.

I didn't know when I'd started pacing, but I just kept at it. "It's not about that. About his job, except it could be. If he's telling me the truth, then... No. There's still something that isn't adding up here. Something that doesn't fit. And I try not to do that, you know?"

He raised an eyebrow.

"Go all detective on my relationship. Assume there's some kind of crime or mystery I need to dig at. Assume he's guilty for something when I know perfectly well that's not how relationships work. It's not about right and wrong. It's about want and need, give and take, support and stepping back when needed. I'm just not...just not good at some of that stuff."

I was staring at a lovely little pot of miniature daffodils, their cheery yellow blooms blown out like trumpets with frills, sturdy dark green leaves and stems anchoring them.

They looked like nothing could hurt them. They looked strong and vital and endless. But I knew. A little too much water, a little too little, and they'd be goners. Dead.

"It's hard to know," Than said. "It's hard to know how much. Or how little."

I stuck a finger in the dirt and found that it was dry on top, but just beneath that, a little scratch and wiggle down, the soil was damp. It was just right.

"How do you know?"

Than stood. I wouldn't have heard him, probably, but the spider eyes rattled with each step, the scrabbly legs scratching and whispering across the polished, dark wood floor.

"These questions are not as uncommon as you may think, Reed Daughter. Among the living, they are legion. Verse, chorus, song."

"I know. Intellectually I know this is nothing new to the human race. But for me. For Ryder and me..." I pulled my finger out of the dirt and dragged the tip of it across my jeans to get rid of the soil.

"How long have you been together?"

"We've known each other since grade school...but if you want to count the six years he was away at college and doing that secret, monster-hunting training..."

"Dating. How long have you dated?"

"Over two years." There was something about that. Shouldn't we be in a better place after years together? More honest, more open, more in love? Not hiding stuff? Or was this the mark in time where we found out all the crushes and unresolved attraction was just a fluke. A fad. Wanted because it was unattainable.

"That long."

The way he said it made me look up at him. Eyes still glassy, nose still red, but the medicine must be kicking in, since he didn't sound as sniffy.

"That is long," I said.

"Is it? Twenty-four months? Must I recount the difficulties you've endured within that time?"

And no, thank you very much, I'd prefer he didn't bring any of it up.

I'd been shot twice, given up my soul to a demon, been bitten by an ancient vampire who was a total asshole, and kind of almost really died for a moment, because of the dude with the head cold standing in front of me.

We'd seen zombie gnomes, chased down and returned Mrs. Yates's penguin a couple hundred times, and weathered some really bad weather. The gods had come, and the gods had gone, not always as per their preference.

People, good ordinary people, had been turned into frogs. One of my sisters had fallen in love with a demon, the other with a half Jinn.

And Ryder. Well, Ryder had found out about all the super-natural stuff that was happening right here in town, joined the force, quit the secret, monster-hunter agency, and become a servant to Mithra—a jerk of a god who didn't like how we Reeds ran Ordinary, and who, as near as I could tell, had forced my boyfriend to pledge fealty to him just to find a way to get under my grill.

It had been...hard. There were days I thought we were just a normal couple trying to decide whose bedside tables worked better in the bedroom (his), and who had the better coffee pot (me). Other days, I knew we were so far from that kind of normal, we might never reach it.

"But how do you know?" I said.

"How do I know what, Reed Daughter?"

I couldn't look at him anymore. "How much water. How much sun." I vaguely waved at the flowers, then crossed my arms over my ribs and nodded at the sturdy daffodils and the little pot next to it where thick, strong triangular leaves speared up through the dark soil.

"Ah," he said. "Life, I find, takes some time and observation. It also takes trials. Those trials bring errors."

"Doesn't look like any errors here."

"Because you only see that which I have accomplished. You have not seen the broken pots, the poor drainage, the moldy bulbs."

I nodded, not having words. It was all obvious, but I needed to hear it. Even if we were still talking about flowers.

"Would you like to?"

I frowned. "To what?"

"See my failures?"

My heart stopped before thudding forward. "This better not be some kind of metaphor," I said. "You better not have some kind of greenhouse of horror back there somewhere. Frankensteined, half-alive experiments in cages. We don't allow that kind of mad scientist stuff in Ordinary."

"I am aware. I've read the rule book. So then, perhaps you should go on your way instead."

"No. Oh, no. You hint at mutated monster plants and

think you can brush me off? Nice try. Take me to your horror show, Reserve Officer."

"You insisted I need rest. And fluids. I am lacking both. Better for you to leave."

"Freak show. Now." I snapped my fingers twice.

He sniffed and lifted to his full height before spinning on his heel and leading me through the dining room, the kitchen, and out to a little mud room space. It may have been built for hanging up wet coats and kicking off sandy boots, but it had been retrofitted with shelves and cupboards, a utility sink in the corner and lots of working space.

In that space were flowers. From the softest buttery cream to the deepest purple-black, the blooms were grouped and spread out, basking beneath grow lights, in seed trays and starter pots, all of them looking alive, well, hearty.

"Not there," he said. "Here." He pointed to the other side of the room.

The narrow table stretched from one end of the room to the other. Clumps of dirt, broken pots, a little row of bulbs that had gone black lined the table in tidy rows. A tangle of roots lumped together to make a small hill in one corner, and dry brown leaves and withered stalks lay in an oddly artistic mat that appeared woven.

"The mutants," he said quietly. "The freaks. The mistakes."

I couldn't help myself, I walked over and took my time looking at each broken failed item laid out on display.

"Why didn't you just throw this all away?"

"I have not finished learning, Reed Daughter. Why would I be rid of my greatest learning experience?"

I stood there a little longer. The chime music was too far away to hear, except for the occasional high tone.

"So I just need to give it a little more time? Pay attention to the mistakes, but not worry about them? Don't throw away all the blooms just because there are a few broken pots and dried leaves?"

"Are you speaking of gardening?"

"Something like that."

"Perhaps you have found your answer. But in case you have not."

He reached across the other countertop, the one with the grow lights, and picked up a small sky-blue pot with dirt in it. He held it out for me.

"What's that?"

"It is known as a flower pot."

"I know that. What's in it?"

"Tend it with water twice a week, enough each time that water collects in this tray beneath it."

"Okay, but what's in it? What's trying to grow?"

"It will need sunlight, but should remain indoors. I would suggest a window sill where the dragon is not allowed to touch it."

The way he said *dragon* like it was an invasive species make me smile. "Aw, c'mon. It's pretty cute for a dragon. Even you have to admit that."

"I must admit nothing." He plunked the flower pot into my hand, and I could either catch it or let it fall.

I caught it of course. "I didn't ask you for a flower."

"That is not what I gave you. I gave you a flower pot. With soil."

"If this is weed... Seriously, Than. I know it's legal, but I don't want to grow weed at my house. Can you imagine if the dragon pig ate it?"

He had already turned and started out of the potting room.

"What if it gets stoned?" I asked. "What am I going to do with a stoned dragon, Than?"

He flipped off the light, and I grinned at his quickly retreating back. "You know it can eat a car in one sitting. Can you imagine it with a case of the munchies? We'd lose buildings. Entire blocks." I followed him out, matching his long stride with my own.

"It won't just want an order from Taco Bell, it will want

Taco Bell. The entire restaurant. And then what am I going to do? Than? Than?"

He had crossed the kitchen at speed, those spider legs flipping and slapping at his ankles like they were trying to send up distress signals. He was halfway through the little dining room before I'd even stepped into it.

"I'll blame you," I called after him. "I'll tell everyone you've been growing pot that was strong enough to make a dragon eat the Bell. Well, I can't tell everyone in town about the dragon, but whatever cover-up I use for the rest of town, I'll make sure you're the reason no one can buy Nacho Cheese Doritos Locos Tacos within a fifty-mile radius. And then what? You haven't seen small-town anger, you haven't seen small-town mobs until you've seen their favorite, cheap, fast food restaurant get eaten by a dragon.

"What I'm saying is you are playing with fire giving me this. Fire. And you should just take it back now so that neither of us, or our beloved Taco Bell, gets burned."

We were in the hallway now, the entranceway to the house. He stopped so quickly the spider eyes rattled like Yahtzee dice.

He opened the door. "Water. Twice a week."

I held the flowerpot out to him. "This is a bad idea."

He waited.

"I've got the black thumb of the Grim Reap...uh..." I shut my mouth. "I don't think I have what it takes to keep it alive."

Those words were hard. So hard. Because suddenly I wasn't talking about the flowers. Suddenly I was talking about Ryder. His love. Our togetherness. Our future. Our relationship. Those words cut through me, punched right through my heart and lungs.

"Water," he said as he reached out and curled his hand around mine, pressing my fingers gently but firmly against the sky-blue flower pot. "Twice a week. If you forget, water. If you do it three times in a week, let it be."

"But..."

"Sunlight. It doesn't have to be direct. But it needs light. And time. And patience. And care."

His hand was still on mine. It felt like it was just our two hands, our fingers and palms holding that little plant together, holding the soil and water and hope all in one small place.

"And if it doesn't work?" I looked up at him, could not hold his kind gaze and immediately looked down at the spiders.

The spiders were looking at the wall, floor, ceiling, a left leg, the corner, but not at me. And that was good.

"Flowers bloom. Even after disaster."

"Is that an inspirational quote?"

"No. It is in the forest ranger comprehensive guide on wildfires and wildfire recovery."

I looked up at him. He gazed calmly back at me. He was not kidding.

"Some light reading?"

"I thought I should be aware of all of Ordinary's rules. And since it is surrounded by national forest land." He just shrugged to finish that thought.

"Okay." I nodded. "Twice a week."

"Yes." He let go of my hand and stepped back. "Good night, Reed Daughter. I will not be at work tomorrow. I shall be taking a sick day." He coughed into his fist, but it sounded totally fake.

"Get well. Don't spread your germs around."

I stepped out onto his porch. It was cold, the wind gusts whipping hair in my face. I pulled the little flower pot toward my chest, unzipped my coat, and tucked it in behind the small safety of my lapels.

I didn't know why I did it. A blossomless flower or weed or whatever it was could handle a little wind.

Still, I held it there close, close to my heart and just kept repeating to myself, *water, sunlight, patience, time.*

Then I got in the Jeep and drove the dark road home.

CHAPTER TEN

I HEARD the key in the front lock, the creak in the hinges I loved and had told him not to oil away to silence. The door closed, locks clicked, deadbolt, then the chain. The rustle of his coat coming off. A soft groaning exhale, as if the full-range motion of shoulder and torso hurt to complete. As if he were sore. Exhausted.

The keys jingled, down into his front pocket, because he never remembered that I'd put a little dish right there on the shelf for his keys, pocket knife, pencil, measuring tape, wallet.

He'd wonder where the keys were in the morning. I'd tell him to check his pockets, just like I always did.

I'd remind him there was a shelf for that, a bowl.

Boots were next, the heavy steel-toed ones he'd been so excited to find on sale, and which I'd teased him about while he'd worked rain-proofing into them with that short, soft-bristled brush.

Then he paused. He was listening for me, I thought. For my breathing. For me to call out his name.

I held my breath and didn't move, lying on my side and staring at the little sky-blue flower pot set off center in our bedroom window.

There'd be morning light. With any luck, there'd be more than enough for it.

With stockinged steps, always heavy in the heel—he had never tip-toed in all the time we'd been together—he walked the length of the hall. But instead of coming into the bedroom, his bedroom, our bedroom, he paused there at the door.

It was half open. I never wanted him to come home and think I was shutting him out. I knew he could see my back from that angle, I knew he could see Spud, who lifted his head and thumped his tail, lying beside me, his back pressed against mine, holding the space where Ryder should be.

I knew he could see the dragon pig curled up on the bench at the foot of the bed, the shark toy Spud had given it tonight propped under its head. Knew the dragon opened its eyes, red light pouring from them, casting the room in fire, flame for a moment, all dragon in its waking. Then, finding itself safe in our house, the twin spotlights of its gaze snuffed, eyes closed. One. Two.

Ryder waited there. I wanted to turn. Wanted to tell him I was awake, that I hadn't really been asleep. I'd been thinking of him, waiting for him.

But then his hand, resting on the doorframe, lifted, the soft *snick* of flesh releasing painted wood distinct in the air, like an exhale. A choice.

He did not step in. His footsteps followed the hallway, down to the spare bath where the door opened and closed, the light clicked, and the water ran, hot, I knew, and full blast.

The water changed to the massage feature, the pulse hard, but not hard enough to beat the soreness out of his shoulders and his left hip he'd been rubbing when he didn't think I was watching.

"Come to bed, Ryder," I said to the wall, to the windowsill, to the little pot that might one day be a flower. If I didn't kill it with too much water, too little water, too much sunlight. All it needed was enough. Just enough.

The water stopped. I waited as he dried his body, ran

fingers through his hair, and pulled the towel around his waist because he hadn't come into the room for clean boxers.

I catalogued his movements through the house. He threw his clothes in the laundry room—the measuring tape in his pocket clanking against the side of the dryer.

I smiled at his soft curse, smiled wider at his sudden stillness. As if waking me was the last thing he wanted to do. As if letting me rest was something he really wanted to give me.

Or maybe avoiding talking to me was the only thing on his mind.

My eyes flicked to the pot. *Water, sunlight, patience, time.*

When he finally came in, he smelled faintly of beer—the good stuff Crow had thrown in the basket—and lemon chicken.

I stared at the bedside clock—an old-fashioned, wind-up thing with glow-in-the-dark squares painted at the tips of the hands and above each number on the face. It was three a.m.

Late. Too late for a job.

This was the quiet fear. That what he was hiding wasn't a what, but a who. That he had found someone else.

My mind, my logical detective, crime-solving mind, went through tonight's evidence. Other than the hour, there was no reason for me to think he had been out with someone else. I didn't smell perfume on him, didn't smell alcohol other than the beer.

Except he'd showered, hadn't he? And not in our shower where I might smell cologne, not in our shower where I might see his clothing in disarray.

No, well, yes. That was all true. It was also pretty paranoid, and there was little to back it up. If he'd been worried about me seeing his clothing, he would have started a load when he was in the laundry room.

So what did I know?

He was working a job out of town. He came home sweaty and tired and sore. There was mud on the boots he loved, and half the time his hair was plastered to his head from sweating under a hard hat.

He was working. That much I knew.

But no one worked a construction site this late at night. Certainly not the architect-slash-foreman.

Even catching up with paperwork shouldn't keep him this late.

Something was going on. Something was probably wrong. I knew that.

What I didn't know was why he didn't want to talk to me about it.

Spud thumped his tail again, but the dragon didn't bother opening its eyes this time. Ryder softly greeted the dog, then used the *come* command to get Spud to move down to the foot of the bed where he was supposed to sleep.

Where he slept when Ryder was home.

Before obeying, Spud got up and waited for pets and scritches, both of which included Ryder gently crooning what a good boy he was and the muted jangling of Spud's tags.

With Spud settled, Ryder just stood there, maybe staring at me, maybe staring at the little blue flower pot on the window sill.

"I'm awake," I said softly.

Ryder *hmmm*ed. "Sorry."

"It's okay."

And this, this was familiar too. Too familiar. Time and patience were well and good, but falling into a habit—a rut— was safe. And it wouldn't solve anything.

"Everything okay?" I asked.

He tugged the blankets back and slipped between them. There was no hesitation, no second thoughts, he just scooted across the bed and curled up behind me. Warmer than Spud, the bend in his knees mimicking mine, his foot nudging under mine until our ankles were all tangled up.

His hand slid down my shoulder, rested on my hip, as if testing cold water. I shifted enough so I could lean back into him. He took the opportunity to drape his arm across my waist and slide his other arm up behind both of our heads.

I leaned my head back and just breathed, needing this, the

contact, the touch. Knowing he was there, right there with me, holding me.

He bent his head so that his face was pressed in my hair. I felt him breathe me in.

"Meetings ran late. Then there was paperwork. And the client dropped in and wanted a tour. I didn't mean for it to go so late. I tried to call. No battery."

I waited. He breathed and breathed, then yawned. "The chicken was really good, Laney. Really good. And I was dreaming about that beer all day. Thanks."

I rolled my eyes. "Beer gets you dreaming about coming home? I'll have to keep the refrigerator stocked."

But before I'd even finished the sentence, his arm went heavy, and his head rocked back a bit. His grip on me slackened. He was already snoring.

I shifted, moving his arm so it didn't feel like I was trapped under a newly felled Douglas fir. I didn't shift away from him, didn't want to move too far.

"Water," I whispered, staring at the little blue flower pot. "Sunlight, patience, and time."

"And truth," I added. "Because you're gonna have to tell me what you're hiding, Ryder Bailey."

CHAPTER ELEVEN

I WAS ALONE in the bed. No dog, no dragon, no boyfriend. The smell of coffee and sausage drifted through the air along with the clatter of dishes being moved from the sink to the drying rack.

The little blue flower pot was right where I'd left it, a finger of sunlight spilling into it.

Hopefully it was enough.

I took a quick shower. I'd need to cover Than's shift and my own today. Jean had covered my shift yesterday, but she had today off.

Myra would be back. I knew she'd want the download on Than's interior decorating choices.

"Morning," I said. "Smells great."

"Pancakes in the oven." Ryder rubbed oil into the cast iron skillet before stowing it in the drawer beneath the oven. He sauntered my way. "Sausage too." He stopped in front of me and oh, how my heart beat harder.

Today's Henley was sage green, and it made his eyes darker. Instead of a flannel, he'd layered with a black, sleeveless jacket.

"Sleep well?" He moved right up into my space, swaying a little as if aiming down a runway, gaze laser-locked on me.

"Eventually."

"Sorry about coming in so late." His hands were a welcome weight on my hips. He drew me closer, pulling me in for a kiss. "You were snoring."

I made an offended noise, and I felt the huff of laughter on his lips. He was here and now and so *right*, I couldn't have moved away from him if I'd tried.

He pulled back slightly. "And you stole all the covers."

"I never—"

The second kiss was harder, deeper. I stopped trying to make whatever point I was trying to make, and just let him kiss me until I was liquid inside.

When he pulled back again, he paused, then caught my lips with his teeth, softly tugging, even though my mouth was swollen and tender.

"No need to dress up, but maybe not the uniform," he said.

I licked my lips and blinked up at him, trying to remember what he'd been saying. Had he been talking?

"Huh?"

He grinned, and it was a wicked thing, wild and happy. I wanted to drag him off to bed. I tugged on his wrist, but he held up his other hand.

"This." He flipped up two fingers with a card between them. A business card.

"What?"

"Our reservation is at six. You come casual but nice, so maybe not the uniform. I'll come casual but nice, so maybe not the work boots. We have the balcony room with the view. No dragon."

He pointed at the dragon pig, who toddled over to sit on my foot and puffed smoke at him.

"Yeah, you're staying home."

"Tonight?" I asked, sand shifting under my feet. Had I'd woken up in the wrong world, with the wrong Ryder?

This was our house, that was definitely the chonky dragon pig sitting on my foot, and Ryder was one hundred percent walking out the door, swinging on his overcoat and whistling.

Spud danced and wagged until Ryder gave him an ear scratch.

"Six!" Ryder said right before the door closed.

"Six," I repeated.

Spud galumphed over to me and danced around, barking at the dragon pig, running away and crouching, then barking at the dragon pig some more. He wanted to play.

Spud's feet were sandy which meant Ryder had taken him out for a run.

"Okay. Dog ran, breakfast made, dishes done. What are you up to Ryder Bailey?"

The business card had THE WESTWIND printed across it in a breezy little swirl. It was a little cliff-edge restaurant where people booked out small special events like anniversaries and Valentine's Day dates.

I'd been told the decor was totally romantic schmaltz, but the food was good and the desserts wonderful. I'd never been there before.

I glanced at the wall calendar. Not his birthday, not mine.

"Maybe he's celebrating the end of the build?"

The dragon pig made little grunty, snuffle sounds and trotted off to the living room.

"You coming with me today?" I grabbed food, poured coffee, and ate breakfast standing.

The dragon pig lorded over the living room, Spud adorning it with toy after toy, each dug out of his personal pile, carried over to the dragon pig, and dropped in front of it.

Spud sat and waited, tail wagging. As soon as the dragon pig grunted approval, Spud barked and ran full speed back to the toys to find the next offering. The dragon pig fluffed and pushed and stacked the growing hoard into the size and shape of pile it desired.

There were days like this when the dragon pig just wanted to stay home and be worshiped by his single fuzziest of fans.

"You two look like you're doing okay here. I'll try to come by in the afternoon in case anyone needs a bathroom break."

The dragon pig *oink*ed twice.

"Okay, fine. If Spud needs a bathroom break. I know you don't work that way."

It was true. The dragon did not poop. That was one of the upsides to having a dragon pig, although his ability to find demons who were hiding and bring them to me had also come in handy.

"Be good." Spud found a skunk with a good squeak in it, and was shaking the holy living stuffing out of it. I hadn't even put my hand on the knob before my phone rang.

"Delaney Reed."

"Boss," Shoe said. "Mrs. Yates called."

"About her penguin?"

"Yup."

"Stolen again?"

"Nope."

"That's…okay. Why is she calling?"

"She's been the target of criminal mischief."

"I can guess all day, but the longer this goes on, the quicker I'm going to put you in charge of the department's Secret Santa exchange this year."

He inhaled, held his breath a minute, like he was thinking it just might be worth it, then he let that breath out. "Someone left statues in her yard."

"Statues?"

"Penguin statues. She wants, I quote: 'All those hideous, phony fakes out of my yard immediately. I will be more than happy to file charges. Especially if that glassblower is behind it.' End of quote."

"Why aren't you out there?"

"I'm on the tip line for the stolen items."

I had forgotten about that. Which was strange. I never forgot the cases we were working.

"Okay, I'll see to it. Keep me in the loop on the robberies."

"Roger that."

I thumbed off the call and was going to get in the Jeep, but found myself at the back of it staring at a box covered with a moving blanket. For a second, I wondered why it was there. I didn't keep boxes and moving blankets in my car. But the thought was gone before it was fully formed.

I stuck my hand in my coat pocket. The tissue I'd used to wipe Than's sweat off my hands was in my pocket. I didn't remember folding it.

Then I was dreaming, all the world a foggy drift.

"This is very good," said the voice of madness, the voice that could make the world stand still. "Place it with the others. Wait until the moon is new. Aren't we lucky that's tonight?"

I didn't speak. I was just standing there, floating, a balloon tied to a fence, bobbing in the breeze.

"This is a critical step, Delaney. Move the blanket to one side."

The voice had sidled up beside me. I could see him at the corner of my eye. It was the same man—

—*not a man, not real*—

—who had spoken before. Only this time he looked excited. As if a great gift, a great treasure, was about to be opened.

I watched my hand push the blanket off the box that should not be in my car.

"Beautiful," he breathed. "Just stunning."

A part of my mind was screaming, hitting the panic button, dialing 911. This was wrong, bad wrong. That part of me was distant and tiny, so easily covered by the sound of his voice, so easily drowned by his words.

"You can look."

I didn't want to. I fought the urge, desperate to maintain some control in this, whatever this was. But my head turned, my eyes tracked as if I had no control over my head.

"Behold the beauty." He pointed, his hand in a black leather glove, the stitches burning like licks of flames, a thin river of lava crawling through heavy black stone.

He pointed at the box, the crate that could have once carried milk jugs or eggs. It was wooden, lined with a soft lap blanket with little moons and stars on it.

I recognized that blanket. It was mine. I hadn't seen it since I'd been attacked by a vampire in my family house on a hill.

Sweat broke out over my body, pooled under my arms.

I didn't remember going home to get it. Didn't remember putting it in this crate, in my car.

I didn't remember the contents either. My brain refused to process what was right there in front of me.

"Can you see it? Can you see these rare and powerful things?"

A Feather. About three feet long, covered in gold and opalescence and glittering jewels. It curved gently, like the lash of a great eye. Like the curve of the horizon under a starry, sunset sky.

There were so few of them on the earth. So few that it would be a rare person indeed who may have seen one.

Or a citizen of Ordinary. Someone who may have walked into the community center and met our very own Valkyrie, Bertie.

This was her Feather, usually displayed on the shelf behind her, recently stolen.

Anyone could have taken the Feather so openly displayed. Even I had been in her office that day, had seen it on the shelf with her other collectables.

Next to the Feather was a statue wrapped in the blanket. My breath caught, my ears rang. I knew that statue. A black wolf surrounded by other wolves, carved out of the heart-wood of an ancient tree.

The stolen Wolfe clan Heartwood.

"The wing of the Valkyrie, the heart of the wolf. You have done so well, Delaney."

I wanted to look him in the eye, and tell him to back the hell off. But my head would not move. My feet would not move. My mouth was stitched.

The world held too still, or we were moving so quickly that this moment was accelerated and wedged between other, steadier moments.

"Now," he said, "the sweat of Death's brow. I didn't know how you would come by it, but oh, how you've come through for me. So many others would not have been able to do this at all. Not find one of these ingredients, much less all three. And here you are, more than capable of gathering all three within the span of a week. I had been prepared to wait for years, many years."

My hand stretched out, fingers uncurling so that the tissue dropped on top of the Heartwood.

It settled there, like a square of used gift wrapping, wadded, smoothed out, folded. Waiting to be useful again, hidden away with the other treasures, a secret, rare and valued.

Something not to be shared.

"Fuck," I breathed, the only word I'd ever spoken in his presence. Or I hoped it was the only word. My memory had obviously been tampered with. I knew he was the one who had been doing the tampering. For all I knew, we'd had long conversations. Yelling matches.

"Had your soul not been owned by my nephew just recently, I wouldn't have seen you. Seen the opportunity that you present. Seen the tiny fissures in your soul I could compromise, small cracks in yourself, your power that I could exploit.

"The vortex opening in Ordinary was a window thrown wide, and oh, how the sunlight poured through."

I could hear the smile in his voice, and I hated it.

"For all of these factors to fall into place so neatly, it might make me suspicious that other hands were involved, other forks in this pie." He paused, thinking it through.

"No, when there is justice to be done, the heavens, the earth, the worlds above and below are simply wheels that need greasing to turn in one's favor.

"Tonight, when the moon is dark, you and I are going to have a celebration. Won't. That. Be. Interesting?"

He didn't touch me but his voice, his will over me and my soul—or the fissures in it—made me want to bathe in bleach.

The instant that thought went through my mind, he stepped away, creating space between us. I could breathe again. It was an odd thing for him to do. Almost as if he were trying to ease my distress.

"Tonight," he said gently. "You have my word this is business only. You will not be harmed. This will soon be over, Delaney Reed. You have my word on that, too.

"Put this away. Cover everything."

I watched as my hand dragged the blanket back over the crate.

Death. Feather. Wood. Death, feather, wood. Death, feather, wood.

My hand closed the Jeep, then I stood there, waiting for his orders. I hated it.

I hated him.

Death, feather, wood. Jeep, Jeep, Jeep. They're in the Jeep. My Jeep. Jeep.

"Go about your day," he said. "Do what you must do. Tonight you will understand."

Then he was gone...

...Jeep...

A voice from my dreams? A voice from my nightmares? My imagination?

...Jeep Jeep Jeep...

I turned my face into the stir of wind and blinked hard. Why was I standing here? I had walked out to the Jeep to...

...Death, feather, wood...

I'd blacked out again. How much time had I lost? I glanced at my phone. Seconds, if that.

Had I lost something else? No, I was sure I'd found something, but I couldn't figure out what it was.

I waited for my racing heart to settle, the sweat on my forehead, the back of my neck drying, cooling, as I sifted my brain for information, for hints of something important. I knew it was important.

A jay screeched. Another scolded in reply. The breeze shushed through the shore pines trailing the clean, green water scents of the lake.

It was a beautiful day. But those missing seconds were vital.

My phone vibrated. A text from Ryder popped up. It consisted of one word: *Tonight*.

I smiled. That must have been what I was thinking about. That was the mystery I was trying to unravel. He'd made reservations for us and wanted me in civilian clothes: casual but nice. But I wanted to do something a little more than nice.

Maybe I'd buy a dress. Picturing the shock on his face when he saw me actually wearing a dress made me laugh.

I sent him back a smiley face with a halo, then got in the Jeep and headed out to Mrs. Yates's place.

CHAPTER TWELVE

THERE WERE A LOT OF PENGUINS. A. Lot. All of them made out of concrete, all of them spread out across Mrs. Yates's yard like an entire waddle had decided to nest here.

Someone had spent most of the night pulling off this little prank.

News spreads quickly in our little town. I was not the only person who had come by to get a gander at the penguin debacle.

Half the town were either driving by, parking in front of mailboxes and driveways, or marching over to take pictures.

"Back it up, back it up now!" Myra yelled.

Myra cut through the crowd from the west, having shown up at exactly the right place and exactly the right moment to get this sudden surge of people in order before they stormed Mrs. Yates's fence.

I started toward Myra. We met at the gate.

"My," I said.

"Delaney. Where's Shoe?"

"Working the tip line."

"Because that's more important than this." She glanced at the crowd doing a risk assessment.

"He's on Secret Santa," I said.

She held up her fist, and I bumped it.

"So," she asked. "How was it?"

"What?"

"Than's house."

I smiled. "Tasteful. Comfortable. Modern."

"Really? Pics?"

"I didn't get any."

She raised an eyebrow.

"It's his home. It felt like I'd be sharing something that wasn't mine to share."

"Fair. So there wasn't any creepy stuff? Weird old books?"

I shook my head. "Just flowers and plants. A lot of plants."

"Huh." She considered that for a moment then lifted the megaphone in her hand. "Shall we?"

"Give them a chance to take a photo. Let's see if we can form a line."

"All right everyone," Myra said, the megaphone at her lips. "We want this to be a safe, orderly event. Everyone will get a chance to see the penguins. Families with kids, line up right here by the mailbox.

"Keep moving. Good job. We've got plenty of time," she encouraged.

I touched her shoulder and thumbed at the house. She waved me that way.

Kelby, the giant we'd hired as reserve officer at our last staffing, was already sauntering our way, taking time to shake hands and smile as she went. She had been a local star in high school, beloved for her talent in basketball, volleyball, and golf.

Everyone liked Kelby. It made her a great asset on the force.

I tried to follow the little winding path to Mrs. Yates's door, but there were penguins everywhere. They were replicas of the town's famous, repeatedly kidnapped water-fowl, but they were either twice as large or half as small. One little penguin statue was cute. But hundreds of penguin statues staring blankly ahead was a little creepy.

Before I could even knock, the door swung wide. Two hands shot out, grabbed my wrist, yanked me into the sunroom, and shut the door quickly behind me.

It was overkill, but Mrs. Yates was not known for subtlety.

"It's that man. That glassblower. I know it is."

For a woman who was always coifed in case she was caught by a camera looking for Ordinary's famous penguin, she looked a little unhinged in pink leggings, a fuzzy white bathrobe, and hair up in huge round curlers.

She was also smoking a cigarette.

That was new.

I took out my little notebook and pen. "Which glassblower are you talking about?" I knew she meant Crow.

"You know I mean Cow."

"Crow?"

"Whatever animal he identifies as." She took a long suck off the cigarette.

"Offensive," I informed her. "His name is Crow."

"Fine. He did this. Crow did this." She leaned her back against the wall and peered out the slight opening at the edge of the curtain, spying on her yard.

"Where's your penguin?"

She jerked her head toward the main part of her house. "I got him just in time. No one had arrived yet. Well, just that family across the street. Such nice, quiet people. Really keep to themselves."

Except they really didn't. They were a family of shapeshifters who wore more than one human face when they were out and about. She'd probably seen them and talked to them a lot more than she thought.

"Did you see Crow do this?"

She sucked the cigarette, then stamped it out. "You know it's him. He's been terrorizing me and my poor penguin for months."

No, he'd borrowed her penguin once and taken it to the beach for a selfie.

Crow was a good-looking guy, and his Instagram post had gone viral. The picture of him and his lonely homie penguin had gotten over a million likes.

It didn't hurt that Crow had been shirtless and knew how to pose.

Mrs. Yates hadn't liked him much, but now that he'd stolen her limelight, she despised him.

"But you didn't see him, did you?"

She pulled a lighter out of her pocket. "Everyone's seen *plenty* of him," she muttered.

"He apologized for taking the penguin. And you agreed, on camera for his Instagram viewers, that you were happy with the arrangement."

"Hmmph. Arrangement," she snarled.

"Arrangement. Any money he makes off those pictures goes toward the local food bank first, wildlife conservation second. To save the real penguins. The newspaper picked up the story and used your photo. Remember that? Remember how they said you were a local celebrity and philanthropist?"

She tipped up her nose. "Well, I got over it."

Myra called out a new order, and a chuckle ran through the crowd.

I should have stayed out there and wrangled the unruly masses. I rolled my shoulders and exhaled one slow breath.

"All right. Let's start from the top. When did you notice there were penguins in your yard?"

"This morning."

"Did you see anyone at your house last night?"

"No."

I didn't think I needed to ask, but I did anyway. "Were you home?"

"Yes." Here her eyes cut to one side.

Interesting.

"Talk me through the moment when you saw them."

"There was a knock at the door. By the time I got here—I was bathing—and opened it, there was a note on the door."

"Note."

"Yes."

"Can I see it?"

She acted like I was asking for the world as she pushed off the wall and stomped over to the small corner desk. She muttered under her breath the entire time. Mostly it was "Crow" this and "picture" that.

She held out a piece of paper like she was showing her parents a D- on her report card.

I took it from her and read the two words: YOU'RE WELCOME.

I wouldn't swear to it one hundred percent, but it certainly looked like Crow's handwriting.

"This was on the door?"

"Yes. And there were people, and I was just standing there, and I was..." She ran her hand down her body to show her current state of dress. "Think of the pictures they have. They'll be everywhere. The internet. They'll be on dark eBay."

I regretted lying to her about dark eBay, but I'd been trying to make a point.

"Did you see anyone taking pictures?"

"Well, no."

"Then we're not going to worry about that unless a photo surfaces." I held up my hand to stop her mid-protest. "If it happens, we'll take the appropriate steps."

She didn't look convinced, but some of her edges had gone softer.

"Fine. But I want you to arrest that terrible man."

"How about I promise to look into it and make sure that whoever is actually behind this is held responsible?"

"And I want those fake, terrible statues gone. I want them off my yard. I want them destroyed!"

"I'll bring in a clean-up crew."

"When?"

"Today, if possible."

"Today?" She glanced out the window at the huge crowd of people. I saw the moment it dawned on her that she was missing a chance at a heck of a photo shoot.

"Well, I know how thin the police are spread these days. If it took until, say, tonight, I'm sure I would manage."

Her hand had moved up to her curlers, fingers pulling the ringlets down, plastic curlers hitting her carpet with soft *thuds*.

"There's several tons worth of concrete out there, Mrs. Yates. It's going to take a crew and heavy-load vehicles to get it all gathered up." I tucked the paper in my notebook.

"So, not tonight?"

"Probably not."

"Can you get it cleaned up by the weekend?"

"During the High Tea Tide?" I hedged.

"Oh, that's right. I forgot about the event. Is attendance expected to be high?"

"Looks like it."

I watched her calculate how many people could stop by her house for a look at her famous penguin. Just like that, her scowl disappeared, and she was all sunshine and bubbles.

"Well, I say, let's not rush it! You have so much on your plate. This little prank can hold until after the High Tea Tide."

"That's very kind of you, Mrs. Yates. But I'm sure I can arrange—"

"No, no. It's fine. Just fine." She had finished with the curlers and cinched her bathrobe tight. "I'll freshen up. Wait a moment, won't you? Half a second."

Half a second ended up being fifteen minutes.

Mrs. Yates swanned out of her bedroom fully appointed in a soft, green, belted pea coat and shiny kitten heels that matched the large purse swinging at her elbow. Her hair curled and bounced, and the fuchsia lipstick was on point.

"Bring me the penguin," she intoned.

I ran my job duties through my head trying to figure out where it said I'd haul waterfowl around for people with illusions of grandeur.

She pointed toward the living room and puffed up her hair with her free hand.

I pulled out my phone and texted Crow. *You owe me.*

I found the penguin in the center of her dining room table which was littered with magazines and newspapers. Most of them were spread open with bits clipped out and gathered in a basket next to it.

It looked like a ransom note production line, but a quick peek at the clippings showed articles and travel guides listing the best things to visit along the Oregon Coast, most of which did not include a certain penguin who was staring me in the eyes.

My phone vibrated. Crow's reply: *??* And a winky face.

A winky face.

I texted: *I know what you did last night.*

His response: *perv*

I coughed to cover my laugh.

"Chief Reed. Now, please."

I pocketed my phone and hefted the penguin. "Don't look at me like that," I said to its little face. "You're the one who had to be so photogenic."

"I am ready," Mrs. Yates announced. "Open the door!"

She snagged the statue, flicked invisible dust off of it, then held it against her chest like an Oscar.

"So, I'll get back to you on the clean up."

"Yes, yes."

"I want you to know we'll do everything we can to find out who pulled this prank."

"Uh-huh. Of course. Door please." She pulled back her shoulders and put on a toothy smile.

I opened the door. Waited.

"Go," she said through her teeth. "Announce me."

I had a good voice and knew how to make it carry. Still, the crowd was a living breathing thing, some people hanging out, talking, others trying to push their way forward to figure out what was going on. Still more posed for pictures.

Myra and Kelsey had it under control. There was no stampeding. The line to get a good look at the yard was moving along at a decent pace.

I put my fingers to my lips and whistled.

"Thank you for coming out, everyone," I hollered.

Myra jogged over, bullhorn in her hand.

Someone yelled, "Louder!"

"Hold your horses, Bill!" Myra called back through the bullhorn.

A chuckle spread through the crowd. Then Myra was there, handing me the bullhorn.

"Thank you for coming out." The bullhorn cast my voice across this block and the next. "This impromptu penguin flash mob is only going to be available for a week. Tell your friends."

I decided it wouldn't hurt to earn a few points with Bertie while I had so many people's attention.

"As a reminder, the High Tea Tide event is Saturday only. Find out more about it by going online, or by checking with local shops. The event will feature tea, coffee, desserts, and delicacies from the finest vendors inside and outside Ordinary. I can also confirm there will be a petting zoo for the kids in the parking lot behind Sweet Reflections candy shop."

"And now, may I draw your attention to Ordinary's one and only concrete star: Mrs. Yates's penguin!"

I started clapping. Everyone else quickly followed.

Mrs. Yates walked out like this was a parade, giving the one-handed float wave while lifting the penguin to show it off.

The crowd ate it up, whistling and shouting.

She strolled through the statues, patting a head here, lowering the "real" penguin down so two statues could see eye-to-eye, making the "real" penguin kiss the fake one. Then, with a practiced bow, she plunked that bird down on the pedestal in the middle of the yard, dead center, without even a wobble.

From her purse, she produced an adorable little bumble bee antenna hat and placed it on the penguin's head.

A little kid yelled "Bee!" and everyone laughed.

Then Mrs. Yates did something I didn't expect. She shouted: "Free Bee Bobbles for the children!" She pulled a fistful of headbands, with bobbing antennas, out of her purse.

Smart. And cute. Maybe even cute enough to get into the bigger papers in the Valley. Definitely cute enough to get her on Bertie's web page.

Myra nudged my arm. "Louder."

I lifted the bullhorn. "Free bee hats for the kids while supplies last, and free pictures with Ordinary's most extra-ordinary penguin."

The crowd clapped, then shifted and shuffled toward the pedestal. Myra took the horn and got them all lined up for the photo op.

I hadn't seen it before, but the penguins were arranged to make a clear path to the pedestal and to create a sort of natural space in front of it for photos.

I'd known Crow all my life. I knew how he apologized. It wasn't with a cute card or, heavens forbid, actual words.

No, Crow said he was sorry with action.

It wasn't always an action you wanted or needed in your life, but he *did* something to apologize when he'd been wrong.

This was his apology to Mrs. Yates. This was him saying he was sorry he stole her limelight (although I doubted he was sorry he'd gotten some of the spotlight himself).

He was giving her back something photo worthy. Something newsworthy.

My phone vibrated.

You're welcome too.

Crow.

I looked around for him, out in the crowd. I saw an arm raise, a hand open my way, and then a flash of a smile as my almost-uncle hopped down from the hood of someone's car and sauntered off, disappearing into the crowd.

I texted: *Perky Perk. Now.*

Can't. Busy.

I'll close down the Nest. Fumigation. Terrible cockroach problem.

There was a pause. I couldn't guess what he was thinking. Didn't care.

I gave Myra the thumbs up signal and spun my finger in a circle, telling her I was headed out. She gave me a thumbs up, then strode over to meet with a reporter. The cameras were clicking, families were smiling, and little kids ran around like waist-high, bobble-antenna insects.

Behind them all, Mrs. Yates preened.

I made it to the Jeep and drove over to the Perky Perk.

The wind was nice, the sun warm, and it only took five minutes before Crow came strolling along, with a smile on his face like he'd been out sweet-talking the other kids into painting the fence.

"Delaney Reed," he declared like we hadn't seen each other in months. "How did the dinner go? Did your man love him some chicken?"

"He did."

Crow slowed, dropped the hey-stranger act. He was suddenly my almost-uncle-god who had explained to the kids bullying me in kindergarten exactly what the insides of their bodies would look like on their outsides.

"Left arm or right?" He closed the distance with easy long strides.

"I— What?"

"Left arm or right?" He lifted each in turn, then stopped right in front of me. "Which one would you rather I break? On Ryder. Which of his arms?"

"You aren't going to break either of his arms."

"Legs? That's a little hardcore. I mean it was good chicken, but I wouldn't say it was the greatest ever made. Not worth two broken legs, but you're the boss. I'll do it near the hospital so the medics don't have to go far to find him."

"Don't break my boyfriend. Any part of him. This isn't going to get you out of being hauled in for that penguin debacle."

"Me? I'm just a handsome, lonely artist—"

"Save it for Tinder. I know you dropped all those statues in her yard."

"Do you have proof, NCIS?"

"I have a note in your handwriting left on her door."

"Note?"

I opened it so he could read it. He leaned in, his hands behind his back. "That doesn't look like my handwriting."

I folded it back into my pocket. "All right. Let's see your hands."

"What?" He stuffed his hands in his jeans.

"Let me see your hands."

"I don't want to."

"Hands. Now."

He waited a moment longer, just to bother me, then held out his hands. His fingers were clean, scrubbed. When I'd seen him in the grocery store, there had been gray concrete-colored dust gathered around the nails.

"Did you pour them?"

"My hands?"

"Did you have molds? Flip them over."

He flipped his hands. "Molds? What are you talking about?"

"I know you put all those penguins in Mrs. Yates's yard. You had concrete dust on your nails yesterday. Were you taking them out of the molds then, or were you just moving them into whatever vehicle you rented?"

"I did not rent a vehicle. I didn't do any of this. I mean, I think it's funny, and I'm sure she's happy with all the attention, but I'm innocent."

I looked away from his hands and met his gaze. "Crow, you've never been innocent."

His smile was beatific and so pure, angels would kill for it.

"Fair. But you don't have enough evidence. A handwritten note won't hold up in court."

"It will hold you up in a cell. While I shut down your business so I can do a thorough search. I'm sure I won't find anything in your back room. No empty concrete sacks, no trowels, no rags with cement on them, no cement dust in the corners."

"Where would I store that many penguins? There must have been dozens."

"I didn't count."

"Well, I did, when I was standing there enjoying the spectacle. So many people. And the reporter, she must have gotten a lucky tip."

"You called it in, didn't you?"

"I'm sure there's no way to ever know."

"They record their calls."

"No way to ever know."

He moved to stand beside me and leaned on the Jeep. "So what do you really want to talk to me about?"

"You putting penguins all over her yard. In the dead of night like some kind of midnight weirdo."

"Sounds dramatic."

We stared at each other for a minute. A seagull flew over, squawking loudly.

"Did she like it?" he asked.

"Mrs. Yates?"

He nodded.

I thought about cuffing him, but Mrs. Yates wasn't going to leave her happy place—in front of any and every camera she could find—to come down to the station and actually charge him.

As long as the statues disappeared—once they were no longer drawing a crowd—she'd probably forget the whole thing.

He nudged me with his elbow. "Well?"

"She didn't like it. She was furious. Outraged."

"Hmmm. And then?"

"And then there was a crowd of people, and her penguin wasn't the center of attention, and she was out for your head."

"Out for whoever left those statues in her yard's head," he corrected.

"She thinks it's you."

"Mmmm. Then what happened?"

"You were there. You saw."

"Just at the end when the bumble bee antennas came out. Weird that she had so many of those on hand. So weird."

"You left her those too, didn't you? She didn't mention that."

"I'm sure she had them hanging around for some other occasion."

"How many of them were there?"

"Three dozen."

"Shall I point out that you shouldn't know that?"

"No, you shall not."

"I had to talk her into it, you know."

"You're good at that. Talking people into things. You always have been. Just really, really good at your job. Everyone loves you."

"No need to butter the bread on both sides, Crow."

He elbowed me gently again. "Did he even come home for dinner?"

"We're doing dinner tonight. His idea."

"All right."

"He made reservations."

"Somewhere fancy?"

"I guess. The Westwind."

"Nice. What time?"

"You're not invited."

"Wouldn't want to be there. So what time should I avoid?"

"Crow."

"Just to make sure I won't be there."

"Six. Don't be there at six."

He gave me a big wink. "Six o'clock. Got it."

"No, you don't got it. Don't be there. At six."

"Sure. Absolutely. I won't be there. At the Westwind at six."

"I will arrest you to keep you out of my private life."

"You know," he said, typing something on his phone, "if he wanted to be really romantic, he would have waited for the full moon."

And for a moment, there was something I almost remembered. Something I knew I would be doing tonight, something about the moon, but it slipped from my reach, leaving a faint memory behind.

"New moon tonight, right?" I asked.

He was still typing. "Ask a Wolfe. They pay attention to things like that." He swiped at the screen a couple times, then pocketed his phone.

"Do you know anything about the other robberies?"

"Now, now. You can't accuse me of all the crimes in town. Well, you can, but it's going to be difficult to live up to that kind of reputation."

"That's not a no."

"What's missing?"

"The Heartwood."

"The pack's heart?" He sounded startled.

"It was in their office at the quarry. Yesterday, or the night before, it was lifted. Since you've been out in the dead of night recently, did you see anyone or anything unusual?"

"Not saying I was, but if I were out, I didn't see anyone stealing the Heartwood."

"You did plant all those penguins, though."

"That's an awful lot for one man to do in one night, don't you think?"

"Not a man like you."

He touched two fingers to his forehead in a jaunty salute.

"Which is why I've decided you're going to be the one to get rid of them at the end of the week. Every last penguin. Every last pebble. Shouldn't be a problem for a man like you." I smiled wide and batted my eyelashes at him.

He scoffed, but before he could say anything, I added. "Two robberies on my hands, remember? Plus the High Tea

Tide, and suddenly, crowd control on an unplanned penguin event. You're on clean up."

He shut his mouth with a click. "What else was stolen?"

"Someone took Bertie's Feather."

He pulled up a bit and tipped his head to the side. That pose and look in his eyes was particularly crow-like.

"Her Feather."

"Have you seen it?"

"Yes. But I'm…Valkyrie Feathers can't be taken."

"This one was."

He shook his head. "No. You can't steal them. I know—not because I've ever tried to steal a Valkyrie Feather."

I gave him a hard look.

"Fine. I've never tried to steal a Valkyrie Feather while I've been in Ordinary."

"When?"

"A long time ago. I was young. Nearly terminally curious."

"Nearly?"

He laughed. "It was pretty close a couple times. One of those was when I tried to steal a Feather. They are almost impossible to pick up once they've been shed—and they are almost never shed. So just finding one took… Well, I spent a lot of years walking the worlds."

I made a hurry up motion with my finger.

"The battlefield was still fresh. The war was still going on. And the Valkyries had descended." He waved his hand through the air, as if wiping a screen clean so I could better see his memory. "That is a thing to see. The power of those women, those amazing warriors, screaming out of the sky and pulling the dead to their feet and up, up to Valhalla." His voice was fond. "What a place. The movies have it all wrong. It's more feet up on the table than polished marble floors. It's a good place."

"I'm surprised they let you in."

"Well, *let* is a strong word."

"You broke into Valhalla?"

"I didn't break into anything. I snuck in like a gentleman. But that's a different story. In what I thought was a random stroke of luck, I found the Feather on a battlefield. I had arrived at the end of the fight, Valkyries shattering the sky into fragments of gold, striding across the land, gathering the brave.

"One of the Valkyries spread her wings and blocked out the stars, her wings were so wide and bright. She was daylight in the darkness. Just…"

He shook his head. I had rarely heard the honest tone of wonder in his voice.

"And the Feather fell. Not light, not floating. It was liquid, pouring downward, as if the air were thicker around it. As if the Feather cut through reality sharpened by different laws, something beyond…beyond." He angled his hand downward, and the movement echoed something unearthly.

He seemed to notice what he was doing and cleared his throat, self-conscious.

"Tell me the rest. The Feather fell—or didn't fall? It cut reality. Then what?"

"You won't believe me."

"I might believe you."

"You didn't believe me about the penguins."

"That's because you are lying about the penguins."

He waggled his eyebrows.

"I'd like to know. About the Feather. Please?"

"You think it will help you solve the robbery?"

"No. Just…you make it sound like a wonder."

He nodded. "It was. I had to have it. I waited for the Valkyrie to rise into the sky, two warriors in her arms. Then I waited longer.

"When I thought it was safe, I stepped out of hiding. The Feather, glittering with jewels I had never seen, stirred on that war-filled wind." He glanced off in the distance, and I could almost hear the battle horns of his memory, could almost taste the heated air, the churned earth.

"I knelt. The Feather seemed so soft, so pliant. So easy for the taking. I wrapped my fingers around it and tugged."

"It was heavy?"

"It was…gravity, stone, an anchor in the universe."

I raised my eyebrows.

"I kid you not. It was connected to that battleground, immovable. Holding that place, bookmarking that point in time. It was a claim. And it was staying there until the Valkyrie came back for it."

"You couldn't move it?"

He put his hands on his hips and tipped his eyes to the horizon again, thinking. "She left it there to claim that space, that battlefield as her own. No one could move it."

"So it stayed there? You left?"

"I hid. I wanted to see what would happen when she came back. It was the first Feather I'd ever found. I wanted a clue so I could steal another in the future."

I raised my eyebrows, and he chuckled. "Your face. I didn't steal Bertie's Feather, because I can't."

"But why?"

"A day and a night and the heavens turned. No, don't roll your eyes. That was damn poetic, thank you very much."

"Leave poetry to the greeting cards."

"A day and a night," he repeated, "and the heavens turned. Then this man, just this ordinary mortal man comes walking up. He picked his way across the battlefield. Looking for something, for someone. A friend. A child. A father. A son. I finally decided he was looking for his father. It was his eyes. They were the very same shade of gray-brown as the warrior the Valkyrie had carried to the sky.

"He called a name. His father's name. His dead father's name. There was something about that young man, with eyes so gray and brown. Something about the arc of his cheek, the cut of his chin. And his hair, golden as wings. As Valkyrie wings."

His gaze held mine, and there was truth there.

"You think he was her child? Her child and the child of the warrior she took to Valhalla?"

"I've thought back on it a thousand times. It would be... rare. But children have been born. Love can be found in the strangest of places. Can be planted and grown in so many hearts."

"Poetry?" I asked, intrigued by the catch in his voice.

He cleared his throat and shrugged. "Just truth."

"Is that what that was? I didn't recognize it coming out of your mouth."

He shook his head and made his eyes wide, like he was surprised.

"As I was saying, the man was their child. I thought so, anyway. Over the years I've wondered if I made that part up, if I saw something I wanted to see.

"But the thing that matters was that he was mortal. I followed him the rest of his life, looked in on him now and then. He lived a very ordinary life. Died a very ordinary death.

"But on that battlefield, he saw the Feather. The Valkyrie's Feather that not even a god could lift."

"Let me guess," I said. "He lifted it. Because unlike you, he was worthy. Geez, Crow. I've heard this story. It's like Thor's hammer."

He scowled. "It's nothing like Thor's hammer. It's a Valkyrie's Feather. Delaney, Valkyries don't *shed* feathers. They are not birds. They don't molt. Ask me how I know, and I'll show you this scar I have right back here on my tight round—"

"—nope, not listening."

"—calf. What did you think I was pointing at, Delaney? Oh, I see. You have a dirty mind, don't you?"

"I get it," I said. "Only worthy people can pick up Valkyrie Feathers."

"No, only people Valkyries *trust* can pick up a Feather. The Feather is left to mark where it lands. Territory of death. Territory of life, maybe. Bertie's Feather marks Ordinary as her own territory. Her own battlefield. She'd know if the Feather left Ordinary's boundaries. And I'm pretty sure there are only a handful of people who could actually pick that Feather up and carry it around."

"Which cuts down the list of possible suspects."

He touched his nose with his pointer finger. "And good fucking luck to them. Having a Valkyrie on the hunt is a one-way ticket to the not-nice Valhalla, if you know what I mean."

"Crap."

"What?"

"I gotta go talk to Bertie." I opened the driver's door. "Before she decides to take justice into her own hands."

"Thank you, Crow," he said. "You just solved my case for me, Crow. I'm sure there's a cash reward and you'll be getting it as soon as I find the Feather and return it, Crow. I couldn't have done this without you because you are brilliant and handsome and *always* funny."

"Clean up those penguins!"

"Don't forget your dinner with Ryder tonight! Six o'clock! I won't be there!"

I sighed and wondered what it would be like to live in a town without nosey uncles.

CHAPTER THIRTEEN

THE COMMUNITY CENTER was Bertie's thing. The events she planned were her thing. Ordinary was her thing.

And the Feather she used to claim Ordinary was her thing.

Why she wasn't tearing the town apart to find the Feather was beyond me. I was thankful, sure, but confused.

Crow had said only someone she trusted could lift her Feather.

But Crow was a trickster god. I knew he wouldn't let a little truth get in the way of mischief.

The interior of the old-school-turned-community center was cool and smelled of lemon cleaner, the floors scuffed from years of students' shoes running through the halls. The hollow, thudding echo of my boots snapped back at me from the empty offices, open spaces, and meeting areas. Another, sharper footfall joined mine, and I knew I was being followed.

"Delaney."

I turned. Ordinary's only Valkyrie wore a blood-red silk blouse, a heavier bolero jacket in a subtle wash of purple. The wide-legged black pants brought the whole look together, as did the knife in her hand.

"Hi, Bertie. I...your Feather? It's stolen?"

One well-groomed eyebrow ticked upward. "Come into my office. Sit."

She arrowed past me and was around her desk and settled before I'd even gotten through the doorway.

Bertie watched me with hawk eyes.

"Crow said he tried to steal a Feather once. A Valkyrie Feather." I dropped into the chair, then sat up straighter. Coming into this office felt like sitting in front of the principal, no matter how old I was.

"Did he?" she said. "I am not surprised." The knife was not in her hand. It was slipped, along with three other blades, into a carving block on one side of her desk. "I reported it stolen yesterday and requested to talk to you."

"I'm sorry you've had to wait. So what can you tell me about it? When did you last see it?"

She was so still for a second or two, I glanced at her chest to make sure she was still breathing.

"The Feather was here when you were here Wednesday afternoon, Delaney. It was gone after that."

I pulled my notebook out and clicked the pen. "Did anyone else come through? To see you?"

"Yes. Many people. I held a local vendor pre-event orientation."

"Can I get a list of who was here?"

She leaned to one side, opened a drawer, and retrieved a single piece of paper.

"Can I keep this?"

"Yes."

"Thank you. So is there anyone you know who would have wanted the Feather...um...anyone you'd trust enough that they could take it?"

Her hands spread across the top of the desk. "Delaney. I think you need to be very honest with me."

"Sure. I'm asking about the trust thing because Crow said you may already know who took your Feather."

"Crow." The way she said it sounded like she needed to rinse out her mouth. "He thinks he understands Valkyrie Feathers?"

"He did try to steal one."

"So you said, but he was not successful, was he? What did he tell you?"

"He thinks Valkyrie Feathers are used to claim territory."

She *hmmm*ed, then dipped her chin. Her hands lifted, fingertips perching on the desk edge, gaze sharp. "That is correct."

"If you know where the Feather is, why did you call it in as missing?"

"I called it in and requested you return my call. Which you have not done. Until now."

"Valid. Do you know where the Feather is?"

"It is in Ordinary." She didn't sound the least bit worried.

"You know where?"

"I have a basic idea. Do you?"

There was something behind that, something I couldn't read.

"I don't have any leads. That's why I came by today. It's a little like Thor's hammer, isn't it?"

"It is nothing like Thor's hammer," she snapped. "Like a sorting hat of virtue." She rolled her eyes. "Valkyries do not need an object to know the heart of any living being."

"So you're telling me anyone could pick up the Feather and walk off with it? That isn't adding up. You wouldn't display it in your office where dozens of people," I held up the paper, "stream through. It wouldn't be safe, and it wouldn't be like you to do so."

A very small smile drifted across her lips.

"I am not telling you any such thing. I would never leave myself unguarded. But Crow isn't the expert he pretends to be. It isn't the worth of a person that allows them to lift a Valkyrie Feather. It is a personal choice a Valkyrie makes."

She was blushing. I'd never seen her blush in my life.

Did Bertie have a boyfriend—or a girlfriend? Was that who she was talking about?

I'd never asked about her private life, hadn't wanted to know. I'd always seen Bertie as a perpetually annoyed woman—an unstruck bolt of lightning who got shit done.

"Personal because the Valkyrie likes them?" I asked, trying not to smile.

Her fingers drummed once. A warning.

"Or maybe it's personal because the Valkyrie thinks of that person as…family?"

The drumming. Harder.

"No, wait. I've got this. It's personal because the Valkyrie is actually quite fond of a person, might even love them a little, and so she trusts them with something precious?"

The drumming stopped. "That is all I will say on the subject."

I couldn't keep the grin off my face. "All right, sure. Good. Will you say who has access to your Feather?"

"No."

"Come on, Bertie. I need a list of suspects. Can you give me a hint? Or text me some phone numbers?"

"No."

"Consenting adults can do whatever they please in Ordinary, as long as there are no laws broken."

"I am aware."

She wasn't denying. She wasn't affirming either. All I wanted to do was find out who she liked so much, she would allow them to burgle her.

"The Feather would not be moveable by most people in this town. Under certain circumstances it is possible a god might be able to move it, but that would be highly unlikely."

I flipped my notebook to a clean page. "And what would those circumstances be?"

"If I were in deathly distress, I may allow a god to use the Feather to find me. It is a hypothetical."

"Have you ever done that?"

She drew in a quiet breath, then pressed her lips together and shook her head.

"So we can rule out the gods being involved?"

"Yes."

"Good. That's good. What about the other supernaturals? Could any one of them move the Feather?"

"I suppose there could be spells, curses. There might be a demon or fae power...but no. I do not believe so."

"You're usually definite on these kinds of things."

"And yet, this is Ordinary. What can and can't happen here is not easily replicated in any other place in the worlds."

I loved that about my little town. We might be Ordinary, but we were certainly not normal.

"So we're down to mortals. Can you give me a list of mortals who might be able to pick it up? Mortals you *like*?"

She just stared at me, giving me a look like I should understand something. Like, maybe, I should be telling *her* something.

"I promise it will remain confidential. I can lock it up so the information isn't accessible by anyone other than me."

Bertie watched. Just watched. "Are you sure?"

I nodded, though there was a knot in my gut. She was getting to the point of something, and I wasn't following her lead.

"I've decided to withdraw my complaint."

"You reported a robbery."

"I reported the Feather had been stolen and requested to speak to you."

"You...that's the same thing."

"No. It is not. And here you are. I've spoken to you."

"But you want your Feather back, don't you? It's still an open case, and the information you've given me will help us find who took it."

"That is no longer necessary."

"I think it is. You might be okay with something so valuable on the loose in the town, but I am not."

"I assumed you would feel that way. Will I have full police support during the High Tea Tide?"

"We've already said we'll be there. Why the subject change?"

"I'm very busy, Delaney."

I glanced down at my notes which were only marginally helpful, back up at her, then at the empty space on the shelf behind her. I had spent the entire time in her office not looking at that space, at where the Feather should be. Seeing the emptiness, the shadow where there should be gold, stirred something else in my gut.

Something that felt like guilt.

"If you're sure," I started.

"I am."

"If you think of anything, give me a—"

"I will."

"If you want me to have our officers drive by to make sure no one is doing anything—"

"That won't be necessary."

I felt like I was in the middle of a conversation and completely missing the point. She made micro-shooing motions with her fingers. "I have appointments arriving any moment."

"Okay. I'll...call me if you need anything, Bertie. Really."

Her gaze tracked me as I stood, as I stepped behind the chair and took a moment to rearrange it. I was stalling to give her a chance to say something. But the click of the front door opening, and the tumble of a woman's laughter and another woman's hushing whisper clued me in that her appointment had arrived.

"Have a good afternoon, Bertie."

I stepped back through the door.

"Oh, and Delaney," she called. "When you do find my Feather, call. You and I will need to speak again."

Her fingers drummed again, hard, small hammers tacking her words down between us, nailing them into places where they could not get dislodged or ignored.

"Sure," I said. "Sure, I will, Bertie."

Then the women—they were starting a new fresh produce shop that was tied into community outreach—gave me a smile as I walked past them.

At least someone was having a good day.

CHAPTER FOURTEEN

MY PHONE RANG. I pulled away from the coffee drive through before answering.

"Chief Reed."

"Got a couple calls," Hatter said. "Shoe's out. I'm on desk. Myra and Kelby are working the crowd at the penguin flash mob."

"I'm north. What do you have?"

"A domestic. Kids playing drums too loud in the garage next door. I've got Jean headed that way."

"And?"

"Traffic light out at 17th."

"How soon until the linemen can get there?"

"About an hour. They're dealing with the blown transformer from that rock slide in Yachats."

"I'm on it."

Traffic was stopped to a crawl near the intersection. I pulled up on the shoulder, half blocking a fire hydrant, flipped on all my lights, and dug around in my glove box for a rubber band.

I tightened the band around my pony tail, then strode into the intersection and positioned myself right in the middle of it, the broken lights above me.

It was a four-way stop, but there were a lot of cars coming up from the beach that wanted to turn against traffic.

To complicate things, the shops lining the street had front parking, and foot traffic was trying to use the crosswalks.

I didn't have a whistle, but I had a voice, so I shouted for the family of six to wait while I pointed at the north-south traffic, and waved them through, holding a palm flat for east-west.

Next, I waved the family across. After that, east-west got their turn. A few shoppers caught the rhythm and rushed to get through on this rotation. I waved them on—gave a car creeping forward a dirty look—and once they were safe on the other side, got back into the flow.

The sun was warm, the breeze light, and traffic unknotted and smoothed out. It didn't look like a job that took concentration and effort, but the cars alone were challenging. There was something about small beach towns that brought out the distracted and grumpy in drivers.

Add in tired kids, distracted shoppers, and I was very, very focused on making sure we all pulled this off without injuries.

"Hey, Chief!" a voice yelled from the side of the street. "Need help?"

Jame Wolfe and a couple of his cousins rambled down the sidewalk like a six pack of good-looking blue collar guys. Jame's fiancé, Ben, was there too, moving without the limp, though still moving slowly. He had on a beanie, sunglasses, and long sweater coat that looked stylish with the scarf he'd wrapped around his neck.

I waved them over. Each of the Wolfe boys took a spot on east-west with the blind corners, while Ben propped himself near the public parking area side of the crosswalk so he could give the okay to pedestrians.

It was a good choice on all their parts. Werewolves were fast, but vampires were faster. If a kid got free and headed into traffic, I knew Ben would be able to catch them before something terrible happened.

It took us a couple rotations through the traffic turns, but then we had it down like an old dance.

Because it was the Wolfe boys, there was good-natured shouting and insults and jokes. They got the drivers and kids in the cars to be a part of it. Honking got into it. One side of the street beeped out "shave and a haircut," and cars on the other side finished off with "two bits."

There was a lot of laughter and cheering when the cars got it right, but I wagged my finger at the Wolfes, and shook my head in mock reproach.

The Wolves threw down a fake protest, right there in the middle of the road, making a big show of begging me for just one little honk. Just one more tiny beep.

A pile of kids in matching T-shirts, on a field trip, who had stopped for a bathroom break, immediately took the Wolfe side of the argument. Dozens of little voices yelled "please" and "boo" and honked like a pack of tiny geese.

I made a show of thinking it over before giving a big thumb's up. The children shouted and cheered and the cars honked out "shave and a haircut," but they were all off beat.

The cars down the road couldn't see our little street performance, but decided they should get in on the honking, and did so. With vigor.

By the time the lineman showed up, sweat was running down my ribs, my neck, and sticking my uniform to my back.

"Glad you could join us," I said to him when he stepped out of his truck.

"Got here as soon as I could. This shouldn't take too long."

"Hour? More?"

"Less. Half hour, tops."

He got to work and had it fixed in thirty-two minutes. Not that I was counting.

"Here you go, Chief." Ben held out a bottle of water. His voice still broke into a whisper without his control. They said it would heal given enough time.

It was good he was a very long-lived man.

I drank the water all down in one go. "Thanks. Did Hatter call you out here?"

Jame sidled up next to Ben and pressed his arm across his lover's back, needing to touch him.

Werewolves were so tactile. It was cute.

"We heard through the grapevine that the light was out," Jame said. "We had the day off, didn't have anything better to do." He shrugged. "And we wanted to talk to you. About the Heartwood."

"Okay." I dragged my sleeve over my forehead, then down my cheeks, soaking up the sweat. "Shoot."

"We want to search your house."

I paused mid-second wipe. "What, now?"

Jame looked a little uncomfortable, but his voice was easy. "Yours is the only outside scent we found in the office from that day. And you…" Here he inhaled, his nostrils flaring, his chest expanding. "…still smell…something. Close. As if you've been close to it."

He turned his face into the breeze, his eyes following the even inhale and exhale of his lungs. Then his eyes landed on my Jeep.

I stared at it too. It looked like it always looked, except it was parked half on the sidewalk.

"What?" I glanced at the shops beyond the vehicle. The statue could be anywhere, among the driftwood knickknacks in the shops, among the second-hand treasures, cast-off memories ready to be discovered again.

It didn't make any sense for someone to steal the Heartwood then drop it off at a second-hand shop, but stranger things had happened. Especially in this town.

"Where have you been?" Jame asked. The breeze had changed. He tore his gaze away from the Jeep.

"I've been in the casino. A lot of people there, but not many of them from Ordinary. Myra was there, and Xtelle."

"Burned strawberries." Jame snapped his fingers. "Xtelle."

"Yeah, and you'll smell her around a lot more. She's here to stay."

He twisted his lips. "If she can follow the rules."

"True. Also I met with the goddess Tala."

Jame nodded, still sniffing, but watching me.

"Came back to town and went into the station. Saw Shoe and Hatter, then Jean and Hogan. Oh, and Stina and Panny. At the candy shop."

He nodded again.

"I also ran into Crow, Ryder, Frigg, Odin, and Than yesterday. Today I was around Mrs. Yates and about half of Ordinary because Crow penguin-bombed her yard. I saw Bertie at the community center and those ladies starting the produce stand?"

Jame shook his head.

"Dana and Joan," Ben said.

"Right. I passed them in the hall, then I grabbed coffee from the drive through and spent the rest of the afternoon in the middle of the street sucking exhaust fumes."

"That's it?" Jame asked.

I ran back through the last two days. "That's it. Other than that, I've been around Spud and the dragon pig and random people walking through the stores and at Hogan's bakery."

"You've come into contact with a lot of people."

"It's a social kind of job."

He inhaled one last time, exhaled, and rubbed his face with the hand that was not around Ben.

"If it doesn't turn up soon, we'd still like to look around your house. We know it's not outside of Ordinary. We don't... none of us think it has been taken that far. But if it has, and if it ends up in the wrong hands..."

This was new territory for me. I didn't know exactly what would happen if it ended up outside of Ordinary.

"What happens if your clan symbol ends up in someone else's hands?"

He grinned, and it was hard and cold and showed just a little fang. "We get it back."

"War?" I asked.

"War's one way."

DEVON MONK

That wasn't unheard of outside our borders. Inside Ordinary, we had rules against that kind of violence. The supernaturals could hold grudges if they wanted, but peace had to be maintained.

"You know to keep that outside of Ordinary, right? These are peaceful streets. And I expect us all to work together to keep them that way."

"You know we will, Chief," he said.

I nodded, because I did know. Part of what made this community work was all the people in the community reaching out, pitching in, raising voices, and listening. Listening went a heck of a long way toward peace.

"All right. We'll back-burner my house search, but if it doesn't show up, you are welcome to go through it. Is there anywhere else you want to sniff out? If so, make sure I or one of the other officers come with you."

"I don't need a babysitter."

"If you want to make sure whoever stole the Heartwood doesn't get off on a technicality, you call on us. Understand? I know this is important to your clan. I know it's precious. And tempers can flare. Let's do this thoughtfully and follow the law. So we don't make any mistakes."

He was still frowning, but he nodded.

Ben, still standing with one arm around Jame, rolled his eyes and mouthed: *werewolves.*

I smiled. "Okay, good. You two let me know if you need anything."

Ben gave me a little eyebrow waggle and tightened his arm around Jame's waist. He leaned in and said something I couldn't hear, but Jame responded with a low growl that almost sounded like a purr. Ben chuckled.

So all good there. Good.

I checked my phone. Five o'clock. I had an hour to kill before meeting Ryder. Time for a shower and change of clothes.

I made my way to the Jeep, and as I was passing a shop, a

160

dress in the window caught my eye. It was a simple A-line with a scooped neck. A summer dress made of whites and a spray of blues that reminded me of the lake, of still water outside my window where the blue heron and turtles soaked in the sunlight.

It reminded me of peaceful times with Ryder, just the two of us on the deck he'd helped his father build, the town all around us, but somehow far away. The two of us in our own little world.

He had said come in casual nice, and since I only owned two dresses, maybe stepping out of my routine a little might be a good thing.

"If it doesn't fit, it doesn't fit," I reasoned, stepping into the resale shop. The little bell tinkled to announce my entrance.

The goddess Tyche, who went by Cheryl, wore a kilt over ripped jeans and a light flowery blouse that showed off her bronze shoulders and the straps of her black under tank. Her springy black hair was tugged into place by a deep turquoise headband. She looked up from something she was embroidering—and the shock that registered over her purple reading glasses was a palpable thing.

"Delaney? Is everything all right? Is it the apocalypse? It's the apocalypse, isn't it? And I wasn't even done with my cross-stitch. Ah, well. Want a drink?"

She tossed the hooped material on the chair next to her and bent to retrieve a large bottle of very nice whiskey. "Glass or bottle?"

She hooked two coffee cups and set them, *clack, clack,* down on the countertop. She was already pouring by the time I walked over.

"No apocalypse," I said.

"You sure?" She paused in the pour. Only one cup had any hooch in it. I picked up the empty and turned it upside down. "Nothing's wrong. Well, nothing more than the normal."

"Then why are you in here? Is it Myra's birthday? Jean's?"

"I'm shopping."

She blinked. Owl like. "For whom?"

"Me."

The silence could have swallowed a whale.

"All right," she finally said. "Sure. Of course. And that's because..." She swayed toward the rack of T-shirts and jeans, behind which were some sturdy overalls and puffy winter barn jackets.

"No, I—"

She changed course and pointed at a rack of boots and a wet suit that I was pretty sure was made out of Kevlar.

"Gods no. No offense."

She winked and took a swig of the whiskey. "How about I stop guessing? What caught your eye?"

Now I was feeling self-conscious. "This was a...bad idea."

"Delaney Reed." Her voice filled up the room with wind and laughter and the sweet call of a bird that didn't exist on this continent, nor on several others. "You will not step one foot out of this shop until you point at the thing that brought you in here in the first place."

She took another sip of whiskey and walked past me to the door. She flipped the sign to the "closed" side, slid the lock, then killed the front lights in the window.

"There. Now it's just us girls. So what did you see? I have private changing rooms down this little hall, and if you don't want to come out of there to look at whatever it is in a larger mirror, you don't have to."

"You're making a big thing out of nothing. You can..." I waved at the lock, at the door, at the lights.

"Nope. This is my store. I set the hours. Oh, plus I'm drunk. Oh, hold on." She held up a finger and took a huge gulp out of the cup. "There we go. I can't serve customers until I sober up, can I?"

I shook my head, embarrassed, but grateful that she'd closed the door and made this a safe place. For some reason, dresses always threw me. They made me feel vulnerable. It's why I only owned two.

"The dress."

She leaned forward. "The what?"

"The...uh...dress. In the window."

She pivoted on the balls of her feet and did a slow scan of her front window. There were half a dozen dresses there and one smart suit with a skirt.

I didn't have to say anything else. She set her cup on the counter and walked straight over to the dress I had seen.

Clouds and blue, with just a little yellow. Now that I looked at it closer I realized it was water and sunlight and time.

It was Patience.

And that was all a part of life, wasn't it?

"Let me put this in the changing room for you. While I do that, I want you to..." She nodded at the whiskey. "One sip. When one is out of practice wearing a dress, a little liquid courage will do one good."

I glanced at the bottle, but didn't pour myself a drink. I didn't drink on duty.

"I'm going to give you two choices, all right?" she said from down the hall. "But I don't want you to come back here yet. Two choices."

I moved away from the bottle, glanced at her cross-stitch —a sweet, grandmotherly, flower-filled frame with the words, "We had sex in this room," in neat little block letters—then moved on to the rack of jackets.

The jackets were practical. Some had a little style, and I thought maybe I should just get one of those and call off the whole dress thing.

But she was back before I could decide between the Army green corduroy and the Army green denim.

Her gaze ticked to the jackets. I dropped my hand back to my side.

"Those are men's jackets, Delaney."

"Uh-huh."

"I'm not going to let you buy one of those."

"I wasn't—"

"Not even for Ryder, who is a fine-looking man, but even he couldn't make those look good."

"Maybe I'll just—"

"Two choices." She held up one finger. Her fingernail was painted with a tiny ribbon and I thought maybe a blue bird. It was cute. I wondered where she had her nails done. And if they might call her away right now for an emergency appointment.

"Choice one: Walk with me through my shop, and I'll show you a few things. I'll let you say no to all of them but three."

"I only came in here for…it was just one dress…"

"You have never been in my shop."

"That's not true."

She raised an eyebrow. "You have never been in my shop to shop. Handing out flyers for Bertie does not count."

"Okay. I don't shop here. But that doesn't mean—"

"I think what it means is that, for whatever reason, today was the day that you thought you could take some time for yourself. Shop for something nice. I don't expect this urge to seize you for another decade. So while you are here, while you have the time— "

I opened my mouth.

"—no matter how short," she went on, "I am going to make the most of it."

I crossed my arms over my chest. "What's the second choice?"

"You can go to the dressing room, and let me bring you six things to try on."

I did the math which was unnecessary since three things I chose was a lot less work than six things she chose.

"One," I said, holding up my finger.

"Excellent," she said.

"You came in for the dress. I'm going to guess you already

do just fine shopping for jeans and practical shoes and shorts?"

"Yes." Buying other clothing didn't bother me, but when I faced dress choices I sort of fell flat.

Myra had always been into dresses. Jean too. I'd followed in my father's footsteps. Tried to mimic him, fill shoes I was much too young to put on.

Maybe it was that, the power of being in slacks, in pants, in uniform that had kept me away from dresses. Or maybe it was just that because my sisters had taken to dresses so easily, I felt like they'd learned a secret language I'd never figured out.

"There are a few things to have in the closet for when the mood hits you. I know you prefer denim and casual on your days off."

"Or my running clothes."

She nodded, her eyes skimming over my body as if she could calculate which things in this shop might be right for me.

"We're going to start easy and go wild. It should take us ten minutes to pick, then you can try on at least three selections besides the dress. Ready?"

Her eyes were bright, her face a glowy flush. She wasn't drunk. Gods, even on vacation, had a high tolerance for things like that. She was excited.

"So ready," I said with zero enthusiasm.

The three items ended up all coming from that circular rack. A sweater in an early morning gray—cashmere, I thought—with just the tiniest hint of beading at the low, open collar. Another dress, this one full length and more loosely structured than my first pick, in browns and greens that reminded me of Tiki heads. Lastly, and to my surprise, a pair of slacks that were high-waisted and so wide-legged they had more material than both the dresses combined.

She waved me toward the dressing room and returned to the main area to turn on music.

I shucked out of my uniform, pulled on the pants and shrugged the sweater over my tank.

They say clothes make the man, but dang, they didn't do too badly for the woman either. The pants fit like a glove, skimming from the mid-hip to ankle so that they actually showed off less than my old, faded, holey jeans.

I liked them. Much more than I thought I would.

"I heard a zipper and you got quiet. What do you think so far?"

"It's...not what I expected."

"Is that a good thing or a bad thing, Delaney?"

"Good?"

"That sounds like a question."

"Good," I repeated.

I changed from the slacks into the brown dress, the top of which was structured just like my tank top. Not bad.

"Brown dress fits," I said.

"But you don't love it. That's what this is about. Finding something you love. Try the other one."

I hesitated, my hand on the cool fabric. What if it didn't fit? What if I looked weird in it? What if it was a statement that I was ready for change between Ryder and me? A change that didn't send him out of town until three o'clock in the morning.

A statement I was ready for us to move out of this rut.

The dress slid on easily, there was a zipper, but I didn't have to undo it to shimmy my way into the fabric. I didn't know if that was a good sign or a bad sign.

I tugged it a bit as it fell into place, delicate across my skin, but strong too, like a kind of armor.

Snug in the right places but still loose enough for full range of motion.

Point one for the dress.

I stared down at it, not quite ready to look in the mirror. I liked how it fell right above my knee, but not so high that I'd have to do that weird, sideways, half slide thing Myra and

Jean did getting in and out of cars and restaurant booths when they were in mini-skirt mode.

The colors were good.

"Do you like it? Does it fit?" I smelled the sweet, smoky hint of whiskey in the air. Maybe she really was going to close the shop for the rest of the day.

"I…um…haven't looked."

There was a pause. I told myself it was no big deal. It was just a—

—*chance for change*—

—piece of clothing.

"Open the door, and I'll tell you if I like it," she suggested.

I opened the door.

Her expression gave nothing away. She had that distant look I'd seen tailors in movies adopt.

"This is your dress."

"What?"

"You can take it off and never look at yourself in it, but this dress is going home with you. It's yours."

"It's not mine until I buy it."

"This was made for you. Now get out of it, and I'll put it in the bag with…" She glanced at the other clothing. "You know what? It doesn't matter. You don't have to take any of the rest of it. But this dress goes in your closet. If you leave it hanging in there for a decade without wearing it, I will personally kick you in the shins."

She gave me a smile with wild hunt mischief in it.

"Come on. Give." Cheryl made a grab for the skirt, but I stepped out of reach.

"Hold on, handsy. I want to see it. Especially if I'm going to be collecting shin bruises for the next decade."

"Both shins." She did a little double kick. I laughed and finally looked in the mirror.

I saw joy, and it stopped me cold.

I had wanted the dress because it made me think of Ryder, of us together, of softer, easier times. It made me think about our future, the one we still hadn't found the time to talk about.

Marriage, I thought, looking at the white of the skirt, soft and delicate. *Rings, vows, and then a life.* One not defined by gods or monsters or duty or jobs. One defined by us.

Relationships didn't come with road maps. Didn't come with rules. If we...

—exchanged rings, exchanged vows—

...really talked about things, really decided to stay together for the long run—whatever that meant to both of us —then we were stepping off into uncharted waters.

"It's too much," I said.

"Okay, it's okay. Just change out of it. No problem."

"Why are you being nice all of a sudden?"

"I've been nice the entire time. I even offered you booze. You are too suspicious for your own good, Delaney Reed."

"Yeah, well, it comes with the job. Do you know how many trickster gods are in this town?"

She just laughed her summer laugh and waved me back into the dressing room.

"A lot," I said as she pushed against the door while I leaned on it, both of us not really trying to win. "Too many!"

"Oh, like you'd have it any other way!"

"I would."

"You'd be bored."

Yeah, I would, but there was no way I was going to admit it.

The door clicked, and I got out of the dress, missing its softness once I was back in my sweaty uniform. I stepped out of the dressing room.

"You have a great shop."

She glanced at my hand. "Did you decide on the sweater?"

"And the pants."

She took both from me to ring them up. "It will be just one minute, if you want to browse. My reader's slow today."

She frowned at her credit card machine and punched buttons. I left her to it and wandered the shop.

I found myself staring at the wet suit wondering if I could dare Jean into wearing it during the High Tea Tide. She'd do it, if there was something she really wanted on the line.

"There we go," she finally said. "Didn't mean to keep you waiting. I know you have that dinner with Ryder tonight." She handed me my card, a receipt, and a reused, clean paper bag. The good kind with handles.

Huh.

"How do you know about my dinner with Ryder?"

She blinked once, gave me the owl eyes. "Oh, I must have heard it from someone."

"Crow?"

She tried for the innocent, confused look again, but her mouth shifted into a mischievous grin. "Trickster gods, amiright? That Crow. He's just so...Crow."

"He is a pain in my neck," I grumbled as I swiped up my purchases and gave her a stern look. "If you see him, tell him he is not invited to the dinner."

"Got it. Not invited." She grinned like a crazy person. "I am sure telling him that will definitely keep him away."

"It better," I said, "if he knows what's good for him." I waved, pushed out the door, and let it tinkle shut on her laughter.

I WAS STANDING at the foot of the bed in my underwear and bra when my phone buzzed. It was a text from Ryder.

6:00 followed by a smiley face.

I tapped the thumbs up icon and went back to scowling at the clothing spread on the end of the bed. Jeans, a clean white tank top, that soft gray sweater.

Or the damned white and blue dress Cheryl had shoved in the bag, and charged me for, when I wasn't looking.

I rubbed at my forehead. The dress was too much, right? It

was pushing things, maybe hinting at things we were not talking about. Rings. Vows. Marriage.

But my eyes kept going to the dress, to the memory of how I'd pulled it out of the bag muttering, "You have got to be kidding me," over and over again. And when I'd thrown it onto the bed, it had landed in pretty little folds and swishes of fabric.

"No. I am not going to make some kind of statement at the first nice meal we've had together in weeks. Nice try, Cheryl."

I scooped the dress back into the bag and put on the tank top, sweater, and jeans.

Eight minutes left. I ran the brush through my hair, patted the dragon pig, patted the dog, then strolled out of the house without a care in the world.

But that soft fog surrounded me, filled my mind again.

I drifted up, still tethered, but somehow outside my body. I watched as I opened the Jeep, got behind the wheel. I watched myself start the car and checked the mirrors before putting it in gear.

What was I doing? I wanted to scream. Tried to. But the me behind the wheel drove safely and conservatively until I pulled up in front of my childhood home, where I'd lived until I'd started staying with Ryder.

It was built on top of a hill where tough coastal pines held out against the sandy soil and hard winds, their branches twisted and frozen in an easterly direction as if there were phantom breezes forever pushing them that way.

The steep concrete stairs were carpeted with pine and leaf debris, soft and familiar under my shoes as I walked up.

At the top, I unlocked the door and stepped into the house.

"Disable the alarm," the voice said.

It was still weird to even have an alarm, but my sisters had gone out of their way to make sure I stayed safe by locking the door when I was home.

See how well that worked out?

I punched in the code.

"Perfect," he said. "Come into the living room."

The living room was tiny. A small table had been set up in the middle of it with a piece of chalk, a candle, and a brass bowl on top of it.

I'd seen enough spellcraft in my life to know something— something bad—was about to go down.

"This isn't...there will be no harm done to you, Delaney," the voice said. "This is so we can talk. Get to know each other better. You can set the crate on the chair."

Crate? I looked at my hands and snapped back into my body and mind, no longer adrift.

The crate wasn't heavy, but I'd carried it awkwardly. I'd also rucked up the sweater sleeves, so bruises were already starting on the inside of my arms.

I tried to resist his command, but couldn't stop myself from putting the crate on the kitchen chair.

There were a thousand things I should be thinking about. A hundred fears, worries, plans I should manage. But only one thing rose to the forefront of my mind.

Had I come up to the house and arranged all these things and not known it? When? When had I done that? How long had I been doing things and not been aware?

What other things had this voice made me do?

The horror of being controlled against my will again, sent me rushing to the kitchen sink, where I ran the water and breathed heavily, trying not to throw up.

"You are thinking too hard, Delaney. You are making this a horror when, really, it is something else. Something much...better."

I spat in the sink, ran the water over my hand, and wiped my mouth. I didn't want to speak. Not yet. I knew words had power. And I was not about to give that away. I stared at the coffee cup at the bottom of the sink.

"You may have just realized that you and I have been together for some time. I regret to inform you, those memories have been hidden..."

I picked up the coffee cup and, in one smooth motion, turned, intending to heave it at him.

But he was close. Too close. He caught my wrist before I could release the cup and crowded into me, pinning me against the cupboard.

Eyes like tarnished gold sparked with light, and one black eyebrow rose. He was old, older than I'd originally thought. An old demon. Perhaps even an ancient one.

"I have overestimated how much of this situation you understand." He smiled, and it was rueful. "That is my fault. One of the drawbacks of selectively erasing your memory, I'm afraid. I am never sure what you might recall in dribs and drabs."

He shifted his hold on my wrist. I still couldn't move it. Couldn't move my body.

I glared at him.

"This is a nice cup." He carefully took it out of my frozen fingers. "You may have sentimental attachment to it, so let's keep it safe." He placed the mug back in the sink behind me then stepped back, not only away from crowding me, but all the way out of my space.

I got a good look at him. Again, maybe, if the whole erasing memories was a real thing. He was in uniform, black and gray. Black gloves. He looked refined, tailored, almost like an actor playing the part of a dangerous man.

"How did you get into my town, demon?" I asked.

His face lifted with surprise, then he nodded and clasped his hands together in front of him.

"I'll tell you. But first, I want to give you my gratitude for having been key to making this happen, Delaney. You will find that I am generous in showing my appreciation."

"How about you keep your appreciation and get the hell out of my town?" I said. I could make him do it. I knew I could. I was the Bridge to this town, and demons were not allowed unless the contracts were signed. But when I reached for the part of me that could shove a creature such as him out of this space, there was nothing.

Blackness where a kindling of fire should be. Quiet where once I contained a storm.

"Hush," he said, and it sounded kind. "I haven't taken anything from you. You are unchanged, you are as you ever were, but this hold I have on you necessitates a certain leverage. Come this way."

I was powerless not to do so. I walked back into the living room, stopped on one side of the table.

"Now, I could ask you to do these things, to cast this spell of your own free will, but I am fairly certain you would not. However, once this spell is cast, you and I will be on a much better footing. Then we will have time to discuss the crime I'd like to report.

"You look surprised. Oh, it is not just because you are a Bridge to Ordinary that I've gone through extensive difficulties to bring us to this moment. I have a crime I'd like to report, and I have decided it will take the law enforcement of Ordinary to bring this crime to justice.

"Convincing you to see my side of things could have been done differently, perhaps, but there was so little chance, so little hope, and I have waited so long..." He stared out the window beyond my neighbors' roofs at a swath of the churning Pacific Ocean.

"I've been inspired by you, Delaney Reed. And by Ordinary. I really had no concept of what it was. Of what it could be. A town like this." He shook his head and the smile was back, softer this time.

It was past six o'clock now. Ryder would know something was wrong when I didn't show up. He'd come out here looking for me.

Or would he?

He'd been staying out until three in the morning without checking in. He'd missed countless dinners. Hell, I'd missed dinners, too.

This wasn't unusual. If I missed our date by a half hour, by an hour, it wouldn't be unusual. I didn't even think he'd worry if I missed our date by two hours. He'd just assume work kept me away. Or worse, that I was staying away because I was angry.

Okay, who else might know something was wrong? Jean? Myra? Not unless their gifts clued them in.

And that was it. Everyone would assume I was where I was supposed to be—off work, with Ryder, on a date.

There would be no one riding to the rescue. This damsel was gonna have to un-distress herself.

CHAPTER FIFTEEN

"PICK UP THE FEATHER, PLEASE."

The demon stood directly across from me, the table between us. Since demons could choose to appear any way they liked, he was no longer in a uniform but instead wore a plain brown suit trouser with a white T-shirt tucked into it. He'd rolled the sleeves on the T-shirt, and instead of a belt, black suspenders buttoned at his waistband.

I took a second to really try to imprint him in my memory. Salt-and-pepper hair, dark brows, he resembled Jon Hamm, if the actor had gold eyes.

"Delaney, please pick up the Valkyrie Feather."

I locked my arm tight against my ribs, but my hand reached out, lifted the Feather.

"Lay it across the bowl."

My gaze shot up to him again. "No."

He frowned. "Do it carefully."

"No." I said the word, but my hand was moving. "No," I repeated, a little panicked.

He sighed, and my hand stopped moving.

"Why not?"

I blinked. "What?"

"Why don't you want to place the Feather across the bowl?"

Here it was, where my words would be weapons, not shields. Carefully, oh so carefully, wielded.

"I want no part of this spell."

"That's non-negotiable, unfortunately. I give you my word that if this could have worked with any other person, I would have chosen that path."

"Why does it have to be me?"

I was buying time. But no one was coming, so hopefully time would give me a chance to think up a way to escape. Or better yet, a way to trap him.

"I am a demon. The only way into Ordinary is by your agreement."

"I didn't agree to you being here."

"True. I seized upon a small opportunity most demons would not have seen."

"Let me guess. My wounded soul?"

He tipped his head. "You are healing very quickly. My nephew was careful in how he held your soul for all that time. It was much less damaged than it might be."

"Bathin?"

He nodded.

"Bathin is your nephew?"

"I was shocked that he released your soul. That boy never lets go of something he likes. Did you know he carried around a dead nebula for centuries? It had a black hole pocket he liked to use to hide things from his father. As if the king didn't know exactly what he was doing. Even when my nephew was called out before the hordes, maligned, ridiculed for keeping a dead nebula, he held on to that damn thing.

"Wept when his father imploded it." He glanced at me and frowned. "No, don't worry, the shock waves won't hit this end of the galaxy for millions of years."

"Bathin?" I said a little more quietly. Of all the things I'd expected, it was not that my captor was the uncle of the guy dating my sister.

"Yes. I was there on the beach when he used those scissors. Brilliant."

"You couldn't have been. There weren't any other demons on the beach."

He lifted his brows.

"In the vortex. You were on the other side of the vortex."

"Just so. Now, place the Feather across the bowl, please."

"The Feather won't burn." I knew that much about Valkyries: totally flame proof.

"Agreed. Nor can it be damaged. Is that what you are worried about?" He smiled. It was weirdly a look I'd seen on Crow's face. An almost-uncle kind of proud look when a child has done well.

"I give you my word neither you, nor I, nor this spell will damage any of the items drawn upon for its making. Does that help?"

"No. Why don't you just skip the spell and tell me about the crime."

"No, that will not work. Your objection is noted. Please, place the Feather on the bowl.

My hand set the Feather carefully across the brass bowl.

"Very nice. You have a touch for spellwork, Delaney. Of course, your wrist action is a little sloppy, but that corrects over time. Now, place the Heartwood—carefully and without damaging it," he gave me a big nod and open-mouthed wink, "—behind the bowl, between you and it."

I bent, pulled the carving out of the crate, and set it—carefully—behind the bowl.

"What spell are you casting?" I asked.

"Just something I cobbled together in my spare time. Please pick up the tissue with the sweat of Death's brow and place it beneath the Feather in the bowl. I know it would have been more convenient to do carving, tissue, Feather, or tissue, Feather, carving, but spells are tricky things that must be followed just so.

"We wouldn't want to implode a pet nebula with one wrong word, would we?

"A little more in the middle…yes. That's it. Very good. And now comes the enjoyable bit, when we—you and I—find out if this risk is worth it. Please hold your palms down over the bowl."

I fought it, every muscle straining. Sweat slipped down my temple, peppered between my shoulders. But no matter how hard I fought, my hands did as he asked.

He shifted his hands so that our fingertips barely touched. I was sure this was the first time I had seen his fingers. They were roughened, scarred, the ring finger on one hand twisted painfully backward, as if torqued there and left to heal incorrectly. The tip of his pinky, ring, and middle fingers on the other hand were missing. Heavy scarring scored from the back of his thumb near his wrist across the entire back of his hand, fingers, and even the small amount of his palm that I glimpsed. Fighting? Torture? Both?

"Delaney," he said softly. "Your attention on this, please." He wiggled his fingers over the bowl, bringing my eyes downward.

"Good then. I've decided not to bring fire into this spell. That is a departure for me. One other way to be sure it will not be tracked by—well, you aren't interested in my recipe, are you? Please, don't bother answering.

"Clear your mind." He intoned, then he chuckled. "I'm joking. That doesn't matter. If I could ask anything of you, it is this: Reserve judgment until you have all the facts."

I braced for it, the chanting, the bloodwork, fire—even though he'd said he wasn't going to use fire. Demons lied about everything. It was just safer and smarter to assume there'd be fire mixed in there somehow.

"The old…" he said in a clear, sonorous baritone, drawing the words out… then, when he finally ended the word, he paused before diving right in with gusto. "…gray mare just ain't what she used to be…"

I blinked, blinked again. What was it with demons and cheesy old songs? Did all their spellwork require it, or just the stuff demons had done in Ordinary?

He stopped. "Bad key? I took you for an alto, what with your...um...rather manly dressing style."

"Nice stereotyping, jerk."

He grinned, and happiness just radiated off of him. He was having a grand old time. "Soprano? Or shall I slow it down a bit? You do know the words don't you? Should I write them down?"

I glared at him and bit at the inside of my cheek. Yes, I was trapped by a demon, and yes, I was the unwilling participant of a spell of unknown outcome. But there was something ridiculous enough about this, that I no longer feared this man, this creature.

There was enough give and take—sort of like an arm-wrestling match—that I knew once this spell was done, I was going to over-the-top this guy and seize control.

"I'll carry the melody. Feel free to jump in with a hum, a harmony, a grace note. You are invited to add your own voice to the spell."

I clamped my lips shut and raised one eyebrow in a "dare me" pose.

He grinned again. "Yes, well." He shook out his hands, stretched his fingers. "Here we go again. And..."

"The old gray mare..." He turned his hands upside down so his fingers were cupping mine. My hands curled into the correct position without my will.

I knew this hand-clap game. Had played it with my sisters for years, though we sang the "Say say oh playmate" words to it. Our mother taught it to me, and I'd taught it to Myra and Jean. The only magic it had ever carried was fun and silliness.

I'd never thought it'd be a part of a demon spell.

"Just ain't what she used to be." He went through the claps—the cross hand-to-hand, the back hands, palms together claps.

"Ain't what she used to be...ain't what she used to be..."

He had a good voice, robust and happy. When our hands

179

touched, he was gentle, so gentle even a toddler would be having fun.

Except I was not having fun. I hated that my hands were nothing but puppets on strings for him.

I was stuck doing a spelled up version of Paddy Cake over a supernatural table setting, but I was ready to pounce the first chance I got to interrupt or stop the spell.

The only problem was, words and sounds were a part of this particular spell. I didn't want to say or do something that would cause the spell to be even worse. To cause something really bad.

Like an exploding nebula.

"The old gray mare she kicked on the whiffletree…"

He was really getting his opera on, so it was no wonder he missed the scratch of a hand at the front door, the subtle rattle of the lock.

It took everything I had not to look at the door.

"Kicked on the whiffletree…"

The door jiggled again. I heard a hard, frustrated exhale.

The demon focused on our hands, executing the last little bit in slow, slower, slowest motion.

"Many long…"

Clap

"…years…"

Clap

"…ago!"

Clap. Clap.

Three things happened in quick succession.

The tissue with Death's sweat went up in smoke that was a living thing, a skeletal hand reaching up to wrap boney fingers around the Feather, and to curl, like a soft river of mist, around the Heartwood.

Then the smoke created a rope that whip cracked around the demon's wrist and mine, clicking down like cuffs.

The door burst inward, and a very angry unicorn charged.

"Asshole!" Xtelle yelled. She barreled at a full gallop, head down, horn in ramming position.

Aiming at me.

I made panicked eyes at the demon. If he didn't let me control my body, I would be gored.

His eyebrows twitched downward, but he did not react nearly quickly enough.

Xtelle shifted the angle of her charge and rammed him in the nearest body part level with her horn—the side of his ass. Sparkles flew everywhere.

"Satan on a saltine!" he yelled.

Xtelle kept pushing, forcing him to take one step, two steps away from me.

His hand dropped away from mine. The spell broke.

No more smoke, no more hold over me.

Sweat covered every inch of my skin, like a fever breaking. I grabbed the Feather and Heartwood and ran to my bedroom where I had stashed my spare gun.

My hands shook as I pulled the weapon out of the safe, loaded it, then put the Feather and Heartwood back in the safe, slamming the door. I couldn't call for help. My phone was in the Jeep, and I didn't have a land line.

I glanced out the window, gauging my options. Run for back up? Go out guns a-blazing?

Luckily, I didn't have to decide. Myra's cruiser pulled into my driveway. The second it stopped, she was out the door, running up the stairs, her face a panicked white, her eyes blinded by past tragedy.

Oh, Myra.

I'd died here. She'd never forgiven herself for showing up just a second too late to save me.

That did it. I knew what I had to do. First, contain the demon-on-demon situation in my living room. Second, find a way to rent out the house.

I never wanted to see that look on my sister's face again.

I wiped my arm over my forehead to get the sweat out of my eyes, then strode into the living room. "Freeze," I yelled. "Police. That means you, Xtelle. And you, whatever your name is." I trained the gun on the non-unicorn.

He was face first against the wall, spread flat, both hands up.

Xtelle still had her horn in the side of his butt. Blood darkened his trousers. "Oh, he'll freeze," she growled. "He'll be so cold, hell won't melt him!"

"Stop!" Myra yelled, coming into the room.

"Easy," I told her. "I'm okay. Everything's okay." I didn't look over at her. I wasn't stupid enough to take my eyes off the demons.

Myra strode up to the new demon and pulled out cuffs with demon-trapping magic worked into them.

"Hands behind your back. Now."

"I assure you, that will not be necessary," he said.

"Hands. Now," she barked.

He lowered his hands and grunted as she snapped the cuffs on them.

"Back up, Xtelle," she said.

"I don't take orders from you." She leaned forward, horn inching deeper, and the demon grunted again.

"Xtelle," I said, "step away from him. Now."

"I don't take orders from—"

"Back up or be arrested," I said.

I thought she was going to push her luck, but wonder of wonders, she stepped back, grumbling the entire time.

"Back here," I told her, "away from the demon."

Myra pressed her hand in the middle of the demon's back and kicked his legs wide. She went through a one-handed frisk. "Any weapons? Any magic items or substances?" she asked.

"I assure you," he said, trying to twist around.

"Nope," Mya said. "Not until I know you don't have anything up your sleeve. Kneel."

Every muscle in his body locked on that command.

The air felt charged, electric. Like atoms were banging into each other: collisions, sparks. It felt like he was about to make a very poor choice.

Bathin stomped into the room and made a quick assessment of the tableau. "I'd do what she says, Uncle, if you don't want to be erased from this existence."

"There is no need to..." he said, but Myra said a short, sharp, twisted word—magic—and followed it with: "Down."

The air sparked between them, little fires catching and extinguishing.

He knelt. Slowly due to the handcuffs, but all the way to his knees.

Xtelle made a soft little gasp. I wondered if it was shock or fear. From the corner of my eye, she seemed...fascinated that he had followed the command.

"All right. Good. Just stay there."

He cleared his throat but said nothing.

Myra took a step back and looked over at me. "You really okay?"

"Yes. He worked a spell."

"What the—?" Bathin lumbered over to the table, pushing past his mother like she wasn't even there. For one strange moment, I wondered if she was invisible again.

"It's so good to see you too, son," she snipped.

Okay. Not invisible. Just ignored.

"Heartwood, Valkyrie Feather," Bathin said, somehow knowing what had been there, even though I'd already taken those two valuable items away. "And the tissue? This is... Oh, Amy, you didn't."

"Amy?" I asked. "Who's Amy?"

"He is," Bathin said. "My uncle. Amy."

"Avnas," the demon in handcuffs corrected archly.

"What are you doing here, Uncle? And how the hell did you even get into Ordinary?" Bathin glowered at the unicorn. "It was you, wasn't it, Mother?"

Her horsey mouth fell open. "How dare you accuse me of such a thing? I followed all the stupid rules this time. Why would I risk my own neck to bring someone like him here?"

"Oh, don't play the innocent. It's never fit you well. I know he lov—"

"—loves to be spoken about as if he isn't even in the

room," Amy said too loudly. "May I please turn so I can explain myself?"

Myra threw me a look. I frowned.

We had Bathin on our side if things went sideways. I was relieved to know we actually had one demon—and not just any demon, the Prince of the Underworld—on our side.

"I'll stab you again," Xtelle said as if she were ordering dressing on the side. "Make any move, Avnas, and I will stab you hard. And not in the ass this time."

He cleared his throat. "So noted, my Queen."

Xtelle's head raised, and she did a mincey little trot in place. "Better," she said.

"We're not going to take off the cuffs," I said.

Myra slipped her hand in her pocket. Whatever kind of root vegetable she had in there was locked and loaded.

"Turn around, Amy," I said. "Slowly."

He smoothly stood, showing his hands locked behind his back didn't make any difference for his balance.

His smile was brief and almost apologetic. If getting stabbed in the butt by a demon unicorn was causing him pain, it didn't show.

Then I remembered his hands. The scars. The missing joints.

This was a creature used to enduring pain. A lot of pain.

"How did you get into Ordinary?" Myra asked.

He nodded toward me. "Her soul."

Bathin growled, angry.

"Oh, you didn't leave many marks, my Prince. For that I would like to commend you. But I was there, on the beach. I saw it just before you cut it away from your hold. I knew I could leave my own mark. Claim just enough to get my foot in the door, if you will."

"You've had a part of her soul for all this time?" Myra asked.

"No. I marked her soul then. I have only just come to collect."

"The mark makes it easy for him to find her," Bathin

explained, moving closer to Myra, shifting his huge bulk so that he was slightly in front of her, pushing himself between her and Amy.

"No matter where he is, no matter where she is, he can access her. Dreams?" Bathin guessed.

"No," Avnas said. "Her subconscious."

Bathin crossed his arms over his chest and glowered at his uncle. He looked like a mountain, an entire range, the world itself. "Talk."

Myra's color had gone up a little. I caught her eye, thinking she was angry her boyfriend had just taken over our arrest. But that was not anger in her eyes. It was another kind of heat all together.

I mouthed the words, "*So hot.*" She blushed, then turned her attention back to Amy.

"What spell did you cast?" she asked.

Amy's eyes shot over to me, then past me as if he could still see the magic items, as if they were not locked away in my gun safe.

"It's something I modified," he said. "You are the sister who guards Ordinary's library, are you not?"

"It's impossible to know," Xtelle mumbled. "They all look the same."

"Why does it matter?" Myra asked.

"If you are the sister who guards the library, I can assume you are versed in spellwork. Some demonology?"

"Spit it out, Amy," Bathin said. "The Reeds aren't basic."

He gave Bathin a curt nod. Like a captain used to taking orders from his general.

"The original spell is a nasty piece of work built to latch and kill. It's a parasite spell, where the host slowly loses control to the attacker and eventually is a zombie, fully controlled by the attacker. Then, of course, the host is ultimately devoured."

"Of course," Bathin went on like this was a discussion so pedestrian, he was waiting for the conversation to actually begin.

My stomach twisted. Was that what had been happening to me? Was Amy a parasite attached to my subconscious?

"But you modified it," Myra said. "Tell us how. What does it do now?"

He shrugged. "It binds me to Delaney."

"No," Bathin said. "There's more. It's not just a binding. I can smell it. Too heavy. Too...death. You used some kind of death, didn't you?"

"Very well done, my Prince."

"Stow the compliments, Uncle. Out with the facts."

"The sweat of Death's brow," he said with barely contained smugness.

Xtelle gasped again. She muttered a fluttery little "Oh, my" which Amy did not miss. He slid a look her way. This time his smile was wicked, dangerous, calculating, inviting her in on the fun. And yes, it was hot.

What was it with demons?

"Obtained non-violently," he added, like that had been the easiest thing to pull off in the world.

"Oh. Oh, my. How very *restrained* of you, Avnas," Xtelle cooed, making the "restrained" sound like a dirty compliment. "How very *soft* and *thoughtful*."

From the way he was looking at her, from the way she was fluttering those ridiculously long unicorn eyelashes, this nice talk was more like dirty talk.

"Gross," Bathin said. "I shouldn't have to listen to my mother sweet-talk my uncle."

"Then you should leave." Xtelle had turned just a bit and was prancing sideways across the room toward Amy, her tail swishing.

"Stop," I ordered. "Stay away from him, Xtelle."

Myra moved in, the stubby red beet in her hand pointed straight at the side of Xtelle's head.

"That's a beet, not a gun. You do know it won't actually fire bullets," Xtelle said.

"I know you keep telling me that. Back up." She gestured with the beet, and Xtelle lifted her lip away from her teeth.

"Stomp you," she hissed.

Myra waved the beet again, and Xtelle grudgingly moved back my way.

"So you changed the ingredients," Myra said to Amy, "or added to them?"

"Yes."

"How?"

"The physical element of Death's sweat helped. I am bound to Delaney now."

"No," Bathin said again. "All of it." He snapped his fingers. It sounded like stones striking. He said a word that slipped and slithered out of my mind the moment I heard it.

Amy stiffened, his eyes locked forward. He stared at Bathin as if the prince had just grabbed him by the chin and forced his gaze.

"The Valkyrie Feather renews the spell, a phoenix rising no matter how it might be worn down, attacked. The Heartwood locks it into the strength of her family, her blood ties. The sweat of Death's brow makes it impenetrable to god interference. That is all. That is all of it."

Bathin snapped his fingers again, and Amy swayed on his feet. A single blood tear dripped from the corner of one eye. "My Prince." He bowed his head.

I didn't know if that bow was out of obeisance or fatigue. He was breathing harder, his shoulders bent.

Whatever Bathin had done had left its mark.

Bathin was flexing his hand open and closed, like a fighter who had just punched a brick wall a dozen times.

"What does all that add up to?" I asked Myra.

"He's connected to you, and he's blocked the avenues through which most spells can be broken."

"Well, Delaney could be killed," Xtelle said. "That would undo the spell."

"My Prince?" Amy said, talking to the floor.

Bathin grunted.

"May I speak?"

"No," Bathin said. "Delaney, Myra, and you, too, Mother, I need a word with all of you. Alone."

"The house isn't really big enough for that kind of priv—" The rest of what I was about to say was cut short.

Because we were no longer in my house.

CHAPTER SIXTEEN

THE SKY, the ground, and the distant walls were all made of a gorgeous, smoky blue with shots of gold burning through it. I'd been in a place like this before.

I sighed. "You planted a stone in my house?"

"Lapis lazuli," Bathin said. "It's good for wisdom, intuition, and clarity. A place where we can talk. In private."

Xtelle had morphed into her human form here, a tall, elegant woman with pink-flame eyes. "I don't recall asking to be a part of this conversation. Nor to be kidnapped."

"You're here because I don't trust you out there with Amy," he replied.

She crossed her arms, her fingers tapping, sharp, pink fingernails clicking against her skin. She turned to me. "Is this allowed in Ordinary?"

"Usually, not without permission. But in this case, I agree with his choice. So why did you need all of us out of Amy's hearing?"

"Can't he hear us through Delaney?" Myra asked him. "Through his connection to her soul?"

I stilled. A sick kind of horror settled in my gut. I didn't want to be used against them. Didn't want to be used at all.

"No," Bathin said. "What he's done is more like a hook

that ties him to her, not a possession that gives him ultimate awareness of her."

Good. Good. That was at least one silver lining on this horror hurricane.

I puffed out my breath and pushed my hand over my stomach to try and settle it.

"Okay," I said. "So spill. What do you want to tell us?"

Bathin's eyes narrowed as he gazed at his mother. "You're a random factor I don't trust. You could be on his side."

"I'm *always* on my side," she said. "You know that."

Bathin held his breath a moment, then started pacing.

"He's modified a very powerful, very damaging spell. He's covered his tracks thoughtfully and well. If there is a way to break the spell, I believe it will be damaging. To Delaney, or Ordinary, or the gods, or the Reed family."

"We've taken on soul-possessing demons before," Myra said. "You, for instance."

The smile he gave her beamed. "And you prevailed."

"Thanks to me," Xtelle said. "I made the scissors that cut her soul free. I made the way to break that binding. Not you." She poked one thin, pink-tipped finger at each of us. "Not any of you."

"Can we modify a spell breaker?" I asked. "We are a town of gods and supernatural people, magic, and knowledge. If someone makes a new lock, we find a new key, right?"

Myra rubbed the bridge of her nose. "I'll go to the library, talk to Harold and the other volumes. See if anyone knows anything that might help."

Xtelle's eyes lit up—literally—and she licked her lips. "Myra, my dearest dumpling. I shall come with you to the library to help speed your search. I am an expert in breaking demon bindings as you may have noticed."

Myra's eyebrows had lifted so high they were completely hidden beneath her bangs. "I would never let you into the library. Never." She said it like that was the most obvious thing in the world. "Never."

"That makes two of us," I added. "Anything else?" I looked at Bathin.

He shook his head slowly. He had a smile for me, too. We'd been connected in a way that allowed him to know more about me than I sometimes preferred. But it also let me know things about him too. I knew he really was trying to change his ways, become something other than what he was expected to be.

He was, at the core of his being, learning to be kind. And thoughtful. And I would hope to say, more human.

He was, at the core of his being, hopelessly in love with my stubborn sister. She was hopelessly in love with him too.

That made me happy.

"What?" I asked.

"I forget how well you deal with things of this nature. Soul possession. Hell's spells cooked up without your permission. Demons threatening everything you love."

"Life's full of roadblocks. You can let them stop you or you can find a way around them, or you can take option three. Option three is blowing right through them. I always go for three."

"He wants something," Bathin said.

Xtelle hummed and studied the back of her nails. "Ordinary?"

He planted his hands on his hips. "Not Ordinary. He could have signed the contract to do that. This is a much riskier action, tying himself to Delaney's soul."

"Maybe he didn't think I'd let him into town if he signed the contract."

"Would you have?" Xtelle asked.

"If he agreed to the rules, signed the contract, and followed the rules, of course I'd let him into Ordinary."

"Oh," she said, as if she'd finally figured something out. "You don't know his reputation." She turned to Bathin. "She doesn't know who he is, does she?"

"You've studied demons?" he asked.

"Generally."

"Myra?" he said.

"Give me a minute," Myra said. "He's the…King's Knight? Is that right?"

"It is," Bathin said. "It means something different in the Underworld."

"He rules over thirty-six legions of demons," she added.

"Yes," he said. "The hidden texts, those we demons don't let slip our grasp, explain he is not only brother to my father, the King of the Underworld, but he is also the king's right-hand man. A confidant. A guide and counselor."

I watched Xtelle while he listed these demony secrets. She still appeared bored with the conversation.

"So what does that make him to you?" I asked her.

Her gaze flicked up, held mine for a moment. I saw something there. It wasn't vulnerability. Demons weren't made that way. Soft and vulnerable was something demons had to learn. But it seemed close to that, maybe the demon version of those things.

Her gaze drifted to Myra. But it was Bathin she was looking at when she answered. "He is not anything to me. Can not be anything."

That last part was a big fat lie. Even though I hadn't known her for long, I could hear it in her voice, along with doubt and longing.

"He is your confidant," Bathin said, "as well as the king's."

"As if I would trust him with anything I didn't want to reach the king's ear."

I didn't know if it was because we were in the middle of a stone made for communication or wisdom or whatever, but there was something more she wasn't saying. Something important.

Bathin frowned. "What plans have you made with him?"

She scoffed. Then too quickly for me to track, she had a knife in her hand. I had no idea where she'd stashed it when she was in unicorn form—

—*the horn*, my brain supplied—

—but it was long and slender and deadly as hell.

Bathin tensed, all muscles set to shut that shit down.

Myra stepped back—a prudent decision in the face of possible demon-on-demon violence. But Xtelle took a step backward and cut her own palm.

She turned her palm down, and her blood—blacker than it should be, and thicker, too—dripped to the ground, sending up puffs of pink smoke that smelled of strawberries and fire.

"I do not have anything planned with Avnas." *Drip. Drip.* "I am not a part of his coming to Ordinary, nor the spell, nor whatever intent he has to bind Delaney."

She tipped her hand back up, drew the blade across it again. Instead of cutting and bleeding, it burned, sealed, smoked. It looked like her flesh had never been broken.

Bathin dropped his hands which he had lifted, poised for something. Maybe more of that snapping he had done that had stopped Avnas cold.

He crowded Myra a bit, as if he needed to know she was near, she was safe, she was there.

Her hand caught his wrist for a moment, a tactile assurance, and then she shouldered him aside.

"Is that the truth?" she asked.

"It's the truth," Bathin said.

"All right," I said. "He told me he wants to report a crime."

They all turned to stare at me.

"What?"

"Why didn't you mention that?" Myra asked.

"Hello, blood palms, magic stone, and horn stabbings," I said. "I've been a bit distracted and just remembered it. He said the spell will do something so he can report the crime to me."

"This is…" Myra glanced at Bathin. "Crazy, right? No one needs to cast a spell to report a crime. Why would he even think that was a thing?"

"Demon," Xtelle and Bathin said at the same time.

"Leverage," Bathin added. "Most conversations in the

demonic world begin with a threat, then a fight of some sort, leverage is applied, and then the actual matter is discussed, which usually leads to a fight of some sort, leverage, threats, etcetera."

"Super interesting," I said, "But can we get back to what the spell will actually *do* to me? Will it kill me? If so, will it be immediate or eventual?"

"It *might*," Bathin said. "Eventually. But there is no advantage to you being dead. None I can think of. Whatever he wants, he needs you alive for it. You are his leverage."

I opened my mouth to argue, but he kept going.

"He might say he wants your family, or your town, or maybe even the god powers, but really, it's you. You are, in many ways, Ordinary's heart. He knows that. And he intends to use it to his advantage."

I shivered even though it wasn't cold here.

"Does it hurt?" Myra asked.

I tipped my head to one shoulder and back, staring at the shifting blue and gold, taking stock.

"It's not painful. I feel better, actually. Things have been drifting and fading lately, and that's been driving me nuts. I think it was him."

"It was," Bathin said. "Subconscious attachment and manipulation distorts time and reality. Now that the spell has been worked, you should be clearer headed."

"Good," I said. "So let's go find out what crime he's so determined to report. Myra, I want you to start looking into spell breakers. Xtelle, I'm assuming you will go back to pony form?"

"Unicorn," she said distractedly. "In disguise," she added.

Which reminded me. "Why did you come by my house anyway? You're supposed to be at Hogan's."

"I got bored," she said to her nails.

"You got bored so decided to break into my house and gore me?"

"I needed attention," she said with a little sniff.

"Well, you got it. So now you can return to Hogan's and

remain bored until Jean takes you out for whatever the two of you negotiate. This is you following the rules like you said you would, remember? This is you learning how the town works and fitting in, remember?"

"I don't understand what the gods see in this place," she blurted out. "There are so many other, better towns, better beaches, certainly better *weather*. Even the ocean is freezing cold here. And don't get me started on the shopping options."

"You can leave any time you want," I said calmly. "That's in the contract too."

"No. There's something to it. There's something I'm not seeing. I'll stay. And...be a good pony." She showed her teeth in what was probably supposed to be a smile, but it came off a little too wild-eyed and crazy.

Bathin snorted. "You won't find it."

"Oh, I will."

"No. You can't even understand what you're looking for."

"If you can understand it, it won't be difficult for me to understand."

He spread those big hands of his. "If you say so."

"I do. Now remove us from this miserable little stone and return us to Ordinary."

"We're not really outside of Ordin—"

Just like that, we were back in my house again.

Amy was nowhere to be seen.

"In the kitchen," he called out. "Is everyone done making their plans and preparing for this little struggle we appear to be locked into?"

He came out of the kitchen carrying my cutting board in both hands. He'd put together coffee and tea, with sugar and dry creamer on the side.

"I am sorry for the rudimentary beverage service, but I didn't want to go wandering the town while you were out. What might you think of me then?" He offered the cutting board. "My Queen? Tea?"

"You know I prefer coffee. And make it sweet." Xtelle, once again in pony form, clomped over to the couch, eyed it for structure, then jumped up on it. It groaned and creaked as she tucked her pony legs beneath her. "The temperature better be exactly one-hundred-ninety-eight degrees."

"Yes, my Queen." He dropped six sugars into a coffee mug and poured the thick black liquid. He didn't mix it, didn't offer her a spoon, just passed her the cup.

She took it with a hoof that should not work that way and sipped it delicately. "Adequate." She turned her head away, making it clear she was ignoring him.

For half a second, I saw the look he gave her: the heat, the desire.

Maybe because we were bound by that spell, I also felt a quick twinge of sadness and longing.

"My Prince?"

"Bathin," Bathin corrected. "I'm not here for tea. I'm here for answers. Why did you bind yourself to Delaney?"

Amy folded his hands in front of him. "I could fetch you snack crackers from the cupboard if you're feeling peckish. They're shaped like little animals. With sprinkles."

They stared at each other, neither man blinking.

"Amy," Bathin said, clenching and unclenching his hands. "You're my uncle. You think you're funny, but you're not."

"I am, though. A little. You've always thought so."

"Maybe I've changed."

"Yes," Amy said, "I think you have."

"Hello?" a voice called out from the front door. "Anybody home?" Panny trotted into the living room and paused, one hoof still in the air, his goat face ticking from Amy, to Xtelle, to me.

"Hello, Delaney," he said, like everything was normal, like he visited me all the time, like no one else was in the room. "I wanted to drop by and talk to you about the event tomorrow."

That was a big fat lie. He had never come by my house in all the years he'd been goating around Ordinary.

"Pan," I said. "You need to go—"

"Oh, Xtelle," he exclaimed as if just noticing she was in the room. "Are you all right, my sweet?" He sidled right on over to her, and smooth as butter, hopped up onto the couch next to her, his silky white hair flowing with the jump.

"You!" Amy said. "Away from the queen!"

Xtelle's mouth fell open, and her coffee cup tipped dangerously in her loosened hoof. She glanced at Pan, then swiveled her head toward Amy. A calculating look tightened her eyes.

"Oh," she said. "Oh, my goodness. Panny. There you are, *darling*."

"Panny?" Amy said. Then louder: "*Darling*?"

"Yes, my dear," Pan said. "Tell me, is that pompous blowhard bothering you?"

"And who are you?" Amy took a step forward, heat and power boiling behind his words.

Pan hopped off the couch and lowered his horns. "Why don't you come at me and find out, you speck of a fool."

"Ooooh," Xtelle said. "Fighting over me? No," she said weakly, "don't." She fanned her face with her free hoof.

"Right, then." Amy rolled his wrist, and a huge scimitar dripping flame appeared in his hand. "It's goat meat for dinner."

"Yes," Xtelle hissed.

"Hey, hey, hey!" Myra shouted, but I was faster.

I pushed my way between the demon warrior and the goat god. "Knock it off!

"You," I pointed at Panny. "Get out of my house. You can flirt with Xtelle at the petting zoo.

"And you," I pointed at Amy. "Put your weapon down. If you harm anyone under my care in Ordinary, I will end your existence."

I squared off against the demon. I didn't make any other move. I didn't have to. He saw who I was, knew the power of Ordinary.

He rolled his wrist again, the sword winking out of sight. He took a step back, his gaze never leaving my face.

"Panny," I said. "Out."

"But—"

"Out. You'll see her tomorrow."

He huffed through his nose, then raised his head and gave me an imploring look.

"No." I pointed at the door.

"Fine." He twisted a bit, looking over his shoulder as he went. "Farewell, my sweet. Until tomorrow. We shall feed from the hands of dewy babes and bite lightly at their tender fingers."

I snapped my fingers for him to hurry it up, and he finally clomped out of the house.

"Is it hot in here?" Xtelle asked breathily once he was gone. "It feels hot in here."

Amy scowled at the door, his fists planted on his hips. "Him?" he said to Xtelle. "That...*god* is who you've been trotting around with?"

"Did you see the size of his horns?" she asked dreamily. "Magnificent."

"They're not that large."

"But for his size?" she said.

I snapped my fingers again, this time at the unicorn. "No. We are not doing whatever you're doing right now.

"Amy, your spell's done," I said. "I'm here. Talk. Why did you bind yourself to me?"

He inhaled, exhaled. He appeared so calm, I would have thought he was putting on the jealous act just for fun, but there was a hard fire kindling behind his gaze.

"I will tell you. But not in front of this audience."

"Try another answer, Uncle," Bathin said.

"Bored now," Xtelle announced.

"We're not leaving you alone with her," Myra said.

"No, it's fine," I said.

"Delaney."

"It's fine, Myra. You'll be right outside the door. It's not like he hasn't been surfing my subconscious for however long. What he wanted to do, he's done."

"You shouldn't be here alone," Bathin said. "Trust me on

this, Delaney."

"Hold on. I got it." I pulled out my phone and dialed.

"Jean Reed."

"Hey, can you pick up something at Ryder's place? I'm out at my house dealing with a demon."

"Xtelle? Did that little minx get out of the house?"

"You had her in the house?"

"Dude. Have you tried to keep her out of someplace she wants to be? She tried to climb through the window. The second story window."

I cut a look to Xtelle who was suddenly very interested in sipping her coffee, her ears rotated slightly toward me.

"Okay, but we've got another one."

"Window?"

"Demon."

"Well, shit. I'll be right there."

"Wait, I need you to stop by Ryder's house and pick up the dragon pig."

Myra shook her head, but at least her scowl wasn't as bad.

"Is everyone okay? Are you okay?" I could hear a door slam and an engine start.

"We're stable at the moment. Myra, Bathin, and Xtelle are here with me. Plus the new guy, Amy."

"Amy."

"Avnas. Bathin's uncle."

"Uncle? What is he doing? Why didn't I get a doom twinge? Holy shit, how did I miss it? Are you sure you're okay? Is he forcing you to call me?"

Yeah, my run-ins with demons had shaken both my sisters. Maybe more than I realized.

"Jean, listen. We got this. He cast a spell to do a binding. No one's been harmed. We're at that part of the movie where the bad guy tells the hero his super brilliant secret plan and makes demands that probably include a lot of unmarked bills and a helicopter. But he wants to keep it private, just between him and me, when he reveals his evil machinations.

"Since we Reeds are the heroes here," I said, "we're going

199

to be smart. Myra's going to keep an eye on the other two demon folk, and you're going to bring me a dragon pig, because I want a dragon under my arm for back up. A hungry, demon-hunting dragon."

"Jesus, Vishnu, Zool," she breathed. "Okay. Okay. I'll be there. Hang on."

"Not going anywhere. Promise." I disconnected the call.

Amy was sipping out of one of my cups, it had carousel horses on it, and a tiny chip in the handle. I didn't like that he'd just stepped into my life so easily. Didn't like that he'd assumed I'd stand aside and do whatever he wanted.

"I got this," I told Myra.

"Okay," she said. "Xtelle, out. You wait outside."

"I haven't even finished my coffee. Delaney, tell your ugly sister she's being rude. Why is your eye twitching like that? Are you unwell? I hope you've washed your hands recently. I don't want to spend my first visit to Ordinary ailing for weeks on end."

"Out," Myra said. "Now."

The pony glanced at me, and the calculations on her part were obvious. She held out the cup, right over the rug in front of the couch and poured the sticky sugary mess left in it onto the floor.

"Oops," she said, letting the cup drop out of her hand. It landed with a clunk. The handle chipped off and skittered to a stop against the leg of a side chair.

Myra was there, right there between me and her, and that was good because I was about to get all up in a unicorn's face.

"This isn't like last time," Myra said to her. "We can throw you out any time we want. Delaney can throw you out. You might want to make some smarter decisions." While she was talking, she was also giving Xtelle the bum's rush, one hand in her mane, one around her neck, pushing her out the door.

Xtelle was making little "Help! Help! I'm being mishandled!" noises, but she didn't sound distressed. Not really. She sounded like she was choking back a laugh.

Myra let go of the unicorn enough to open the door, then shoved Xtelle out and slammed it closed.

"Rude!" Xtelle yelled, but it was ruined by the laugh she couldn't quite cover.

Demons were annoying as hell.

"Okay, we'll all wait here for the dragon pig," Myra said.

"I don't think a dragon is necessary," Amy said.

"Oh, it is." Bathin shut him down before Amy could even oil the conversational wheels. "You've seen it, I assume, while you've been stalking Delaney?"

"Observing is not the same as stalking, my Prince."

"That shit doesn't float here, Uncle. You know the Reeds are god chosen. Gods have never been your concern, but it's hard not to see their connection to the Reeds, isn't it?"

"Vacationing gods are powerless."

"Oh, sure," Myra said. "A god on vacation, who wants to get a little break from the demands of his or her power, is a walking, talking weakling."

He sipped coffee, and gave no argument.

She raised one eyebrow. "Tell me stupidity doesn't run in the family."

"It's on his mother's side," Amy said quietly.

"Hey!" Xtelle shouted through the door. It sounded like she had her horse lips pressed right up against the door latch.

Bathin coughed to cover a laugh.

"I'll consider what you've said, Myra. There are gods in Ordinary, and they may not be as helpless as they appear."

That was interesting. Foolish, but interesting. I might see the gods as lazy or eccentric or frustrating, but I would never, not even once, think that any of them were helpless.

While they could actually get sunburned, break a limb, or be killed once they had laid their power down to live a mortal life, they were only a thought away from that power. To underestimate their reach, to underestimate their strength, and frankly, to underestimate their tempers, if their vacation was interrupted, was a fool's game.

Underestimating gods. There was some leverage.

"The dragon's non-negotiable," I said. "You want me alone, you get me alone with the dragon."

He shrugged like it wasn't worth the air to argue.

Good enough. Because the one thing I had learned from Bathin possessing my soul was that connections and bindings worked both ways. Amy might have gotten his hooks into me, but that meant I had access to him too.

He was about to find out just how far I would go to keep my family and town safe.

CHAPTER SEVENTEEN

JEAN STOMPED INTO THE ROOM, her glare instantly aimed at Amy, even as she crossed the room to where I was sitting in the chair. Amy was in a chair to my left, Myra on the couch to his left, and Bathin loomed like stage security at a rock show.

The dragon pig in her arms puffed smoke out of its nostrils. It was still a little pig, still cute, but it was not playing it up.

No, this was serious dragon. This was the dragon who could tell I was angry, and yes, a little frightened. This was protector dragon, maybe even destruction dragon.

"Hey," I said to it as Jean handed it over to me. I held it up so we were eye level. Fire blazed in those adorable black eyes. "I'm okay right now, but this isn't going to be a long-term situation. I need you to make sure this demon is never outside our reach. And if you're a good dragon, you might get to eat him."

The dragon growled. Out of the corner of my eye, I could see Amy go very, very still.

I turned the dragon in my arms so it could get a good look at its future meal.

Amy's shoulders were pulled back, but at an angle, as if

he were prepared to jump out of that chair and fight for his life, if necessary.

Good. He should be worried. He had picked the wrong damn person to try to overthrow.

Jean stood right in front of me, her back to the demon. "Are you really all right?"

"I am. I want to hear his demands or plans or whatever. I've got the dragon. So I'm good."

"I called Ryder," Jean said.

Ryder. The date. The reservations. I had forgotten all about it.

That hit me harder than I expected. I was right here, going through another possible life and death situation involving a demon and my soul, and I hadn't once thought about calling Ryder.

What did it say about me if my boyfriend, the man I loved, was the last thing on my mind when my life was going to hell?

"Good," I croaked out through a suddenly dry throat. "That's super good."

Jean squeezed my shoulder and gave the pig a pat. "You keep her safe. If he tries to harm her in any way, you have my permission to chomp him to mush."

"Jean."

"Eat him in small bites so he feels it longer."

I shook my head and made wide eyes at her. "Not necessary."

She turned to Amy, then marched right up in front of him. "Fuck you." She kicked him in the shins. Hard.

It was the stress, the sudden break in that boiling, building pressure in my chest. It all came out in a laugh, a gasp, and it was like I could breathe again. I could think again.

For his part, Amy's face went a little greenish, his eyebrows knitted, and his hands clenched the chair handles hard enough to make them creak. That had hurt. She liked to wear steel-toed boots, and the girl knew how to kick.

"You must be Jean," he said, his voice a little thready.

"Just in case you think this is going to be some kind of cakewalk, you asshole, I want you to get this real clear. You are screwing around with the wrong place and the wrong family. We will crush you and blow the dust of your bones off our palms."

She turned again, not giving one damn that her back was to him again, and threw a glare at Bathin. "You a part of this, hot stuff?"

"Nope."

"Good. Myra, I say we give them two minutes, then come back in here and lock this down."

Myra stood, glanced between Amy, the dragon, and me. "Good?"

"Don't let her kick a hole in my house, okay?"

She nodded. "Come on, Jean."

They walked out the door, Bathin last, lingering for a moment, before uttering one word—not in a language I recognized, something slithery and guttural—before shutting the door.

Amy jerked at the word, jerked again at the door shutting. Then he took a second to unclench his fingers and to breathe out, slowly, as if triggering the release valve.

"What was that?" I asked. "The word?"

He shook his head. "It's demon. Difficult to interpret. We have two minutes before they return. I have demands. Well, one, really."

"This is my excited face."

He lifted an eyebrow, then leaned back in his chair, a little less flight, but not quite fight yet.

"I would have signed the contract. No, you don't have to believe me, but in any other circumstance I would have. Ordinary is interesting. Following you, even in the tangential manner in which I have, has made me aware of the uniqueness of the place, the...harmony."

"You're a warrior. A general of legions. You'd get bored here."

"I had thought the same. But not now."

"Just get to the demand, Amy."

"The crime," he said.

"All right. Get to that."

"It is a contract. An illegal contract. I want you to break it."

"Between you and whom?"

"Not me," he said. "Two others."

"Time's ticking."

He took a breath, weighing his options. Through that hook between us, I could sense a sort of deliberation of my worth. Deciding if he had chosen correctly. Bet on the right horse. Thrown his chips on the right number.

And through that same connection I felt his decision. Felt the *yes.*

It was strange how a part of me liked that. Strange how a part of me would have been offended if he thought I couldn't deal with the issue, solve it, and send him packing.

"Vychoro, the King, is bound to Xtelle. Not a marriage, nothing so simple or pure as that. It is more a claiming, though in some circles of demons, it is a great honor."

"You think highly of your king?" I asked.

"He is my brother. Powerful. Ruthless. Vychoro dominates with horror and fire. There are none who oppose him. Not if they desire to live."

I couldn't tell if that was an endorsement or not.

"I do not agree with his ways. He has become ravenous. His hunger to rule, to oppress, to destroy—endless. He is not the brother I once knew."

"And?"

"I want you to break the contract between Vychoro and Xtelle."

"You want…you want me to make him divorce her?"

"No. I want you to break the contract."

"I heard that. Look, Avnas, this is your chance to get me on your side. I mean I'm still going to break this spell binding us, and kick your ass, but if you want mercy, or empathy, or understanding, tell me why the King and

Queen of the Underworld breaking up is so important to you."

His nostrils flared. Yeah, truth was a hard swallow for demons.

"I can pay you. Such riches as you've never known."

"Pass."

"Power, more power than you can dream of."

"Don't care."

"I can bring your father back."

The silence ticked by. I raised one eyebrow. "No," I said, "you can't. I'm not naïve, Avnas. I know how this universe works."

"You know what the gods have told you. What they want you to know of the universe. There are things even they don't have access too."

"Stop stalling. You didn't answer my question: Why do you want that contract broken? What's in it for you? Revenge? Reward? Are you after the throne?"

His eyes went hard, every line of his body more solid, heavier, somehow. The demon features were a thing out of a nightmare behind the polite human mask he wore.

"I could force you to break it."

The dragon pig grunted, and I snorted. "Oh, yeah. Do that. See how that goes for you. You still haven't answered my question."

He glanced at the clock on my wall. We had about twenty seconds left before my sisters barged back in.

"I won't agree to anything unless you tell me the truth. Now, not later. Why do you want the contract broken?"

He watched the clock's second hand tick. Then, at the last moment, he said, "Love."

The door opened. Everyone shoved their way into the house like they'd been watching the clock just as closely as Amy.

Neither Amy nor I looked at them, both caught by the word he'd spoken. Truth vibrated through that word, through our connection.

Love. He loved someone enough to want the contract broken.

I was pretty sure it wasn't his brother, the king. But there were many kinds of love. It could be fatherly. It could be companionable.

"I would like to remind all of you that I have not been treated well." Xtelle barged through the door last, her hooves edged with mud, little bits of grass, and something lavender stuck to them. She'd been stomping. I had a feeling my heather plants were goners.

"As a citizen of Ordinary, I am filing an official complaint!"

I still hadn't looked away from Amy. That truth held, stitching a silk-fine thread between us.

Love. He loved her. He was in love with Xtelle.

What was I supposed to do with that?

Xtelle was essentially married to the King of the Underworld, who was Bathin's father. Avnas was Vychoro's brother, and lusting after one's sister-in-law was pretty uncool.

"Hello," Xtelle called. She clicked her hooves together like snapping her fingers.

Something must have shown on my face, because Amy's eyes widened as he realized I was putting two and two together and coming up with a unicorn. Then he shut all emotional reaction down so hard, I felt the mental slam in the back of my molars.

"Are you deaf? Did you both lose all ability to hear?"

"Not at all," Amy said smoothly. Like he was just a guy, there to serve. Somehow he hid that fire, that passion I had seen when he'd spoken his truth.

Love.

"Finally." She clopped over to me. "What does he want?"

"I'm not going to tell you."

"You really should tell me, Del-*lame*-y," she said through gritted teeth. "He's a demon and he cast a spell on you."

"How does this work?" I asked Amy.

"Which part of it?"

I pointed at myself, then pointed at him. "The connection. Do you have to be around me all the time?"

"You want me out of your sight? A demon, set free in Ordinary, without having signed any contract to follow the rules? Just think of what I might do."

"Did that, got the broken soul to show for it. So not doing that again." I lifted the dragon pig so my mouth was right by its soft little ear. "Hey, buddy. I want you to take Avnas to the special jail, okay?"

Avnas drew his head up, "What are you—?"

Too late.

The dragon pig flew out of my arms—no wings, just a pink projectile of tiny pig that should not have had that kind of buoyancy. Before Avnas could raise a hand to fend it off, there was a big showy poof of white smoke, and they were gone.

I coughed at the hot coppery taste that filled my mouth and waved at the smoke.

Myra opened the front door. I opened the nearest window.

"Oh, that was beautiful!" Jean crowed. "I am so glad I was here to see the look on his face." She chortled, then coughed her way to another window.

Xtelle looked absolutely flabbergasted. Her pony mouth was opening and closing. Her head kept turning to me, then turning back to where Amy had just stood, then back to me again.

"But...he bound you," she finally said.

"Yep."

"And you just...disposed of him."

"Locked him up tight so I know exactly where he is."

"But you let Bathin roam around Ordinary. Free."

"Bathin possessed my soul," I said. "I wasn't thinking as clearly. Also, it was my first run-in with a demon. I've learned."

Bathin, the cocky jerk, just gave me a small salute and a wink. "You're welcome."

"Suck it," I said.

That just made him smile, because he knew what I really thought about him: I knew he wouldn't take my soul now, if the same choices were given to him.

I knew how much he loved my sister, and how hard he was working to find his place in Ordinary so he could stay here with her.

"So he just…just sits in a jail cell while you just…aren't you afraid he will use your connection to…do something terrible to you?" said Xtelle.

"I think he's my problem not yours."

"But—"

"Unless you know how to break the spell he cast on me, you should be doing pony stuff in Hogan's yard. Getting ready for that petting zoo gig you got."

Bathin coughed, and it was not because of the smoke. "Petting zoo? You're," he shifted his gaze to me, "she's in a *petting* zoo? For children? Please tell me it's for children."

Jean frowned. "It's not like there are adult petting z— You know what? Never mind. I retract that statement."

"It's behind the Sweet Reflections," I said. "She'll be there bright and early during the High Tea Tide and will be there all day."

Xtelle sucked her nostrils in and narrowed her eyes.

"All," I enunciated, "day."

She muttered something that sounded like "stomp stomp stomp," then turned toward the door. "I refuse to spend a moment more in this dismal place."

"Ordinary?" I asked hopefully. Maybe a little too hopefully.

"This house." She *stomp, stomp, stomp*ed across the floor, each hoof hitting harder than necessary, her pony butt swishing.

"I got her." Jean stepped over to me and wrapped me in a fierce hug.

"I want you to stay here," I said. "I need to talk to you and Myra."

"But what about Miss Stompy?"

"Congratulations, Bathin," I said. "You get to babysit your mother. Make sure she gets to Hogan's and stay with her. If she demons out or runs off with that goat, I'm holding you responsible."

"All right," he said. "Let's go." He pointed at the door.

To my surprise, Xtelle actually listened and trotted through the door. Although the goat bleating at the bottom of my stairs might have had something to do with it.

"We still on for tonight?" Bathin asked Myra.

"I'll be at the library. Looking for spell breakers."

"I'll come by with dinner." He glanced out the door. "Hey. Step away from the goat." And he was gone.

I exhaled and pressed my palms over my eyes. "This sucks."

"You let him into the library?" Jean asked. "When did you take your relationship up to that huge level?"

"He doesn't come in yet. That's…it's too soon. So we eat dinner or lunch outside. Or in the car."

Jean snorted. "You don't have a romantic bone in your body, do you? Good thing Bathin has one: a romantic bone. Okay, I just heard what that sounds like." She flopped down in the chair where Amy had been sitting.

Myra took out her notebook. "What are his demands?"

"He wants me to break a contract."

"He thinks you have some kind of authority to do that?" Jean asked. "I mean the safer bet would have been Ryder, right? Mithra's chosen one. But Amy should have known that if he was really following you around."

"He was really following me around. It's fuzzy, but I've got a faint memory of hearing his voice before, of seeing his face."

Myra jotted down notes. "The fade out episodes?"

"Yeah."

"What contract does he want broken?" she asked.

"The one binding Xtelle to Vychoro."

Jean popped the gum she was chewing. "For real?"

"The King of the Underworld," Myra said.

"Yes."

"He wants you to break up Bathin's mother and father," she said.

"Yes."

"He wants you to destroy the contract between his brother and his sister-in-law."

"Harsh," Jean said, "Do demons actually marry each other?"

"There are rituals," Myra said off-handedly. "And contracts. It's all about the contracts."

"How are they broken?" Jean asked.

Myra put the little notebook back in her pocket. "Bathin says the only way a demon will let go of one thing, is if they can control something of greater value to them. Contracts are sacred to demons. A lifeblood of their identity. A map to their existence. I haven't come across anything that says a contract was willingly ended between demons. Murders and killings, yes. Amicable split, no."

"Terrific," I said.

"I'll go through the library." Myra stood. "And I'll get everything I can out of Bathin too."

"Good. Jean, I want you to come with—"

The front door flew open. Ryder strode into the room.

His hair was styled back, and he was freshly showered. He wore a button-down, silver-gray shirt and the black slacks I loved that made his ass look amazing. The scent of fresh air and sawdust and the cologne he only wore when he was dressing up for fancy events swirled around him as he made his way to me with laser focus.

He looked like he was about to shovel his way into hell to kick some ass.

He stopped. Right there in front of me, but not touching. His gaze was everywhere on me, searching, frantic.

"I'm okay," I said.

He let out a breath—choppy and fast— as if a yell had been building, steam, anger, pressure—

—*fear*—

—that had had no other release.

"Laney," he whispered.

I was in his arms. My body pressed against his, and his arms locked behind me and pulled me just that slight bit closer as if he were afraid I'd fall away, as if he were afraid I was already too far out on the edge of a cliff.

He anchored me, grounded me, solid and steady, his heartbeat fast under the softness of his dress shirt, my ear and cheek pressed against his chest, the heat of him, the scent of him soaking into me.

"I missed our dinner," I said.

"Yeah."

"Another demon thinks he can push me around."

Ryder grunted. It sounded good there, so close to my ear, so close to my own heart. "He obviously doesn't know you."

He held me a second more, then his hands went flat against my back and his arms loosened. He drew back enough he could see me. "How bad?"

"He cast a spell binding us together. We're working on how to break it."

He glanced over my shoulder, looking at my sisters. "How bad?"

I pinched his side. "Hey. I'm telling you the truth."

"She is," Myra said, "but what she's leaving out is we don't have the scope of what we're up against. At this point, it's a pretty tight spell. We don't know the consequences of breaking it."

"Of course we don't," he said. "So what's our move?" That was directed at me.

"You," Myra said, "take Delaney home and keep an eye on her. She left the dragon pig with Amy at the other jail."

"Amy?" Ryder frowned. "She our demon?"

"Avnas. Bathin's uncle," I said.

"Brother to the King of the Underworld?"

"Yeah, I don't like it either," I said. "Jean, you and I are going to go—"

"Nope," Jean said. "You missed your very special dinner. I can't believe I didn't know about it, Ryder. You promised."

His expression didn't change. Really, if everyone in the room hadn't gone completely silent, I wouldn't have even noticed anything weird about that comment. My sisters were always butting into my business.

"Oh-kay," I said, studying Ryder's non-reaction. "Why was dinner something Jean needs to know about?"

"It wasn't."

"Ha-ha," Jean fake laughed. "You know me. I love it when you two go on dates and stuff. I even write it in my diary. If you two are going out for something fancy enough for your man to smell so good, I need to be in the know."

Ryder just gave me a long-suffering look. "She's your sister," he said.

I smiled, because it was cute how much he was pretending she annoyed him.

"I like Myra's idea," Jean said. "Go home with Ryder. I'll deal with the pony demon. Make sure she stays where she's supposed to stay so Bathin can help Myra with her research. Do you even know what was in the spell?"

Suddenly I remembered Jean hadn't heard all this, nor did she know what I'd locked inside the safe.

I stepped all the way out of Ryder's arms and faced my sisters, who were both standing.

"Yes. Bertie's Feather and the Wolfe's Heartwood."

No one moved. Well, Myra blinked.

"Really," Jean said. "Were they destroyed?"

"No." Time to fess up. I'd committed a crime: theft. If Bertie or the Wolfes wanted to press charges, it was within their rights to do so.

"I stole them."

"You stole them." Jean tugged on one of her ponytails. "Want to run that back around the track again?"

"I don't remember stealing them, just flashes that add up to me knowing I was the one who took them. The components for the spell were a Valkyrie's Feather, the Heartwood of a werewolf clan, the sweat of Death's brow."

"You stole something from Death?" Jean's eyes were huge.

"Yes? Than has a cold. I touched his forehead to see if he was running a fever and wiped my hand on a tissue. Sweat. Brow. I guess it was enough."

"Wait," Jean said, holding up one finger. "This is important. I want to see the pictures of the inside of Than's house."

I blinked, having forgotten I hadn't told her about it yet. "I didn't get pictures."

"What? No! You promised."

"It's modern," Myra said. "Clean and no weird stuff, or so she told me. Okay? Let's stay on track here. Where are the Feather and the Heartwood?" Myra asked.

"In the gun safe in my room."

"On it." Jean jogged to my bedroom.

"So, this is a little awkward," Myra said. "I should bring you in. Find out if the injured parties want to press charges."

"I know. But I'd rather you go to the library."

"You weren't going to make Jean arrest you, were you?" she asked.

"No. Jean's going to return the items and explain the situation. She'll get statements, and bring people to the station to fill out paperwork if need be."

"I'm what now?" she asked coming back into the room.

"Returning the stolen items to the owners."

"Uh—"

"Which means," I said, turning to Ryder, "you need to arrest me. I'm turning myself in, Reserve Officer Bailey."

He blinked. "You know this is serious?"

"Absolutely." I held up my hands, wrists together, and waggled my eyebrows. "Cuff me, Danno."

"I'm not going to cuff you."

"Not even in a sexy way?"

"No. This— Delaney. How did you let another demon do this to you?"

That was when I realized my man wasn't worried, he was furious. Furious at me for getting snookered again.

But I had nothing to be ashamed of. Avnas had found a vulnerability in me, in Ordinary, and abused it. My job was to keep him locked down until I could undo his damage.

I was doing my job.

But apparently Ryder thought I was stupid enough to hand my soul to any demon who happened by.

"How did I *let* him?" I dropped my hands, my stomach clenching with the familiar mix of anger, sorrow, and disappointment.

He was pushing away. From us. From me. I didn't know where he was trying to escape to—

—*what was he hiding*—

—but I was tired of walking the extra miles he put between us to try and stay close to him.

"Forget it. I'll go to the station myself. Hatter or Shoe can process my statement."

I walked to the door, hurt stewing in my gut.

"That's not—" He sounded exasperated. "You don't understand. Okay, you do, but not what I'm saying."

"Don't you have work to do?" I asked. "Something out of town? Might as well get back at it. I'll see you tomorrow morning while you're running out of the house before I get up."

That was a petty jab, and I knew I was off my footing. But dammit, how could he just assume I wasn't fighting with every scrap of my being to keep Ordinary—and myself —safe?

"Delaney," Ryder said. Warning and frustration. Neither would do him any good.

I grabbed the doorknob, but before I could take another step, a whistle pierced the air.

"Hold it," Jean said. "We have a problem to solve."

I pressed my lips together to keep from yelling at my sister. She did not get to armchair coach my relationship. "What problem, Jean?" I snapped.

"I can't pick up the Feather."

My head was so full of anger and hurt, it took me several seconds to figure out what she was saying.

"The Valkyrie Feather," she said slowly. "It's stuck in the safe."

I closed my eyes and took a breath. Then another. I wanted to yell, I wanted to cry, but no matter what I wanted, I had a job to do. "All right. Okay. We got this. Here's what we're going to do. Myra, you're still on the library."

"I agree," she said.

"Ryder, if we're in close quarters, I'm just going to fight with you. So I'd like you to go home, or to work, or go find Bathin and make sure he's not doing anything he shouldn't with his mother. Xtelle signed the contract and is here legitimately now."

"I still think you should let me go over the contract again," he said. "Demons always find a loophole. Let me look through it one more time."

"With your buddy, Mithra?" He knew how I felt about that god who hated my family. He knew how I felt about Mithra trying to mess around with anything in Ordinary, including my boyfriend.

He just pressed his lips together and shook his head. Disappointed.

"Jean," I said, "you and I will return the items. I'll apologize, I'll explain, and if they want me arrested, you can take me in."

I made eye contact which each of them in turn, lastly Ryder, who dropped his gaze after a very short stare down.

"Understood?" I asked.

Myra was already walking my way. "Understood, Chief. Come on, Ryder. Let's do our part." She touched his arm as she walked past him, but didn't drag him with her.

Ryder walked toward me. He took his time, stretching out that small space into what felt like hours.

"We need to talk," he said, quietly, his head bent so he was sure not to lose eye contact with me. "After you get done with

Jean, we need to talk. I'll go check on Bathin and make sure things are fine on that level, then I'll be home. I'd like you to be home too. Let me know if you can make it."

Then he stepped forward and dropped his arms around me again. I didn't lean as hard into him this time, but I didn't pull away. He shifted so he was just a little closer, one last gentle squeeze, and then he let go, not fast, not angry, every inch of his body transmitting he might be angry, but he wasn't done with this yet. Wasn't done with us.

"Yeah," I said. "Okay."

Then he was past me and out the door.

I closed my eyes and counted my heartbeats, trying to steady the ache in my chest.

"I think you're reading too much into everything," Jean said. "He's worried. That's all, Delaney. We're all worried. And his worry came out a little angry. And condescending. I'm worried too."

"I know," I said. "But it's not like I was going around looking for another jerk who wants to use me as a bargaining chip."

She made a rude noise. "I'm not worried about that. Demons are old news. We've taken them on and defeated them. I'm worried about what Bertie is going to do to you when she finds out you stole her Feather." She gave me a wide grin. "You are so doomed."

"Well you're about to have a front and center seat for that delightful event. Let's get the Feather."

She did a short bow, her hand toward my room, and I strolled back to the bedroom to retrieve the Feather of my doom.

CHAPTER EIGHTEEN

THE WEREWOLVES WERE NOT AMUSED. I carried the Heartwood carefully out in front of me, having decided that my scent was already on it, so putting it in a cloth or other carrying case wouldn't make any difference.

Plus, I didn't want it harmed. If I kept it in my tight grip, I could get it back to the Wolfes safely.

Before Jean and I even reached the front door of Granny Wolfe's house, half a dozen family members had silently joined us. They walked beside us, walked behind us, men and women caging us in with their bodies.

It wasn't threatening, but the message was clear. They knew we had the Heartwood, and they weren't going to let it, or us, out of their sight.

The door opened before I could raise my hand to knock, and Jame filled the entrance. His eyebrows were drawn down, his gaze hard as stone.

"Delaney," he said.

"Jame. We have the Heartwood."

"I know." He stared at Jean, who just wiggled her fingers at him in a little wave.

Jame was breathing hard, inhaling the scent of us, the

scent of the Heartwood. All the Wolfes were doing it, had been doing it since we first showed up.

I didn't know what they smelled, but if it was death, demons, and one Valkyrie Feather, then they were pretty much putting the puzzle together without having to see the box top.

Finally, Jame stepped aside. "This way."

We were ushered—bodies beside us, bodies behind us, Jame ahead of us—into the house through the main entry, then through the wide open entry into the living room.

Granny herself sat in the padded loveseat, two little boys, maybe about three years old, sitting on either side of her, their furry bare feet stuck out straight in front of them. They each were gnawing on a bone with a thick knot on the end like they were lollipops. Sam and Dean were twins and the youngest of the Wolfe clan. They obviously knew it was okay to wolf-out a little here at Granny's.

Jean and I were corralled to the overstuffed, patchwork-covered, velvet sofa. Wolfes dropped down on either side of us, stood behind the couch, and crowded into the other chairs and floor space. All of them breathing, sniffing, scenting.

I leaned forward and very carefully placed the Heartwood on the table in front of us.

Jame moved to stand behind Granny, his hands resting on the back of the loveseat on either side of her head, while he stared at me.

Granny ignored me, Jean, the family around her, and just sipped her tea. Jean and I were not offered any hospitality other than a seat and being allowed to remain breathing.

Once her tea was done, she set the cup on the table between us, sat back, and folded her hands in her lap. "You tell me, now," she ordered evenly. "All of it. True."

"I took the Heartwood that night when I came to check on the office. I did not take it willingly. I was being controlled by a demon, who has now bound me to him by using the Heartwood in a spell. He is demanding my services before he will free me. After he used the Heartwood for the spell, I took it away from him, locked it in my safe, and am now bringing it back to you."

"And your sister there?" she asked.

"I'm here as an officer of the law," Jean said. "I need to know if you want to press charges against Delaney for stealing your property and using it to invoke unsanctioned magic."

"Uh-huh." Granny lifted her hands and stroked those short, strong fingers over the twins' heads, a loving pet they leaned into.

The ticking of a clock in another room—maybe the kitchen —drummed through the silence, broken by the quiet snarls and the clicking of Sam and Dean's teeth as they punctured the bones.

Jean and I waited. More family appeared and lounged against walls. One man sat at the bottom of a staircase that led to the upstairs communal sleeping space and smaller private bedrooms.

Then, at a signal I could not sense, a man and two women near the wall shifted into wolf form.

I wondered what order they'd been given.

"Take it home," Granny said.

All three came around her loveseat and a woman still in human form—Tiffany—picked up the Heartwood from the low table.

The three wolves followed Tiffany up the stairs. The two youngsters stood on the loveseat and peeked over the top of it. All Wolfe eyes followed the Heartwood until it was gone from sight.

"The Wolfes and the Reeds go back way a'ways." Granny had not watched the Heartwood being taken from the room. She had kept her gaze on me. "Ain't that the right of it, Delaney, daughter of Robert?"

"Yes, Granny Wolfe."

"And there are rules all those within these borders must

DEVON MONK

follow. No matter who we be. No matter what we be. No matter what we are to this land."

"Yes, Granny Wolfe," I repeated.

"So, you say I can send you to jail for taking the Heartwood of our clan from my people, my *blood*?"

"Yes, Granny Wolfe."

I maintained eye contact, because I knew better than to look away. It wasn't so much that either of us needed to bow to the other, but the authority each of us wielded created an uncertain power dynamic. She recognized my place upholding the law for all. I recognized her place upholding the law within her clan. It had been this way for years. I didn't want it to change.

"It stink of demon," she said.

Took me a minute to follow her line of thought. She was talking about the Heartwood.

I nodded. "He didn't touch it, but the spell did. Smoke touched it."

"It stink of death."

I nodded again.

"And Valkyrie."

My head was still bobbing. Yes, yes, yes. All those things.

"And it stink of you. You fighting against all those things. Especially fighting against that demon."

I stopped nodding because I did not know that was something a werewolf could smell. An action? An emotion? An intention?

"I didn't agree to the spell. I didn't agree to steal the Heartwood either, but my hands picked it up. My hands carried it away from you."

She blew air through her teeth, disparaging my words. "Can tell it wasn't your will behind it, Delaney Reed. You don't have to tell this old wolf things she can see with her own eyes and smell with her own nose." She was still staring at me, and it was uncomfortable to hold her gaze this time.

I felt like a little kid who had just admitted to eating all the cookie dough.

"If you want to press charges, you'd be right to do so," I said. "You can get me on burglary and damage, both mental and emotional, and illegal magic use. I won't fight you on any of it. I'm sorry this happened. I'm sorry I was the one who put your family through this violation."

To make my point, I very purposely turned my eyes away and down. Down to the ground. It was more than respect I was offering her. It was surrender.

They all knew it.

All the Wolfes moved a little. I was no werewolf, but it was clear they were shocked.

I waited, just breathing, breathing, breathing. Let them understand my regret. Let them choose my penance.

"Well, then." Granny cleared her throat. "I understand my rights under your law, Delaney Reed. Always have. But now you need to understand my rights under Wolfe law."

I looked up, but didn't meet her gaze. It was a sign of respect. Of deference. "I'm listening."

"I don't care about locking you up for a demon playing you bad. Won't do me or mine any good having the one Bridge to town out of order. But this affront can not go unanswered. You took something from me and mine. Now I take something from you and yours. You brought back that which you stole, and that makes me pause. Makes me notice you a way I don't see you before.

"You are like your father, I always known that. But you are something else too. You held our heart in your hand. Only yours. That demon didn't once touch it. Because you stood there, keeping it safe, so he didn't soil it, didn't change it.

"I don't know if your papa woulda done the same. Maybe. Maybe not. But now I know the truth of you. Of your heart. That needs to be known to all of my kind, in clan or out."

I had no idea what she was talking about.

"It gonna take a little pain, Delaney Reed, to settle this between us. You understand that, now, yes?"

"Hold on," Jean said.

"No." I put my hand on Jean's leg and squeezed. She was

worried, but I trusted Granny when she said it was only a little pain. I could give that for what I'd cost them. I could give that if it meant they would trust me to keep the law in Ordinary. "It's okay."

"Well, I need to know exactly what you're going to do to my sister," Jean said. "And if I don't like it, it's not happening. Understand?"

Granny flashed her teeth in a small, tight smile. "Yes, Little Reed. I understand you sisters bleed for each other. I said it was a little pain, and that's truth. Giles?"

Giles was a big guy. A big wolf. Easily six four, shoulders meant for felling trees, hands the size of catchers' mitts. It had always surprised me that he chose none of those kinds of big, physical jobs, but instead made his living as a tattoo artist.

He stepped forward from the wall to my left and walked across the wooden floor and a scatter of overlapping rugs far too silently for a man that big. He held a bag that looked like a physician's house-call bag and a short, three-legged stool.

"You take from us, we take from you. A little blood," Granny said.

"All right." I sat up straighter and did my best to keep my gaze on her not on the hulk who put the stool down, sat, then placed the bag on the coffee table where the Heartwood had been.

He began unpacking things, laying them out on the table.

"This should have been done years ago," Granny said. "But the past can't be pulled back to us, so we just gonna do this now. You understand?" She tipped her head down a notch.

"Blood?" I guessed, since the pain was a given and she'd mentioned blood.

"Yes, that. A mark. That says you are one of our own. And we won't be crossed. Never again."

Nope. Still wasn't getting it.

My confusion must have been obvious.

She *tsk*ed but didn't look as stern. The twins were curled up beside her, Sam putting his head on her lap, Dean laying

his head on her shoulder. They were both drowsy, eyes closing, lifting for a second, then closing again.

Her arms wrapped around both of them, pulling
them close.

"We are marking you, Delaney Reed. Permanent."

That's when it all clicked.

I'd been expecting punishment, pain, and blood. A pound
of flesh kind of thing. But that's not what she had been saying
at all.

She'd told me I'd done everything I could to protect the
Heartwood of her clan. Now she was going to put her own
protective mark on me. So it couldn't happen again. So if it
did happen again, they would know. She would know.

I wouldn't be alone.

When a demon, or any other creature, tried to use me, use
my soul, I wouldn't be alone.

I'd have the entire Wolfe clan at my back.

"You don't have to—" Suddenly my throat was tight. I
had to take a deep breath so I didn't accidentally sob.

"Hush yourself, Delaney Reed. I've made my decision.
This is the price. You carry our mark. Now. Forever." She
nodded like the queen she was, and Giles gave me a wink.

He had finished unpacking. Now he placed his palms on
his knees. "Where do you want the mark? It's tradition for it
to be on the arm or hand where it's easily visible."

"How big is it going to be?" Jean asked. "Colors or
black only?"

I flashed her a thankful look. I hadn't thought about any
of that.

"It needs to be big enough that it can be seen by
Wolfe eyes."

I took off my sweater, baring my arms, considering.

Not my inner wrist over my pulse. That felt too personal,
too near my heart. Any tattoo there would be so close to my
veins, it would be like it touched my heart. Any tattoo there
would be a statement of what makes me me.

This tattoo needed to be a sign that the Wolfes were my

protectors, that I belonged to their clan. They didn't hand out this mark easily.

It wasn't a mark of shame, it was a mark of pride.

I wanted to honor that.

"Here." I held out my left arm and pointed at the back of my wrist where a watch might sit, if I wore one.

It was the most obvious place I could carry it. Everyone would see it for the rest of my life.

Granny Wolfe stilled. Giles twisted the bulk of his huge body to the side to quirk his eyebrow at her.

"Yes," she said. "This is good. This is good."

Behind her, Jame grinned a little crookedly. He nodded, and I knew I had made the right choice.

"I'll need you to move over a bit and put your hand on the arm rest." Giles was all soft, easy-going, professional. "Ty, can I get some music in here?"

A shadow slipped away, then something between trap and country started playing over hidden speakers. A few Wolfes groaned softly, apparently not liking his musical tastes, but none of them left.

Jean took my other hand in hers, and started up a conversation with Giles and Jame and some of the other family members who settled on the floor to watch the event.

I heard them, but wasn't really listening. There was something hypnotic about Giles' motions. I couldn't stop watching that needle trace a path against my skin, dip into the ink well, then trace over my skin again.

As Giles worked away at inking a black, stylized ocean wave that swirled and curved into the profile of a howling wolf, more Wolfes paced into the room, both in fur and skin.

Every line Giles inked made me a little more settled, a little more grounded. While the needle buzzed and buzzed, I felt each person in the family breathing, felt them tied closer to me, felt their emotions. Or at least the high points of what they were feeling. And the high points were satisfaction, happiness, pride.

They were proud to claim me. To keep me. To make me theirs in this way.

I was happy to carry their mark. Proud and humbled.

"That's it." Giles rubbed the cloth over the symbol one more time, then sat back and settled his gear. "Take one last look. I'm going to cover it."

I blinked my eyes open. I'd been drifting. I shifted my arm to get a better look.

It was beautiful. An ocean wave coming out of the curve of a crescent moon, and in that wave, the wolf howling.

"It's amazing. Thank you."

"You're welcome," he said. "Welcome to the family."

He spread goo on it and topped that with clear wrap.

I couldn't take my eyes off it, couldn't believe it was there.

"Delaney Reed."

I glanced at Granny.

"This is settled between us, you understand?"

The awareness of all the Wolfe emotions faded, replaced by one strong thought: *peace*.

I nodded. "Yes. This is settled between us."

As soon as those words were out of my mouth, the clan stirred, stood, and oh-so-casually found a way to touch my shoulder, my arm, my hand as they left the room.

I was a part of them in a way I'd never been before, and I was in a little bit of awe about that.

It wasn't until Jame had escorted Jean, laughing, and me, drifting, out the door, that a prickling fear hit me. What if them claiming me and being a family at my back put them at risk?

I turned around to ask Jame how long this protection would last, and if there was any way out of it. Before I said anything he shook his head.

"Nope. This is forever. Nothing changes that. If you need us, we're there. Other than that, nothing changes from how it's always been."

"But…"

"No." He opened the door of Jean's truck for me.

"Just— I don't remember seeing this symbol before."

"You haven't." He gave me a little shove into the cab of the pickup. "You're the first to ever wear it."

Then he shut the door, gave me a wave, and walked away.

～

THE VALKYRIE WAS WAITING.

Bertie's office was a closed vault at the end of an impossibly long hallway. Even from this far away, I heard the *clack-clack-clack* of her hard gold nails drumming against her desk.

I gripped the jeweled Feather in my sweaty hand.

She knew we were here.

"Wait," Jean pulled me to one side before we'd even gone halfway down the hall. "Your will."

"What?"

"Have you updated it?"

I made a face at her and pulled away.

"I want those new T-shirts you bought from that fancy online store. And the dragon pig. Think of the dragon pig!"

"You suck," I said with a smile.

I paused outside the closed office door, pulled my shoulders back, and knocked softly before opening up the door and walking onto the battlefield.

"I took your Feather."

Bertie was perched behind the desk, dressed in a robin-egg blue power suit over a pale yellow blouse. Her hair was styled in tight curls, and her make-up was fresh and perfect.

The High Tea Tide was tomorrow morning, but it looked like she was already in full PR mode.

"I didn't know I was stealing it. There was a demon involved. Avnas, Bathin's uncle. He used your Feather, the Wolfes' Heartwood, and Than's sweat to cast a binding spell on me. But the binding spell was after I'd taken your Feather. So I committed the crime before I was bound to him, though he had me in some kind of thrall using the dings in my soul."

She just sat there, her gaze shifting once from my face to over my shoulder where Jean stood waiting.

Jean took that as a prompt. "If you want to press charges, I'm here. This is like any other crime we'd process in Ordinary. We'll follow the letter of the law. She's admitted her guilt. It's your right for restitution."

Jean tucked her thumbs into her belt, waiting.

Bertie was silent, so I boiled it down to basics again.

"I took your Feather. I'm sorry." I held up the Feather over my head like Thor's hammer, and it sparkled and shone.

"I am aware," she said briskly. "Sit down. You look ridiculous."

Jean made a little face and dropped down into one of the chairs in front of the desk. I followed suit, carefully placing the Feather in the center of the desk first.

Bertie's eyes tracked the Feather, but as soon as my plastic-wrapped wrist came into view, she finally tipped her hand.

"You went to the Wolfes' first?"

She did not sound happy about that.

"Uh…yes?"

"I suppose you took something from them too, didn't you?"

"Yes."

She pursed her lips and shook her head, curls jiggling.

"What was it? A claw? A bell? A little tuft of fur?"

"The Heartwood."

She sat back in her chair, and her hands went to the edge of the desk, fingertips perched there like birds on a line.

"I see." She dropped one of her hands and opened a drawer beside her. "And the Feather? Why did you steal it again? A demon, you said?"

"Avnas. He wants me to break a contract for him and thinks binding us together will make that happen."

"And where is Avnas?"

"In jail. The strong one with the magic cell that even a demon can't break out of."

The corner of her lip quirked slightly. "You locked him away?"

"I sent the dragon to put him there and keep watch on him."

Her eyes were sparkling, as if I were letting her in on a delightful little secret instead of just reporting on doing my job.

"He is the King's Knight, you know."

"I know. Bathin's uncle, brother-in-law-ish to Xtelle. We're keeping our demon scourge all in the family, apparently."

"You are here to arrest your sister?" she asked Jean.

"I will if you want to press charges. She stole something from you."

"Which could not have been stolen by any other living creature in Ordinary," Bertie said.

"Wait," I said. "You knew? All this time you knew I had your Feather?"

"Of course."

I swallowed back the groan and managed a reasonable tone. "Why didn't you tell me?"

She *blink, blink, blink*ed. "Tell you that you stole something from me? Why was I to assume you didn't know what you'd done? I'm not your guidance counselor, Delaney."

"But it was your property. Weren't you…worried?"

"You are the only person in Ordinary who could have moved it. That speaks of the trust I have apparently misplaced in you."

It was the nicest thing she'd ever said to me.

Jean snorted, then cleared her throat.

"Thank you?" I asked.

She ignored that. "Since you are both here." She drew a folder out of the drawer and placed it on the desk. "I would like you to commit to the next six months of community events."

Jean squeaked like she'd just been punched in the gut. I tried not to smile.

It had taken time, over a year, but it looked like the little cat and mouse game between Jean and Bertie—where Bertie volunteered her to work an event and Jean found a way to wiggle out of it—was over.

To no one's surprise, the Valkyrie had won.

Bertie produced a pen and clicked it once.

"Oh, you first," Jean said to me.

"Happy to." I took the pen, more than willing to choose the events I wanted instead of the ones Jean left behind.

"So many choices." I sighed dramatically.

"Wait." Jean grabbed for the pen.

"Nope. No, I got this. This is good. Super good."

"You've done so much more, and I should—" She made another swipe for the pen, but I turned my shoulder and chortled as I checked off the easiest events.

"That's not— Delaney, I want—"

"And...done!" I pushed the folder her way and held up the pen.

She scowled and snatched it out of my hand.

"Swamp Cowgirl!" Jean glared at me.

"It's the Wild Wild Wetland tour," Bertie said. "Explaining the importance of our wetland habitat."

"Yes, Jean," I said. "Are you saying our wetland habitat isn't important?"

"No. It's important. Especially in the spring time. When the mosquitoes rise like blood-thirsty fog banks to feed upon my flesh."

"There's the rootin'-tootin' spirit," I said. "Saddle up for swamp fun!"

Jean scratched her cheek with her middle finger, flashed Bertie a totally fake smile, and filled out the form.

"Delaney," Bertie said, "I have decided not to press charges at this time."

"All right," I said, waiting for her to follow up on that.

"However, I want you to show me your hand."

Jean stopped writing and looked between us.

I extended my left hand—the one with the new tattoo—toward Bertie.

"Not that one. Your right."

Oh, this couldn't be good. I extended my right hand sideways in a sort of handshake position.

One minute Bertie was nodding encouragingly like a first-grade teacher who was impressed I'd remembered which limb had a hand at the end of it, and the next, she stabbed me in the base of my thumb.

"Ow!" I jerked back and shot up to my feet. "What the hell?" I tucked my hand into my chest pressing my left thumb over the cut.

Bertie pulled two tissues from the little flowery box next to her and wiped my blood off her tiny apple knife. "It's just a scratch."

I moved my thumb. The blood was still welling. "It is not just a scratch. This is going to scar."

"Oh, yes," she said. "I would hope so. How else would certain people understand that crossing you, means crossing me? Did you expect a tacky tattoo? You already have one of those."

I opened my mouth. Closed it. "What? Why? You know what? If you want people to know something, you could just tell them. Verbally. By using your words."

"No, this is much more efficient. I can't follow you around all day waiting for you to fall prey to the next nefarious person. I'm a very busy woman, Delaney. Which you'd know if you volunteered more for the community events that are vital to our town's financial and social standing."

"I— What social standing?"

"Boring has stepped up their outreach."

I shook my head, having no idea what another town over a hundred miles away had to do with anything.

"They have acquired a...person of my acquaintance. A Valkyrie."

"What does that have to do with our social standing?"

"Robyn has always tried to one-up me. If I pulled ten warriors off the battlefield, she pulled twenty. If I drank from the skulls of my enemies, she devoured their brains. If I padded my nest with a hundred virile lovers…"

"I get it." I reached across the desk and pulled tissues, packing them on my cut and holding it tight. "Your arch nemesis is in Boring, Oregon, for no reason I can imagine."

"No kidding," Jean said. "Who wants to live in a town with that kind of name?"

"Right?" I agreed. "At least it isn't Drain."

We all nodded, having been to that town too.

"She thinks she can out-event me," Bertie announced.

Chills ran down my spine, just thinking about how many community events Boring was about to be subjected to.

"That's terrible," Jean breathed. "I'm so sorry for them."

Bertie raised her eyebrows and turned the little knife in her hand. "Oh? And why are you sorry for that town, Jean?"

Jean swallowed and looked at me. I just widened my eyes, not knowing how to unspring the trap she'd just stuck her big mouth right in the middle of.

"Because there is no chance they're going to win," Jean said. "Everyone knows you are the best at this, Bertie. And you've been doing it so spectacularly for so many years. You're practically famous for it."

"No need to lay it on that thick," Bertie said. "But I agree. She is a rank amateur. If she thinks she's going to make her Boring little town anything more than my amazing Ordinary, then she has another think coming." She punctuated by stabbing the air with the little knife.

For a moment, Bertie was a lot more than just a woman in her eighties with impeccable suits. She was taller, even though she was still sitting. She was sharper, all the angles of her, gem cut. And she was so, so much more frightening.

Valkyrie. All the way down.

"Murder's against the law, Bertie." I slipped into my role as Chief of Police. "If she shows up dead, you're my first suspect."

"Pish-posh, Delaney," Bertie gathered the folder from Jean. Jean leaned back to stay out of her reach. "If I killed

Robyn, you'd never find the body." She glanced at the pages, tapped the edge of the folder on the desk to even them out, then hid it in the drawer.

"Is there anything else?" Bertie asked.

"You're sure about the charges?" Jean asked.

"I am. Now if you'll please leave, I have a photo shoot scheduled."

And just like that, we escaped the Valkyrie's nest with only one small wound between us. I called that a victory.

CHAPTER NINETEEN

JEAN DROPPED me off at the cabin on the lake. I told her I wanted to go to the station and write up a report, but she'd given me a hard look she never used to have. She told me I'd been attacked by a demon, which made me a victim of a crime. I needed to go home to relax with my man.

Since my man and I were maybe still fighting, I wasn't sure how much relaxation was going to happen. But one thing was true: I had been attacked by a demon, had been under demon attack for quite some time now. I was tired, angry, and wanted to take a long hot shower then crawl into my pajamas and eat a carton of ice cream.

The lights were on when I got home. I knew Ryder was in there. He had told me he'd be there, waiting.

I took a deep breath, the air zinging with that explosion of smoke and green and salt I'd only found in little seaside towns.

Music. It was the first thing I noticed when I walked into the house. Something soft by the Neutral Milk Hotel. The lamps were on, but the overheads were off.

Spud trotted to me from the living room. I gave him a head rub.

"Good boy," I said.

Spud wagged his tail.

"Dragon pig will be home soon. It's doing a little guard dogging in the magic jail for the night."

At the words "dragon pig," his mouth dropped open into a happy smile. He dashed off to his stuffed toy pile and started rooting around for tonight's offering.

"Hey," Ryder said, soft, questioning. He stood on the other side of the kitchen island, a mug and plate in his hands. "Hungry?"

He looked so at ease right then, wearing the T-shirt, the one with holes across the shoulders he loved too much to get rid of, his hair mussed up like he'd been pulling at it.

I couldn't have stopped myself from going to him if I'd tried.

His concerned frown lifted as I came near. He had just enough time to place the cup and plate on the counter before I was in his arms. He pulled me in tight, moving his bare feet so I could better fit against him.

I leaned my head on his shoulder and just breathed him in.

He didn't say anything. He didn't have to. We were together, hearts beating, bodies warm, until our breathing slowed, and fell into sync.

"I miss you," I said.

He swallowed before saying, "I miss you too."

He held on for a moment more, then rubbed my back. "I heated up the chicken. And the coffee is fresh."

I was exhausted. All I wanted to do was to fall into bed. But my stomach growled. I leaned back so I could see him. I really didn't want to fight. I just wanted to have a nice night at home with him. I just needed to smile and sit down for a nice reheated dinner.

"Not gonna run off all night again, are you?" I said. "I'm beginning to think you're trying to hide something from me."

Every muscle tensed. His easy expression went flat as a wall, hard as armor.

"Why don't we eat?" he said. Another non-answer. He'd been giving me those a lot lately.

"Yeah. That's fine."

"You don't want it?"

"I said it's fine."

His arms dropped, and I took one of the stools on other side of the island, leaving him standing in the kitchen.

He placed the plate in front of me and poured me a mug of coffee. "So how did it go? With the Feather and Heartwood?"

"No one wanted to press charges."

"Good. What happened to your hands?"

I glanced at them. One was wrapped in cellophane, the other sported a bacon-shaped Band-Aid Jean had insisted I use.

"They wanted my blood instead."

His shoulders jerked. "You gave it to them? Is that a tattoo? Did you let someone mark you?"

"Why are you angry? You have tattoos."

"This isn't about the tattoo."

"Then what is your problem?"

"My problem is you keep letting other people just—*do* —this kind of shit to you."

"That's not fair. You aren't angry that I got attacked by a demon—again. You're angry that I'm finding my way through this without you. Well, you're only in town about three hours a day. Sorry you couldn't fit me into your schedule."

Every word was even and steady. I wanted to take them back the moment they were out of my mouth. Before then. I wanted to go back to months ago when everything between us was easy and okay.

My heart pounded like a battle drum, shaking me, shaking the world around me.

Ryder stood so still, I wondered if I'd actually spoken out loud. Then he looked away, over my shoulder, at the ceiling.

DEVON MONK

"I'm sorry," he said tightly. "I shouldn't have said...it that way."

"No," I said. "You shouldn't have. I don't let anyone do things to me without my permission and without knowing the consequences—which I'm willing to live with. I was attacked, Ryder. I didn't invite that demon to set his hooks in my soul."

He pressed his hand against the back of his neck and squeezed. That's when I realized how tired he looked. How thin. He nodded, but still wouldn't make eye contact.

He pushed the food around with his fork, spreading out that stupid pea-filled salad.

My stomach clenched in a sour knot, but I lifted my coffee and took a drink. We were both aiming for normal, trying not to let the words break the evening, but it was too late.

"You're not getting much sleep," I said. It was stilted and soft, but was the best I could do.

His eyes flicked up to mine, searching for anger, for blame and finding none. He looked away again, back to separating peas from pasta.

"I'm not at my best right now either," I said. "I'm sorry I didn't make it to the fancy dinner tonight." There, that was my white flag. That was all I had in me.

"I'm sorry I didn't make it to dinner last night." He forked salad into his mouth and chewed.

I sighed and pressed my fingers over my eyes. "Is this about us?" I asked, not looking at him yet. Not able to. "Is this about wanting different things?"

"It's not...that isn't what...Delaney, you can look at me. I'm not...I'm sorry I was angry."

I took one breath, savoring the darkness behind my fingers. I wasn't hiding because he was angry. I was just trying to prepare myself for the truth. For whatever we were about to tell each other.

There was choppy water ahead. The kind of water broken and sharpened by hurricane winds. The kind of water that tore a ship into tiny splinters before sinking it forever.

A storm. Unavoidable.

I dropped my hands and opened my eyes.

He was watching me, his plate pushed aside. He looked like he had a stomachache, a headache. He looked like a heartbreak ready to crack.

"Oh, gods," I exhaled, knowing the ship was taking on water, but uncertain if I should bail it out, or hold my breath and swim for shore.

"Hey, no, hey." He reached, his hand catching mine. The familiar scratch of callouses, rougher now that he was spending every spare minute on one job site or another, calmed me.

"We're good, right?" he said. "This, us…it's good?"

"It's good. We're good," I said.

"So there's no reason to…worry. I think there's no reason for us to worry. About us. What we are to each other. What we mean to each other."

"Good," I said. "I can get behind that."

He was nodding now, like this was a script he'd run through his head over and over, and I'd answered appropriately.

I was on board. We were bailing water.

"So that means right now, for a little while, we don't need to worry about the choices we're making. We trust each other." He must have seen the shift in my expression, though I wasn't sure what was coming through. Confusion? Fear?

"Because we're good," he added hastily. "As a…together. We might want something…different…more…promises later. But that would just be icing on icing, because we're already cake. And icing. But good, right? We're already good."

He stopped and swallowed. He was sweating now, his color up. If I didn't know him better I'd say he was just one more "good" away from a panic attack.

It felt like my heart was being squeezed between two bricks. We weren't talking about a sinking ship or cakes and icing. I was pretty sure we were talking about marriage. And he was telling me, without telling me, that he did not want the same thing I wanted. Not now.

Was that why he was avoiding me?

I took a breath and remembered the pot on the window sill. Remembered a little plant that hadn't bloomed yet.

Patience.

"I think you're talking about more than cake," I said calmly.

He nodded.

Sunlight.

"I heard you. So what I'm going to do is step back. Give us time to think. We can talk about it more. Later. Are you okay with that?"

The nod again. His hand squeezing mine was hot, tight, sweaty. This was tearing him up inside, a conflict I could not understand. I hated that the simple idea of us exchanging vows, of us promising to be together forever, was kicking his needle into the red.

Water.

"I love you, Ryder Bailey."

His breath came out hard, caught on a hiccup as if he'd held it too long. "Yeah," he said, wobbly with unshed tears. "I love you too. I'll be home more. The job…it's almost done. I promise. It's almost done. Just, please, wait for me. Don't give up."

"I am not giving up." I inhaled, exhaled, settling the emotions crashing around inside of me. It had been a long damn day. "How about dessert and a movie instead of dinner?"

He closed his eyes for just a second too long, dealing with his own inner storm. Then he raised his head and gave me a smile. "I'd like that."

I retrieved a carton of ice cream from the freezer while he dumped the dishes into the sink. With two spoons in one hand, ice cream in the other, I headed to the living room.

We sat on the couch, close, touching from shoulder to hip. I threw a leg over his because I was lost at sea, the ship having fallen into splinters that were washing away on the waves.

I needed to hold on to someone, to hold on to him. He wrapped his arm behind my shoulders and pulled me closer, shifting so we touched as much as possible.

Spud jumped up next to Ryder, laying his head and the stuffed french fry in his mouth on our laps. He wagged his tail slowly, like he did when we were sick and he was in bed waiting for us to get better.

I handed Ryder a spoon. He turned on the TV.

We shared the ice cream, adrift and looking for shore.

I WOKE ON THE COUCH, stiff and cotton-mouthed. The sound of Ryder's footsteps, his boots, crossed the floor to the door. I blinked at the ceiling, waiting, listening.

It was still dark out.

The door opened, and he hesitated. I wondered if he would turn, come back, stay with me. Instead, he walked out. The door closed softly as the scent of saltwater drifted into the house on a damp wind, cool where it touched my face with ghostly fingers.

Spud, sitting on the floor next to me, tapped his tail.

I could lie there. Wait for a repeat of the same morning we'd been living on a loop, or I could do something about it.

"It's not stalking if we're living together, right?" I asked Spud.

Spud waved his tail a little slower, as if he weren't sure I had that right.

"Wanna go for a ride, boy?" That got me an enthusiastic tail wag. He ran over to the little box near the front door where we kept his leash, dug it out, and held it up for me, wriggling with delight.

I stretched, hooked the line to his collar, then grabbed my coat and phone. I looked out the window as Ryder's truck pulled off down the dark road.

Then I was out the door and in my Jeep, Spud riding shotgun.

I followed Ryder, but not too closely. Ordinary didn't have a lot of traffic this time of night, and Ryder was not only a reserve officer, he had also trained in some secret government monster-hunting program. He was aware of his surroundings.

But I didn't think he'd expect me to follow him. I hadn't any of the other times he'd snuck out of the house, so there was no reason for him to be suspicious.

Spud settled in, laying his head on my thigh. I blew out a breath, and ran my hand over his soft fuzzy head.

"I shouldn't be doing this. I trust him. I do."

Spud didn't move his head, but his tail thumped on the back of the passenger seat.

"This doesn't look like trust. I know that." Ryder was through Ordinary now, headed northeast, and I followed. It wasn't like me to leave town and not let my sisters know. But I had my cell on me and the police radio in the Jeep. If anything came up, they could find me.

He cruised along Hwy 101, then took the exit toward Otis, following Hwy 18. I thought maybe he was headed to the casino. For a minute, I wondered if this was about something other than the construction job, something other than him not wanting to be home.

Gambling. He could be going out to gamble every night and staggering back home in the early morning. Maybe he was in debt. Maybe one of his construction projects had gone bad. Or maybe he was addicted to gambling and didn't want me to find out.

But he slowed miles before the casino, turning left into the parking lot of the little Rose Market. I pulled in behind the trash dumpster, hidden from his view by the low, one-story building itself.

In the daylight, the little white building with the red roof did a pretty good business from the locals scattered in the hills and fields around it, folks who didn't want to make a longer trip for basic needs. It also served people driving between the casino and the beach.

Right across the street from it was one of the fire and rescue district stations.

But in the middle of the night, both buildings were dark and quiet.

I gave Spud one more pat, then got out of the Jeep and shut the door as quietly as I could. Voices, both male, I thought, were carrying on a conversation, neither voice particularly hushed. They were coming from the other side of the building, right about where Ryder had parked.

I made my way around the back of the building, still hidden from view, straining to hear.

"You know what I want, Ryder."

I knew that voice. Mithra. I didn't know Ryder had been meeting him outside of Ordinary.

"You want to either rule over Ordinary or destroy it. Because you made me the Warden, you think that means you can be judge and jury over everyone in town. Oh, and you want to remove the Reeds and their entire bloodline from ever holding an authority position in the town because…" He blew out a breath. "I'm a little fuzzy on the details. Was it because no one listened to your last Warden in the 1850s? Or because you don't like it that all the other gods got together to decide on Ordinary's laws and rules, and you refused to join them?"

Oh, my man was salty.

"Respect me, Ryder Bailey."

"Or what? You're already using me as a puppet so you can bust people for spitting on the streets of Sheridan, or doing occult arts in Yamhill, or selling brightly dyed baby chicks in Eugene."

"If you would just do as I ordered—"

"I never signed a contract with you to be your lackey. I never signed a contract with you at all."

"You entered into an agreement with me to become the Warden of Ordinary and to do as I instruct you to do."

"No. I volunteered to be Warden of Ordinary because you were trying to bully Delaney into letting you rule the town. That's it. Full stop. As far as I'm concerned, being a Warden means being an impartial witness and observer of good contracts. To make sure people inside Ordinary are being treated fairly, no matter who tries to boss them around."

"Stop."

Ryder sucked in a breath and made a little choking sound. I eased forward just enough to see what was happening.

Mithra looked the same as I'd last seen him: Salt and pepper hair that had never met a comb, tightly trimmed beard, buggy eyes, and flat, round face that reminded me of a pug.

Instead of wearing tattered, cast-off clothing, he was in a black, wide-sleeved robe, symbols and power and words scrolling through the folds.

Ryder's back was to me, but I'd never seen him stand so stiffly.

"I no longer care to hear your opinion, Mr. Bailey. Lift your right hand."

Ryder jerked, as if an invisible rope tied to his wrist suddenly pulled his arm up.

"Lift your left foot."

Same jerking motion. And now his foot was sticking out in front of him at an awkward angle.

"I am showing you mercy, Ryder Bailey. I do believe you and I can come to an agreement. But I demand your respect. Do you understand?"

Ryder was silent.

"I haven't taken your voice this time, Mr. Bailey."

This time? I moved to step in, to get between them, to pick a fight with a god, but then Ryder spoke.

"I understand. Let go."

Mithra flicked a finger. Everything about Ryder relaxed and went back to normal. His hand lowered, his foot lowered, and his shoulders squared.

"I want out of the contract."

"You want something, I want something. But the contract between us isn't what you called me out here for, is it?" Mithra said.

"Yes, it's the contract. I'm done being sent out like a dog on the hunt every damn day and every damn night. I'm done being your puppet."

"No, you called me here because of Delaney."

Ryder went silent.

"I agreed to be your follower, Mithra, and I have been. I want out."

It was Mithra's turn to be silent. "She wants more from you," he said, as if this were something they'd been talking about. An old issue.

"You don't know her."

"I have been studying her family line since they first took guardianship of Ordinary. I do know her. She wants a commitment from you."

"And I want one from you. I want to break our contract."

"She wants you to marry her."

My heart tripped, then kicked so hard, I pressed my fist against my chest to hold it in place.

Mithra was a god. He might know I was hiding behind the building.

But because he was a god, I was betting he didn't expect anyone to actually spy on him. Most deities thought themselves above such petty skullduggery, or didn't care if it happened. We were all beneath their notice.

"You don't know Delaney." Ryder's voice was the roll of the ocean, strong, low. I pressed my palm against the building to keep from going to him, standing behind him. I'd had a lot of practice staring down gods. I wanted him to know I had his back.

"I know her better than you want to admit," Mithra said dismissively. "I've been thinking a lot about her lately."

"The contract," Ryder said. "I'm here for our contract. If you refuse to talk about breaking it, then I'm leaving."

"You want to break the contract," Mithra said, bored, like

a predator playing with its food before swallowing it whole. "I want you to marry Delaney."

My heart stopped. The world zinged oddly as if every atom in the air had been hit with jumper cables, everything in that moment, a buzzing darkness with pinpoints of light.

"You want me to marry Delaney."

"Yes. You assume I have nefarious plans for taking over Ordinary—"

"—which you do," Ryder said.

"—but no matter my ultimate intentions, I also want what is best for you, Ryder Bailey. My loyal follower. Therefore, I want you to marry Delaney Reed."

This buzzing wasn't much better, but I could see again, could breathe. I scanned the grassy area behind the store, stared at the sky where clouds scuffed the stars. I rubbed my fingers on the building. It was solid and hard and real.

This was real. This was really happening. He had really said that.

And then Ryder spoke. "No."

Mithra chuckled, and it was not kind. "I rule you. I own you. You will do as I command. And would it be such a hardship? You've been thinking about it for months."

"Fuck off." Ryder's voice was no longer the ocean. It was lightning. It was fire burning through steel. He was angry. Furious. "You don't know my mind. You push me around like a puppet, shove my head under water until I'm gasping for air. I want our contract ended. My mind, my life is my own."

"Do you think so?" Mithra baited. "Then why haven't you proposed to Delaney? Why haven't you married her? You've had all this time. Why won't you ask her?"

"As long as I am under your command, I will never marry Delaney. Never."

Those words hammered, striking the steel around my heart, sparking embers before cracking through to pierce.

Never. He would never marry me. Never.

I knew truth when I heard it, had known him long enough

to hear a lie in his voice. This wasn't something he was saying for Mithra's benefit. He didn't want to be married.

Somewhere in the back of my mind, I reminded myself that we had a pretty good thing going even without wedding rings. I wasn't the kind of person who needed to be married to know I was loved. But it was the way he said it.

It was that *never*. The anger in it, the hatred.

I was cold, suddenly freezing. I shivered and sucked down air, my breathing gone choppy and shallow.

Okay. Okay. So now I knew why he'd been gone so much. Mithra was running him ragged. Mithra was controlling him.

I didn't know why he hadn't just told me, but I didn't have the mental capacity at the moment to work that out.

The only thought stabbing through the buzz in my ears was home. I needed to get home, needed to drive away, needed to be gone before Ryder found out I'd been spying on him.

I moved quickly, trying not to kick the gravel, got into the Jeep. Spud's tail was going strong, and just seeing his goofy, happy face set the center of me back in place again.

The steel around my heart might be broken, but it was still there. I inhaled, exhaled. Settled my fingers on the steering wheel. Worse had happened to me in my life. I could deal with this.

"Okay," I said. "Okay. I got this. Okay. Just…we should go. Wanna go home, Spud? Let's go home."

Spud positioned himself so he could look out the window, and I started the Jeep.

I didn't remember driving back to Ordinary, but when I got there, I didn't want to go home. Not to mine, where a demon had decided to cast his stupid spell, and not to Ryder's, because, pot on the window sill or not, I just didn't have it in me to think about sunlight and water and patience.

So it was maybe no surprise that I pulled up in front of a little aqua cottage that I'd only been to once.

Spud was very interested in our stop, sniffing at the glass

of the window as if there were a smell right outside the car that he really, really liked, but couldn't quite get.

"I should just go home." I stared at the door. "Or over to Myra's or Jean's. Jean's probably at Hogan's. So Myra. I should go to Myra's."

I had almost turned on the Jeep's engine when the porch light flicked on and the door opened.

A familiar tall, lean figure stood in that doorway, spider slippers akimbo.

Than waited a moment, then moved sideways in that space, inviting me in.

I rested my head on the steering wheel for the count of three, ran through my options again—Myra would worry and mother me, Jean would worry and try to fix whatever was going on between Ryder and me—or Death.

I chose Death.

Than didn't move as Spud and I got out of the vehicle and strolled up the walk. He just watched me, his dark eyes glittering, his face placid.

I stopped on the front step. Spud wagged his tail excitedly, but stayed at my side because he was the bestest of good boys.

"Can I stay here for the night?"

Than blinked. Something crossed his face, some emotion, but I was too tired to try and figure it out.

"You don't have to say yes."

"Come in, Reed Daughter." He waved at the interior of his house.

"Spud too?"

His gaze drifted down, and Spud instantly sat, whining and eager, tail swinging.

"He is a 'good boy'?"

"Yes."

"Well, then." The hand again, the wave.

We rushed into the house, Spud the happiest I'd seen him since the dragon pig had let him lay on its hoard of stuffed toys.

Than wore striped pajama bottoms with a matching striped, button-up pajama shirt. The spider slippers looked even more alarmed than the last time I'd seen them.

"Is this a business call?" he asked.

"No."

That thing traveled across his face. Something like interest? Delight?

"Then this is a social visit?"

"Yes."

"In the middle of the night?"

"Well, what's left of it, yeah."

"Are you staying?"

"I thought you said I could?"

"Until morning, Reed Daughter."

"Delaney," I automatically corrected. We were still standing in the front entryway, and his couch and the tidy throws draped across it were looking pretty appealing right now.

"Since morning is only a few hours away, yes," I said. "Until morning."

"I see," he mused. Then he stilled. "This would be considered a *sleepover*?"

That's when my muddled brain clicked together the clues. The look of anticipation he quickly smothered, the gleam in his eye, the slightly elevated breathing.

He was excited. This might even be what giddy looked like on him.

"Maybe," I hedged, trying to look stern. "Do you have hot cocoa?"

"With pink mini-marshmallows."

"Then this, Than, is a sleepover."

He didn't smile, but shifted his stance so quickly, the slipper spiders waggled their legs in panic. Than bowed slightly and extended his hand toward the interior of his home. "This way, Reed Daughter. I shall fetch a bottle to spin."

"We really don't need a bottle."

"Oh?"

"It takes more than two people to play that game."

"Ah." He led me to the living room, gestured at the couches, then withdrew the controls for his media center from a side table drawer.

"Instead, we shall have to gossip. I am sure we have many judgmental observations to share about people who are not here. Or I would assume you do."

"No, I don't want to gossip."

He lifted one eyebrow and waited.

"Tonight. I don't want to gossip tonight. I don't want to talk about anything. Or anyone."

"Not even Ryder Bailey?"

I shook my head.

He *hmmm*ed.

Gods. Sometimes they really did know what we humans were thinking.

When I found the pillow next to me suddenly more interesting than his endless stare, he handed me the remote. "Choose a movie while I pop the corn and brew the hot cocoa beverage. Do you require leisure clothing?"

"No," I said quickly. I did not want to know what clothing he might think was appropriate for a sleepover. "I'll just kick off my boots."

"Boots will be left at the door, please." He walked out of the room. Spud scrambled to catch up to him, and when the dog matched his stride, Than's long fingers found the back of his head and patted him softly.

Spud moved in even closer, gluing himself to Than's leg.

I worked off my boots and left them by the door, then returned to the couch. I wasn't really in the mood for a movie, but I scrolled through the selections anyway. When I found an old Danny Kaye I hadn't seen in years, I queued it up.

I checked my phone while the sound of popcorn popping drifted to me on buttery, salty whiffs. No texts from Ryder or anyone else, so I set the phone on the side table, curled my feet up under me, and dragged the throw from the back of the couch to my lap.

"Here we are."

Than had a fancy serving tray that was probably real silver. On it he had placed two mugs filled to the brim with chocolate and extra-tiny marshmallows in a frothy pink foam, a large wooden bowl of popcorn, and two smaller matching bowls. There was also a little dish of strawberries, and another of chocolates that I assumed had raisins in the middle of them.

He placed the tray on the table, then considered the empty chair, the space beside me on the couch, and to my very great surprise, chose the couch.

He oh-so-casually drew the other throw off the back of the couch and placed it in his lap, exactly like mine, staring straight ahead at the screen where the movie was paused on the opening credits.

Spud sniffed at the spider slippers, sniffed at the blanket, then sat and stared adoringly at Than.

Than placed one hand on the cushion between us. That was all the invitation Spud needed. He hopped up, squooshing between the two of us. I thought he'd want to snuggle me, but he put his head on Than's lap and sighed like he'd just found his favorite bed in the world.

Than bent, gathering a mug of cocoa, a bowl of popcorn, and a strawberry for himself.

He hadn't said anything more, I hadn't either, but the mix of cocoa and popcorn was too good to resist. I took a mug and a bowl and tried the cocoa first. It was delicious.

"I see you've chosen a film?"

"We don't have to watch it," I said.

"Oh?" Than turned to me now. "Would you prefer other sleepover activities? Nail paints? Pillow forts? A mirror in which to call forth that bloody child Mary?"

"You've really done your research on sleepovers."

"Becoming a part of Ordinary entails learning the local

customs. Blending in." He dipped his strawberry in the marshmallow foam and took a neat bite.

I stuffed my face full of popcorn so I wouldn't tell him that blending in was not his strong suit. He was trying. That counted.

"Or, perhaps you would reconsider...gossip?"

He sounded so hopeful, I laughed, spraying popcorn bits. I slapped my hand over my mouth, chewed, swallowed. "Sorry," I choked out. "I never thought you'd want to talk trash about people."

"Shall we try it and find out?"

"I don't...no. I don't think so. Hey, didn't you have a cold yesterday?"

"Apparently common viruses do not survive long in my presence. Would you like to talk instead about the hell spell that demon bound you with?"

I scowled and crunched more popcorn. "You see that, huh?"

"Yes."

"It's Bathin's uncle."

"Yes."

"I stole the sweat of your brow for the spell. I didn't know I was doing it, though. Because my stupid soul still has stupid holes in it."

He waved long fingers as if that wasn't a conversation that interested him. "It is healing as it should. Where is he?"

"Jail. The dragon pig's watching him."

Spud lifted his head when I said dragon pig, looked around for his buddy, then settled his head down again, sighing.

"I don't recall the dragon being deputized."

I smiled a little at that. "Not that jail. It took him to the other jail."

Than put a piece of popcorn—just one—in his mouth and chewed while watching me. "Other jail."

"We have a...um...magic jail. For the people who need that type of containment. Honestly, we don't use it very much, but Myra rigged it up for demons after that whole Bathin and Xtelle thing."

Another piece of popcorn, and still the intense focus. As if he expected me to say more, to spill the beans.

"Ryder snuck out tonight." I grimaced and corrected myself. "Mithra called him out of Ordinary. And I followed."

Two pieces of popcorn in those long thin fingers this time, deposited one at a time, *plunk, plunk,* in his mouth.

"They met up at the Rose Market on Highway 18. Mithra was his normal asshole self. From what I heard, he's been sending Ryder out to enforce obscure Oregon laws. Something about no spitting in Sheridan. Things like that."

Death picked up his mug, took a deep drink, then lifted it a bit, a suggestion that I, too, take a drink.

So I did. It really was amazing. Than knew how to brew a fine hot cocoa beverage.

"I thought Mithra was punishing him for something, but he's enough of a jerk just to want to pull strings and watch Ryder dance. I was going to leave, to just…leave it at that, but then Mithra told Ryder he wanted him to marry me, and yeah. So, okay. That. And then I left."

I shoved popcorn in my mouth so I would stop talking. It tasted like packing Styrofoam. There was a stinging prickle at the back of my eyes. I would not cry. Not over a manipulative god who Ryder was doing his best to manage.

Without me.

Without even telling me.

I will never marry her.

Death twisted, and without disturbing Spud's nap, plucked a tissue from the box by the lamp.

"Did you spy on him long enough to hear his reply?"

"I wasn't spying." I took the tissue. "Okay, I was spying." I wiped at my eyes which should not be leaking, then took a big breath and let it out. "I feel so stupid. All of this. Just. Stupid."

"Mmmm."

I dropped my head back on the couch. "Spying on my boyfriend. Who does that?"

"Would you like a list?"

"No." I rolled my head to meet his gaze. An awful lot of humor in those eyes. "Are you laughing at me?"

"Whatever would make you think that, Reed Daughter?"

"He said no."

Death paused, and I wondered how many millions of data points that statement could be applied to.

"Ryder," I clarified. "He said no. He wouldn't marry me. He said he never would, so that's all settled now I guess." The last came out too loud and too cheerful, and for just a second, I felt like yelling and throwing things, or putting on my jogging shoes and running out the door, out of Ordinary, out of my life and never coming back.

Marriage didn't have to be my future. I hadn't obsessed over it as a child, hadn't thought myself ready for it until Ryder came swanning back into town with that great smile, clever brain, and gorgeous heart.

Over the last two years, I had thought about it more. Now that we were living together, I thought it might be our tomorrow, our someday.

Than placed his bowl on the silver platter, the mug following with a little *clink*. He slid out from under Spud and stood.

"Where are you going?" I asked.

"This is the part of the sleepover that requires wine, is it not?"

I laughed again. "No, don't. I'm fine. I have to go to work in a few hours. Wine is a bad idea." I reached for his sleeve and tugged at it, tugged him back to sit on the couch.

He tipped his head to one side, studying me. "Did he say no to you?"

I fluffed a pillow and propped it behind me so I could curl my feet up and sit sideways on the couch. "I just said he did."

"You said he said no to Mithra."

"Same difference. Mithra ordered him to marry me and

Ryder said he would never." I curled the mug into my chest, enjoying the warmth that soaked through my shirt.

"He told Mithra he would never marry you."

"I like how you're catching on so quickly, and I don't have to repeat myself."

Point Delaney. One-zero.

His eyebrow twitched. "One feature of humanity that has never changed in all of time is their sarcasm."

I toasted him with the mug.

"And their ability to lie."

"I'm not lying to you."

Than sighed. It sounded like he had run out of patience for the entire world. "You aren't the only human on the earth, Delaney. I was speaking of Ryder."

"He's lying. To Mithra?"

"Are sleepovers always so mentally stimulating?"

Point Than. One-one.

"Yeah, this is about how it goes."

"And?"

"What?" I asked.

"Do you recall everything he said?"

"Yes?"

"Did you tell me all of it?"

I hadn't. I'd left one part out. "He said he wouldn't marry me as long as he's under Mithra's command, but since Mithra is never going to let him go…" I shrugged.

"Might he be lying to Mithra?"

I rolled that around while I finished my cocoa. "Maybe," I admitted. "He's been so absent. I don't really know what's going on in his head right now."

"You've asked him, of course."

I felt the blush roll across my cheeks. "As much."

"Perhaps you should apply more specific effort in your word choice. Might I suggest something along the lines of: Ryder Bailey, do you intend to marry me? Enunciate clearly and use careful listening skills. You must also insist on the same level of conversational skill from him. It is known as a clearing of the air. Conflict resolution. Maturity."

"Did you just accuse me of being childish?"

"Only of being human, Reed Daughter."

He sipped cocoa, watching me over the top of the mug.

It made sense. Ryder was no fan of Mithra. He might be lying to the deity. But I had heard his voice, the tone of it, the conviction. If he were lying, he was doing a damn good job.

"How about we watch the show," I suggested.

"The Court Jester," Than read from the title credit. "Is it a tragedy?"

"It's a musical. Kind of. And an adventure. And a comedy. So quotable. You're gonna love it."

"I see." He settled back, one hand smoothing over Spud's soft ears. "Go on."

"Oh, wait. Before I forget, Tala says hi." It was a casual comment, no big deal. If I hadn't been sitting on the couch right next to him, I might have missed his reaction.

He was still, but the color in his face seemed to warm. Not a blush, because I was pretty sure Than didn't have the capability to feel embarrassed.

"Who?"

His voice cracked. *Cracked*.

I fought down a grin, because this was suddenly so much more interesting than the show.

"Tala. She's a goddess. Of the morning and evening star. I met her out at the casino Thursday."

"She mentioned me?"

"She wondered if you were vacationing."

"Ah." He didn't say more, but I could see it in him. The strain to remain uninterested. "And you told her?"

"Yes, you're vacationing here. Then she told me to say hi. So I have. I've told you your girlfriend says hi."

"She is not my girlfriend." He almost, *almost* pulled it off. The affronted look. The raised eyebrow.

But that not-blush was still there. And his breathing was a little quick.

"Is she your enemy?" That hadn't occurred to me.

"No." The word was slow, stretched out.

"Well, whatever she is, she seemed *very* interested in contacting you."

He swallowed, and I heard the click of his dry throat. "That is very cordial of her."

"Isn't it? Isn't it so nice of her to want to know where you are? To want me to pass on that message. I enunciated it clearly, didn't I? Are you sweating?"

"Why? Is there another hell spell in which you wish to participate?"

Sassy. I just shrugged. "I am sorry about that. Do you want my blood too?"

"Your blood?"

"Seems to be the preferred form of payment for my crimes."

"Who has taken your blood?"

Ah, yeah. There he was: the scary guy. The Death who wasn't as much on vacation as he might think he was.

I showed him my hands. "Werewolves, because I used the Heartwood in the spell, and Bertie, because I used her Feather in the spell."

"Ah." The looming thunder in his eyes faded. "Wood, feather, and sweat. A very traditional spell. I can imagine the demon assumed using those items from citizens within Ordinary would give it power over you."

"Wait. What? It doesn't?"

He nodded toward my hands. "The demon grossly underestimated how much the citizens of Ordinary care for you."

I waited for him to continue. When he didn't, I shook my head.

"The marks," he explained, like I was new to language. "You are claimed by the Wolfe clan, you are protected by the Valkyrie. And, it should go without saying that I am... minutely fond of you."

"Minutely," I breathed, in a sort of wonder.

He almost—almost—rolled his eyes.

DEVON MONK

"But that doesn't really mean anything—the marks," I added quickly, watching the thunder roll in. "The marks don't change the spell. He's bound himself to me."

"Oh?"

"Yes. He's bound to my soul."

"Yet the moment I add my claim to you, the spell will be broken."

"What?"

"What?"

"What are you talking about?"

"Is that not why you came here this evening?"

"You can break it?"

"It's rudimentary demon-soul, three-ingredient hellwork, Reed Daughter. He claimed the power of wood, feather and sweat. When wood, feather, and sweat claim you instead, the spell will be broken."

"Claim me? Is that why Granny and Bertie did this?"

"I wouldn't guess to know their ultimate intentions, but the facts remain." He reached over and drew the controller off my knee as if expecting me to bite his hand.

"If I want the spell broken, all I have to do is let you claim me?"

He lifted the remote and pointed it at the screen. "Comedy, you say? With music?"

"Than."

He lowered the remote. "It is, I believe the quickest way to break the spell. Is that not why you allowed the other marks?"

"No, I was apologizing. This is what they demanded in payment. They could have pressed charges. Put me in jail."

"For a demon binding himself to your soul?" He *tsk*ed.

"For theft. I stole the Heartwood and Bertie's Feather."

"You stole the sweat of my brow too. Should I prosecute?"

"You could."

"I see no reason to engage in foolishness." He pressed the remote and the movie began, declaring the new Vista Vision High Fidelity over orchestral music. "Is it a stage play?"

"It's a movie from 1956."

"Ah. And there is the fool."

Danny Kaye was on screen in his jester suit singing about how life couldn't be better.

"About you claiming me," I said.

"Shh."

"You know I won't let that happen."

He thumbed up the volume.

"Than." I touched his arm.

He paused the movie and looked at me.

"I can't be claimed by a god. Can't be...beholden to any. As the Bridge to Ordinary, I must remain impartial. No god can rule me."

"I've read the laws. All of them. I am very aware of Ordinary's boundaries and your own."

"Right. So breaking the spell is out of the question. You can't claim me with a mark or blood or whatever. That's not happening."

"Must we settle this before we can watch the film?"

"I just...no. That's all. That's all I needed to say. We can watch."

He held my gaze, and two long fingers fished in the small breast pocket of his striped pajama shirt. When he withdrew his fingers, a small business card balanced between them.

I stared at the paper, which he wiggled at me until I took it.

It was heavy card stock, bone white with tasteful gray lettering. One word was precisely centered on the card, written in an elegant font.

Death

"You have a card?"

"I believe the fool is singing the plot to us." He turned back to the screen.

"Why do you have a card? No, wait. That's not what I want to know. Why are you giving your card to me?"

His thumb hovered over the pause button. "I am taking you on as a client."

"A client."

"Yes. As my client, my full offering of services are available to you. At your discretion."

"What does that mean? Is this some kind of *contract*?"

He sighed and pressed pause. "It means, Delaney Reed, that we agree we are friends. When a friend calls, when *you* call, I shall offer you my full abilities."

"So this isn't a claim?"

"Nothing so slight. This is a promise."

The air seemed just a little colder, all the shadows of the room deeper, all the lights sparking hard and bright.

Then he blinked and gestured with the remote. The world reset to normal mode. "Shall we observe?"

I nodded and settled back to watch the show. It was a good thing I'd seen it a couple dozen times. My thoughts were too scattered to follow the clever wordplay, wheeling between Ryder's declaration—

—*never marry her*—

—and Than's promise—

—*we agree we are friends*—

—I wasn't sure which one worried me more.

CHAPTER TWENTY

W<small>HEN THE MOVIE ENDED</small>, Than insisted on doing my nails. "Sleepovers require it."

My nails were now "Sugar Bunny" pink. I gleefully applied the polish to Than's nails telling him: "Twinsies. It's a sleepover thing."

Afterward, he bade me a goodnight and retreated into his bedroom, spiders scrabbling at the edges of the doorjamb before being thrust into the darkness. The door closed behind them with a quiet click.

Tired as I was, I didn't sleep, my thoughts returning again and again to the problems at hand: Xtelle and the never-ending chaos around her, Amy and the bond he'd forced on my soul, Mithra using Ryder as a puppet. And Ryder. Why hadn't he told me what Mithra was doing? Why did he think he had to fight the god alone?

Spud was up before dawn needing a bathroom break, so I took him for a walk, then left a note on the kitchen table thanking Than for the sleepover.

Spud came with me to the station, where I changed into the clothes I kept there.

"Long night?" Hatter asked as he squinted at the screen and hunt-and-pecked his way through a report.

"And long morning. What's the update on the High Tea Tide?"

"Starts at eleven, but folks are already out getting early bird deals on breakfast and hitting the beach. Did you know there's a petting zoo at the candy shop?"

"I did know."

He grunted and went back to pecking.

I filled my travel mug with coffee. "Myra's coordinating personnel," I said, even though he already knew that. "Come on, Spud, let's go."

Hatter looked up. "Where are you going?"

"Need to check on a demon. Don't get up. I'm not going to see him until I have Jean and Myra with me."

"They're already out there waiting for you."

I gave him a look.

"It's not that we don't trust you on your own around demons, Boss. We know you're completely capable of going hours, maybe even days without being possessed."

"Consider stowing the smart remarks. You have a yearly review coming up." I snapped my fingers, and Spud stopped nosing around in the garbage can and bounded my way.

"Wait," Hatter said. "I take it all back. We've seen you go whole minutes at a time without being possessed."

I lifted a finger in response and shut the door on his laughter.

THE MAGIC JAIL was out beyond the parking lot behind the station in an unimproved wooded area that sprawled across a few blocks. It didn't take very long to walk through the grass and weeds, then under a few trees, following the dirt path that wasn't visible to most people.

It was cool this morning, but the breeze still carried the softness of a summer that had been holding on extra long this year. Perfect weather for an outdoor event. Bertie had, once again, planned impeccably.

Myra and Jean were leaning against the front of the cruiser at the edge of the field where it gave way to thicker clumps of trees and viney undergrowth. My sisters had a box of Puffin Muffin pastries propped on the trunk.

Jean waved.

"Ladies," I said, as Spud bounded around Jean, whining and wriggling for scritches.

"How are you feeling today?" Myra asked.

"Good. How about you?"

"I'm okay. I spent most of the night going through the books. I haven't found a way to break the spell."

"I might have a bead on that." I dug around in the pastries and chose a chocolate glazed. Took a huge bite and moaned at the flaky, deep-fried, chocolate-covered goodness. I savored, then chewed and swallowed.

"Than says he can break it. Well, they can break it. With the marks," I held up each hand in turn, "and his card." I patted my back pocket.

Myra made a rewind gesture with her finger. "Back up. What card?"

I shoved more donut in my face and handed her the card.

"What does Hogan put in these?" I asked with my mouth full.

Jean grinned. "Amazing, right? He told me never to share the recipe. But it's butter and cayenne."

"Why does Than have a card?" Myra asked. "No, wait, I don't care about that. How can this break the spell?"

"He said that, to break the spell, the people connected to the elements used in it have to claim ownership of me in some way. So, the tattoo from the Wolfes," I held up my hand, "and the love pat from Bertie are their marks showing their claim. If Than marked me or claimed me, then the spell would break."

Myra turned the card back and forth, held it up to the light, and rubbed her thumb over the letters. "But he can't do that. You're the Bridge."

"Right. That card just means we're friends."

A passing seagull screeching out a give-me-the-french-fry call filled the long silence.

"But you're already friends," Jean pointed out. Spud found a pine cone the size of a fist and dropped it at her feet. She chucked it out into the field.

"He said if I call, *when* I call, he will offer his full services. As if I hired him or something."

Myra's eyebrows went up.

"I don't know what he meant by it either. That's all he would say. When I pressed, he got all godly and mysterious."

"Okay," Myra said. "Okay. That's...not bad." She gave me the card.

Jean swiped dirt off her hands, and petted Spud on the head instead of picking up the slobbery half-destroyed pine cone again. "How does a card help?"

Myra picked up half an apple fritter and broke off a piece of it. "The marks left by the Wolfes and Bertie act as protection against anyone wanting to use their power against Delaney."

"Than didn't use his power on me."

"I know. Friendship might be more like..."

"Adoption?" Jean grinned. "Did you just get a new deadly daddy, Delaney? Are we in-laws to Death? Because I'm so going to put that on my social media profile."

"He didn't adopt her," Myra said. "It's more like he's offering protection services."

"Ooooh," Jean cooed. "Delaney's got a bodyguard."

"Delaney doesn't need a bodyguard," I said. "But a spell breaker? That I can use." I tucked the card back in my pocket and started off toward the trees.

"Aren't you going to call him right now?" Jean asked, matching my stride.

"Not yet. Now that I know I can break this, I want to interrogate our prisoner."

"Poking demons isn't a good idea, Delaney," Jean said. "Unless it's for sexy fun times, right, Myra?"

"No comment." Myra finished off the fritter. She was ahead of me, working her way through the brush and trees.

Inside these woods, lay a specific kind of magic. The kind the gods who had first created this vacation space had decided would be warded and hidden and spelled up. A small building was built here.

Just big enough for two rooms—one outside the bars, and one, flexible in size due to the nature of the prisoners it had to hold, inside the bars.

Our magic prison. Our spelled jail. Our hinky clink.

One minute we were walking among the trees and ferns, and the next there was a small brick building in front of us. We were the Reed sisters. Protectors of the rule of law of this very special town. The only way this building ever revealed itself was when one of us was in front of it.

"There it is," Jean said. "I love how it just *shooshes* into view. How long has it been since anyone has used it?"

"Before Dad..." Myra winced and looked at each of us in turn.

"Before Dad left us." I squeezed her arm. "Bigfoot, I think, wasn't it?"

Jean grinned. "That's right. Midnight magic mushrooms with Odin. What a mess."

They'd thought it would be funny to film Bigfoot riding around town peeking into shop windows. Odin hadn't been caught, but Bigfoot had gone ahead with Odin's "Oscar-winning inspiration" and stolen a car for his joy ride.

Thank goodness he hadn't gotten any farther than the curb before he hit a trash can and passed out. That's where Dad had found him.

"Ready?" I walked up to the door.

They both nodded.

I pressed my palm on the door, and it opened for me. We stepped inside.

The fresh air and soft sound of wind chimes always surprised me. Just because it was a magical jail didn't mean it wasn't also a decent place.

From the outside, the building had no windows. But inside, the light came through high, wide windows that made the daylight look even sunnier.

The walls were brick. Across each brick was scrawled a mark or line—the unique magic and power set into the place.

Magic could be used here, outside the cell. But inside the cell was a magic-free zone.

The bricks closest to the jail cell, which took up the far corner of the room, had new marks carved into them. Marks put there by Myra, so that we would have something extra to hold demons.

The dragon pig had pulled all of the metal objects in the room into one pile and was perched on top of it like an eagle on its nest. I could make out several wire baskets, an antique fan, a slightly newer desk lamp, the base of two swivel chairs, all the silverware, including a giant novelty spoon that I didn't remember being stored here.

I walked over and scratched the dragon pig's head. "Hey, good job keeping an eye on him. Spud is outside. He misses you."

The dragon pig yawned, showing way too many sharp teeth, then stood. It looked over at Amy, then back at me.

"No, I got this. We got this. Go ahead."

The dragon pig hopped down off the pile, pulled the giant spoon out of it, then trotted toward the door, dragging the spoon along the ground. With a small poof of smoke, the dragon pig disappeared.

I turned to study our prisoner. He didn't look the least bit rumpled or inconvenienced.

"Delaney and all the other Reed sisters," he said. "How pleasant to finally see you again."

"We saw you yesterday, Amy." Jean positioned herself between Myra and me and the demon. "I'm surprised the dragon pig didn't eat you."

"Yes, well. We did have a long conversation. Not a big talker, that dragon. Has a bit of a temper, doesn't it?"

"Run me through your demands again," I said.

His eyebrows rose. "I already told you, in private, what I want."

"Refresh my memory in front of my sisters. We're all in this." I folded my arms over my chest. Jean and Myra crossed their arms too.

He glanced at Myra, then Jean. He seemed to make a decision and stepped back from the bars to pace, hands behind his back. "I am requesting you break the contract between the King of the Underworld and the Queen of the Underworld."

"And if we can't find a way to do that?"

"I will make you, your family, and your town suffer."

"How?"

"I am bound to your soul. Since I have a piece of you, I have leverage over you."

"You'd think, right? Okay, tell me. Do you want to stay in Ordinary?"

"Yes?"

"We have a contract you can sign that will allow you to stay here."

He stopped pacing and strolled up to the bars again. "So you have said."

"But?"

"But I have...inflicted myself upon you and your town."

"And?"

"And I do not expect you'll offer me citizenship out of the kindness of your heart." He scoffed.

Jean groaned. "Oh, you really don't know her, do you?"

"Between the King of the Underworld," Myra interrupted, "and the Queen of the Underworld. We aren't in the business of forcing those kinds of changes without full cooperation from at least one of the parties involved."

"If anyone in this world could manage such a feat, it would be the Reed sisters."

"Not the god of contracts?" she asked.

"He and I are not on speaking terms." Final. Angry. Oh, he did not like Mithra.

Join the club.

"You think pretty highly of us," Myra said.

"So does my nephew."

There was a beat of silence.

"What does Bathin have to do with this?" I asked.

"I've spoken to him. When he was forced out of Ordinary, he returned to my lands and told me about this town. He told me about each of you."

Bathin had possessed my soul for over a year. He probably had a lot to say.

"Well, let's just get this clear now," Myra said. "We can't break the contract, and we won't without permission from Xtelle or Vychoro. All this," she waved at me, at him, at the room, "is for nothing. Bad move on your part."

"I'll remain bound to Delaney until you come up with an answer. I have time."

It all hit me at once.

He said this was about breaking the contract, but the real reason was he loved Xtelle. He wanted to live in Ordinary to be near her. If he set us Reeds on an impossible quest to break an unbreakable contract, he'd be here in Ordinary with Xtelle forever. Since he was bound to my soul, theoretically, I wouldn't be able to throw him out either.

New plan.

"You have one way out of this," I said. "Just tell Xtelle you love her."

Jean and Myra startled. Right, I hadn't told them that part yet. Oops. "Tell her you want her to break the contract with the king so you can court her. Use small words and enunciate. Clear the air. Be mature. "

Gee, where had I just heard that advice?

He looked like I'd just popped his brain balloon.

Jean coughed to cover a laugh. Myra rubbed at the bridge of her nose and sighed loudly.

"Xtelle?" Myra demanded. "Him? He loves…her?"

"So he says." I pinned Amy with my gaze. "The problem you've got here is that you are assuming Xtelle wants what you think she wants. That's not your place. Xtelle can make up her own mind. If she wants to be bound to the king, she's going to stay bound."

"But if she just—"

"Stop. Just stop right there."

He shut his mouth. I walked closer, but didn't cross the line of symbols carved into the floor. I probably should have been mad, but at this point, I was only mildly annoyed.

"She makes her own decisions. Period. You need to tell her how you feel."

"I...can't." His expression was cool, but I felt the anguish in his words.

"Then we'll just leave you here for awhile to think about what you've done." I nodded to Jean. She strolled to the wooden stand with a large, flat-screen TV on it and wheeled it over to face the cell.

"What is this? Entertainment?"

Myra snagged the controller off the cart and flipped through channels until she found the one she wanted.

"No," he said.

"Yes," she said.

Amy pressed his back against the far wall. "You wouldn't."

"Think about your decisions. You have two options for getting out of here." I said. "Break the binding between us, or talk to Xtelle."

"But your soul..." he said.

"Just because you think you have me in a lock, don't forget that I have you in a lock." I gave him a toothy grin. "You're mine, Avnas, until I throw you out of town."

Myra turned up the TV. The sweet meowing and purring of tiny kitties got louder along with the little puppy yips and growls.

The cute animal channel was a delight.

"They're...so...fuzzy," he said weakly.

"Wait until they add the bunnies," Jean said. "Ooooh. And baby otters."

"Baby otters." We all swooned at the same time.

"You wouldn't."

"We already have," I said. "Make a decision, Amy, or it's cute animals for days."

He scowled at me, but when I opened the door for my sisters to leave and glanced back, he was staring at the screen, his expression a mix of horror and fascination.

It wasn't torture, but all those cute fluffy creatures were bound to get annoying eventually.

I stepped out and shut the door. The building disappeared in a *shoosh,* leaving behind nothing but scrub brush and trees.

A crow called out. Another answered. We grinned wildly at each other, then burst out laughing.

"Did you see his face?" Jean asked.

"Baby otters was brilliant." I high-fived her.

We headed back to where the cruiser was parked.

"Why didn't you just call Than and break the binding?" Myra asked.

I shrugged. "I think Amy actually has feelings for Xtelle, and he didn't think I'd let him into Ordinary. He needs some time to decide what's most important to him. Love or power. I hope it's love."

"Aw," Jean said, slugging me gently on the arm. "You old softy."

"I know he's a demon," I said. "I know he's here in a breach of Ordinary's rules. But so was Bathin. And look how that turned out."

Myra made a little thoughtful sound. "Not every demon is like Bathin. Amy used you to steal things and cast a spell. I don't like that."

"Oh, I don't like it either. But I plan to use it to my advantage."

"How?" Myra asked.

"I don't know yet. I just have a gut feeling it's good to have the counselor to the King of the Underworld on our side, if push comes to shove."

Jean paused, and we stopped and looked at her.

"Jean?"

"No," she said, "I'm okay. It was just a...like an echo. Not a doom twinge, but almost."

"About the King of the Underworld?" I asked.

"I think so. I think that's going to be a problem."

I took a deep breath and blew it out. "So there's a reason demons close to him are suddenly looking for a place to hide out."

Myra nodded. "War?"

"War," I agreed.

"Great," Jean said. "Just what we need. Ryder hasn't even asked—"

"—for a raise," Myra said, too suddenly and too loudly.

"What are you talking about? Why are you being weird?"

"It's not weird," Myra said. "He's our longest standing reserve officer."

"We don't pay any of our reserve officers. It's not in the budget."

"We were going to talk to you about that," Myra said. "Right, Jean? About Ryder asking her for a raise?"

"Yes." She nodded. "That is what we were going to talk to you about. Money."

They were lying. I just didn't know what they were lying about. "Is this about Mithra?"

Myra tipped her head. "You mean how he's got Ryder going every damn direction all the time?"

"Wait. You knew about that?"

"I figured it out."

"And you didn't want to let me in on it?"

"He didn't tell you?" Jean frowned. "Why didn't he tell you?"

"Maybe he was going to get around to it," I said with confidence I didn't feel.

Myra stopped. "Are you okay? Are the two of you okay?"

"We're good. It's just, you know. Relationship stuff."

"Uh-huh."

"And now I'm changing the subject. Is everything in place for the High Tea Tide? Is Bertie bossing everyone around?"

"When isn't she?" Jean groused.

I grinned. "Let's not make the Valkyrie angry, ladies. This High Tea Tide isn't going to happen without us."

"I just remembered. Hogan said he needs my help at the bakery," Jean said.

"Nope." Myra pushed her ahead of us. "Don't make me frog walk you to your volunteer duties."

"No, really." Jean twisted so she could see us over her shoulder. "He super needs help, and since you two are available for traffic flow I should just—"

I stumbled as sharp pain knifed through my chest. I caught myself before falling to my knees, and just stood there, palm flat on my breast bone, breathing hard.

"Delaney?" Myra grabbed my elbow.

"What?" Jean's blue, blue eyes were suddenly too wide. "What's wrong?"

My heart drummed. Hard. I knew that hook-in-the-bone, that tug. There was a god in Ordinary. Not on vacation. A god here to do business.

CHAPTER TWENTY-ONE

"GOD," I said. "Here. Full power."

"Where?" Jean scanned the forest.

"Station, I think." I had my breath back now, the initial pain fading. I waved that way. "Yeah, station."

We jogged to the cruiser, where Spud and the dragon pig were snorting and sniffing their way around a bush.

Myra opened the doors. I called for Spud and the dragon pig and was the last one to jump into the cruiser.

"Who?" Myra said, flooring it, throwing me back in the seat.

"Mithra."

"Well, shit," she said.

We made the station in seconds. Before she'd even put the car into park, I was out and striding toward the front door.

I strong-armed it. "What are you doing here?" I demanded.

Ryder stood to the right, arms crossed, squared off against the god. He looked gorgeously furious, hard muscles locked across his shoulders, bulging along his forearms, his jaw clenched.

I could feel the heat of his anger, the force of his strength.

My love for this man shot through me like a bolt of summer lightning.

He slid a look my way. There was heat in his eyes—something more than anger. Something deeper that licked with passion and need.

In that second, he and I were together. Connected in a way we hadn't been for what felt like months. Forget gods. Forget demons. This—he and I joined—was all the power in the world.

"Ah, here we are now," Mithra said. "The Reed sisters. I only need to speak to you, Delaney. The others are dismissed."

"No," Myra said. "You get her, you get all of us."

I nodded slightly at Ryder, unable to take my eyes off him. *Are we okay?*

His answer was a quickly quirked eyebrow. *Yes.*

"What are you doing here, Mithra?" I asked again, finally turning my attention to him.

"A god can enter Ordinary on business. I have business."

"Make it fast. We have work to do."

A flash of anger rolled across his face—a burn so fast, it devoured itself before it could catch.

"I demand you recognize my connection to Ordinary through the Warden Ryder Bailey. I demand you recognize that that connection gives me the right to rule over and enforce all contracts in this land."

"No."

"I am a god, Delaney Reed," he went on as if I hadn't spoken. "Even you must bow to me."

"Not here. We have rules about gods coming here and throwing around power. This is a vacation town. Gods vacation here. They want to do so peacefully. So," I repeated, "no."

"Perhaps this contract, and the rule I have over it, will change your mind." He held up a document I was very familiar with. A wedding license.

274

Everything in me went still for a moment. All I could hear was the rushing in my ears.

How dare he dangle that in front of me? Threat or bribe, I didn't care. He had no say over my future.

I took three steps forward and grabbed the paper out of his hand.

"Delaney," Ryder said. "Don't—"

I ripped the paper in half.

Mithra blinked. Stunned.

Ryder rubbed his hand over his mouth. I glared at him. "Don't what?" I asked.

He shook his head, his hand still over his mouth. From the curve of his eyes, I was pretty sure he was trying to stifle a laugh. "Nothing. Carry on."

"You have no authority in my town, Mithra." I waved the shredded paper at him. "The contracts we enact are legally solid and morally clear. I can't say the same about your motivations for trapping Ryder into serving you, or for trying to force me into handing Ordinary over to you. Yes, he's a Warden. But this land was made by the will of thousands of gods. This land follows the laws they set in place. You can join us, but you can't own us."

"Do not put yourself above me. You are nothing. Demons bind your broken soul. The man you're living with won't even marry you—yes, I know you were spying on me last night."

"He what?" Jean said.

"Wait," Myra said.

But it was Ryder who took over. "You heard Delaney. She told you to leave. Leave."

Mithra just scoffed. "How pitiful you are. You have no control over me."

"Maybe not," I said striding up to stand in front of Ryder. "But I do. Business hours are over. Go away."

"Little girl, why would anyone listen to you?" That smug smile. That sweaty superiority. I wanted to punch him in the face.

The Reeds were an old family. Old blood chosen by gods long, long ago. We were not gods. Not even close. But we were the protectors of this precious land, this place of refuge for deities and supernaturals and all those who called this little town home.

I could not fight a god whose reach extended beyond universes.

But I could hold the line of my home for those I loved, for the community I was humbled to serve and grateful to keep safe.

"I am this land," I said, setting roots into the thick volcanic basalt. This land, my feet, the trees and wind and storming ocean, my body, the arc of sky, sun, and shatter of stars beyond, my head. "I am the Bridge by which deities rest their burden and breathe in peace.

"I am love. I am strength. Chosen and bound to serve all who gather to create this town, who make this our home.

"I am Delaney Reed."

I called on the power of Ordinary, and it answered with a roar.

Gold and green and branch and bloom, twisted forests, great growling crash of toothy foam and wave, hurricane wind carving mountains to blacken bone. The voice, the shout, the song of every heartbeat, every soul in this beautiful town, rose, up, up, up.

They were my breath, my pulse, a thousand spinning threads of beautiful color and hue and song. These beating hearts a power, a tapestry of life, a magic unbreakable.

My people.

My town.

"You will leave Ordinary now, God," I said, the power of Ordinary in every word, the magic and song and lives sparking lightning through my nerves, burning fire over my skin.

This was my power. This was our power.

This was Ordinary.

Mithra's eyes widened.

"Leave." I pointed at the god.

Mithra fizzed like an out of focus picture. Fire caught at the edges of him, red to orange to burning yellow and scorching hot white as if he were plummeting through the atmosphere too fast to survive.

And he was gone.

I exhaled hard, the push of power and magic and love and lives and *sound, sound, sound* gushed out with that breath. I was a tap suddenly turned off, power draining from me quickly— through my fingertips, through my feet, through my pores—back into the land, into the living, into the thrum of blessings that bound this place to me.

I blinked, tingly and itchy, and the world toppled sideways.

"Hey, now." Warm arms, strong arms, wrapped me, steadied the world. The scent of Ryder's skin filled my breathing. I leaned into him. Just for a moment. Just while I caught my breath.

"I've never seen you do that," he said, wonder in his words.

"First time." My voice had gone to scratch. "Saw Dad do it. Twice. It's. A thing. Bridge thing. We can make gods go. Leave. Bye-bye. With...power thing."

"Let's get you sitting down, love. Here we go. Just like this."

By the time I lined up my brain cells to tell him I was fine, I was already sitting in my desk chair, Ryder and Jean and Myra hovering around me.

"Water?" Myra passed it to me.

I was thirsty, a desert, so I drank it down in one go.

"Are you okay?" Jean asked. She chewed at her thumbnail, which I hadn't seen her do in years.

"Good." I cleared my throat. "I'm better. Good. My brain was kind of...offline for a second."

"Are you sure?" Myra's brows were tucked down, her eyes sharp. She looked like it took everything she had to keep from checking my forehead and packing me in bubble wrap.

"I am. I really am okay. Ready to get to work. Um, High Tea Tide. Go team."

"You should take her home," Jean told Ryder.

"Way ahead of you." He had his keys in his hand and was giving me that look.

"Wait," I said. "You can all actually hear me, right?"

"Yes," he said. "You want to work. We've all decided you should be home, resting."

"But I said I'm good," I whined.

"Delaney, you just shoved a god out of Ordinary for the first time." Jean bent a little so she could stare me right in the eyes. "That was…wow." Her smile was crazy big.

"Just part of my job."

"Okay, but it was still wow, and now you should go home."

"You don't send me home when I write speeding tickets."

Jean scoffed and stood, hands on her hips.

Myra handed me a cup of tea. "Let's agree those are two different kinds of jobs," Myra said. "Since you've never thrown a god out of town before, we want you to go home and take a minute to regroup."

"I threw Crow out a couple years ago."

"Yeah, but Crow loves you," Ryder said. "He left when you asked."

Myra just pointed at Ryder while she stared at me.

"I'm fine. I really am. Bertie's event—"

"Don't worry about the event," Jean said. "I'll cover your shift. And yes, this is probably the one and only time I'm actually going to volunteer to help Bertie and not try to get out of it. So you'd better not waste it."

"I still think—"

"Delaney! Delaney! Pay attention to me!"

Xtelle pushed her way through the front door and trotted across the lobby until she was right next to my desk. On her heels was a very familiar goat.

"Ponies don't talk."

Xtelle blew her rubbery lips. "Everyone here knows I'm more than a pony. I am a magnificent unicorn!"

"You certainly are, my sweet," Pan said.

"Goats don't talk either," I said.

He lifted one hoof and made a little locking motion in front of his mouth.

"What do you want, Xtelle?" I asked.

"Oh, now I can talk? *Now?*"

"Yep. I'm giving you ten seconds."

She flattened her ears and showed a little teeth, but then she took a deep breath.

"You can't keep Amy in jail because Vychi will be looking for him and when he finds him and finds him trapped he will attack Ordinary with legions of demon hordes and even if you think you can beat them I will remind you that Vychoro will not care if there are human casualties especially those outside of Ordinary like that person at the casino you yattered on and on to about his child and college and *boring* I do not like children with their sticky hands and tiny screechy voices and they kick and they bite and a petting zoo for children is the *worst* thing I have ever experienced in my life and I have not one but two houses in hell."

Pan nodded along and scooted closer to her, his side against her side. He bleated a little *baa* that sounded like "babe."

She made her eyes wider and stuck out her lower lip, which made her look ridiculous, and leaned into him.

"Vicki?" I asked, somehow stuck on that name.

"Vychi. Vychoro, the king of course." Xtelle sniffed.

"Got it. Well, whatever the demon king does won't change how I do my job. Avnas is in jail. That's what happens when you break the law in Ordinary."

"Oh," she said. "Then don't worry. I thought you actually cared about human life."

"Xtelle."

"I thought that person at the casino was someone you liked. Someone you thought should remain alive."

"Xtelle," I warned.

"But if you're fine with The Brute tearing the world apart at the seams and killing everyone you care for, then by all means, keep Avnas behind bars."

"Who's The Brute?" Jean asked.

"Her husband," Myra said.

"King of the Underworld," Jean said. "Why are you still married to him?"

Xtelle's mouth fell open, and her eyes dashed between Jean and me. "Because...you wouldn't...he's very...I can't... well, it's not like I *wouldn't*...it's just. Complicated."

"Is it?" I was going with my gut here.

"What?"

"Is it complicated?"

Her ears flattened half way. "It always has been."

"You know you have a home here in Ordinary, Xtelle, if you follow the rules."

She held very, very still. Those pony eyes suddenly looked much more human, or maybe just demon. Vulnerable. Hopeful. "Do I?"

"Yes. You signed the contract. Our contracts are good."

Pan moved closer to her again, leaning his shoulder against hers. I thought I heard him whisper: "I told you so."

"Well," she said. "Well. I see."

Ryder clapped his hands once. "Great. Now that we've got that figured out, Delaney is going home for the rest of the day."

"Delaney isn't going home," I said.

He frowned.

"Xtelle." I stood and waved away everyone's helping hands. "You need to come with me."

"I don't want—"

"This way." I took it easy for the first few steps, but it was immediately clear I really was feeling fine.

Ryder fell into step next to me. Myra was on her phone, and all I caught was, "now" and "the station." I didn't know who she was calling, but that didn't matter. What mattered was taking control of this demon situation once and for all.

"But where? Where, Delaney?" Xtelle shouted as she trotted along beside me, the goat attached to her like Velcro. "Where are you taking me?"

"To the scene of the crime."

"Which one—I was never even with that monkey!"

I let that go, because there was only so much I could handle at one time. And right now, I was going to handle the demon who had bound himself to my soul.

CHAPTER TWENTY-TWO

"THIS ISN'T A FOREST," Xtelle grumped.

"Enough of one," I said.

"There's something more here, isn't there?"

"Yep." I kept walking through the grass and underbrush. Ryder walked with me and so did Jean. Myra had stayed behind.

"What is it?" Xtelle prodded. "Is it a secret? It's magic of some kind. I know it has to be magic."

"It's magic." I took one more step, and the building appeared.

Xtelle stopped so quickly, she left little skid marks in the dirt. "No. I've followed almost all the rules. I demand a lawyer. The cute one on TV."

"I'm not locking you away. But you are coming with me." I pointed at her, and took another step, passing right through the door and into the jail.

Xtelle passed through the door with me, caught by my command. I hadn't expected Pan to come with her, but he must have been standing close enough, he'd ridden on her coat tails.

Pan whistled. "I've always wondered about the inside of this place."

Jean opened the door for Ryder, whose gaze immediately found me, then took in the demon behind bars, the pile of metal the dragon pig had left behind, and the screen of baby ducks that Jean turned off. He walked to one side of the room, closer to the cell than the door and waited.

"My Queen," Avnas said, startled.

"Avnas," she replied, bored.

"Some demon knight," Pan snorted. It had a weird musical quality to it, like he had a horn stuck up his nose. "Not impressed."

"Delightful," Avnas said through his teeth. "The goat who thinks he's a god."

"That is so enough of that." I pointed at Pan. "You. Be quiet, or I'll throw you out." I pointed at Xtelle. "You, listen. Avnas, now is your chance to talk."

Everyone was quiet, except for Ryder who brought me a wooden chair and positioned it so I could sit and keep them all in my sight. Not that I really had to guard them. It was impossible for anyone to leave without Reed permission and help.

"Talk," I repeated.

"I do not know what you expect me to say to you," Avnas said stiffly, shoulders back, head held high.

"Not to me," I said. "To her."

He glanced at Xtelle, but his facade did not crack.

"Tell her what you told me. Tell her what you want. Tell her why you really bound yourself to my soul. Tell her what your real goal is."

"My current goal is to be out from behind these bars and to never see another adorable baby mammal chase its tail again."

"Here's something you may not have figured out about Ordinary," I said conversationally. "Truth works here. It's a good thing. Conversation works here. Tell her real things, Avnas."

Ryder stood behind my chair, and even though he wasn't touching me, it was good to feel his strength at my back.

"You have one chance at this," I said. "Why not try the truth this time?"

His eyes cut to Xtelle, than back to me. They were steel hard. "Or what?"

"No or. Whether you talk to her or not, I'm going to break your hold on me. Close your mouth, because whatever you're about to say, you're wrong. The hell spell you put on me had a few flaws that worked to my advantage." I leaned forward, elbows on my thighs, hands loose between my knees.

I had all the power here, he just hadn't figured it out yet.

"Let me tell you a truth," I said. "Trying to use my friends against me in that spell was a fatal miscalculation."

"You underestimate my power." Fire flickered gold in his eyes and burned there just under his skin.

Even though he was on that side of the bars, and I was on this side, we were still bound. I felt the connection, tight behind my breastbone, behind my lungs. Somewhere deep, my soul fluttered and stretched, trying to pull free, like lungs bound too tightly and unable to draw air.

"With one flick of my finger, I can crush you, Delaney Reed. Crush you with the very rules and magic by which you live."

"Yeah," I said. "I don't think so."

"Shall we try?" he asked, still angry, but softer, as if this were intimate, just between the two of us. As if Xtelle, Pan, Jean, and Ryder weren't in the room. As if there weren't bars and layers upon layers of magic separating us.

"You can't use magic in that cell. That's kind of the point. So. Last chance, Avnas. Tell her the truth."

His eyes narrowed. He raised his hand. He was so going to do magic no matter what I told him. Idiot.

"Delaney," Myra's voice was a little breathy, as if she'd been jogging. "I have someone to see you."

My sister: right place, right time.

"Good afternoon, Reed Daughter," Than's voice was as dry as rice paper.

My sister: right place, right time, and right equipment.

Which in this case was a god wearing an eye-watering pink shirt polka-dotted with neon-green olives.

Jean, who had moved over by them, said, "Nice nails."

"Sleepover," Than said.

"Sweet." Jean made a fist. Than considered her fist a moment, then bumped it with his own before moving to stand next to me, facing the demon.

Amy's hand didn't lower, but the tension in his muscles shifted. He looked more like he was getting ready to retreat instead of attack.

"Avnas," Than intoned. "It has been some time."

Yes, he was on vacation. But even so, all the gods carried residue of their power, the weight of it always at the ready to use in an instant, if they so desired.

"What's the plan here?" Myra asked. "Are you setting him free?"

"I'm giving him his one chance."

"You told me I have three chances," Xtelle piped up. We all looked at her, and she recoiled, squishing her head back, wrinkling up her neck. "Well, you did."

"You get three chances because you signed the contract," I said. "You are a citizen, and there's a learning curve to living among mortals and gods."

She cut her eyes to Avnas.

"He forced his way into town, attacked me, took part of my soul, stole precious items, meddled with my memories, and cast a spell to use as leverage over me to get his way."

She shook her head like she didn't understand the difference.

"He's not following the rules," I said.

"That's all that matters to you, isn't it?" she asked.

"Yes." My answer was swift. Rules really weren't the only thing I cared about, but for right now, she and Avnas needed to know I would absolutely die on this hill.

"But lucky for all of us, I'm going to simplify things." I reached into my back pocket and pulled out Than's calling card.

"Than?"

"Yes, Delaney?"

"I would like to hire you."

"I see. When?"

"Are you free now?"

Avnas had gone a strange gray-green color, his face glistened with flop sweat.

"I am," Than said. "Shall we agree upon the conditions and terms previously settled?"

"Yes." I rolled up my sleeves and turned my hands so Avnas could get a gander at the tattoo and knife wound. "Should I call for backup?" I jiggled my hands.

Avnas was breathing hard now, his jaw locked, his nostrils flared. He looked like a man preparing to step off a plank into an awful lot of alligators below.

"I don't believe that will be necessary," Than said.

Good, because I didn't know how I was going to fit the entire Wolfe clan in the building, and I didn't want to deal with the years of hard time Bertie would put me through for interrupting her event.

"Shall I?" Than asked.

"What?" Avnas and Xtelle said in unison. The demons locked eyes.

Before Than could do whatever it was to break the spell, I held up a finger.

Than stilled, though he hadn't done anything except fold his hands together.

Avnas must have known the jig was up. He'd been outsmarted, outmaneuvered. I had the Wolfes behind me. I had the Valkyrie on my side. They'd marked me as their own.

And here was Than, at my call, his services at my discretion.

All three ingredients of his binding were about to be corrupted. As soon as Than threw his weight behind my request—to break the spell, of course—Avnas was all out of leverage.

"I came here for you," Avnas said in a rush.

Xtelle looked over her shoulder, at each corner of the room, at Pan, who shook his head in short jerks, and finally back to Avnas.

"Me," she said. "You came here, to Ordinary. For me."

Yeah, she did not believe him.

"Let me guess," she went on, gathering steam. "The Brute wants to know what I'm doing and wants you to spy on me. Vychi wants to know my every move so he can kill me all the way this time? Is that what this," she waved her hoof, "is? Are you trying to take me down so The Brute can rule without me in the way?"

I could see it, Amy's struggle. It was all over his face. Also, we were still connected so I could *feel* his frustration, his need to tell her the truth, and his utter survival instinct to lie, lie, *lie*.

"Tell her," I said, gently. "What do you have to lose?"

Than lifted one hand, and Avnas rocked back a step. All Than did was scratch at the side of his nose. Still, the threat was clear: Avnas could come clean, or he could go away.

I saw the moment he made his decision. He straightened, tugged on the sleeves of the suit he was wearing—a very nice black with a deep blue shirt that showed the width of shoulders and chest.

For a moment, for a flash, I felt something…good in him. An intent. A desire for change, to make his life different.

To *be* different. Maybe, to be who he hoped he could be.

I'd felt the same thing in Bathin when he'd possessed my soul. When I looked back on it, I thought that was why I had never fought him as hard as I could have. Why I'd given him time to figure things out—himself, this town, and yes, his love for my sister.

Maybe that was clouding my decisions now. Maybe I was thinking it had worked out okay with one demon, it will work out the same for this demon.

Maybe Avnas was nothing but evil, a spy, a foe. Hungry for the kill.

But being a Bridge to Ordinary gave me insight many

others didn't have. I could *feel* the basic nature of people. I knew what was a danger to my town, to all those within it.

My gut told me Amy might be dangerous—of course he was dangerous—but he was not the kind of danger that would tear my town apart.

"Xtelle," Avnas said, suddenly all leading man on the silver screen. "I came to Ordinary for you."

"To kidnap me? Well, you're about to be disappointed, buddy."

"No, I didn't come here to spy on you or kidnap you or report back to the king. If I had my way, I would never return to him."

Pan snorted, a very musical *bullshit* in the middle of it.

Avnas turned, as if he had just noticed the goat in the room. "You have something to say, Goat?"

Pan puffed up his chest. I swear his horns got bigger. "Avnas. You are some kind of fool coming here and trying to hurt Delaney."

Than cleared his throat and studied the back of his Sugar Bunny nails.

Avnas looked between the goat and the guy in the olive-covered shirt.

"The place is crawling with gods," Pan went on, pushing himself in front of Xtelle, getting closer to the bars of the cell. "We don't like it when our vacations are interrupted by scheming, self-serving, two-faced jackasses."

Xtelle cooed dreamily.

"What was that?" Avnas asked.

"What?" she asked.

"You sighed. Like you like him. You don't...you couldn't...he's a god in goat clothing!"

"And I'm a unicorn in pony clothing."

"Demon," Myra and I said at the same time, but Xtelle was on a roll.

"Are you going to report that to Vychi too? That I've finally let my unicorn fly free? That I'm living upworld, happier on four hooves than I ever was downworld on eighteen tentacles?"

"I'm not telling him anything," Avnas shouted. "I don't belong to him anymore. I've broken my contract. I've turned against him. I've betrayed him. And I've come here. For you. I've followed you because thinking of an existence without you is..." He stopped suddenly, as if his own words had finally caught up to him.

"What?" Xtelle asked, confused. "What *exactly* are you saying to me, Avnas?"

But he pressed his lips together and stared straight ahead.

"Than," I said.

"Yes, Delaney?"

"I'd like to hire you to break the spell Avnas cast. The one where he tried to use the people who care about me against me. I'd like you to break the part of it where he used the sweat of your brow against me. Can you do that without using your god power?"

"Yes, I can."

Than lifted his hand. This time Avnas' head jerked up and he stumbled backward. Than didn't snap his fingers or wave his hand. He just crooked one finger in a "come here" motion.

Avnas didn't move, but a light mist, softer than smoke, drifted away from the middle of his chest.

My own chest was warm, then hot, like I was standing in full August sunlight instead of inside an invisible building in an untended forest.

The magic in the building responded to the magic Than wielded. Symbols on the walls, ceiling, floors, and window glowed softly yellow and blue. They were soothing colors, sand and sky colors, beach colors. Than held his hand out toward me.

I had no idea what I was supposed to do.

"Um?"

"The card, Reed Daughter."

"Right." I dropped the card onto his palm.

He reached into his pocket and withdrew a little metal hole puncher, then snapped a hole in the card.

The magic in the room snuffed out with a sweet little chiming sound, like someone had triggered a shop door bell.

"Thank you," Than said with absolutely no inflection. He offered me the card between his fingers. "Come again."

I blinked. Was that a joke? Had he just made a joke?

"I have information," Avnas said in a panic, "on the king of hell and his plans to attack Ordinary. And information on his son."

"Bathin?" Myra asked.

"No. Well, yes, I have information on the eldest, but I'm speaking about his other son, Goap."

"Let me guess," I said. "He wants to come to Ordinary, too, and has decided getting a piece of my soul is the best way to do it instead of just showing up and signing the damn contract. Why is this so hard for demons to understand? We have a contract you can sign. We've been saying this for decades. Myra probably has one in her pocket right now."

Myra tapped her jacket pocket. Ryder, who had been quiet through all this, snorted a laugh.

"Demons don't believe anyone is telling the truth," Ryder said.

"We do here!" I said.

"I have information on the second son in line for the throne," Avnas said, once again ignoring the contract he could sign.

I threw my hands up in frustration.

"If Bathin is killed," Avnas said, "or if the king steps down —which will be never— "

"Never," Xtelle agreed.

"—Goap will take the throne. The right information will make it much easier to kill the King of the Underworld. Done quickly, and without Goap's knowing, Bathin would become king."

I looked at Myra. She just shrugged like it was news to her.

None of this had anything to do with me. It did, however, have something to do with Ordinary, since members of the Underworld's royal family were hiding out here.

"I'm not going to kill the King of the Underworld," I said. "If that's what you're hinting at, you can just stop right now."

He frowned. "He will bring war to your border."

"If he does, we'll deal with it. Ordinary does not involve itself in the matters of demons, unless said demons are residents of our town. You still haven't told Xtelle why you're here. If you want to stay in Ordinary, tell her everything."

"If I want...you'd let me stay?"

Jean groaned a little. "Wow. You really weren't listening were you?"

"If," I said, "you sign the contract and tell Xtelle the whole truth, then yes."

"Whole truth?" Xtelle turned to face me, her big round butt toward the cell. "What did he say about me? Because if he's talking about the donkey and the pudding factory, I was not there."

I ignored her. "Stop stalling, Amy, or I'm throwing you out."

I crossed my arms over my chest. So did Jean, Myra, Ryder, and Than. I had to bite the inside of my cheek not to laugh. Avnas was totally getting Ordinary's version of the Care Bare Stare.

Amy cleared his throat and squared his shoulders. "My Queen." He bowed, and you better believe she trotted a sharp circle to face him.

"This is the whole truth. I came to Ordinary to leverage Delaney Reed's soul. For you."

She lifted her nose and looked down it. "I don't want her soul. It's so...sticky and righteous."

He shot me a look. I just shook my head and pointed at Xtelle.

"There's more," he croaked. "I wanted, still want, the contract between you and the King of the Underworld to be broken. But I also...I also care...of course, you understand

I've been a part of your court for many years, how could I not? Care. For you."

He looked like he was about to pass out. His voice had gone all thready and his breathing was choppy.

Did demons have panic attacks? I was pretty sure demons didn't have panic attacks.

"You care." Xtelle strolled forward, homing in on him like an apex predator. "Why?" Her eyes were narrowed, and her nostrils flared. If she'd been in human form, she'd have had a fist cocked and ready to swing.

"Because...I...you...because you are...everything. I lo... long to see you free. From him. Your...um...fire burns bright. And you should choose...find...decide the lov...level of...life. Yes, the life of happiness you seek."

Worst speech ever.

But somehow, Xtelle was impressed.

"My fire burns bright?" she cooed. "How...poetic, Avnas. I've never seen this side of you." She batted her long eyelashes, and bent her knee so her hips cocked.

Pan decided to push his way into the conversation, crowding the space between them. "Poetic for someone stuck behind bars and ordered to tell the truth a dozen times before he got...poetic. That little monologue was straight from the heart, I'm sure."

"Demons don't have hearts," Avnas and Xtelle said automatically.

Xtelle giggled and dipped her head coyly, looking up at Avnas through her eyelashes.

Avnas smiled, and it was a wicked, handsome thing.

Pan narrowed his goat eyes and lifted his head into pre-ramming position.

Oh, dear gods. A farmyard love triangle was the last thing I needed to deal with.

"No ramming the cell," I said.

Pan didn't step back, but he rocked so all his weight was on his haunches. "I wasn't going to ram the cell. I was going to ram him."

"No ramming at all," I ordered.

He grumbled, but lowered his head and squished up even closer to Xtelle. But she had, amazingly, forgotten him for the moment.

"You were forcing Delaney to break the contract between the king and I?" Xtelle asked, in that flirty voice that made Pan's ears flatten and his lip curl. "How very *forward* of you."

"I was going to do it behind your back," he said with a dirty chuckle.

She giggled louder. "Oh, *you.*"

"But," I interrupted, "that's not happening because no one gets to make decisions for how you want to live your life or who you want to spend it with. Xtelle. Xtelle, are you listening to me?"

"What?" she murmured. "Is someone talking?"

I tapped her rump. "I'm not breaking the contract for you."

"What?" She finally twisted to look at me over her shoulder. "Don't you have a pudding factory to de-mule? Why are you bothering me?"

"No one is breaking the contract between you and Vychoro."

She scoffed. "I know that. Why even bring it up?"

I closed my eyes for a second and indulged in the image of taping her mouth shut with one of those pallet-wrapping machines.

"Avnas was trying to force Delaney to break it," Myra said. "That's why he's in jail."

She swung her head, stared at Myra for a second then lifted a hoof and somehow snapped, like she had fingers. "There."

She hadn't done magic. I would have known if it was magic. But she had done something…supernatural. Something tied to her. Something tied to the Underworld.

Thunder crashed so hard the entire building shook. The rumble rattled bricks and spells. The floor shivered and rolled with an earthquake shimmy.

A whiskey-hot wind whipped through the room, and a high, warbling voice called out, "Doom! Doom!"

Before I could tell anyone to dive for cover, it was over.

The wind dropped, the voice silenced, the floor settled, and the thunder faded, faded, and was gone.

"Everyone okay?" I asked. I got nods all around, except for Than who just yawned.

Pan had taken the brief distraction to put his goat arm around Xtelle's neck. It was probably supposed to be comforting or protective, but it just looked awkward.

"What was that?" I asked Xtelle.

"Oh, I just broke the contract between the king and myself. I am a queen without a realm. Woe." She batted her eyelashes at Avnas again, but leaned her head on Pan. "Who shall protect me now?"

"You broke the contract with a snap of your fingers?"

"Yes?"

"You could have done that at any time?" I went on doggedly.

"Of course."

"Then why didn't..." But I didn't finish the question.

She wasn't paying attention to me anyway. Avnas was glaring at Pan, his eyes burning with jealousy. Xtelle was eating that up like whatever it was demons prefer to eat, which I was beginning to think might be pudding and donkeys.

"The thunder, earthquake, and doom warning?" Myra asked.

"I'm sure it's nothing," Xtelle said breezily. "Woe to me. All alone. A queen without a country." She shifted closer to Pan while throwing sideways glances at Avnas to make sure he was catching the act.

"Delaney Reed," Avnas said, looking away from Xtelle with some difficulty. "I have done as you required. I told her the whole truth. And now, I'd like to sign that contract."

Myra, of course, really did have a copy of the contract in

her pocket. She raised an eyebrow in question. I rolled my eyes, but nodded.

She clicked a pen and took both over to the demon, careful not to step on or interrupt any of the magic symbols, though I knew a simple touch couldn't change them or their effectiveness. They were stronger than that, deeper than that. Fused to the foundation of Ordinary's creation.

Avnas scanned the contract quickly. "Really? This is the contract you signed?" he asked Xtelle.

"I found it to be adequate," she sniffed.

"It's...more than adequate. It is very thorough." He shot me a look that pinged off my bored expression to Myra. "I'm impressed."

"Sign it and live by it. After all this, you only get two chances while you're acclimating to Ordinary instead of three. And if you so much as breathe on a soul while you're here, you are out on your ass," Myra said with a bright smile.

His gaze lifted to Than and waited.

"Yes?" Than asked.

"I offer you my apology."

"I'll consider accepting it."

The temperature dropped. The magic in the room didn't flare so much as deepen.

Avnas bent the contract so it was stiff in his hand, and signed on the dotted line.

I could feel it, that rush of heat that stung my lungs. It had only happened twice before. When Bathin signed the contract, and just the other day, when Xtelle did the same.

There was now, officially, another demon in Ordinary.

Gods help us all.

He passed the sheets of paper through the bars to Myra. She read through them, then handed them to me to do the same. It all seemed to be in order.

"All right," I said. "You are now a citizen of Ordinary, and as such, you must follow the rules, both mundane and supernatural."

"I will," he said, staring straight at Xtelle, like he was repeating wedding vows.

"You understand you can't bind anyone's soul. Can't even touch one?" I asked.

"I do."

"I'm going to hold you to that," I said.

He finally looked away from Xtelle. "I wouldn't expect anything less of you, Delaney."

Weirdly, it sounded like gratitude. Like *thank you.*

Myra shot me one more "Are you sure" look, and I nodded. Anyone was welcome in Ordinary if they followed the rules. Even love-sick demons who were desperate and full of threats, but who had otherwise not done any of the things he had threatened he was capable of doing.

I didn't think Avnas was a good guy or a bad guy. I thought he was going to prove, over the next few months, if he could live in Ordinary. If he could thrive here. We had had just as many people leave the place as those who came to stay.

A vacation town for gods, which held to strict rules, wasn't everyone's idea of bliss.

I placed my hand on the bars. There was no lock, because this was a place built solid, with power and magic and will. My palm vibrated with the power of this place, a soothing sort of pinging, of knowing, like glass ringing in sympathy with a bell.

"You can go," I said.

Just like that, the bars were gone. All of them. And while the magic symbols were still visible, they were fading to a soft, watery blue.

"That's it?" Avnas asked. "Just like that, you trust me and let me go free?"

"Oh, I don't trust you. You haven't earned that yet. But the rules of Ordinary apply to me and my job too. There is grace for first-timers trying to enter the town. But after that, things become much more by the book."

"You'll need to choose your shape," Myra said.

He had taken a step, then paused. "What?"

She shrugged. "It will need to be something that easily blends into the mortal world."

"Such as a man," he said.

"Sure," she replied.

"Yes," Pan said.

"Or a pony?"

"No," Pan said.

"That's an option." Myra threw Pan a look. "But your behavior will need to match the form you choose."

"I see." Avnas took two steps forward. "Then I choose this."

The air blurred around him. Between one blink and the next, Avnas the man was gone and in his place was a small, black bull. A little taller than Xtelle, Avnas was wide and muscled and thick. A single white star was centered on his forehead, and his horns reached out and curved upward to deadly points.

He posed. Muscles popped in huge lumps and swells like a pillowcase stuffed with bricks.

"Oh," Xtelle said.

"No," Pan breathed.

"My Queen," Amy said.

"Bulls don't talk," I said. "Neither do ponies or goats. Understand?"

They didn't look at me, not one of them. Amy was too busy staring longingly into Xtelle's eyes, she was too busy ogling his ass, and Pan was too busy snorting musical curse words.

Yep. What we had here was a full-on barnyard love triangle.

"Out," I ordered. "I have work to do. You all should be at the petting zoo like you promised you would be, Xtelle. That's a second count, if you don't follow through."

"Is someone inconsequential speaking?" she asked. "Did I hear my name?"

"Yep. No petting zoo, no staying in Ordinary."

That got her attention.

"But it's so children-y," she whined.

"You should have thought about that before you stole the chocolate."

"I shall be there with you, my Queen," Amy said. His voice, low and soft, weirdly matched the whole bad-boy, miniature Spanish Fighting Bull form he had going.

"That's not necessary," Pan said. "We don't need you there. Do we, my sweet?"

Xtelle blushed. It was really weird to see a horse's hair turn just a little pinker at the cheeks. "Well, I suppose I should go to the dance with the one who invited me," she hedged.

"And...I'm done," I said. "Myra, would you make sure these two—"

Amy snorted.

"—or three get to the petting zoo?"

"Already have the extra halters and lead lines in the back of the car."

"Of course you do."

She gave me a wink. "Want me to see if I can find someone to adopt Amy?"

"Adopt?" his head swung, and he lifted his nose, nostrils flaring. "I am not a child."

"No, but you're apparently a cow of some kind," Myra said. "Cows are owned around here, kept outside for most of the day, and sleep in barns."

"Bull."

"No, it's true," Myra said, purposely misunderstanding him.

"No, I am. A bull."

"The living conditions are barbaric," Xtelle said. I couldn't tell if that was horror or glee in her tone.

"Who is your adopter, my Queen?" Amy said.

"I haven't decided yet."

"Jean," I corrected. "For now, Jean is in charge of her. You know that, Xtelle."

"What? Where is that annoying sound coming from?" She turned a tight circle staring at the ceiling.

"That's it." I strode to the door and opened it. "Everyone out."

The entire parade marched through the door—Myra, the goat, the pony, the bull, Jean and Ryder, and finally, Than.

"Than," I said before he was more than a step outside the building.

"Yes, Reed Daughter?"

"Thank you."

"For which thing?" he asked.

"Breaking the spell."

"Ah," he said. "Yes." He inclined his head and strolled off. He made it about six steps before he froze.

A song of silver and pastels strummed through me. God power. A god was in Ordinary. A new god.

"Delaney Reed," a gentle voice said.

I knew who it was, even before she stepped into visibility from between two trees.

"Hello, Tala."

CHAPTER TWENTY-THREE

I LET the door swing shut behind me. The magical jail disappeared before the lock clicked shut. I strolled over to the goddess.

"Deities usually meet me on the edge of town," I said.

Myra had managed to shove the pony, the miniature bull, and the goat into the back seat of her squad car, and she was already on her way back to me.

Than, I realized absently, had frozen in place, halfway to the squad car, but turned toward me.

No. Correction. Turned toward Tala.

I wanted to ask him what his problem was, but I had a new god on my hands. Even though she came across as serene and gentle, her powers were just as potent as any other god.

"I came to you as you requested. Am I in error?" She didn't move toward me, so I closed the distance.

"No. This is good," I said. "I'll need you to accompany me so we can store your powers. Do you understand the contract means that you must follow all of Ordinary's rules?"

"Yes, I do."

"Good. Welcome to Ordinary. Let me give you a ride out

to Frigg's place." I started toward the station, but paused. She was not following me.

As a matter of fact, she hadn't moved at all. She was still standing there, a vision of beauty and light. Soft sunbeams fell green and gold through the leaves spilling around her like dawn's breath.

Than hadn't moved either. His breathing had gone deep and steady and even.

"Hello, Thanatos," Tala said.

Hearing his name seemed to break the spell holding him. He straightened just slightly, his hands coming behind his back to clasp loosely there, as if reminding himself that he should not reach out. He should not touch.

I threw a look at Myra. She looked gobsmacked, her eyes darting from Than to Tala to Than to me.

Yeah, I wasn't sure what I was seeing either.

Could it be that there was bad blood between them? Or was it something else? Was it what it looked like—Than startled to see her? Startled and pleased and oh so awkward about the whole thing.

Did they have a different kind of history together? Something more romantic?

If his body language was anything to go by, or that long, soft look she was giving him, the odds were good.

This. Was. Awesome.

"Hello, Tala." His voice was smooth and cool. More indifferent than I'd heard him in a long time. Nervous? Overcompensating much?

Tala did not looked fooled in the least.

"I asked Delaney if you were vacationing here."

"Oh?" He threw me a look I couldn't quite read. Exasperation? Panic?

"She told me you were here. You, and many others."

"It is a destination open to many. At the Reed family's grace, of course."

"Of course," she said. Her gaze finally moved from his face, slowly taking in all of him—his body, his stance—before returning to his eyes. "Grace looks good on you," she said quietly.

Than's head came back, just a fraction. "Yes. Well."

"Boring!" Xtelle yelled. She'd rolled down the passenger side window of the cruiser. "Kiss her or stab her or *do* something!"

Tala's gaze fell to me. "The demon is still bothering you?"

"She signed the contract. So far, she's only broken one law. Three chances," I answered before she asked. "The other demon is new here. Newer," I corrected. "He's been arrested once already. He's down to two chances."

Her small smile carried a lot more mischief than I expected. "Well, it appears your grace is quite generous."

"Oh, you have no idea." I made big eyes and nodded slightly toward Than. "So, let's get this show on the road. Tala, you and I will find Frigg…"

"She's on her way," Myra said.

I grinned. "Thanks. We'll get your power properly stored so you can remain here, and then I'll go over a few details."

"Details?" she asked.

"Things like you'll need a place to stay. We have a few houses and apartments available for new arrivals. You need to choose a name for us to call you, and you'll need a job or volunteer work in the community. If you like volunteering, Bertie's the woman you want to talk to."

I noticed Ryder and Jean had leaned in toward each other and were talking in hurried whispers. I wondered what they were up to.

"Acceptable," she said. Then, without looking away from me, said, "It is, however quite a lot to take in. I am wondering if you might recommend a guide to me? Until I am acclimated."

I saw exactly what she was doing. It was obvious she wanted me to pair her up with Than. Have him show her around town.

Than was my friend. I mean, he was the god of death, there was no doubting that, but he was also my friend. I knew there was something between him and Tala. It might not be friendly, but my gut said it *might* be friendly, and maybe a little more than that.

Tala was the goddess of the morning and evening star. Legend said she used her light to ferry men to safety. If that legend was true, then Tala had spent a lot of time caring for others. I could see why she wanted a vacation.

And I could see how she might just be patient enough to want something else. Might be patient enough to follow him across the heavens, or maybe across the Earth, to a little place called Ordinary.

Than was staring calmly at the mossy branch of a tree in the distance, acting as if he couldn't hear a word we were saying.

I certainly didn't want to make him uncomfortable. Didn't want to make him feel awkward or put him in a bind.

Oh, who was I kidding? I couldn't think of a better way to thank him for breaking the spell than throwing his maybe-possibly-ex-girlfriend/unrequited crush at him.

"Than," I said, all boss in my tone while I struggled to smother a smile. "Are you free for the next week or two?"

One eyebrow arched. "You are my boss. I believe my schedule is in your hands?"

"Yes, for your reserve officer duties. But the kite shop? Are you working all week?" This was it. His chance to let me know he didn't want to be with Tala. His chance to say he was just too busy to show her around.

I mean, I might want to see him squirm a little, but I did not want to actually put him in a position he'd find personally distasteful.

"I will attend my shop," he hedged.

"Kites?" Tala said. "Do you fly them?" She sounded...happy.

His eyes narrowed. The look he gave me was one that would wake me up in the middle of the night, if I hadn't grown up around gods.

I gave him my biggest, brightest shit-eating grin.

"I do," he said turning to Tala. "I am also the proprietor of the shop."

She smiled. And oh, how the world around her brightened.

Goddesses were a thing of beauty and strength and power. When all of that was focused in a smile and aimed at one very dour vacationing reaper, it was pretty amazing the air between them didn't sizzle and catch fire.

"Would you be my guide, Thanatos?" It was like she was asking him to the prom. Very sweet and a little teasing.

Myra cleared her throat. Than shot a fast look her way. I wasn't sure what he read in the look my sister gave him, but the two of them had developed their own language. If I had to guess, I'd say she was telling him not to be a dumbass. She was telling him to say yes.

"Here," he said, stepping forward and offering Tala his arm, "it's just Than."

She blinked, then smiled again, softer this time. She walked out from between the trees to stand beside him and placed her hand on the crook of his elbow.

"Than," she said with a nod, as if they were just now meeting for the first time in their very long lives.

"And you are?" he asked.

"Talli," she said. "Will it do, do you think?"

"It is an adequate adaptation."

Myra cleared her throat again. Than sighed. "It is lovely. Though I am partial to your original name."

Tala gave Myra a curious look. "Thank you."

I didn't know if she was thanking Than or my sister, but that didn't matter.

What mattered was the song of silver and soft pastel mornings clanging louder and louder through my head. Tala's power needed to be stored if she wanted to vacation here as Talli.

I opened my mouth to ask Myra the ETA on Frigg, when the familiar rumble of an engine coming closer filled the air. It cut off as she parked in the lot behind the police station.

"Who is that?" Xtelle leaned on the horn once, twice, three times, the last blast going on and on. "Myra? Delaney?" She let off a short honk for each word. "Pay." *Honk.* "Attention." *Honk.* "To." *Honk.* "Me."

"I got it," Myra said. "See you at the crowning?"

I blinked hard, trying to remember who we were crowning.

"Contest winner," she said, right when I put two and two together.

"Best tea and dessert combo, right?"

"Yes," she said. "You know, if you had asked, I would have been happy to be on the tasting panel."

"You want every local tea maker except the winner to put you on their shit list for a year?"

She grinned, one hand on the door handle, one on the TASER on her hip. "Oh, I would have let them down easy." She yanked the door and pulled the TASER all in one smooth go. "Back away from the horn before I find out what barbecued unicorn smells like."

Girly screaming was accompanied by the cruiser rocking on its springs. Myra pointed at the back seat. "The crowning," she repeated. Then she ducked into the car and drove away.

Frigg had been walking our way through most of this. She was tall, taller than me. Her blonde hair, so often in a braid, was loose today, catching honey in the sunlight. She was also wearing a flowy sort of floral number in dark green with sunflowers at the hem and waist and thin shoulder straps. I was used to seeing her in jeans and button-up shop shirt with her name stitched over the pocket, but she must have had the day off from the towing company she owned and ran.

I realized I didn't see Jean or Ryder anywhere and wondered when they'd left.

Frigg stopped close to me, facing both Than and Talli, who stood poised as if ready to be announced to the king.

"Hey, Tal," Frigg said. "You here for work or pleasure?"

"Vacation," she said.

"All right. Good. Good. So we have some powers to stow?" Frigg asked me.

"Yep. Do you want us to follow you out to your place?"

She shook her head and dug around in the crocheted sunflower satchel that hung crosswise over her shoulder and rested on her hip.

"Myra said I should bring a transfer vessel."

I looked at the item in her hand. "Why did you bring a bobbin?"

"Easier to carry than the whole spinning wheel."

I rolled my eyes. "But you don't have the powers stored in a spinning wheel. They're stored in the ground in the middle of your grove."

"Yes. And my power is there holding them. The easiest representation of my power is a bobbin."

"Not mistletoe or silver?"

She jiggled the ordinary-looking wooden spindle which was anything but either of those things. "Easy, light, tied to the powers."

As she turned it between her fingers, I could see the light of powers flash and flow down the lines of the threads. I could hear the soft collision and chorus of powers singing through creation.

"That's pretty handy," I said.

"Yeah, I don't know why I didn't think of it before. It's easier to store them here and just take them out to my property instead of having everyone come by."

"You know I don't mind going there—"

"No, we're good," she assured me. "I know you've been… uh…busy, and you have a…uh…the tea event—some kind of crowning thing?—still to take care of. So this keeps you… uh…nearer town for, you know…"

I'd never heard her stumble over her words so much.

It made me instantly suspicious.

"No, I don't know. Why am I staying near town?"

"For the High Tea Tide. There's a crowning. You're supposed to be there, aren't you?"

I thought back on it, and really, no. I'd never said I'd be there. "Bertie didn't say I had to be there. I have time."

"Huh," she said. "Weird." She shrugged. "Well, if we're going to my place, we'll have to use your car, because I brought the tow truck and don't have enough room for all of you. Drive out to my place, do the hand off, drive back here, drop me off at my rig, and hope we get back in time for me to be at the crowning."

"You really want to be at this crowning thing, don't you?" I asked.

"Yes," she said, elongating the word. "I really do. Want to be at the crowning. Don't you want to be at the crowning, Than?"

"Desperately," he said so dryly, I thought I saw the grass wither around his feet.

"There you go," Frigg said. "If you really want us all to miss the crowning…"

"Okay. I'm going to let it slide that you are absolutely trash at bullshitting."

She laughed, and it was a big, warm sound. "Oh, when it counts, I can bullshit the spots off a leopard."

"So putting aside you all seem to really, really want me to be at the crowning, which I will assume is because Bertie is still angry at me and looking for a little public revenge, I need to know, with total faith, that the bobbin can carry the power to where it should be stored. After that whole thing with Crow, I am not taking any chances with how the powers are kept."

"Crow?" Talli asked.

"Long story," I said. "Ask him sometime, he'll make it longer."

"It's more than just a vessel," Frigg said. "Here. Feel it for yourself." She dropped the bobbin in my hand. I closed my fingers around it.

Where I had seen the colors and heard the songs of the powers before, now that I was holding the bobbin, I could feel the song rush through me, carried on a welcoming wind.

For a second, I wasn't just Delaney, standing in a grove of trees behind the police station. I was also Delaney, the Bridge to Ordinary, standing in Frigg's grove, in front of the hollow tree where all the god powers lay at rest, dreaming.

I could feel the connection from the grove to the bobbin, as if each were a part of a larger mechanism. Both a piece of a spinning wheel connected by pedal and band and flyer and maidens.

The bobbin in my hand wasn't a separate piece or separate vessel to transport the power, it was a part of the storage, a part of that place brought here, to me.

It was a very lovely little bit of magic, and fully within the rules of Ordinary.

"Does that clear it up?" she asked.

I knew it had been less than a minute. Only a few seconds since she had dropped the bobbin in my palm, even though it felt like I'd been ringing with that revelation for hours.

"Yeah. Yes," I said. "It's a direct channel, not a vessel."

"Well, not *just* a vessel," she confirmed.

"Okay," I said. "Yes. This works. So, Tala. To enter Ordinary you must agree to set your power down and live your life as close to a mortal life as possible."

"I understand."

"There are risks. Without your power, you can be injured. In extreme instances, you can be killed and your power will have to be transferred to another mortal. I will be the way in which your power is transferred if that happens."

She stepped away from Than and stood in front of me and Frigg, the perfect point in our triangle. "Delaney," she said kindly. "I fully understand my actions and the consequences of them. I agree to the terms. Now, shall I shed this power so I can see the color of your ocean with my own eyes?"

I nodded. Some gods needed a lot of reminding of what they were getting into. Especially those gods who didn't like to follow rules, or who had never followed rules.

I'd been dealing with demons a lot lately too. Demons who hadn't found a rule they couldn't wait to break.

"Frigg, do you agree to harbor and keep safe Tala's power?"

"Yes. Happy to."

I nodded at Tala.

She reached for me, and I took her hand as she offered Frigg her other hand. Frigg took it and also pressed her palm against the back of my shoulder.

I inhaled, exhaled and then—

—*light, rising soft and pure, no heat, silver trill of birdsong, of starsong, a call, a hope*—

—opened my mind, my soul, the path of me that was Ordinary's heart—

—*a single note, a pulse point, silence held, then a breath*—

—power, Tala's power, the goddess of the morning star fell silent and liquid through my veins, flowing like a mercury river into the bobbin, into the grove, into the welcoming arms of Frigg's spinning wheel, another thread, another string weaving the fabric of the universe.

Then it was done.

"Good," I said, still vibrating with the aftermath of carrying such exquisite energy. "Welcome to Ordinary, Talli. Than, would you please show her around?"

She smiled. Even though she wasn't carrying power, it was brighter somehow, better somehow.

Free.

"Thank you. Both." She gave Frigg's hand a squeeze. Frigg removed her hand from my shoulder so she could give her a quick pat on the shoulder.

"Us girls have to stick together," she said with a wink. "So, Delaney. The crowning? I'll see you there?"

I closed my eyes and shook my head. "If for no reason other than I want to see what you're lying about, yes. You'll see me there."

She waggled her eyebrows and started back to the rig. "If you two want a ride, I'll take you," she threw over her shoulder to Talli and Than.

Talli turned to Than. "Should you like a ride?"

"I should rather a walk," he said. "A stroll."

"Well then." She offered her hand, poised to take his arm. He strode forward, his face carefully blank, slotting his elbow in place.

Without even one more word, they strolled off, leaving me behind.

"Okay," I said, watching them go. "Don't worry about me or anything."

An *oink*ing by my feet drew my attention. Dragon pig sat there, looking up at me with its adorable face.

"Hey, buddy. You did a good job with that demon back there." The dragon pig *oink*ed again, hopped up to its feet. "You wouldn't want to tell me what the crowning's all about, would you?"

It just grunted and smacked its lips.

"Yeah, yeah," I said. "I think I have some spoons in the car."

CHAPTER TWENTY-FOUR

BERTIE HAD OUTDONE HERSELF, which was really saying something, because I'd been to almost every one of her events since I was a kid, and she went all out on all of them.

The streetlights were hung with pennants in softly contrasting colors. She'd done up the light poles with flowers and leaves, little teapots and cups scattered here and there in the flowers to give another pop of bright color. Flag-like banners were staked in front of shops on every block. Suspended from the trees and awning were little paper wheels and streamers in flashy copper and silver.

And the flowers. They were everywhere. Potted and hung vines and bushes created paths between the businesses, circled little cozy eating areas and a gazebo that hadn't been there yesterday. There was a stage where an empty lot had been this morning.

The area around the petting zoo seemed greener somehow. Children were playing badminton without a net and running with ribbons in their hands.

It was beautiful. Not a fairy land, not an amusement park. It felt more like she had transformed this stretch of town into a garden filled with little tables and benches and nooks where sitting for a cup of tea and bite of pastry seemed like the most normal thing to do.

It was October in Oregon, but right now, today, it was summer. It was long warm days with friends and family. It was a moment no one in their right mind would want to miss.

From the look of the crowd wending its way through all the little grottos and groves, no one in thirty miles was missing it.

The vendors were just as cleverly scattered throughout the event, some operating inside shops or in little alleyways between buildings, even a few lining the streets and side streets, creating mini food courts.

I had no idea where the crowning was supposed to take place. I kept pulling my phone out and staring at the screen, expecting a message from Ryder, but there was no message there.

After repeating that half a dozen times, I sighed and shoved the phone in my pocket. He'd left right after the magic jail incident and I hadn't heard from him since. I wondered if he was out doing Mithra's bidding again.

Whether he was or not, today wasn't the day I could try and fix that. I needed to be here, doing my job.

I walked out into my town and worked the crowd, breaking up disagreements, helping a little boy find his lost daddy who jogged up behind him with a relieved look on his face. I held their ice cream while he explained that hide-and-seek wasn't a game they were playing today.

I drank tea. A lot of tea. Vendors waved me over and offered it "on the house" as if I were going to be one of the judges. The pastries were amazing, and after the fifth sample, I decided I really needed to pace myself.

Hatter and Shoe rambled by once or twice, a hand lifting in a wave, as they continued their route. I wondered how many miles they would put in before the day ended. They were totally going to win the department mileage contest.

As the day rolled on, I didn't see Jean or Myra, but they checked in via text, so that was good.

Really, it was a pretty good day all around.

Then I found myself in front of the dress shop.

For a minute, the crowd wasn't my happy place, the day wasn't summer bright. No. In that moment, I remembered getting excited about going out to dinner with Ryder. I'd even ended up with a dress just for the occasion. I had been looking forward to it.

I had been looking forward to him.

I had hoped he would carve out at least a few minutes in his life for me.

For us.

"Looking for some shoes?" Cheryl leaned in the doorway of her shop. "I just got some sandals that would be darling with that dress you're not wearing."

"No, thanks. I'm onto your ways."

"Oh?"

"If I walk in that shop, I'm coming out with stuff."

"Gasp, I say. You *are* onto me. I don't suppose you'd like to say that a little louder for the crowd?" She grinned, and I shook my head. "So why no dress?" she asked.

"I'm working."

"Okay. Later, maybe? I mean, if you can't wear a dress to a fancy tea party, then why have a dress at all?"

I had a reply, which involved me griping about missed dinners, demons, gods, and an absent boyfriend, but I pushed it away. "Maybe I'll put it on later."

"Sure."

"When I'm not on duty."

"Uh-huh."

"I do like it."

"Right. I can see that." At my scowl, she tucked her thumbs into the pockets of her bright green capris. "You know a dress can just be worn for fun, no strings attached."

"Well, that's good to know because buying one second-hand has been a hoot a minute."

She laughed, and I couldn't help but smile. "I'm just saying, maybe you were saving the dress for something special, and maybe the special is just this. A nice day. A nice town. A *very* nice shop owner."

"If I wear the dress will you stop badgering me about it?"

"Maybe. If you send me pics. Oh," she said, as the idea hit her. "Wear it to the crowning. You're off duty then, aren't you?"

"When is this thing? I swear everyone's telling me to be there."

"Tonight? I'm not sure. Sunset?" If she was lying, she was amazing at it. "Hang on, I have the flyer thing Bertie dropped off." She ducked into her shop, then came back with a flyer that had been folded in half lengthwise. "I really don't pay much attention to the itineraries. Clothes shopping is sort of hit-and-miss at these kinds of things."

"Not much traffic?" I asked, taking the paper.

"Halloween is my big season. Well, and Christmas. And prom. But high tea after everyone's already done their back-to-school shopping? Not so much. Give me a week."

I opened the flyer. The crowning was at six. Right before sunset. It would be the cap to the event, the big announcement of the tasting winner, and raffle prizes from local businesses would be given out.

"Hi. Happy High Tea Tide," Cheryl said.

I glanced up and moved out of the way as three young women—sisters, I'd guess—all funneled past her into her shop, already cooing over how retro the place was.

"Could be worse," I said nodding at the girls.

She gave them a long look. "I think there are a few items they'd like."

"Well, go ahead. I wouldn't want you to miss out on your retail threatening."

She barked a laugh and waved at me, disappearing into the shop with a jangle of the bell over the door.

FORMAL DRESS PREFERRED

Right there, in all bold, after the line item that explained what the crowning would be.

I looked around the crowd, and yes, there were more

people in dressier clothes than the normal yoga pants, shorts, and flip flops we usually got.

"Hey, Boss," Shoe said as he came down the sidewalk toward me.

"Shoe. Are you in on the whole crowning thing too?"

"What, at sunset? The prize giveaway? No. Why? Should I be? Did one of the judges drop out?"

Okay, he wasn't lying. "No. People just keep telling me I should be there."

"And you think that's suspicious."

"In this town?"

He sniffed in agreement, then scanned the crowd. "I haven't seen anything out of the normal. The uh…petting zoo has been…entertaining."

"Tell me they aren't talking."

"No. Stina is ruling that pen with an iron fist. She's good at keeping her thumb on the troublemakers."

The troublemakers were undoubtedly the demons.

"Good. There's a new god in town. A goddess. Tala."

Shoe scrunched up his wide face. "I'm unfamiliar with her."

"Morning star. Than seems to have some kind of history with her."

His face split into a smile. "Well, this is going to be fun, isn't it?"

"I hope so."

He nodded, then spotted something over my shoulder. "I better get rolling. Say, where's Ryder?"

"He hasn't checked in."

"Want me to slap some smart into him?"

"I can take care of my personal life all on my own, thank you."

"Sure, Boss. But if you need back up." He tapped his chest, right over his badge and his heart. Then he was off, moving like a slow-rolling bulldozer through the crowd.

A whistle down the street made me turn that way. Since it was Hogan, pointing at a cup in his hand, a cup that was probably filled with coffee, I more than gladly headed that way.

"Hey, Delaney," he said, holding out the cup.

"Is that more tea?"

"Not even a little."

I took a sip. Coffee, rich and black. Not the way I usually took it, but with all the sweets and floral tea I'd been noshing, it was a welcome change.

"Wish come true," I sighed.

He chuckled. "I aim to please."

"How's it going?" I asked.

"Great. Lots of new people coming in." He glanced back toward his shop. "How much do you think a delivery van costs?"

"Why?"

"I've had six offices and five hotels ask if I'd keep them stocked in pastries."

"Sounds like a good way to expand."

He frowned, but he was nodding. "I'll have to hire on."

"We got a new god in town. She'll be looking for a job."

"Who?"

"Tala."

He smiled. "Nice. Yeah, if you see her, send her my way."

"So that's nice." I waved my finger at the light tan jacket he wore over a coral shirt, both of which put rose undertones in his dark complexion and made his blue eyes pop. The outfit was finished with casual jeans and Chucks, but somehow that worked perfectly.

"Bertie asked us to fancy up a bit," he grinned, and held his hands out to the side, then did a slow turn.

"Very nice."

"You're looking…official." He nodded.

"I would hope so. It's my uniform."

"Sure, but Jean and Myra are changing for the crowning."

I just raised my eyebrows.

He laughed. "Yeah. Bertie put her foot down. She wants a

certain look for the reporter coming in to do the article about it. Something about good advertising."

"Everything's about good advertising for her."

"Maybe not everything. Nice tat, by the way."

I rolled my arm, unable not to look at the ocean wolf. I loved it. More than I thought I would. "Thanks. Wolfes gave it to me."

"Yeah, I can tell."

"Delaney?" Bertie popped out of a trinket shop. She was draped in a smart, square-neckline ruby dress that flowed below her knees in an explosion of lacy gold and peach flowers. "We need to speak."

"Good luck," Hogan murmured.

"Coward," I whispered. "Hello, Bertie. You're looking lovely today."

"Yes, I am. As are you, Hogan."

"Thank you, Ma'am."

"Delaney your clothing is an insult." Those hard eyes narrowed. "Are you on duty?"

"Everyone's on duty during your events. You know that."

She slid a look toward Hogan. He shook his head just slightly.

"All right," I said, drawing out the word. "What's going on?"

"What's going on is the crowning at six o'clock," she said.

"I've heard about that. A lot."

She gave me another scathing once over. "I would prefer you in your dress uniform. Lacking that, I fully expect you to be there in a dress. You do own a dress?"

"I'm not going to be a part of your advertising, Bertie."

She stilled, and her head lifted up, her shoulders went back. "Delaney Reed, you owe me a debt."

"Pretty sure we settled that." I lifted my hand where the cut was quickly healing and scabbing.

"No, that was a reminder. Of what you are to me."

"You don't own me, Bertie."

"Thank the stars for that. Can you imagine?"

No, I could not. I shuddered.

"However, you owe me a debt for not turning you in for burglary."

A family of four squeezed past us, one of the men, with a baby strapped to his chest glanced at me, tapped his husband's arm, and pointed at me.

I pivoted, and moved out of the middle of the sidewalk toward the building where there was a little more privacy.

"What do you want, Bertie? What," I clarified with one finger raised, "favor?"

She exhaled with so much obvious exasperation it almost made me smile.

"Wear a bloody dress. That's it. That's all I ask. Put on a dress and attend the crowning ceremony. I don't expect you to stand out from the crowd, but I want you there because I am expecting many of the tourists to have already left by that time, or be inside the restaurants for their evening meals, or down on the beach watching the sunset."

"You're afraid people aren't going to attend the closing ceremony?"

"Of course not."

But there was the angle of her chin—stubborn—and the restlessness of her hands clasping and unclasping. She was worried. Worried the event wouldn't end the way she wanted. Worried it wouldn't bring the tourists back. Or maybe just worried she wouldn't get featured as the main article on the local paper's web pages.

Or: "Is this about Robyn in Boring?"

"That soft-claw sister of mine thinks she's the height of class. I'll show her Ordinary has so much class she can shove Boring right up her—"

"I'll wear a dress!"

Her shoulders immediately lowered, and she nodded. "Of course you will. Good. I will see you at the pavilion at exactly six o'clock. No later."

"Yes, Ma'am."

"You will also be there," she told Hogan.

"Wouldn't miss it."

Bertie gave us both one last look, probably to decide if we were lying, then smoothed her hands down the riot of lace and flowers. "Excellent." She surveyed the crowd around us, found her next target, and was off.

"So, see you at the crowning, eh?" he asked.

"I guess so."

THE DAY GOT WARMER, the crowd switched from hot tea to iced, and pastries became ice creams and sorbets and bonbons.

Everyone was too blissed out on all the free sugar to cause any problems, and other than traffic—both foot and vehicle—being about triple what we usually got on a pretty Saturday in October, everything was buzzing along like normal.

I still hadn't seen Myra or Jean, though Hatter waved at me from where he was carefully rescuing a kid's balloon out of a tree.

I looked for Ryder, too, but he was absent. I wanted to be angry at him for that, but all I felt was a sort of acceptance. He had pledged his fealty to Mithra, and that god would do anything to make sure my life was complicated, messy, and...lonely. Unless I gave Mithra rule over Ordinary.

Since I would never do that, I had to get comfortable with a relationship that was complicated, messy, and sometimes lonely.

THE DRESS WAS where I'd left it, folded in the bag I'd intended to use to take it back to Cheryl. I pulled it out, shook it a little to free the skirt.

"Damn it," I said. Because I did like it. Even if it reminded me of Ryder and how our relationship was a little off the rails.

Even if it reminded me that though I was living with the man of my dreams, I was still a little lonely.

"Time for a fresh start," I said out loud. "You're going to be my Bertie dress. My event-going dress. The thing I pull out that means I'm doing my job, and damn prettily, thank you." I gave it another shake, not sure I could make it feel like a uniform, but determined to try.

"Let's do this."

I stripped, took a quick shower to slough off the day's sweat and magic, slung on the dress and brushed my hair. I braided it back, took it all out, thought about leaving it down, then went for the middle ground and pulled it to one side in a loose, messy kind of braid.

Shoes. I had running shoes, my work boots, or flip flops.

"Sorry, Bertie." I couldn't imagine having to deal with crowd control or some other emergency in flip flops, so I put on my work boots.

They looked…well, it could be worse.

The little plant Than had given me drew my eyes. I'd been good about keeping it watered. But just in case, I stuck a finger in the soil. It was damp. And right there in the middle, a tiny green sprig curled up out of the dirt. Whatever it was, it was starting to grow.

"Good job, buddy," I said as I turned the pot so the indirect light from the window fell on the tiny leaf. "You got this."

I made sure I had my phone and keys. On the dresser, I found the envelope I'd picked up Thursday at the casino. I groaned. So much had happened, I'd forgotten to deliver it to Bathin.

I tucked it in my pocket just as a message buzzed on my phone. I tapped the screen. A text from Jean saying she and Myra were already at the crowning and had saved me a place. She added a little emoji of a fancy dress, a crown, and the barf face.

I grinned, sent her the thumbs up, then checked for anything from Ryder. Nothing. I dropped the phone into my pocket and nodded. That was about right.

CHAPTER TWENTY-FIVE

"CROWNING," Jean mused, sipping from a Puffin Muffin travel mug. "I get it now."

I looked away from the stage where a table was set, long-stemmed flowers scattered across the white lace tablecloth. In between those flowers were silver stands, and on each of those was a type of tea and pastries.

Off to one side, on a golden pedestal, sat a crown. It was made of golden leaves and vines, the flowers pegged in the center with jewels. It was costume jewelry, but it was still a crown and looked very fancy. Next to it were two smaller crowns, silver and copper, simple rings made of leaves, no jewels or flowers.

There was also a mic up there. The background was taken up by a lattice of wood and fairy lights.

I had to admit, for a quickly constructed stage, it somehow carried a fairytale vibe.

"What did you think crowning meant?" I asked.

I had a cup of coffee too. Jean had insisted on it. Since I'd replaced lunch and dinner with my weight in pastries, the unsweetened, but cream-added, coffee was perfect.

Really, everything about the day was perfect: the weather,

the soft breeze, the crowd that was still upbeat, excited, happy.

Jean wore this gorgeous orange print, boho maxi-dress with a swooping turquoise hem. She gave me a crazy grin and a wink. My other sister was walking my way in a 1940s-style navy blue dress that showed off her curves, her demon boyfriend looming behind her and scowling at anyone who gave her the side eye.

Hogan worked his way over too, looking sharp in that jacket, his smile for Jean filled with adoration.

I smiled at each of them and tried not to scan the crowd for Ryder. I knew he wasn't here. Was probably off doing errands for Mithra. I knew I had to get comfortable with that.

"Hey," Myra said. "Wow. I can't believe you're wearing a dress."

"Like it?" I stuck my hands in the pockets. "It has pockets."

"You look amazing," she said.

"You do," Jean said. "Like it was made for you. It's perfect." Then Hogan was behind her, and she spun to give him a big hug.

"Shh…" Myra said. "Pay attention. Here we go."

Bertie strode across the stage. She lifted the microphone from the stand and thumbed it on.

"Hello, everyone. Welcome to Ordinary's first High Tea Tide. I am so happy to see you all here on this beautiful day." She smiled, and it was softer than usual, kind.

She really did love these things, and I was glad for it. There was something satisfying in seeing people find their place in this oddball little town. Bertie had not only found her place, she'd thrived in it. In doing so, she had made our community better.

"I hope you've enjoyed the amazing teas and treats brought to us by all the vendors. Let's give them a hand." She led the applause. Everyone joined in.

I leaned toward Myra. "Where are the judges?"

"Shh."

"This festival, like so many others, would not be possible without our amazing volunteers." She clapped, and everyone followed suit, looking around for the suckers. Several people lifted their hands to acknowledge they had survived said volunteering.

"I'd also like to take a moment to give thanks to our law enforcement. When a small town hosts large gatherings, it is an extra task of safety brought upon our officers' shoulders. A task they handle with aplomb and humor. Please join me in thanking Chief Delaney Reed and her officers." Bertie clapped. Jean, Myra, and I all waved but I couldn't see Hatter or Shoe in the crowd.

"Delaney Reed, everyone," she said. The applause raised for a moment. I waved and smiled some more, then the crowd quieted, turning their attention back to Bertie.

"Oh, crap," Jean said. Her hand pressed against her breastbone. "Something."

"Doom twinge?" I asked, glancing around the crowd for whatever disaster she had sensed.

"No, not exactly. Not...no." She narrowed her eyes. "I think something, though."

"I need a little more than that, Jean," I said. "Is something dangerous about to happen?"

Myra grabbed my arm. "Beach. Now."

Since her gift was always being in the right place at the right time, I let her drag me through the crowd, Jean, Bathin, and Hogan right behind us.

Once clear of people, Myra kept on walking, down several blocks toward the ocean. "You can let go of my arm," I said. "Myra. Mymy. Let go. I'm with you."

She glanced at me, as if just noticing I was still there, then nodded. "You have to be there. Promise me. Whatever this is about, I know you have to be there."

"Couldn't keep me away with a ten-foot club," I said.

"Beach, right?" Jean said. "I mean...uh...I think that way? Down the stairs?"

That way was one of the public beach accesses that jagged

back and forth down and down to the beach below. Here, the grassy hill on either side blocked much of the view both up and down the beach.

Once we hit the sand, we wouldn't be able to see what was coming. It was a great place for an ambush.

"Move," I said to Myra, pushing her behind me.

"You don't have to— Fine." She let me pass. I was wishing I had my gun on me. Damn Bertie and her fancy dress. Damn Cheryl and her perfect salesmanship. Damn this town for choosing this one moment, on this one perfect day to screw everything up.

But then, it wouldn't be Ordinary if something ridiculous didn't happen right in the middle of another ridiculous event.

I patted my pocket. Nothing but the phone and the letter I still hadn't given to Bathin.

"Here," I said, shoving the letter at Myra, who glanced at the name on the envelope and handed it over her shoulder to Bathin.

"Who's it from?" she asked.

"I don't know. A god, probably. I picked it up at the casino Thursday."

Thursday seemed like forever ago. As my boots clomped a steady beat down the stairs, everything that had happened since Thursday rolled through my mind.

Ryder making breakfast, Ryder leaving quietly in the mornings, coming back quietly in the night. The stolen Heartwood, the missing Feather. Than's planting room, all the mistakes carefully cared for, and maybe not really mistakes at all.

Growth is growth, after all.

My breath went steady and even, my gaze searching the sand below. Nothing to see. A normal beach with footsteps denting the sand, lots of traffic since the last high tide. The sound of town fading and fading with each step, the ocean hush rising and rising, as if someone had their fingers on two different volume buttons and was adjusting them in time.

Faster then, the flash of images. Ryder's eyes, the hurt in them, the anger. Mithra's mocking, his demands as he tried to use our connection against us.

The demon Avnas' quiet admission of love for Xtelle, accompanied by his pained look as she trotted in with a god in goat form.

More. The needle and ink, the Valkyrie's knife, Than's ridiculous spider slippers, and Tala, her serene mischief, his awkwardness.

It all spun together, these last few days, and for a moment, it was like I couldn't get enough air in my lungs.

All the world was happy—the tea, the treats, children laughing, families walking hand in hand. My sisters were happy, Jean and Hogan building their life out of bright, quirky colors, Myra and Bathin stepping a dance of patience and passion, of darkness and heat.

Then there was me and Ryder. Except when I thought about us, all I saw was a drawer full of notes. An empty bed. And apologies that never turned into changes.

We needed change. We needed to find a way to break Ryder's connection to Mithra, though I had no idea if it was even possible.

I was on the last turn of the stairs. No more time for moping, no more time for worry. With smooth efficiency, I switched into cop mode and pushed everything else aside to focus on the beach. On the surroundings and possible threats. Jean had said she didn't think it was a doom twinge, but her grasp on her gift wasn't as well practiced as Myra's.

She might be wrong about how bad it was.

The first thing I noticed was the paper scattered in the sand. Just a small piece here and there, caught on the rounded rocks, half buried. They seemed to be in a line, a path of little multicolored bits.

Then the breeze picked up, and the paper stirred. One flipped.

It wasn't just a piece of paper. It was a paper star.

I slowed, taking in the scatter of white, silver, gold, and pink. All of them stars, all with the words "I love you" written across them in Ryder's handwriting.

"Wait," I said, my head spinning and reality doing a poor job of keeping up. "Wait." Softer this time as I pieced the clues together.

Ryder was doing something romantic. Apologizing? Maybe this was the dinner we'd missed, the time we'd missed.

Or maybe he'd been planning to do something romantic and it had gone wrong.

Jean's quasi-doom twinge could be about Ryder.

Was he hurt? Was Mithra forcing him to do something against his will? I hadn't sensed Mithra in town, but I'd had a demon attached to me for weeks and hadn't known it.

Now I really wanted my gun.

"Uh, Delaney?" Jean said. "You mad?"

"Hold up," Myra said. "Maybe you should just—"

"Screw this." I strode through the sand, no sense of subtlety, no worrying for what might be waiting for me once I stomped through paper stars and sand, once I turned that corner enough to finally see the whole, wide beach.

I didn't even care that I didn't have a gun. I didn't need any weapon other than the blood in my veins and the power of this place I called home.

"What in the hell...?" The words died on my lips.

Dozens of driftwood poles were stabbed into the ground to create a natural grove-like design. Instead of branches, bits of twisted wires arched outward. Hanging from each copper and silver wire, strung on silk ribbons, were paper stars.

Hundreds of them stirring on the soft wind.

Distantly, I registered there was music. Noticed, absently, Hatter and Shoe there, playing guitars.

Those things, all taken in a flash, at speed. Those things ticked off a list, as if I were cataloging a crime scene, or setting a place to memory for later investigation.

Because while none of that—

—*lovely*—

—stuff mattered right now, there was one thing that mattered very much.

One person.

Ryder Bailey was wearing a suit. It was a green so dark it was almost black. That contrast with his golden skin and mossy eyes made me stop, welded in place from the heat that flashed through me.

Ryder Bailey was wearing a suit.

His hair had been styled too, brushed and held into place with enough product that the wind wasn't tossing it around wildly like when we used to walk the beach in the mornings.

He'd put some time into that hair and into his beard, which I noted he'd trimmed.

Ryder Bailey was wearing a suit, and the look on his face was just as stunned as mine. Then it shifted, flashed with something deep and passionate, before simmering down to nervous energy. Energy that made him shift his feet and tighten his hand around something in his palm. Tighten his hand so hard, knuckles popped.

Ryder Bailey was wearing a suit, on the beach, with stars all around him. He held a small box in his hand. Bells were ringing somewhere inside of me, but my heartbeat was too loud in my ears, louder than the ocean.

"Delaney," he breathed, like he'd been waiting to say the word so long, it was worn down, roughened, then polished to a fineness. He visibly swallowed.

Time went spongy. I knew I should respond, I knew I should do something, but I was drowning in the roar of my heartbeat. I was drifting away from my bones.

Ryder Bailey was wearing a suit.

"Delaney?" Myra's hand landed on my shoulder, just her fingertips. It was enough. It was everything. The world snap-crackle-popped back into place.

"Yes." I had no idea who I was answering.

The song Hatter and Shoe had been playing ended. The wind shifted a bit, but was still soft, still gentle. The sun was beginning to go down, and the light was as rich as amber, thick enough I could taste it, honey and sea salt.

People were gathering now, I could see their movements in my peripheral vision. I recognized them. Crow, Odin, Frigg, Athena, Zeus. Than and Talli were there, as were Ben and Jame, all of their clan around them. The vampires showed up, the entire family, including Old Rossi, in suits, tuxedos.

I'd never seen my town look so fine.

"You look beautiful," Ryder said. He took three steps. I counted each one against the thudding of my heart, against my breath which was going short and fast.

"So do you," I said, not even recognizing my voice. It was a happy voice, it was a soft voice. It wasn't pinging between disbelief, hope, and fear like my thoughts.

Was this an apology? Just a gift, a romantic…whatever this was?

He had a small velvet box in his hand.

My sisters were here.

And they were wearing dresses, almost zinging with soft exuberance. Images, clues, filtered through my mind. Jean laying her head back on Hogan's shoulder. Myra wrapping her arm around Bathin's waist, a dreamy look in her eyes. As if they knew something romantic was about to happen.

Another clue: Bertie making me change into a dress. Would she go so far as to make everyone in the entire town dress in formal clothes just to force me into it?

Well, that answer was easy: Yes, of course she would.

So she must have known about this too. It was why she'd made me meet my sisters at the crowning. It's why the big event was so late in the day, much later than Bertie liked to wrap things up in October.

My thoughts pinged back to it again and again. Was this a romantic apology? Or was it… a proposal?

"Delaney," Ryder said again, smoother this time. The

nervous energy was still there, radiating off of him like sunlight. Sweat pricked across his forehead, a drip tracking the edge of his temple, all the way down to the hard edge of his jaw.

"I've loved you for what feels like forever," he said. "Since the first time I saw you punch Jeff Baron for stomping on the good box of crayons. I thought to myself, 'She's so cool.' And brave. And thoughtful. Because after you punched him, you found the other crayons and made sure everyone had enough. Even then, you were making people feel safe."

I huffed a laugh. He flashed a grin so bright and sweet, it brought tears to my eyes.

"A lot of years have passed, and I've made some good decisions and some dumb decisions. But today, right now, I know I'm finally making the best decision in my life."

He was still clutching that box in his hand, but now he seemed to notice it. He didn't look away from me, hadn't once since he'd started talking, but his hand loosened. I could see it in the angle of his shoulder, in the slow inhale and exhale.

"Ready?" he asked.

I had no idea what he was asking me, so I nodded.

I heard a soft sound, a scratch, a whisper behind me. Like paper stars rubbing together.

No, louder. Like an envelope ripping open.

Several things happened at once.

Ryder began lowering himself, as if he were about to kneel, but he paused, his eyes going wide at something behind me.

I was already turning, Jean's hand pushing my shoulder, Myra shouting as she pulled her gun.

Everyone was moving, all the werewolves, the vampires, the gods, and—Hell. There were so many more people here now, people who I'd known all my life, almost the whole town of supernaturals and gods. They'd gathered while I'd been lost in Ryder's eyes.

I got a brief look, just a glimpse, of Bathin, the envelope caught between two fingers, his eyes narrowed, furious.

Furious at a man—no, demon—standing in front of him. Furious because that demon—same dark hair as Bathin, same royal bearing, but the rest of him thinner, leaner, all whipcord and hatred—plunged a sword through Bathin's gut.

CHAPTER TWENTY-SIX

THE AIR WAS KNOCKED out of my lungs, and sand was every-where—in my mouth, my eyes, my hair and ears. Sand smooshed down the neckline of my dress and slithered into my boots. I pushed to get up and realized there was a body covering me. A very familiar body.

"Stay down," Ryder growled, his breath hot, his beard scratching my cheek.

"Get off—" I started, but then the strangest thing happened.

Bathin laughed.

Not one of those weird, shocky giggles some people went into when they were in pain. No, this was a derisive bark. A challenge. Loud and hearty.

"Is that it?" Bathin demanded. "Myra," this in a much softer tone, "put the gun down. It won't work."

"I'll shoot him, and we can find out." She sounded furious.

"Ryder," I grunted. "Get off of me!"

He shifted—smart, because I was about to go for an elbow to the ribs if he'd held me down a second longer.

I wormed out from under him at the same time he stood. We sort of tangled up there for a minute, but ended standing, more or less side by side, even though he kept trying to put his body between me and the demon.

"Myra," Bathin tried again.

"Turn around asshole, so I can shoot you in the face." Wow. My sister was more than furious. She was...I'd never heard that kind of cool violence from her.

Bathin must have caught onto her tone too, because he took a couple steps forward. Right *through* the demon who was still standing there, back toward us.

"Baby," he said, walking into the muzzle of her gun and putting his hand on her wrist. "I'm good. I'm fine. Don't shoot me."

She blinked like it was the first time in an hour. Angry tears slipped from the corner of her eyes.

"What in the hell, Bathin!" She dropped her gun back in her purse and reached for him, but didn't seem to know where to put her hands since the sword hilt was still sticking out of his gut. "He stabbed you. Holy shit, we need an ambulance. Delaney, get an ambulance."

Bathin threw a look over her shoulder at me as I strode up to them. "I'm fine," he told me, because Myra was done listening to him, scared beyond reason.

If I'd ever doubted just how deeply her feelings for him ran, this would be the moment when I finally understood.

She loved him to the point that her calm and cool was busted as soon as she saw him injured.

"You have a sword in your gut," I said. "Talk to me."

"Oh." He glanced down like he'd forgotten about the thing, then wrapped his big mitt around the hilt and yanked.

"No!" Myra said, just as I said, "Wait!"

He should have had to step back to clear the blade from his body and not hit Myra. She jerked backward instinctively as his fist went by, but there was nothing in it.

Nothing but smoke.

"What the hell?" Myra repeated. She pointed at his stomach. Her hand trembled, but her words were angry. "Why aren't you bleeding?"

"It wasn't a real sword," Bathin said. "Well, not for long. It's a projection. It hurt, momentarily, but he can't maintain the hatred over this distance long enough for it to stick. The wimp."

"What?" she asked.

"Who?" I asked. Ryder was next to me, had been for quite some time. He pointed toward the demon man who stood as still as a projection on pause.

"My brother," Bathin said. "Goap."

"And that's him?" I asked.

"It's a message from him. But yes, that's one of the forms he takes." Bathin caught Myra's hands, covering them with his own. "I opened the envelope. I should have waited, but I didn't recognize the handwriting. I didn't know it was from my brother."

"He stabbed you."

Bathin rolled one of his big shoulders. "Siblings."

She shook her head slowly, but I could see the color coming back into her cheeks. "What an ass."

"Takes after my father."

Xtelle neighed and whinnied as she trotted down the beach, a string of fake flowers draped around her neck bouncing with every step. She glanced around at the supernaturals and gods gathered, somehow figured out correctly that these people were in the know about the magic of the town, and said, "Why wasn't I invited to this gathering? It looks important. Why isn't it about me?"

Bathin tipped his head. "And my mother."

Finally, Myra smiled, but she was still shaking her head.

"Is that Goap?" Xtelle asked. "What is he doing here? Is this about him? This can't be about him. I haven't had a party about me yet."

Bathin let go of Myra's hands and walked around so he stood in front of the projection of his brother. "You might as well watch too," he told me.

Of course I moved over to see. So did most of the rest of the gathered crowd. Myra stood slightly in front of Bathin. He had to shift her more to the side. "Otherwise, it won't work, babe."

I felt the crowd shift as Xtelle pushed her way through until her head was next to my hip.

Then Bathin pulled out the paper and envelope he'd stuffed in his pocket, scanned it, and said, "This is my first and final warning."

The image of Goap snapped to life. He was...colder, somehow, now that he was moving, and harder. He looked real, but my instincts told me he wasn't really here in Ordinary, wasn't really alive and breathing and glaring at his brother.

"Hello, Goap," Bathin said. "What do you want?"

"I want you to die, but slowly, and somewhere where I can watch."

Bathin made a rolling finger motion so his brother would hurry it up.

"You have a betrayer in your midst."

Bathin rolled the finger again. "Get to the marrow. I have things to do."

"Father wants you dead."

"Still waiting for news."

Goap shifted his stance, linking his fingers in front of his waist. "The king knows you're here. He knows Xtelle is here. He knows Avnas is here. He's coming. The Reed family won't be enough to keep you safe. These hollow gods won't be enough to keep you safe. He will tear this place apart with his bare hands."

"Why tell me?"

Goap looked startled. "What?"

"The king's wanted me dead for eons. Why send this message now?"

"I just told you: He's coming for you."

Bathin shrugged. "Maybe he is, and maybe he isn't. But you're here, and that's interesting."

Goap threw his hands up. "Fine! Don't listen to me. You never have. But when you're gone, there will only be one son in line for the throne." He sneered and pointed at his own chest.

He held that pose, but as the seconds ticked by, his sneer turned into a frown and he straightened. "Is this still on? How do I turn off?" He patted his arms as if looking for a button. "I thought I put the switch—" His hand tapped his elbow, and he winked out and was gone.

"Ass," Bathin grumbled.

"Okay," I said. "Let's take this somewhere more private and work out a plan. Bathin, I'm going to need you to tell me everything you know about your brother and your father's resources. Xtelle, I want—"

"No," Ryder said.

"You can—" I turned toward him and he wasn't angry. He was smiling. It was soft and so familiar, I felt a sweet pressure building behind my breastbone.

"That can wait just a little while, don't you think?" He reached out for me and took one of my hands.

"You have sand on your face," I said.

"Yeah?" He brushed one side of his face. I pointed to the other, and he swiped his palm over it. "Better?"

"Yeah. Yes. Good. Me?"

"You look perfect."

I smiled because I couldn't not. "Are you trying to butter me up for something, Ryder Bailey?"

"Is it working?"

"Let's hear all of it, and I'll let you know."

He squeezed my hand. Then, without looking away from me, he lowered down until he was kneeling, one knee down, one foot flat. "How's it looking so far?"

"Good. Nice form. Great choice of slacks too. Thigh muscles are a nice touch."

"Thanks. That's why I picked them. Also for my butt. They make my butt look amazing."

"Maybe I should be the judge of that."

"Only you," he said. "Delaney. I love you. You're the only person in this world who I want to judge my butt."

335

I snorted a laugh and shook my head a little, tears pricking the edges of my eyes. "Is this what I think it is?"

"Butt talk?"

"The butt talk isn't quite what I was hoping for."

"Okay. I can take criticism. Less butt talk more heart talk. Got it." He cleared his throat. I thought I heard someone make a dreamy sigh, but really, it seemed so far away it wasn't worth paying attention to.

Right now there was only Ryder, only his hand on mine, only his smile crinkling his eyes. He looked happy. Nervous, but happy.

He'd never been more handsome than this moment.

"Delaney, I've wished on a lot of stars, but I never thought you'd come true. Please let me be your husband." He opened the box. The thin gold band winked like a drop of honey and sunlight nestled against black velvet. "Please be my wife."

"What about Mithra?" I whispered. They were not the words I expected to come out of my mouth. From the look on Ryder's face (and the muffled tittering from the crowd), they were not the words he expected either.

"I'm not proposing to Mithra," he said.

"This will give him what he wants," I said. "Us, in a contract. Him, trying to get a piece of Ordinary so he can rule over all of us. You said you would never marry me."

"Not while I was connected to him," Ryder said, calm but so sure. He shrugged. "So we're going to have to find a way to end my connection to him."

"We?"

"I want to be in every part of your life, and want you to be in every part of mine, Delaney Reed. Even if that means I'm dragging you into a fight with a god."

"Yes," I said.

"Good, because I'm out of ideas of how to deal with that problem. Shouldn't have even tried to do it alone."

"I'm not agreeing to the god stuff—I mean I am, of course I am—but I'm also saying yes."

He blinked. Then he held up the box just a little. "To?"

"Yes. To that. To you being my husband. If I can be your wife."

And oh, the smile he gave me as he stood, sand shushing off his suit.

He pulled the little gold ring from the box. He kissed it, his gaze on me. Then he placed the ring on my finger. His hand was shaking. My hand was shaking.

More than that, everything in me was shaking, tremors strumming through me like sheets of rain against window glass.

I was crying, the tears warm and swift, but my heart beat loud, louder than the ocean, so loud I didn't know how the whole world couldn't hear it.

Then Ryder Bailey leaned forward, tipping his face down, just as I lifted up.

"I love you," he whispered against my lips. I exhaled a small, held breath.

"I love you." I kissed him, and he kissed me back, soft and promising at first, then his hands cupped my face, and I was sheltered there, in his kiss, in this private world created between us.

My hand slipped down to his butt, and I gave it a squeeze, eliciting a huff of laughter from him, before he doubled down and kissed me harder. Kissed the breath out of me, kissed the tremble away until I was lightness, I was air, I was joy.

The world was cheering. But that was far away, that was some other reality.

Mine, the real world, was the man smiling down at me, his hands still cradling my face.

"How'd I do?" he asked.

"Ten out of ten," I whispered. "Want to go for eleven?"

"With you?" he asked. "Always."

Then he kissed me to eleven.

EPILOGUE

It was a Sunday morning, and Ryder was not in bed. There was, however, a lot of noise coming from downstairs in the kitchen.

A *lot* of noise.

The oven door thumped open and closed, cast iron clattered, metal on metal scraped and whisked, then the downpour sizzle of eggs smacking a hot griddle.

I smelled pancakes, bacon, maple, and blueberry. I smelled coffee.

He was really outdoing himself down there.

But it wasn't just cooking sounds that had woken me. Music was playing.

Loud.

Ryder was singing.

Louder.

It was a Beach Boys song, and he was really giving the "good vibrations" part of it all his lungs. He had a good voice, but I could tell he was distracted, because his voice faded now and then, and he started getting the words wrong.

I was so going to tease him about that.

I thought about going down there, but the bed was warm,

and it looked like October had finally decided to get on with the rainy season, sending little claw-clicks of rain against the windows.

I was cozy. Content.

Cupboards opened and closed, dishes rattled, and the snap of burners turning off filled the air.

Another song came on, quieter and softer—"Work Song," Hoizer, singing about the woman of his dreams.

I thought he'd call me down. Instead, I heard his bare feet on the stairs, the clink of dishes shifting as he made his way to our bedroom.

I rolled over so I could watch him walk into the room.

He pushed the door with his elbow, both his hands supporting the tray he was carrying, a carafe of coffee hooked on his fingers.

"Morning," he said.

"Morning," I said. I couldn't stop smiling. He wore a pair of ratty athletic shorts and a T-shirt with da Vinci's illustration of an archer shooting an arrow through a shield.

"Breakfast?" He lifted the tray a little.

"Did you make pancakes?"

"Nope. For my new fiancé, it's waffles all the way."

"Aw." I sat and flipped the covers back, making room for him beside me. "What happens when we get married?"

"Then it's Belgian waffles."

I laughed and helped hold the tray, then set the coffee on the night stand while he settled into the bed next to me, mattress dipping under his weight.

"This is amazing," I said, looking over the spread. He'd made waffles, scrambled eggs with basil and feta, sliced cherry tomatoes, sliced oranges, bacon, and a little pot of blueberry compote. Along with that was maple syrup, butter, and enough coffee to keep me happy for hours.

"Good enough for breakfast in bed?"

"I don't know," I said. "I've never had breakfast in bed."

"We'll have to do something about that."

"Maybe. Let's see if these eggs hold up." I took one of the plates he'd put together, handed him the other, and got busy adding the toppings I wanted. And coffee. He'd wisely brought up two of our biggest mugs. I filled them to the brim.

We ate in silence, other than the muffled sounds of appreciation, the rain on the window, and the music drifting up from downstairs.

Spud finally came into the room, yawning, and got a couple pieces of bacon for being a good boy and staying on the floor while we ate. Dragon pig was downstairs somewhere sleeping. I could hear its rumbling snore every now and then.

"So?" Ryder asked, mopping up blueberries and bacon with a fork full of waffle.

"I vote we make breakfast in bed a new Sunday tradition."

He grinned. "Seconded. But what about when you're working the weekend shift? Or I'm out of town?"

I sipped coffee, already on my second cup. There were still things we needed to work out, things we needed to say to each other. Maybe now was the time to start on that. I could ease into it. Slowly warm up to all the things I needed to say to him.

"Why didn't you tell me Mithra was using you like a puppet?"

Okay, so much for slow and easy.

He crunched bacon and leaned his head back against the headboard, staring at the ceiling.

"I think it happened so infrequently that I thought I could just handle it. You have so much on your plate."

"Never too much for you. Never too much that I wouldn't drop it all to help you. Do you believe me?"

He rolled his head, still against the headboard, to look at me. "Things have been hard the last couple years."

I swallowed, breakfast a lump in my gut. "I guess so. But there's good things happening too." I lifted my left hand where the simple band encircled my finger.

He smiled, and his eyes twinkled. "Yeah, that's good."

"Yeah," I said. "It is. But you trying to deal with Mithra alone, isn't."

"You took on a demon. Two. No, three."

"Not alone. I never wanted to take them on alone."

He shifted so his arm was behind my shoulders and pulled me toward him. "I don't want that either. So let me fill you in. Delaney, Mithra's been a total ass and thinks me being the Warden, or me marrying you, is some kind of leverage he can use over your family and Ordinary. I've tried to leave, but he's told me more than once he'll appoint a new Warden if I do."

"Hmmm. I'm not sure he can do that."

"I'm not sure either."

"My turn. Ryder, my soul is almost healed, but even though it's still a little broken, demons have some stupid idea that I'm weak and can be used to hurt Ordinary and the people within it. Also, there's probably a ruler of the Underworld on his way to start a war."

"Sounds messy."

"That thing with Mithra sounds messy too." I tipped my head closer into the crook of his shoulder and rubbed my palm across his chest.

"We'll figure it out," I said.

His thumb gently stroked the side of my arm to the beat of Crosby Stills and Nash singing about their house being very very very fine.

"I know we will," he said.

"We'll figure it out together."

"Agreed. We'll figure it out together."

"No matter how messy it gets."

"No matter how messy. Speaking of messy, we have a wedding to plan."

I groaned and turned my face into his chest. "We could elope?"

"Not even a chance. This is going to be the wedding of your dreams."

Before I could automatically reply that I was dreaming

about eloping, his words sort of sunk in and settled inside me.

We were getting married. It still didn't feel real.

"We're getting married," I said.

"What?"

I looked up at him and blew random strands of hair out of my eyes, sure I looked an absolute mess. "You're marrying me."

"Damn right I am."

"What if we don't get along?"

He frowned. "What are you talking about? We've known each other forever."

"Well, I just found out today that you think the line in "Good Vibrations" is 'She's giving me a citation.'"

"Because that's what they're singing."

"They are not. They're saying 'excitation.'"

"Bull. That's not even a word."

"Bet you I'm right."

"Bet you're not. What does the winner get?"

I sat up and pulled off my T-shirt. "How about sex?"

His gaze roved over me, hot, hungry. Then he reached over his shoulder and clawed his shirt off over his head, wadding it up and throwing it to the floor. "How about we just cut to the chase?"

"No way, Bailey. We've got a bet going. I'm not going to let you—" I shrieked as he lunged for me. I twisted out of the bed, running down the stairs to find my phone, Spud barking his head off, and Ryder hot on my heels.

I was fast. But even I wasn't fast enough to search for the lyrics to a song before I got tackled onto the couch.

"Oof," I huffed, landing on my back, the fall softened by the cushions and Ryder's hands at my back, at my hip. "Hey," I said, looking up at him.

"Hey," he said back, low, sexy. His gaze dropped to my lips, then rose to my eyes. He smiled. "Okay?"

I nodded and let the phone fall to the floor so I could wrap my arms around his neck. "How about we call it a tie and both be winners?"

"Together?" he said.

"Together." He kissed me, and I kissed him, and it was *love*, and it was *together,* and it was *magic.*

ACKNOWLEDGMENTS

This book kicks off the next multiple book arc in the Ordinary Magic series, which is not bad for a little idea that started life as a short story years and years ago. There will also be a fun short novel, SEALED WITH A TRYST coming up in the DIRTY DEEDS anthology. The short novel is about Delaney and Ryder trying to get away on vacation while Ordinary is dealing with one wacky disaster after another.

In the same anthology, you'll find a tiny short story: AT DEATH'S DOOR. The short is from Death's point of view, and I gotta say, it was super fun to write.

I'd like to thank my unflappable and delightful copy editor, Sharon Eileen Thompson for catching all my grammar fouls, and my amazing sharp-eyed proof readers, Eileen Hicks and Louis Maconi for catching even more of those slippery errors.

To my beta reader, Dejsha Knight–thank you for wading through the roughest drafts. You don't know how much your input keeps me on the right path.

Shout out of gratitude to the extraordinary artist Lou Harper at Cover Affairs who not only gave me a pink unicorn, she also totally nailed the dragon pig for this book. (That adorable face! Those dragon-y wings!)

Big fuzzy thank you to my family, for putting up with all my writerly weirdness, including listening to me go through all the same (but different!) complaints about the challenges of writing this book as I do (but differently!) with every book. Thank you for not running out of the room when you saw me coming.

To my husband Russ, and my two sons, Kameron and Konner, I love you all. You are the best part of my life. I'm so proud to be a part of yours.

And a huge thank you to the Travelin' Rats, for all the laughter and adventures. Y'all keep me sane (let's find that next horizon!)

Lastly, I'd like to thank you, dear reader. Ordinary wouldn't have a chance to exist if it weren't for you giving this silly little town a try. I hope you will come back soon to see what mischief everyone gets into next!

To keep up with news and release info, click the link to sign up for my (infrequent and non-spammy) newsletter here: Devon Monk's Non-Spammy Newsletter or simply go to: www.devonmonk.com

ABOUT THE AUTHOR

DEVON MONK is a national bestselling writer of urban fantasy. Her series include Ordinary Magic, Souls of the Road, West Hell Magic, House Immortal, Allie Beckstrom, and Broken Magic. She also writes the Age of Steam steampunk series, and the occasional short story which can be found in her collection: A Cup of Normal, and in various anthologies.

She has one husband, two sons, and lives in lovely, rainy Oregon. When not writing, Devon is drinking too much coffee, watching hockey, or knitting silly things.

Want to read more from Devon?

Follow her blog, sign up for her newsletter, or check out the links below.